Ruth Hamilton was born in Bolton and has spent most of her life in Lancashire. Her first novel, *A Whisper to the Living* and her second, *With Love from Ma Maguire* are also published by Corgi Books. She has written a six-part television series and over forty children's programmes for independent television.

Ruth Hamilton now lives in Liverpool with her family.

Also by Ruth Hamilton

A WHISPER TO THE LIVING
WITH LOVE FROM MA MAGUIRE

and published by Corgi Books

NEST OF SORROWS

Ruth Hamilton

CORGI BOOKS

NEST OF SORROWS

A CORGI BOOK   0 552 13755 3

First publication in Great Britain

PRINTING HISTORY
Corgi edition published 1991

This book is set in 10/11¼pt Plantin
by Kestrel Data, Exeter

Corgi Books are published by Transworld Publishers Ltd, 61-63
Uxbridge Road, Ealing, London W5 5SA, in Australia by
Transworld Publishers (Australia) Pty Ltd, 15-23 Helles Avenue,
Moorebank, NSW 2170, and in New Zealand by Transworld
Publishers (NZ) Ltd, Cnr Moselle and Waipareira Avenues,
Henderson, Auckland.

Made and printed in Great Britain by
Cox & Wyman Ltd, Reading, Berks

For Meg Cairns, who listens

He that loves not his wife and children, feeds a lioness at home and broods a nest of sorrows.

BISHOP JEREMY TAYLOR 1613–1667

NEST OF
SORROWS

I

View Street, in the town of Bolton, Lancashire, sat like a monarch frowning down on those subjects who seemed to flee from her, four little streets set on impossible slopes that ran parallel with the main road, the latter being called Derby Street. These four cobbled ways were populated in the thirties by 'good little houses' containing 'good little bodies', for they were proud streets where there lived weavers and others with proper trades, such as high-earning coal-facers, ironworkers and skilled tanners.

Every step in the thoroughfares was cleaned and stoned daily, while windows and doors showed no signs of cracks or wear in paint. Pavements were swept clean, and the back alleys reflected a similar interest in cleanliness. This was the place to live if you were up-and-coming. Those who eventually arrived, usually through saving and a long history of self-denial, often moved on to View Street itself, or to the top of Deane Road where the houses had bathrooms and inside toilets.

Number 39 Maybank Street was as proud as the rest, though its inhabitants were young, just a pair of ordinary recently-wed workers who had set their caps at a decent house. From older and settled relatives, these two had taken rugs, a table and chairs, a flock bed and an old sofa that was worth re-covering, while from Rachel's dad, who lived at 33 View Street, they had gladly received some pots, a few pans and two good chests of drawers. The Murrays were set up; they had been set up for the past two years.

It had all begun in 1932 with a rush of great happiness

and enthusiasm. Rachel O'Leary, anxious to escape from a house still filled by half her motherless brothers and sisters, had flung herself headlong into love, while Peter Murray had known that he had got himself the best-looking girl for many a mile. That her price had been a wedding ring had neither surprised nor deterred him, for a decent girl would never settle for less than this full amount. So now here they were, settled for life, one baby in its cot upstairs, another about to emerge at any minute from his mother's womb.

The certainty that this second child would be a lad could not be questioned in Peter Murray's mind – he had never even considered that he might father a second girl. Judith was a smasher, she would turn heads in time, would his bonny little lass. Aye, girls were all right, girls were necessary. But to really make a place in life, a man needed three things. A good wife, a good job, and a son. The first two were lined up all right – Rachel was a tidy body, a good cook and a sight for sore eyes. His job at the ropewalk carried plenty of responsibility and a good wage. All he wanted now was his boy. He, above all men in this street, needed a son, because his life's ambition was to 'make somebody into somebody' and you couldn't do much with a girl, even in this day and age. Lasses just got wed at the finish and made more kids; there was no future in educating a girl. Of course, Peter would have got an education himself, given half a chance and a couple of better days in his impoverished past. It was just lately – since he'd turned about twenty-ish – that he'd come to realize, through library books and suchlike, how much he might do for a young Murray.

He glanced at his wife who lay groaning by the fireplace. He had brought the bed down as soon as her waters had gone at tea time. She looked pale and sweaty, but it would soon be over. All women went through this, didn't they? Mind, she hadn't been as bad this time last year when Judith was born. Happen this one wasn't going to come easy.

'I want the doctor!' This statement emerged from a mouth contorted with pain.

He gulped down the last of his hot brew of stewed tea. 'Nay.' His voice was as calm as he could make it. 'I've booked Bessie Hargreaves. Everybody has Bessie, she's reckoned to be the best. She'll be here once she's seen to her own, never fret.'

'Doctor!' She was panting now. 'Doctor! This minute!'

'We can't afford . . .'

'Get him!' Her eyes were wild and the red-gold hair, usually light and fluffy, was plastered against her head like an auburn cap. 'Get me a doctor, or, God help me . . .' She screwed up her face against the stabbing in her abdomen, then went on, '. . . I'll lose this one. I will! I watched me mam for days before she went, and I know . . .' She screamed loudly, words he could not understand because they were not really words. When the paroxysm had passed, she glared at him steadily. 'Do as I say. Do it!'

He flew from the house, cap and scarf ready to be donned against a bitter November wind.

Rachel Murray lay still as a stone while poor little Judith cried out from upstairs. With excruciating slowness, the woman eventually managed to roll over and use a tin cup to hammer on the party wall until Eileen Foley put in an appearance. 'Take Judith,' commanded the voice from the bed. 'Take her. Keep her till this is all over.'

Eileen studied her next-door neighbour. The poor thing was only a lass herself, barely twenty-one, but with the face of a sixteen-year-old. Young for her age, was Rachel. But not healthy. Not at the moment, anyway. 'You're not doing so good, are you? Shall I get Bessie for you, luv?'

'She's . . . she's . . . coming. Oh, dear Lord! That one hurt.'

'And where's yon feller?'

'Doctor.'

'Oh. I see. Well, if there's nowt I can do for you . . .'

'Take . . . Judith.'

After Eileen had removed the howling child, Rachel mopped her fevered brow on the yellow woven quilt, then reached under the pillow for her beads. 'Holy Mary, Mother of God . . . Oh sweet Jesus, help me . . . ! Pray for us sinners now and at the . . .' He wanted a boy. He has to have a boy. 'Oh God! And at the hour of our death. Amen.' And it is dead, I know it's dead. 'Glory be to the Father and to the Son . . .' It's a dead daughter. She hasn't moved for days. Days and days. 'And to the Holy Ghost . . .' The rosary slipped through slick fingers and clattered to the oilcloth. 'Mother!' she screamed now, and it was not Christ's mother she screamed for.

Isabel Street. She was suddenly back in Isabel Street with all the fleas and the ringworm and the flies. But she wasn't really there, was she? No, she couldn't be. She was in Maybank Street having a baby . . . But look! There was Jimmy, her favourite brother. His boots didn't match and he'd been to the clinic to get his head shaved. Yes! She could reach out and feel the stubble, she could see the circle of degradation on his scalp.

The stabbing pain was there again, but it was all tied up with something else, something she hadn't remembered for years. Jimmy and John were together in the street, heads bent to jacks and bobbers. Agnes and Frances had come back from the Theatre Royal where the management was holding a twins' week and twins could get in free. But because Agnes and Frances looked so unalike, they'd been refused free admission and had come home for birth certificates. Frances' face was down to her clogs. 'It's not worth it,' Rachel heard her say. 'Show'll be over by the time we get back.' Vera was being marched hurriedly up the street by Annie and Nellie. She'd been playing knock-a-door-and-run and was not favourite with the neighbours. Theresa was in the house, too young for street-playing. Mam was in the house too. With a new baby called Joe.

It was all so clear. Etched deep in her mind, it was, nearer than the pain. Other children were about too, playing with hoops and sticks, tops and whips, skimstones and hopscotches. A few mashers were setting off for the town centre, lads with hair parted down the middle and plastered to their heads with grease. Some older girls came past; Rachel could hear the giggles, could smell the essence of violets with which they had covered the smell of their bug-spoiled clothes.

'Oh, Mam!' she screamed in both times, though no-one in Isabel Street heard her. Maybank Street listened and kept its counsel – women in labour often called for their mothers.

Locked inside the delirium, Rachel cursed her invisibility. Because in Isabel Street she could make herself neither seen nor heard. She ran from one to another, bare feet scarcely touching the burning flags. It had to be real – she could feel the heat. And if it were real, she could save Mam! To Frances and Jimmy she called, 'Run! Run for the doctor! Mam's dying!' But they carried on with their stupid games.

Then it arrived in Isabel Street, that awful sound she could only liken to the scream of a mortally-wounded animal. And still everyone played. While Molly O'Leary howled her final torment, while her life-blood soaked the sheets, ropes turned and children sang their skipping songs. After all, the noise could have been anything, couldn't it? Kiddies playing Indians often made a cry just like that.

Rachel echoed that sound all the way to the hospital. Neighbours stood aghast while she was carried out of the house for what looked like – certainly sounded like – the last time.

Throughout the days that followed, Rachel remained

in that other time, sometimes managing to save her mother's life, usually failing completely due to lack of cooperation on the part of others in her dream. When she finally regained her senses, she learned that her child had lived, that it was another girl, and that she, Rachel Rose Murray, would never again be fruitful.

That such a minute scrap of humanity could have caused such agony was a source of great bemusement to her. Judith, at eight and a half pounds, had been easy to part with. But this poor little red-haired soul weighed no more than five pounds, was frail and ill. The tiny child had taken away much of Rachel's fight and strength, and had caused the destruction of her mother's reproductive system, not to mention her father's hopes.

So if Rachel Murray had ever been forced to answer a question which was seldom asked outside her im- mediate family, she would have pinpointed the start of her husband's downslide then, right after the birth of Katherine. He took no interest in the child, bought no gifts, stayed away from the hospital, was absent from the baptism of his daughter.

After this event, the O'Learys gathered at 33 View Street for what they called a family conflab. Things were getting serious, out of hand, it all was. Joseph O'Leary Senior stroked his tobacco-streaked white moustache and thought about how serious it was. For a man to fail to attend the naming and blessing of his own baby, well, such things went beyond all understanding! Ten children he had reared single-handed since his own good wife's death, and although three of them had been of working age, the other seven had required constant attention. Especially Joe, who had been just ten days old when his mother passed away.

'He'll come round at the finish.' Joseph tapped his pipe against the chimney breast. 'There's no man on earth could turn his back on the little mite she is. Would you ever look at her now, Annie?' he asked his eldest daughter. 'Like a fairy queen, she is. Rachel, where is your man just now?'

Rachel shrugged listlessly. 'Drinking, roaming the streets with his mates, who's to know what he's up to? He wanted a lad. It's not his fault it wasn't a lad . . .'

'And you can't have no more?' Theresa's eyes were round with questions. As yet unwed, she knew little of the workings of the female body.

'No more.' Rachel's voice was expressionless. 'And that's what's upsetting him.' She looked down at her sleeping daughter. 'So unlike Judith, she is. Judith was a mass of black curls and big blue eyes. But this one, well, I don't know who she looks like.' Judith gurgled and stumbled about on the peg rug in front of a roaring fire, but still Rachel's eyes remained fastened to the younger child. 'It's as if they ripped the heart out of me and placed it in my arms. It's funny, the way I love her. As if she's the last piece of me, I suppose.'

'You must not prefer her over Judith.' The old man's tone was stern. 'Ten I had, and never a pick or a choose did I make between them. Every one had his or her own needs. Back in Ireland, I was taught by me own mammy never to show a preference once my children were born.'

Rachel sighed loudly. 'I've no preference. I'm just lucky to be alive, and so is Katherine.'

'Aye.' John's serious face glowed in the firelight, making him look even more earnest and concerned than ever. 'But what are you going to do about Peter? He can't carry on this road. There's been rumours of him messing about drunk all over town.'

'Wetting the baby's head, I don't doubt.' Vera sounded angry. 'Wetting it all by himself, or with his daft friends. He should be here, Rachel. You should have made him come. Lad or no lad, he should have come to the church like everybody else. And where's his family? His mam and their Harold and their Bert? I bet he never even invited them. Just because our Katherine's a girl!' On this, they physically closed ranks, standing in a semi-circle around Rachel and her two children.

Agnes was the first to speak. 'If he gets awkward, Rachel, over money and such, you'll have to tell me dad and we'll all muck in with a shilling a week. This little lass is too frail for anything but the best. So you just tell us if Peter keeps you short of owt.'

Jim almost growled, 'He'll not turn awkward, Agnes. Me and our John and our Joe will stop him turning awkward.'

'No fighting!' cried Rachel. 'And there's three of them, don't forget. Their Harry and Bert are both handy when it comes to punching. Anyway, Peter'll get over it. Just you wait and see.'

But Peter didn't get over it. As the months and years went by, he held his deep hurt to himself, nursing it like some unmendable wound that had been deliberately inflicted by life, by ill-luck and by his own wife. It was almost as if she had conspired with factors elemental to deprive him of that which he had most deserved, and he took it out on her by sulking. Time and again, she attempted to shake him out of it. Whenever there were a few coppers to spare, she bought herself a new blouse or a cheap skirt, tried to make herself presentable and clean when he came home from work. But he would have none of her.

Judith was fortunate; she remained acceptable in her father's eyes. But poor Katherine was ignored from birth, because he could not find it in his heart to forgive the one who had killed his unborn sons. Also, while the child was not exactly ugly, she was puny and pale in comparison to her more robust sister. It was not unusual, therefore, for him to take the four-year-old Judith out for a romp in Queens Park, though he never offered to take Katherine.

At last, after three years of stretched patience, Rachel snapped. To be around when Rachel Murray snapped was not a good idea. She had an Irish temper that had been carefully cultivated and handed down through generations of Dubliners, and while her level of control was usually good, a breaking point was inevitable.

She faced him across the table on a fine Sunday in June 1937. Judith was all done up in her royal-blue bonnet and coat, while little Katherine, who had begun to take things in, stood to one side as if she knew her place already. 'Where do you think you're going?' began Rachel, her dark grey eyes flashing ominously.

'I'm taking her down to look at the crown green bowling.'

'Oh aye?' A foot tapped sharply against the flagged kitchen floor. 'And what about this one?' She waved a hand towards the younger child.

'Eh?' His mouth fell open as if she had asked a totally pointless question. 'What about her?'

'Why can't she go an' all? Come to that, why can't we all go?'

'She's nobbut three! She'll only get in everybody's road.'

'You took Judith when she was only three.'

'Aye, well.' He drew a hand across his upper lip. 'Judith's got sense – haven't you? She likes a bit of bowling, does my lass. And you don't enjoy it, Rachel, so don't carry on as if you're missing summat.'

'Missing summat? Missing summat?' Her voice rose in pitch as she bundled both children into the safety of the back yard. 'I'm missing a husband, that's what! And yon lass is missing a dad, a dad she has a right to.'

His mouth fell open. 'What the hell's got into you at all?'

Rachel studied the handsome man she had married. He was nearly six feet tall, dark-haired, blue-eyed, strong-limbed and muscular. Yet at this moment, he looked gormless, like a big soft lad with his jaw hanging loose in that silly way. She spoke quietly, her teeth gritted together as if avoiding the bad taste created by her words. 'Since I had that child, you've treated me like a dog. No, worse than a dog! A dog gets thrown the odd bone, eh? But not me, oh no. I'm nowt a pound, me. Just because I can't have any more kiddies, just because I'm wrong inside. And my little baby can't be blamed for that!'

'I never said anybody was to blame, did I?'

She shook her head vigorously. 'No. You've said nowt, because you're not man enough to speak your mind. But I could cut through your resentment with a blunt butter knife.'

'Not a man!' he screamed. 'It's you that's not all there. It's you has the bits missing. I can father a son . . .'

'Prove it! Go on, get out and prove it! Look at Jimmy Pickavance down Canon Street – nine girls he had. Nine! And a finer fellow you couldn't meet. But you . . . oh aye . . . it has to be my fault. How do you know you'd have had a boy, eh? Can you show it me in writing? Cos it's the men what gives a child its sex, our doctor told me that. A woman's eggs are neuter – they can be anything. You made the girls, not me!'

'And I've no chance for a son now, have I? Not since that one ruined you!' There, it was out. He stood panting, as if he had just accomplished a five-mile run, yet there was a kind of terror in his eyes, for he knew now that he had annoyed his wife beyond endurance. Only once had he seen her angry before, and that had been over a man too. Bessie Hargreaves' chap had, while in his cups, threatened to beat his wife to within the last inch, and Rachel had saved her. Aye, she'd taken a shovel to him, and the whole street had come out to watch the man run like the devil all the way up to View Street.

Rachel straightened her short spine. 'I've had enough,' she announced softly. 'More than enough. I shall take the pair of them back to my dad's house. At least at my dad's house, they'll both get treated as human. How do you think our Katherine feels, eh? What must she think when she stands by and watches you playing with her sister?'

'You'll take our Judith nowhere!' His bright blue eyes were shaded by fear and temper. 'That lass is definitely mine.'

'And the other one?'

'She looks nowt like me. She could be any bugger's!' He knew he had gone too far, yet still he stood his uncertain ground. 'Thin and ugly, she is. Not a sign of Murray in her. She looks like nothing else on this earth.'

'What?' Her voice rose to a scream now. 'Are you accusing me of . . . of . . . ? Right. That's it, Peter Murray. You can keep your few bob a week, cos I'm off to my own folk. That child is the spitten image of my mother! Not that I should have to explain things like that. A proper man would know his own child, no matter what it looked like!'

'You'll not go! Except over my dead body!'

'Oh aye? And who's to keep me here? Will you stop off your work and watch me every minute? Will you lie awake all night to make sure I don't sneak out? Remember, my dad's is only a stride from here, I can be there in half a minute!' Even then, at the eleventh hour, she could probably have negotiated had he shown the slightest sign of remorse or shame. But he simply turned on his heel and left the house by the back door, collecting Judith on his way through the yard.

Rachel watched him disappearing through the gate, then she opened the door and brought in her younger daughter. 'Come on. I'll read to you.'

'Daddy gone.' The child's pale face was creased with sadness.

'That's right. Daddy gone. Get me your story book.'

'Judy gone too.'

'Yes.'

'Kaffrin still here.'

Rachel bowed her head. 'Yes. Katherine with Mammy

and a nice story book.' She could not meet those sad green eyes; she could not force herself to look squarely into the face of a three-year-old. 'I'll read you that one about Little Red Riding Hood.'

'Big bad wolf.'

'Yes.'

Katherine fetched the book and reached up to be lifted to her mother's knee. Rachel clung to the infant, her own body shaking with dry and silent sobs. 'Don't cry,' whispered the little one. 'Daddy come home. Daddy always come home.'

Little Katherine knew her place all right. She knew it, but did not truly accept it. When Peter came home with a dress for Judith, or a pair of ribbons with which to adorn the older girl's pretty hair, Katherine would stand to one side and watch while these gifts were passed over from father to daughter. Although she had achieved an adequate level of verbal expression, the younger child never said anything. She simply watched and envied her sister.

Rachel, ever vigilant, would scrimp and save to furnish Katherine with similar presents, but these always arrived later, always from Mam, never from Dad.

Katherine decided to do something about it. She was not loved, so she must make herself lovable. There were differences between herself and Judith, differences that must be remedied. Late one afternoon, she balanced herself precariously on a dining chair and studied her reflection in the fireplace mirror. The main thing, she concluded, was her hair. Judith's hair was black; her own was a strange colour that people called red, though it looked nothing like the red in her crayon tin.

It was a Saturday. Judith was out with Dad, while Mam had just nipped next door to help Mrs Foley turn mattresses. Katherine had been advised to sit and draw till Mam came back. She reached down and picked up a black crayon, peeling back the paper cover so that she would have enough wax to work with. Furiously, she rubbed the crayon against her hair. Nothing happened. She rubbed harder, but still her hair shone red-gold, bright and horrible as ever.

With a deep sigh of sadness, Katherine clambered down to terra firma. Something black. She had to get something black so that she would look like Judith. Quickly, she ran through the kitchen and up the stairs, throwing open the tallboy that contained Judith's folded clothes. After a moment's deliberation, she chose a pretty pale blue dress with smocking on the bodice, all gathers and silky roses and pink threads. When she had donned the frock, it came down to her ankles, so she hitched it up unceremoniously before changing clogs for ankle-strap shoes.

But she still needed something black! Tripping and stumbling, she flew down the stairs, her face glowing as an idea took root in her three-year-old brain. There was plenty of black! Out in the back street, there was loads of black! And it had been a hot day, so it would be squidgy and soft like thick paint.

Slowly and silently, Katherine let herself out of the house, crept down the yard, opened the tall back gate and squatted down at the edge of the shallow pavement. Tar oozed out of cracks between cobblestones and kerb, and she scooped up the precious bounty, plastering it thickly on to her hated hair. She smiled to herself. Now she would look like Judith, now Dad would love her and buy her ribbons and frocks.

Picking up her voluminous skirt, Katherine skipped along to the end of the block. Dad and Judith would be home soon. It was nearly tea time. She knew it was tea time because the pie in the oven had smelt ready, while her stomach felt empty and hollow. Hopping happily from foot to foot, the child waited for her father and her sister.

A few passers-by stopped and stared. One old lady clad in long black skirt and shawl tutted loudly, 'It'll take more than a pound of butter to get that stuff off thy head, lass,' but Katherine wasn't bothered. She looked like Judith. Looking like Judith was the only important thing.

They came round the corner of Derby Street, father and daughter hand in hand as usual. Throwing caution to the winds, Katherine launched herself towards Dad. 'Look!' she screamed. 'Black hair like Judy! Dress like Judy!'

He stopped dead in his tracks. The vision before him was almost unholy, like something from an unclean world. A white face stared out from between greasy locks that looked strangely green, while the dress, covered in fingerprints, was a tar-stained ruin.

'Like Judy!' repeated the child, but Peter was too shocked and angry to hear the words.

'Get home!' he spat sharply.

Katherine, feeling very puzzled, stood her ground. She had black hair; he had to love her.

With a howl of despair, Peter Murray abandoned Judith and picked up his younger daughter, gripping a handful of the spoiled dress and holding the child at arm's length.

She struggled. 'Put me down! Daddy put me down!' But he marched up the back street till he reached the gate of number 39. With tremendous force, he hurled the little girl into the yard just as Rachel opened the door.

'What the . . . ?' began Rachel, her voice failing as she noticed the state of the child who lay in a crumpled heap at her feet.

'Look at her!' Peter forced his words through clenched teeth. 'She's ruined that frock – two quid it cost me. And her hair! What's she done to her bloody hair?'

Rachel shivered as a sudden shaft of comprehension entered her consciousness. 'She's tried to dye it,' she whispered. 'She's trying to look like her sister.'

'What?' he yelled. 'That? That try to look like our Judith? No bloody chance.' With the toe of his shoe, he turned Katherine over. 'She doesn't even look human,' he sneered.

Rachel crouched down. 'Her knees are bleeding,' she said quietly. 'And her elbow. You threw her, didn't you? You threw her into the yard. You might have crippled the poor little thing.'

He laughed mirthlessly. 'She's not right in the head,' he muttered. 'Putting tar in her hair and stealing Judith's frock. She's bloody mental.'

'She's three years old,' sobbed Rachel. 'You're a bully, Peter Murray. A great big stupid bully!'

Judith stepped between her father and her little sister. 'Don't hit Katie,' she said in a firm clear tone. 'Katie can have the frock. She's only little. She doesn't know what she's doing.'

Peter paused, glanced at the three distressed females, then stamped into the house.

By nightfall, Katherine's head had been practically shaved. So firmly had the tar stuck that there was no saving her hair. Rachel tucked her younger daughter into bed. The poor little soul would have to wear a bonnet, would have to go about looking like somebody with a bad case of nits. All for the love of Peter, all to gain his approval – or even his attention. 'Good night, love,' she murmured.

'No hair,' said a tiny voice. 'No hair like Judy's, no hair like Kaffrin's. No hair at all.'

'It'll grow,' said Rachel weakly. But would Peter grow, would he ever grow up?

As she straightened from the bed, a vivid picture entered her mind, the memory of his face distorted by hatred for this child. If Rachel and Judith had not been there, he might have kicked this little baby to death. It was time to teach him a lesson.

*

Rachel left Maybank Street with her two children at the end of June. It was a rainy day; she felt as if the sky were doing the crying for her, because there were no tears left in herself. Since the Saturday of the tar incident, Peter had spoken scarcely a word to anyone, and the atmosphere in the house had become yet more leaden than before. Even Judith had had very short shrift from her dad during these past weeks, so neither child was upset on being told that they would stay with Grandad for a while.

Grandad was universally loved. He had a happy face with lots of white hair on it, tickly hair that made children squeal during hugs and kisses. Grandad had a nice big house too, the sort of house where hide-and-seek was played, where there was a proper bath with taps, and a Hoover that sucked dirt off the floor. There was a wash house at the end of the yard, while the view from the front street was awesome, all the way to town with the big clock stuck high in the sky right opposite Grandad's front door.

They were received with arms not exactly wide open, because Joseph O'Leary had the usual Catholic respect for marriage, yet he understood his daughter's dilemma well enough to offer shelter for the immediate future. 'This will show him his stupidity,' he announced. 'You can all sleep in the front bedroom. Theresa and Joe still need their privacy. God knows they waited long enough for it in a house so crowded. And with the two of them working, Rachel, you will take over the cooking for the while. It won't last. Believe me, the man will not carry on long without the three of you.'

Peter carried on without them just until he got home from work on that first day. On discovering an empty house and a cold grate, he set off immediately for 33 View Street, throwing the interior glazed door so wide on his arrival that this item almost parted company with its hinges. 'Where are they?' he demanded of his father-in-law. 'She's got no right . . .'

'Hasn't she?' The older man lit his pipe and sat back in the horsehair rocker. 'The girl has taken enough of your nonsense. If you can be father to one child, yet no father to another, then she must keep both away from you.'

Peter Murray groped for words to say, but his temper was too high for any sense to come out of his mouth. 'She belongs down yonder,' he snapped at last. 'She's my bloody wife!'

'Do not curse in my house! Rachel may be wed to you, but she is still a free spirit. The Lord gave us intelligence, did He not? And my daughter's intelligence tells her that you are doing no good for Katherine. In fact, you are also harming Judith, for a favoured child is always spoiled. Now get yourself home until you come to your senses!'

'I want to see her!'

'Then you will be disappointed, because she is away at her sister's house.'

'Which one?'

'That I will not tell you. And don't be waiting in the street for her, because my son and my son-in-law will escort her home. I suggest you go and pray for some guidance, Peter. Unless you can treat my daughter and her children right, they will be staying here with me.'

'You . . . you high-handed old bugger, you! I was never good enough for her, was I? Nobody's ever been good enough for your precious lot! Well, I treated her right. She didn't have to get wed, not like most of your other girls. I kept her clean right to the finish, I did . . .'

'Then later you dirtied her because of her illness. I don't need my daughter to tell me, Peter. I know you are no longer a husband to her. She cannot give you a son, so you leave her cold and alone in the night. You have two fine daughters, clever girls the both of them. Why can you not take pleasure from what you have? Why must you grieve over what cannot be?'

27

The visitor inclined his head slightly, the wind suddenly taken from his sails. 'I don't know. There's no rhyme nor reason without a son. I had plans for a son. I thought if I saved up, I'd happen get him off to college, give him a real start, like a career. With girls, there's nowt to aim for.'

'Why not?'

'Well, they just get wed, don't they?'

Joseph nodded slowly. 'They get wed, they have sons. Your grandchildren will perhaps fill this gap for you.'

'No! They will not be Murrays!'

'Ah. I see. So there's the crux, is it? Family name? What did your family do to deserve such glories?'

'Well . . . I . . .'

'Well exactly. You are in danger of losing everything, Peter Murray. No matter what my children have done, I have always stood by them. Girls, boys, it mattered not to me. Because they are people, people with souls. Where is your soul, man? Is it buried just because your wife cannot bear you a son?' He struggled to feet made uncertain by wounds received in combat during the Great War. 'Go from my house now. Do not return until you are a man.'

'I am a man! It's your daughter who's only half woman! She's the one who . . . who . . .'

'Who failed you? By getting sick?'

They stared at one another in silence for several seconds, then Peter Murray stormed out of the house slamming every door behind him.

Joseph O'Leary sat down again and stared into the fire. 'God help you, Rachel,' he said quietly. 'For I will not always be here to protect you.'

The years that followed were the happiest in young Katherine's life. Grandad was the most awful torment – Rachel herself described him on occasion as 'mortallious troublesome' – because he certainly knew how to excite her younger daughter to the point of desperation. Katherine would come downstairs on Sunday mornings, cheeks glowing from the bath, hat and coat clutched in her hands ready to be donned for church, hair tied back with a clean ribbon, shoes shining like black glass. And Grandad would approach her with the white rosary and the specially bought pearl-backed little girl's Missal. 'Oh dear me!' The white head would shake sadly. 'Here's you all done up for church on God's good day, and clogs still on your feet. However could you think of going to Holy Mass in clogs?'

'Grandad! These are my best ankle-straps.' She was beginning to learn that he was neither blind nor daft. 'You know these are my ankle-straps. I never go to church in clogs.'

'Ah, well. They look like clogs to me. Shouldn't you go and check with your mammy?'

'No. Mam's getting herself and our Judith ready. And you know she gets mad with you for toe-menting me. She says you've not to toe-ment me.'

'Oh.' A large hand would scratch his head thoughtfully. 'If I were your mammy, I would not allow you to mass in the clogs . . .' And so it went on.

Weekdays were the same. 'Katherine, why are you wearing the good shoes and this a school day? If your mammy finds you ready for school with the ankle-straps all shining for Sunday, won't you get a scalping?'

Katherine learned how to cope with him. It took time, but by her fourth birthday, she had him well in hand.

'Will you sing for me, Katie?'

'I don't know.'

'Go on, child, sing for your poor old Grandaddy.'

'Can I sing on the stairs so you can't stare at me?'

'Yes.' A long pause while the child made no move. 'Will you sing for me, Katie?'

'Can I have an ice-cream cornet and one for our Judith if I sing on the stairs?'

'You can.' Still no move from Katherine. 'Will you sing for me?'

'With raspberry on?'

'Yes. Will you sing for me now?'

'Doubles? Can we have doubles off Manfredi's cart?'

'You can have doubles with raspberry on the both of them. So, will you sing for me?'

Solemn green eyes would gaze up at him. 'No. I won't sing for you.'

Then, crippled though he was, he would chase her round the table until she allowed him to catch her.

Judith took no part in these games. Judith, at five, was a studious child with a terrible need for books, and Grandad spent many an hour begging and borrowing from neighbours to keep the little girl's appetite sated. And, of course, Judith had her father. Every Tuesday evening, Peter would arrive to collect his elder daughter for an outing.

Rachel had tried on numerous occasions to make peace between her husband and Katherine, but nothing seemed to work. And Katherine, sensing that her mother wanted the rift mended, did her childish best in the first few months of the separation. She saved sweeties for her daddy, would sidle up to him and push barley sugars into his pocket, but he never smiled or thanked her. Once, she even pinched some marigolds from a neighbour's front garden, arranging them into a bouquet with a bit of ribbon, but Peter forgot the gift and it sat for days on the box-top of the Singer sewing machine, drooping, unwanted, forgotten.

So when, in a somewhat belated attempt at peace-making, Peter offered to take both girls, Katherine disappeared in an awful tear down the back yard, locking herself into the wash house until her father had left. She had finally accepted that he did not love her, but with that acceptance came a level of fear and insecurity that bordered on neurosis.

Grandad talked to her seriously that night. 'The man is your daddy, Katherine. You should have gone down home with him.'

'This is home.'

Joseph inclined his head thoughtfully. 'This is where you are living for the while. Your home is where your father is.'

'He don't want me.'

'And why would you be saying that, now? Hasn't the man left you here with Mammy because he thought you were too young to be out at night?'

'He only wants Judy. He never plays with me, not like you do. He never says my name and asks me to sing. I am the bestest singer in all the nursery, but he never listens to me singing. I want to stay here with you and Mam and Auntie Theresa and Uncle Joe.'

'Not for ever?'

'For ever and ever, Amen. That's in a prayer at school. I don't like my daddy. You can't make me like him, Grandad.'

Joseph O'Leary looked at his small granddaughter and knew that he could make her do nothing. There was a streak in her, a touch of Rachel, he supposed. Rachel did not suffer fools and neither would this one. Dear Lord, what would become of them all? Now sixty, Joseph had retired early from the iron foundry, giving up his job as moulder because he simply wasn't up to it any more. With one shoulder weakened by surgery after a fall from a horse, and one leg still filled with tiny bits of shrapnel, he was a man older than his years. Old, tired and ready for the long sleep.

'I love you, Grandad.'

'And I love you. Will you sing for me?'

'Yes.' And she sang, in her clear bell-like voice, songs from the old country, songs he had taught all his grandchildren from babyhood. He held her close and stared into the red depths of the fire. A war was coming. His war had not been the one to end all fighting. This next would change lives and perhaps he would not be here to watch such changes. A tear fell into the child's thin red-gold hair. In his mind's eye, he watched young men being mown down like a field of fragile corn, every face white in death, every blade of grass stained dark with immature blood. Why would they never learn? Why? A whole generation wiped out in one fell swoop, another raised now from its leavings. So they would take the sons, everybody's sons, and make them sacrifices to the god of greed. There was no sense to any of it.

On a grim Monday in 1939, Peter Murray presented himself at number 33. His hair was cropped close and his face was ruddy from recent shaving. Joseph's weary eyes began at the army boots, making their slow way over khaki socks into which were tucked trousers of the same colour, up and up over belt and tunic, finally coming to rest on the cap. 'May God have mercy on you,' the old man said quietly. 'Come away in. The children are at school and Rachel's taken a job in the mill canteen. You are going into it, then?'

'Tomorrow. I'm off for training. She'll have to keep the house on while I'm gone.'

'She will. I'll see to it that she does.'

'I . . . I want her home, Dad.'

Joseph swallowed hard. This was the first time Peter Murray had acknowledged their relationship by marriage. ' 'Tis a time of severe turmoil, Peter. She will feel safer here, but I'll try to get her to go back one or two nights a week.'

'Thanks. And it doesn't look all that safe here, does it? I mean, View Street's nearer the sky than anything else round here. There'll be bombs, you know. Has Ju . . . have the girls got their gas masks?'

'They have. We all have. Lancashire Fusiliers then, is it?'

'Aye.'

'Front lines, I shouldn't wonder?'

'Eeh, I don't know, do I? I mean – we'll be the last to know when and where. Same as you've said over the last lot – we're just the cattle, we go where we're put. Only I'm going to try and get on, pass some classes if there's chance.'

'You're looking for education? Out of a war? It might have been possible had you been a regular, but as a call-up . . .'

'I've not been called up. It's not my turn yet. But a few of us decided to go whether or not. I mean, it's our country, isn't it? He'll be wanting more than Poland, you know. Next news, he'll be prancing past the Eiffel Tower and that's only a cough and a spit from England. I just thought I might take advantage . . .'

'Of a war?'

'It's the only bloody chance I'll ever get. Mind, as a Fusilier, I might not go far. The other feller'll have a gun too, I suppose.'

'He will. He most certainly will. Don't think about it, Peter. I never thought about it. God alone knows how many lads I killed before they brought me down. It does not bear imagining. When you go in there, when it comes your time, just keep the tin hat on and the gun blazing. Does Rachel know you've joined up?'

'No. She'll not be all that interested.'

'Ah, now, I wouldn't be saying that, man. This is your chance now, not just for an education, but to see things right between yourself and my daughter. Though the damage to Katherine is probably beyond repair . . .'

'Eh? What damage? Who's been hurting her?'

Joseph breathed a long drawn-out sigh. 'How will they educate you when you can't see past your own nose? The child is terrified of you, frightened to death. Where she expected love, she got coldness. Sure I've tried to be a father to her, but it's not the same. Unless you can get round Katherine, the child is a wedge between you and Rachel for evermore.'

Peter's lip curled slightly. 'She's only a kid! How can a kiddy come between man and wife, eh?'

'She resents you. For not loving her. Peter, she resents your resentment. Even at five years of age, she knows she was a disappointment to her father. Can you put that right?'

'I don't know.'

'Do you want to? Do you love the little girl?'

Peter hesitated. 'No,' he said eventually. 'I don't love her. I suppose this is the time for truth, what with the war and all. No point in lying over these things. No. At first, I thought she wasn't mine. I know she is mine – I do know that now. Only I can't get near her. It's not just me. I know there's something wrong with me if I can blame a baby for not being a boy and for its mother turning barren. But it's her too. There's summat about Katherine. It's a way she has of looking at me . . .'

'As if she knows everything?'

Peter shot a grateful glance in the old man's direction. 'That's it! As if she's got all the answers.'

'Her mother was the same. Rachel bested me from infancy, she had me heart scalded every day of her young life. And my wife's mother back in Dublin used to tell me that Katherine's granny was the same as a child – all eyes and no comment. But if only you knew Katie, Peter! If only you knew your own daughter! She sings like an angel and her drawings are like the pictures of a child twice her age. Judith is a clever and industrious girl, but I'm convinced that Katherine has a brain that will shame us all. Ah well. Perhaps after the war . . .'

'Aye. Happen when it's all over there'll be no problem. If Rachel's a widow, then . . .'

'Away with your bother, man! I wasn't meaning that at all! A war changes everyone – even children. Perhaps

34

it changes children most of all. When you come back at the end, you can have a fresh start – all of you.'

'We'll see.' He rose to leave.

'Will you be back to say farewell?'

'I will. And I'll get some leaves before . . . before whatever.'

Joseph O'Leary stood at his front door and watched his son-in-law marching away from him in the ill-fitting uniform. Poor Rachel! Poor Judith and poor Katherine! But most of all, his thoughts were with Peter Murray. He was the one going into the 'whatever'. And only a man of Joseph's experience could begin to know what that meant.

The war meant little to Judith. At worst, it was an inconvenience, because she liked her bed and did not enjoy the many nights spent in a communal shelter at the back of Grandad's house. They lived in Maybank Street during the days now, full days at the weekends, and during the week coming home from school for tea, then sitting awhile to listen to the wireless when the battery was working. After dishes were washed, all three of them made their way to Grandad's for the night, and Judith thought this was all very silly and time-consuming. No sooner did she settle with a book than someone moved her from one place to another.

Katherine was terrified. The wail of the sirens made her jump almost out of her skin, and she became even more 'nervy' and 'highly-strung' during that first awful year, that year of silence, dread and rumour. A further problem was that she seemed to take an unhealthy and very mature interest in the progress of the fighting, pushing herself to read daily and local presses, worrying herself ill when the Battle of Britain started and all those poor men went up in aeroplanes.

Rachel dragged her off to the doctor. 'She doesn't sleep, she won't eat, she's always in a corner worrying and she's driving me out of my mind and all.'

'Is she taking her cod-liver oil and orange juice?'

'Yes. And malt on a spoon. I dose her up with malt every morning.'

'Good . . . good.' The man listened to the child's heart. 'She's thin, Mrs Murray, very thin. Does she have a cough?'

'No, not really. Only the same as everybody else – when she has a cold, like. But she won't behave, Doctor. I can't get really good food, you know how we're all fixed with rationing. But we've got a few hens in the wash house and she won't even take an egg. I can get her to eat a bit of yellow on dipped bread, but she won't eat no white. Then when me dad kills a chicken, this one goes into mourning, won't eat what she calls her friends. I'm at the end of me rope, can't do a thing with her.'

Dr Barnes stared with mock-severity at the child before him. 'Won't eat your friends, eh?'

'No. They ate Martha last week. Just because she stopped laying eggs.'

The doctor struggled not to smile. 'Do you want to die, Katherine?'

Rachel stepped forward. 'Nay, don't go frightening her, she'll only get worse!'

'Shush!' He placed a finger to his lips, then spoke again to Katherine. 'If you don't eat, you will starve to death.'

'The spuds is all green,' the child said clearly. 'I will not eat green spuds.'

'Neither will I. Green potatoes are dangerous. Tell you what, will you eat my chickens? My chickens have no names. If I eat yours and you eat mine . . .'

A half-smile played over Katherine's mouth. 'You're daft, you are.'

The doctor straightened. 'Well. That's me put in my place, I suppose. Katherine, will you eat anonymous chicken?'

'A chicken without a name, you mean?'

'Yes.'

She pondered. 'With stuffing on the side. I'll eat it with stuffing on the side, but not out of its bum.'

The doctor threw back his head and laughed heartily. 'What you have here, Mrs Murray, is a child over-endowed with intelligence and sensitivity.'

'Aye, and without a pick of flesh to her bones. The cruelty will be having me up about her. You could play a tune on her ribs.'

'Wait outside, Mrs Murray,' he said quietly. 'I want a private word with my patient.'

When they were alone, the young doctor watched as Katherine pulled on her clothes. Then he squatted on his haunches so that his face would be level with hers. 'What are you afraid of, child?'

'The war.'

'Just the war?'

She nodded quickly. 'Mind, there's other things I don't like. I don't like boys with irons on their clogs and I don't like soldiers.'

'Oh? Why not?'

'They frighten me. Their clothes are rough and a horrible colour. Boys kick. Soldiers kill each other. People kill hens too. Even nice people like my grandad. Sometimes, I don't seem to like anything at all, except for drawing.'

He took her tiny hands in his large palms. 'What about Daddy? Do you like him? Are you afraid of him?' He knew enough of the family's circumstances to ask this very leading and dangerous question.

'I don't like my dad. He doesn't like me, see? He only likes our Judith. She's a good girl, never does owt wrong.'

'But what wrong have you done, child?'

She suddenly seemed to age, for the eyes of an old woman stared blankly from her face as she said quite simply, 'I got borned. And I got borned a girl. I heard them talking about it – my mam and Grandad and Uncle Joe. After me, my mam can't have any more babies. I should have been a boy.' She studied their intertwined fingers for a second or two. 'I tried being a boy for a few days, pinched some keks off a line at the back of Hillside Street. But wearing keks doesn't make you a boy, and I've got a bit missing. So I put the trousers back on the line.'

John Barnes suddenly felt a hatred for Peter Murray, a hatred that made his stomach churn with anger. 'You're a fine lass, Katie. There's no need for you to try to be a boy.'

'And no need for me to try to like my dad either. If he doesn't like me, then I shan't like him. So there.'

'Things will be different once it's all over, love. When he gets back safe, he'll be glad of his little girl.'

'No!' She stamped her foot sharply. 'And I'm still not eating green spuds.'

He released his hold on her. 'My God,' he whispered beneath his breath. 'Six years old! Whatever are you going to become at all?'

She raised her chin. 'Not a boy, I do know that. Partly because I can't, mostly because I don't want to. Anyway, who wants irons on their clogs?'

There was no answer to that, he thought as he opened the door to allow Rachel in. There was no answer at all to this precocious child.

2

Peter came home on leave several times. When he did, the family lived at 39 Maybank Street, and things looked fairly normal on the surface. But each time he came home, Katherine ran away at least once to her grandfather's house. Joseph brought her back on every occasion, and she returned to her proper home without a great deal of protest. It was as if the child had a point to make and, come what may, she would make it and be damned.

School was all right – Katie quite liked that. It was a place where she could be just like everyone else, where it didn't matter that daddy didn't love her. At school, she could do things, pretend about things. There was story time for a start, she loved that. Then there was composition and drawing – even arithmetic held a certain logical charm.

But there were also the bullies. It was about them she had expressed her concern to the doctor. They were big, loutish lads with irons on the wooden soles of their clogs, and they took pleasure from frightening anyone who seemed smaller and defenceless. Katherine Murray was certainly small, definitely defenceless in the physical sense. But what the lads hated most particularly about her was that she was cheeky. When they threatened her, she conceded no ground, showed little fear and gave them a load of lip, so they decided, in their infinite wisdom, to teach her a lesson.

The lesson involved a length of rope, a lamp-post, and several six-year-old thugs. At four o'clock one October afternoon, they fastened the protesting child to the lamp standard and threw stones at her. She faced them, eyes

39

wide and unblinking as they hurled abuse and missiles in her direction. 'Pig-face!' they shouted. 'Ugly red-head cow, silly teacher's pet, scrawny kid.' She bit back the threatening tears. If her fear showed, they would have power over her forever. Even when a sharp stone grazed a corner of her eye, she stood her ground.

Then suddenly her father was there, his arm in a sling from a recent practice accident that had resulted in extra leave. With an almighty roar, he lifted a brick from the pavement and threw it at the lads. 'Never touch my daughter!' he roared at their disappearing backs. He stared at her in silence for a while. They were both tied up, she to the post, he to a rigid splint. With much difficulty, he unfastened the ropes with his one good hand. They eyed one another cautiously. 'Why?' he asked at last.

'Because I'm only a girl.'

'Katherine!' He paused. This was the child he did not, could not love, yet he somehow wanted to protect her. Was this paternalism? Had it arrived at last – too late? There was despair in his eyes. 'It's OK to be a girl. I'm sorry.'

'So am I. If I were a boy, I'd knock the shit out of them.'

His mouth twitched. 'You shouldn't say words like that. Judith never says those words.'

She looked up at him, yet her eyes held such an air of arrogant superiority that he felt as if he were the shorter of the two. 'Judith never does anything interesting,' she said, clearly. 'Judith is boring.'

He realized with a terrible jerk of his heart that this was the first time he had had a conversation with this child. And she was walking away, cool as a cucumber, covered in blood – the kid was walking away from him. 'Wait!' he called.

Immediately, obediently, she stopped. But she did not turn her head in his direction. Instead, she simply stared ahead and waited for him to catch up with her. 'What do you want?' she asked now.

'What do you mean, what do I want? We're both going home, aren't we?'

'You want to walk with me?'

'Why not?'

'I don't know.'

They walked along a few paces, then Katherine sniffed and said 'Thanks.' Her tone was subdued. 'They get me cos I'm cleverer than them and I do all the sums right. They can't fight with words, so they use their hands and feet and stones. Like soldiers.'

'I'm a soldier.'

'Yes, I know.'

'And I can't fight with words?'

She stopped and looked at his bandaged arm. 'You never say words, not to me. And you're not doing so well with the other sort of fighting, are you? Does it hurt?'

He smiled uncertainly. 'I haven't done any fighting yet. I got this falling off a wooden horse in the gym. It was an accident.'

'Oh.' They resumed their walk. 'Does it hurt?'

'A bit. Does your face hurt?'

'A bit.'

He coughed. 'So, what are you going to do about the bullies?'

She shrugged. 'They'll get fed up now. They'll move on to somebody else. If they don't, I'll find a way. I ripped Tommy Holland's sum book up last week and he got the cane. There's always a way to get back.'

'Katherine?'

'What?'

He cleared his throat self-consciously. 'We've had a bad start, you and me. But we're both in the wars, aren't we? Me in real muck and bullets, you stuck with that crowd at Peter and Paul's. Don't you think it's time we . . . well . . . made up?'

Her eyes were round as she asked, 'Friends, like?'

'Yes. Friends, Katherine.'

'Oh.'

'Well? What do you say?'

'We can be friends.' It was obvious that the words were being chosen carefully. 'Even though I'm not a boy, and even though I'm not Judith, I suppose we can be friends.' It wouldn't be easy. She knew with an unwavering certainty that it would not be easy. 'We can try to like one another, then Mam will be happy.'

Peter Murray's breath seemed stuck in his throat. She was bright, clever and – yes – infinitely more interesting than her older sister. Not that his instinctive love for Judith could ever be lessened, but this was . . . different. Possibly more valuable, because it had needed learning, had come about through a process of pain. 'Forgive me, lass,' he whispered. 'For God's sake, forgive me.'

And she looked at him with a smile of such sadness and beauty that his heart was almost cut from him. She was a stunner! In repose, her face was ordinary, un-remarkable, even plain. But when she smiled, it was as if the sun had been turned on by God's magic switch. 'You can't help it,' she said quietly. 'Grandad said you'd come round in time. And Grandad's always right.'

So began the relationship between father and daughter, though the latter was six years old. It was a tentative start to a love that would never come easily to either of them. For what no-one realized was that Katherine's faith in humanity had already been shaken, that it was too late for her to form a complete partnership with Peter. Almost from birth, she had missed her father's love, and those six missing years formed a hole that would never be healed. More than that, her ability to give of herself and of unquestioning love had been sorely diminished during her infancy. But on that October day in 1940, the whole family rejoiced in the peace treaty that had apparently been negotiated between father and daughter.

Rachel was particularly pleased. Peter had gone back to fight for King and country, and Katherine had cried when the train pulled out of Trinity Street. 'Why are you crying?' Judith had asked, her own blue eyes dry and wide with surprise. 'Why is she crying?' she had asked her mother.

'Because she's found summat and they've took it away.'

After this, Katherine's obsession with the war took on massive proportions. She wept copiously over fallen countries whose names she could neither read nor pronounce, and on the week beginning 12 May 1941, she took to her bed 'forever', would not eat and refused to attend school. The whole family was forced to remain in Maybank Street, because the child's hysteria kept them there. When Joseph arrived to lift her from the bed, she kicked and screamed until the frail man gave in to her.

Dr Barnes was sent for. 'What is it now?' he asked the pale-faced patient. 'There's a war on – what the hell are you doing in bed when there's trouble enough?'

She studied him as if from a distance. 'London,' she said quietly.

'Oh. And you stopping in bed and not eating will build all the bridges up again and stop the city burning, is that it?'

She stared at the ceiling. 'If I am very, very good, nothing will happen. If I stay very still, everybody will stop getting hurt and things will go right.'

'What are you? A bloody student Buddhist monk?' He shook his head as if to clear it. Why was he asking such a question of a child not yet seven? 'Good God!' A large hand passed over his face as he wished, not for the first time, that he'd paid more attention during psychology class. 'Tell me about it, Katie. Come on, spit it out.'

The child in the bed was weeping softly now. 'Over five hundred bombers. They killed one thousand and four hundred people in just one night! They hit the big clock!' Hysteria bubbled nearer the surface now. 'It won't get put right till they've got me! I should never have been born . . .'

He opened his mouth to interrupt, but she continued, 'They hit Parlyment. That's where they do all the plans . . .'

'No!' He shook her quite fiercely. 'Plans are done under the ground in a secret place.'

But she brushed aside his words and, with her teeth chattering while he continued to shake her, she went on, 'In the paper, it says London can't take no more. They are crying in the streets, little girls and boys with no house and no mam!'

He allowed her to fall back on to the pillow. 'And is this your fault?' he roared. 'Is it?'

'Yes!' This word was elongated until it became a scream. 'If I was a good girl, God wouldn't let it all happen.'

'Bloody Catholics!' he cursed. 'Bloody newspapers and wireless! What have they told you at that daft school, eh? That you can finish the war by praying?'

'I don't say my prayers at night,' she moaned. 'And when I did, I prayed that . . . that . . .'

'What? Tell me, girl. You will tell me what is at the bottom of this or I will take you to the hospital. Well? What did you pray?'

'I can't say it. I can't!'

'If you don't, you will be very ill. And I will stay here until you tell me what you prayed. While I stay here, other people are needing me. You are keeping me away from sick people.' He cursed himself inwardly, because wasn't he doing the same thing he blamed the nuns for? Wasn't he playing on that over-developed sense of guilt? 'Tell me, Katherine Murray.'

She turned slowly to face the wall, pulling the cover over her head before beginning to speak. 'I prayed . . .

44

I prayed for us to stay with Grandad.' Her voice was muffled.

'What?'

'I wanted to stay in View Street.'

'What's wrong with that?'

'HE HAD TO DIE!'

The doctor frowned. 'Who did? Grandad?'

'Don't be silly!' She jumped up in the bed, her eyes wide and staring. 'My dad! I prayed that the Germans would kill my own dad! That is the most wickedest thing I could ever do! And I never told in confession and I went to mass and holy communion with it all inside me, all the sin! So the bombs still come!'

He faced the window while he pondered. This one was too clever for her own good, but not clever enough yet to work out all these mixed feelings. That parents could make such a God-awful mess of rearing a child . . . 'You are not . . . significant enough to be responsible in any way for this war, Katie. A man called Hitler started this mess, a very evil man. The sins are his, not yours. And you're not the first person who hasn't liked his or her father. I didn't like mine. When he died, I felt like celebrating.'

'But I like him now. I try very hard to like him. I said the prayers before, when he wouldn't talk to me. The prayers are all saved up in heaven. When the Germans kill my dad, it will be my fault!'

The doctor swivelled on his heel and marched towards the bed. 'I am a doctor,' he said gravely. 'I am a very important man. Right?'

'Right.'

'Do you think God will listen to me?'

'He should do. Being as you save people.'

'Then get down on your knees with me, Katie. I, as a very imporant man, will un-pray your prayers.'

'Will it work?'

'Yes.' He gritted his teeth. If Peter Murray went and

got himself killed, then this child would never believe in anything, would she? Deity, the medical profession, people in general . . . her whole life would likely go down the drain. It occurred to him that he must cut a comical figure kneeling by the bed with a small child. But medicine, he told himself firmly, comes in all kinds of bottles, and this was medicine for the soul.

'Dear God,' he began, his voice suitably sombre. 'Look down on this little girl and bless her. You gave me the gift of healing, and now I seek to mend this child's tortured soul. She prayed for her father to die, but this was a mistake. Guard the life of Peter Murray against all aggressors, and forgive Katherine for her error.' He then threw in a bit of Latin, a *quod erat,* a couple of *ad infinitums* and a *Deo gratias.* After all, the child was a Catholic. He glanced sideways at her. 'OK?' he asked.

Her face positively glowed. 'Yes. Ta, Doctor. I thought I could never tell nobody about what I'd done.'

He left her there on her knees and went down to tackle Rachel. 'That bloody man of yours doesn't deserve a girl like Katherine! She's whipping herself because of the way he's treated her.'

'I know.'

'And look how he treated you too, eh? Like a rag for the cart, like something to be cast away as worn out. Bloody fool, he is.'

'Things are better now, Doc,' she said lamely.

'Better? They'd better be better. I'm not having her blaming herself for London burning. He can never mend what he's done, never! If she carries on like this, I'll have her removed to the Cottage Homes. She needs peace from all of you, especially those stupid nuns. You're a sensible woman, Rachel. How can you let the old crows put so much nonsense into your children's heads?'

'It's our Faith. You can't dictate our Faith!'

'I can if it's killing her! Now. Keep the wireless switched off at news time and don't let her near a paper.'

'Eh? She reads the headlines on her way to school. I can't stop her knowing what's going on. And you'll not take my child away, Dr Barnes. I shall write to Peter this very day and tell him what you've said. I shouldn't be at all surprised if he goes AWOL if he thinks you're putting his daughter away.'

'His daughter? Huh! He never recognized her existence till recently. The damage is done, Rachel. No matter how nice he is to her in the future, that girl will never forget how she was spurned. This could alter her whole life. Fortunately, she's young enough to pull herself together, but it's no thanks to either of you.'

'What was I supposed to do?'

'You could have left him. Permanently!'

'I'm a Catholic . . .'

'Ah. You see? We're back to that again, back to your bloody religion. Well, you mark my words, Rachel Murray. That child is disturbed and a disturbed child makes an unstable adult. On your head be it!' He picked up his hat and stormed from the house.

Judith arrived home from the library. 'What's for tea?' she asked.

'Tea?' roared Rachel. 'Tea? Your sister's up there ill, and all you can think about is your stomach.'

'She makes herself ill.'

Rachel stared hard at her older daughter. 'Happen she does, Judith. And happen she just can't help it.'

'Why can't you behave yourself like Judith does?' Rachel Murray stood in front of the grate, her hand outstretched towards her difficult daughter. 'Judith never gets in trouble. And look how smart she is in her uniform. She never comes home looking like the cat's dragged her out of the river. Where've you been? We'll be on blackout in a minute, I've been past meself worrying. And there's your Grandad poorly too up yonder. We've got to hurry up.'

Katherine wiped a smudge of mud from the end of her nose. She didn't care. It was 1944, she was ten years old and she was in love. 'I've been playing with Mike Wray. We got a bit interested in building a house, so I forgot the time.'

'Forgot the time? You've been on that bombsite again, haven't you? While our Judith's been up at Grandad's for an hour or more. She's likely done all her homework by now! And how are you going to shape if you pass your scholarship, eh? I took the doffing job for you and your sister! Five days a week I work in that mill to save for your education. And what do you do? Sneak off with Michael Wray!'

'He's my best friend.'

'You shouldn't have a boy for your best friend. You should have a girl like . . .'

'Like Judith does,' mimicked the unrepentant child. She was happy. Happy, happy, happy! And she wasn't going to let Mam spoil it. Rome was free again, British soldiers were on their way to Paris, everything was going to be all right! And Dad was coming home with a bad foot – he probably wouldn't have to go back again. And Mike had given her a hairslide with a flower on it, and he'd blushed when he gave it her, so he loved her and Mam was such a pest. 'Are we going or not?' asked Katherine. 'You keep telling me I'm late, then you keep standing there. What's the matter?'

'Grandad.'

'Oh.'

'With everybody wed now and him on his own all day, well, he's let himself go. The doctor says it's pneumonia, Katherine. Our Nellie's with him at the minute . . .'

'And Judith.'

'Yes, but Judith'll be doing her . . .'

'Her homework.' snapped Katherine. 'Is he going to die?'

Rachel's head drooped. 'They think so, lass. He's not so good.'

Katherine studied her shoes sadly. 'I love my grandad. He used to go on about shoes and clogs. He took notice of me.'

'I know.'

'Why do people have to die, Mam?'

Rachel shrugged weary shoulders. 'To make room for more, I suppose.'

'Then why can't it be just the bad people? And Grandad doesn't take up much space.'

'You're ten now, lass. You know the answers as well as I do. Grandad's old. He's never been all that well since the last war ended. I reckon he's had longer than what we expected.'

'Do we have to go up and look after him?'

'Aye. We'll lock up here, then we'll stop with him till it's all over one way or the other. Our Nellie'll have to get back home, so it's down to us.'

'It's always down to us. Last time Grandad was ill, it was down to us. Not that I mind, Mam. But he's their dad too. You'd think they'd want to be with him.'

'Yes. Yes, he was a good dad. A very grand man, he was. Eeh, I wish you could have seen him, our Katie. Done up in his good suit and with me mam on his arm. His moustache was dark then, all waxed at the ends, it was. And me mam, well, she was just beautiful.'

'Was she?'

'You're like her.'

'I'm not beautiful.'

'You will be, lass. Aye, you will be. Now get that fire doused with tea and make sure all the gas is off. Your clothes are already up there, our Nellie carried them. I'm just going next door to tell Eileen to keep an eye on this place – for the post and that. And for God's sake, don't start your worrying. I've enough on without you ill on top of everything else. And get your face rinsed, you look like you're straight out of a midden feet first . . .'

When Rachel had left, Katherine stood and stared at the photograph of her father over the mantelpiece. He was a sergeant major now, and he wore his crested stripes with an air of great pride. There was a commission waiting for him at the War Office, he only needed to pick it up when he was ready. He'd intended to ship the whole family off to India where they could have had servants and a posh house, but his recently wounded foot would put a stop to all that. Katherine breathed a sigh of pure relief. Mam hadn't wanted to go to India and neither had she. It would be too hot there for people with red hair and fair skin. Judith hadn't said much, Judith never did. Life seemed to leave the older girl untouched, but Katherine guessed that her sister would not have wanted to give up her place at Mount St Joseph's Grammar School for Girls.

So, they would be staying here. Some posh bloke from the regiment had got Dad a promise on a job over at the paint and varnish works, a sit-down job too on account of all the exams he'd passed during his training. Only now, to spoil everything, poor old Grandad was going to die.

They walked together up the darkened street, mother and child hand in hand as usual. People came out of their houses with little gifts, poultices and inhalations for the old man, teacakes and bits of precious meat for the rest of the family. Rachel thanked them all soberly, then she and Katherine walked those last paces towards a house of death, a house that had once been so happy.

Rachel perched on the edge of her father's bed, her mind going back to the day when they'd first moved here, little Joe in his father's arms, the rest of them taking care of each other. The sheer luxury of the house after Isabel Street had been breathtaking. And when Dad had got a bit more money, he had bought a secondhand crystal set and they had all fought over who got a listen to it.

She remembered bath nights, first come first served, last in dirtiest out. And kneeling over a paper while he fine-tooth-combed her hair with the dry comb for 'walkers', then with the wet steel comb for eggs. He had been a good dad, the best dad possible. Women had set their caps at him, for he had been a fine-looking man, but as far as Rachel knew, Joseph O'Leary had remained celibate since the death of his beloved wife. Aye, that was a dad. That was a real man.

He stirred in his sleep. 'Rachel?'

'I'm here, Dad.'

'Look after the little one. And Judith too. Say goodbye to them all for me.'

'I will. Hang on, Father Gorman's coming.'

She left priest and dying man together so that the last confession might be made in privacy and with dignity, then, as she came towards the stairs, she saw a dark shape huddled against the banister. 'Katherine?'

'Has he gone, Mam?'

'No. He's getting extreme unction.'

'They should all be here.'

'Yes.' Yes, after all he'd done for them, his sons and daughters should have been with him at the end. But they had their own lives to lead, children to mind, husbands away at war. So it was left, as always, to Rachel because she was geographically closest.

'Can I be with him, Mam?'

'At the end?'

'Yes. If it was me, he'd stay at my bed, wouldn't he?'

'He would.'

'Judith's not bothered. She slept through the whole war, didn't she? Why does Judith never worry, Mam?'

Rachel sighed heavily. 'We're all made different, lass. And thank God for it too. It wouldn't do for every one of us to be worrying and mithering like you do. Judith would likely sleep through an earthquake. You're the worrier, Lord help you. Aye, it's all gone in one bucket, hasn't it?'

'Can I be with him?'

'Aye, when the Father comes out, you go and sing them nice songs for your Grandad.'

So Joseph O'Leary slipped into the afterlife with a smile on his face, because his granddaughter was standing with her back to the window, a hand reaching down to clutch his, that clear voice achieving without effort the final notes of 'Danny Boy'. And as she promised him, in song, that she would be here in sunshine and in shadow, he breathed his last. Although Katherine knew he had gone, she carried on to the end, telling him with sweet purity that she had 'loved him so'.

Rachel came in and found her daughter lying across the foot of Joseph's bed, as if preparing to sleep where she had slumbered so many times during her infancy. 'Come on, lass,' whispered Rachel. 'You can't do nothing for him now.'

'I can be here.' There was a stubborn note in her voice. 'I can be here till they come to do whatever they do.' She rubbed her eyes fiercely as Rachel drew a sheet over her dead father's face. 'He was a nice man, my grandad.'

'Yes, he was. Now get to bed.'

Katherine rose to her feet and stared down at the still shape of her grandfather. 'I'm staying to pray for him,' she said. 'Judith can sleep enough for both of us.'

'Judith's got sense.'

Katherine looked her mother straight in the eye. 'I know that. I do know that. You don't have to keep telling me about Judith's sense. Grandad says I'm not like Judith, and that I don't have to be like her, or like anyone else. I am me. He told me that.' She waved a hand towards the bed. 'And he's always right. He was right about my dad, wasn't he?'

'Yes, I suppose he was.'

Rachel Murray looked into the dark tunnel of the life

that lay before her, a life she could do little to alter. Not liking what she saw in the blackness, she busied herself about the room, tidying and hanging up her father's clothes. But the pictures would not leave her mind. The love she had used to have for her husband was dead, as dead as the man in the bed. Peter Murray had killed that love just as surely as if he'd taken a knife or a gun to some living creature. All because of Katie. And now there would be no Dad here to take the edge off things, no grand old man to keep the peace between herself and Peter.

Rachel turned then and saw her daughter sobbing alone in a corner. That was the trouble, thought the mother as she held out her arms. No-one ever noticed Katherine weeping in a corner. Not until it was too late.

Judith was just about sick to death of their Katherine. For a start, she was a show-off. Everybody at Mount St Joseph's said that Katherine Murray was a show-off right from the first day and Judith, as a second-year, had to bear the brunt of all the jibes. 'Who's got a little sister who doesn't know her place?' they all asked when Katherine took first prize for art. And she didn't just take the prize for her own year, oh, no, Miss Clever Clogs had to walk off with the Missal for the whole lower school, beating everybody up to and including third years.

Then there was Katherine's fixation with Michael Wray, which was becoming a terrible pain both at home and at school. The whole assembly seemed to know about Katherine's assignations in Queens Park. Notes were passed around classes, 'Katherine Murray = Michael Wray', with love hearts drawn all over them in pink and purple. The fact that Michael Wray was a third-year at Thornleigh didn't help either. Many sixteen-year-olds at the Mount didn't have boyfriends, so for an eleven-year-old upstart sister to flaunt one in the park every weekend was a source of desperate shame.

Judith decided to tackle Mam about it. 'She's round the duck pond with him every Saturday.'

'Oh, I see.' Rachel pushed a lock of hair from her face. 'Pass me the Brasso, will you? She's not doing anything wrong, is she?'

'She's showing me up.'

'It's just her way, love. She likes Michael, that's all. It's only like you and Joan Atherton. How would you feel if somebody tried to separate you from Joan?'

'It's not the same! Everybody's laughing at me, saying my little sister's fast. How do you think I feel? She breezes in and takes all the art prizes, never does a stroke of work and comes in the top three of the class. She makes me sick. I wish she'd never passed!'

Rachel glanced briefly at Judith. This was not like her at all. She usually didn't notice what went on around her. 'I'll talk to her.'

'Yes. But will she listen? Does she ever listen?'

'Just don't tell your dad about it.'

'Don't worry, I won't.' Judith knew that the situation between Katherine and Peter was on a knife edge these days. For some reason beyond Judith's comprehension, Dad had got it into his head that their Katherine was 'unusually gifted'. This meant that he put a lot of pressure on the child, and even in anger, Judith would not set him on her little sister. He was already annoyed about the homework, to rile him over Michael Wray would have been well beyond a joke.

Peter put his head round the front door. 'Right!' He stepped inside, hands rubbing together in glee. 'We're off! I got made up to foreman, Rachel. An extra two quid a week and all the paint we can use. Sam Pilkington's found us a house too, up Hawthorne Road. It'll be handy for the girls' school, and there's nowt to keep us here now, is there?'

Rachel looked at him askance. Leave Maybank Street? Leave all her friends and neighbours? 'Oh, I see. When are we moving?'

He frowned. 'Nay, there's no need to go overboard with enthusiasm. What would you want to be stopping here for? You know it upsets you seeing somebody else living in your dad's house.'

'I'm just used to it here.' Rachel finished polishing her brass plaque. 'And so are the girls.'

He looked at Judith. 'Do you mind moving?'

'No. Not if it's nearer school.'

'And Katherine? Where is she?'

Judith studied her shoes. 'Out.'

'Out?' His face darkened. 'What the hell's she doing out at seven o'clock on a Monday night? Ah, I see. You all thought I was away for the evening, didn't you? Well? Where is she?'

'Borrowing a book,' said Judith hastily. 'I think.'

'Rachel?'

'I don't know. I just turned me back for a minute, then looked round again, and there she was, gone.'

He hobbled over to a fireside chair. As always, as if to demonstrate outwardly the size of his emotional wound, his foot played him up just to keep pace with the hurt he now felt at his younger daughter's 'betrayal'. Hadn't they given up a lot to get these two educated? Wasn't he a fine man placing such store in girls, wasn't he making the best of things? And him a war hero too.

Rachel noted the saintly expression on his face and sighed inwardly.

When Katherine returned at a quarter to eight, Judith was in the kitchen working at her geography books. There was no escape for Katherine. The living room was just a stride off the pavement, and she found herself face to face with her father as soon as she entered the house.

'Well?' he asked, his tone trimmed with sarcasm.

'Oh.' She stopped mid-step. 'I didn't think you'd be here.'

'I am here, though. Where've you been?'

'Sketching in the park.'

'Sketching in the dark, more like. And where's your pad?'

'My friend has it.'

'I see.' He shifted his bad leg into a better position on the ever-ready footstool. 'And what's your friend's name?'

'Michael.'

He shot out of the chair. 'Eh? You've been out with a lad? You're nobbut eleven. What the hell are you doing messing about with lads? Do you think your mam slaves in that bloody mill so's you can start courting now and get wed at sixteen? Our Judith never goes with lads.'

Rachel spat on her rag and took her temper out on the brass rose bowl. 'Leave me out of it,' she muttered. 'I work because I want to.'

Katherine bit her lower lip and put her head on one side. 'I've done nothing wrong,' she said eventually. 'He's my friend . . .'

'And how old is he?'

'Thirteen. He saved me from the bullies after you'd gone back to the war.'

'Thirteen? Thir-bloody-teen?' he yelled. 'He's old enough to . . . to do things! You'll stop away from him, lady!'

'I won't.' A defiant chin was raised. 'He won't hurt me. Michael would never hurt me. He's a Thornleigh boy . . .'

'Bugger Thornleigh! He's too old for you. And you should be with girls, girls your own age!'

'He looks after me.'

Peter stared aghast at his daughter. 'Don't we look after you? Me and your mam?'

She hung her head slightly. 'Yes, I suppose so. But

Michael's interested in art, we both draw pictures. He wants to be an artist and so do I. We've got . . . things in common.'

'Aye, but have you got homework in common? Monday's maths and English, isn't it?'

She nodded just once.

'Then bring your work here and show it me.'

Katherine scurried through to the kitchen and dug around in her satchel. 'Did you tell on me? Did you?' she whispered to Judith.

'No. But I will if it carries on. My whole class is laughing at me because my ugly little sister can get a boy and I can't.'

'I'm not ugly! I'm not!' hissed the smaller girl.

'Huh. Look in the mirror, will you?'

Katherine stared at the twelve-year-old beauty before her, all luscious dark curls, violet eyes and skin like cream. She knew what she herself looked like; she didn't have to go poking about in front of a mirror. Thin red hair, freckles, greenish-yellowish eyes, no flesh on her face. Life was grossly unfair. 'Sometimes, I don't like you, Judith Murray.'

'Ditto.'

Katherine placed her work on her father's knee. 'Oh, I see.' It was obvious that his sails had deflated. 'When did you do it?'

'Tea time.'

'Is it right? Have you got all the answers?'

'Yes.'

He thrust the books back at her. 'Then why didn't you stop in and study like your sister does? If you studied, you could go to university and get a degree. You don't need boys.'

Katherine tilted her chin. 'You needed them though, didn't you?'

Rachel's hand slowed in its polishing of a candlestick. 'Shut up,' she growled.

'Well, it's true! He never bothered with me till he saw me tied to a lamp-post! He never cared till he found out I was as brave as any lad!' Her temper teetered on the edge now, and Rachel grabbed her daughter's arm tightly, but still the girl continued. 'I used to listen when you were arguing. All about me not being a boy and Mam not having any more children. I thought things were all right between us now, but they're not, are they? Oh, no, you're going to pick on me all the while. Miss Goody Two-Shoes in there can't do any wrong, can she? Well, I'm not having you telling me what to do all the while. And I shan't go to university, I shan't. So there!' She stamped her foot against the rug. 'Just because you never went, you force me. It's all right for Judith, she's like a big soft dog, she does as she's told. But I remember things. I'll always remember things!'

Peter Murray struggled to his feet and dealt to Katherine's cheek a blow that sent both mother and daughter reeling, so fierce had Rachel's restraining hold become. But she didn't hold on for long, because the girl ripped herself away, picked up the large brass plaque and clouted her father full in the face with it. 'Don't you hit me,' she snarled as the man put a hand to his nose. 'Don't you ever, ever again hit me. You're always hitting me when Mam's out. Never Judith. Always me!'

With this, she ran from the house, leaving her sobbing mother lying on the floor and her white-faced sister standing in the kitchen doorway.

Rachel picked herself up and stood shaking in the centre of the room, her hand straying along the table's edge as if seeking support. 'You've done it now, Peter,' she said, her voice quivering with tears. 'She'll fetch somebody, you mark my words. I've known ever since I had her that she'd take nowt lying down. Judith, get up to your room. Go on. Don't stand there as if you're practising to be a tailor's dummy!'

Judith turned and fled from the unpalatable scene.

'The little bitch!' With the back of his hand, he wiped a drop of blood from his upper lip. 'Just wait till she gets in.'

Rachel composed herself, straining to listen as Judith's footsteps reached the upper storey. 'Right,' she said. 'You've been hitting her again. While I'm out, you hit her. You're always going on at her, aren't you?'

'She gets what she deserves,' he snarled. 'I only thump her for clarting about when she should be studying.'

Rachel sighed heavily. 'I've had enough, Peter,' she said finally. 'I know you're drinking again. I know you can't control yourself when you're drinking.' He turned his face towards the fire as she went on in a whisper, 'I know what you're like. Nobody knows better than me what you're like. Thank God the two girls don't know the half of it. But I'm your wife, I've had to put up with your temper. Oh aye, and I've the marks to prove it too!'

'That's nowt to do with this,' he mumbled shame-facedly.

'No,' her voice was ominously low. 'Happen it isn't. But if you hit my daughter half as hard as you hit me . . .'

'That's private,' he snapped, turning to face her, though he could not quite meet her eyes. 'And I don't mean it. I don't want it to happen. It's just when I'm . . . when I'm . . .'

'When you're drunk.' She paused fractionally. 'It can't go on, lad. I shall have to go and stop at our Annie's. And you can just forget about Hawthorne Road. Even if we did keep this family together, you'd never manage that rent, not with the amount you drink and put on horses.'

'But I—'

'When she gets in, I get out. And Katherine and Judith too. Our Annie'll take us in. I'm not stopping here for you to use my daughter as a target.'

'Oh aye?' His voice arrived muffled. 'And what about their education? Who'll pay for that once you've hopped it? I'd like to see you putting the pair of them through The Mount on a doffer's wage, especially after you've paid your Annie. She's a grabber, is that one. There's more Irish navvies kipping at her house than there is in all Liverpool.'

'Then the girls will have to leave the school.'

He was suddenly sobbing, head in hands, back shaking violently. 'Oh God,' he moaned, 'I don't know what gets into me. It's something about her. Like she's defying me.'

Rachel sniffed. 'No excuse to hit a little girl. No excuse at all.'

'Please?' He was pleading now, tears coursing freely down his cheeks. 'Give me a chance, Rachel. Just give me a chance . . .'

She hesitated. 'Right,' she said at last, her tone firm and determined. 'We'll stop together on one condition, Peter Murray. Leave our Katherine to me. If you can't deal with her without hitting her, just leave her to me.'

'What? And let her get away with what she's done?'

'You hit her first. And you can't expect a wiry lass like her to put up with being clobbered. She might be thin, but she's strong. Remember how she dealt with the lads? She got them in more trouble than enough when they kept going for her. She'll have you, Peter. She'll get the police or the cruelty – just you wait and see.'

But Katherine didn't bring anyone to the house. She simply stalked in, head held high, her eyes bravely meeting her father's as he sat huddled over the fire nursing his sore nose. And he knew when he looked at her that she had won. Whatever he did to her, she could and would do worse. His defeat did not come with the battered nose, oh, no, the battle had been lost as soon as he raised his hand to her.

Without a word to anyone, the girl walked stiffly through the room and into the kitchen. It seemed that no-one breathed as she opened the stairway door and went upstairs. Judith received her without comment. The drama was over and she had a book to study.

'You've lost her.' There was a note of finality in this statement from Rachel. 'What ground you made up, you've just lost. There'll be no getting her back now. You are the biggest damn fool I ever met in my life.'

'Aw, shut up. She'll get over it.'

'She won't. And neither will you, you big soft lad. Shouldn't you go to hospital and see if your nose is broke?'

'It's not broke.'

Rachel began to set the table for breakfast, her mind filled by a picture of Katherine's determined face. His nose might not be broken, but that tenuous link with his younger daughter had been severed, possibly forever. Yet they loved one another, Rachel knew that.

After that night, no further mention was made of a house in Hawthorne Road. Peter knew that Rachel had been right. As expected, he spent his extra money on whisky and horses, coming into the house only to sleep and eat. His downslide had begun again.

Michael Wray ran his fingers across the clear handprint on Katie's face. 'He did that? Your own father did that?'

'Yes.' Her head was bowed in shame. 'I couldn't go to school today in case anybody noticed it.'

'I'll kill him.' The boy's tone was restrained in spite of the severity of his words. 'Or I'll set my father on him. He's a sergeant now, you know. The other police think a lot of my dad, they'll listen to him.'

'No! I don't want . . . I don't want my dad in trouble.'

'Why not?'

Her mind said, 'Because I love him', but she spoke aloud, 'Because my mother couldn't stand the shame. He's never been happy because I was a girl. He seems to want me to be like a boy, successful and everything. It's with me being ugly. He knows Judith will get married and her education will be wasted. But me, I'll be on the shelf.'

'Rubbish. You're not ugly.' He knew his face was burning with embarrassment. 'You'll get married, Katie.'

'Huh! Who'll have me? I've got stringy hair, eyes like a cat's, great big feet and . . .'

'A very nice smile.' He hesitated and turned away slightly. 'Yours is the sort of face painters like. It's got lots of angles and planes, very good bone-structure. After you'd been to tea that day, my mother remarked on your cheekbones. Very high, she said. Very elegant.'

'Oh.'

'Anyway.' He kicked a stone across the path to hide his acute discomfort. 'I'll marry you.'

'Will you?'

He nodded. 'We'll have a farm with a duckpond, lots of mallards to paint. And in a barn we can make a big studio with good lighting and hundreds of canvases. I'll use oils and you can use water-colours. We'll have seven children and they'll all be artists and actors and stuff like that.'

'Nice. But we'll have to wait years.'

'What will you do till then, Katie? What if he turns on you again?'

'He can't help it. At first, he didn't love me at all. Now, I sometimes think he loves me too much.'

'If he loved you, he wouldn't hurt you.'

'And if he didn't love me, I couldn't disappoint him and make him hurt me. You can't understand, Mike. Nobody but me can understand about me and my dad. I'm special to him. If I let him down, it really gives him pain.'

'If he hits you again, we'll run away and hide till we're old enough to get married and be famous artists.'

She smiled broadly. 'For thirteen, you don't half talk daft.' But the smile remained on her face all the same.

3

Peter Murray leaned on his walking stick and glared at his annoying daughter. She was a mess and no mistake. Blue jeans rolled up to the knees, a sleeveless striped blouse with a flyaway collar, the whole lot covered in streaks and splashes of paint. Her hair, too, was paint-spotted, that beautiful red hair that had thickened out something wonderful during the past few years. 'What do you mean, you're going to Didsbury? Didn't you get an offer for Newcastle?'

'I'm doing teaching,' she said with quiet determination. 'We're both doing teaching so we'll have plenty of spare time for our painting.'

'Both. I see. So it's still you and Mike Wotsisname riding off into an orange sunset, is it?'

'With a touch of burnt umber, yes.'

'Don't you come the clever lip with me, lady! Your mam isn't here to protect you now, is she? Why can't you be like Judith? She's doing so well at Oxford . . .'

'I'm not a linguist. I'm an artist.'

'I see. So you'll be living in a garret next news, all candles and boiled spuds.'

'No. We'll do OK.' She turned as if to leave the room, but he waved his stick at her and she stopped in her tracks, back towards him. 'I hope you're not threatening me, Dad.'

He shook his head sadly. That he could love her so much, that he could fail to tell her how much. He brought the cane down on to the table, noticing how she didn't even flinch at the crash it made. 'Katherine! Study art at

Newcastle or wherever. Study fine art – you can always teach it if you want to.'

'No. Mike and I have it all planned out. I'm going to teach juniors and he's doing seniors. We shall get married as soon as we leave college.' The catch in her voice was caused by the need to explain to him, to tell him that she loved Mike, that she loved her father too, that there was no need for all this animosity. But things had gone too far for that. And things hadn't been right from the start, had they?

'Katherine, why do you have to throw yourself away? Judith hasn't got a boyfriend – she lives for her studies.'

She faced him now. 'Good for Judith. It's all working out wrong for you, isn't it? You thought I'd be your nearly-son and Judith would get married and give you those male grandchildren you're setting so much store by. Well, Judith can't get a man. She might look like an angel, but she's a cold fish. You spoiled her. You made her take and take until she didn't know how to give. As for me, well, I started off as a disappointment, so I might as well carry on in the same vein. I'm not going to be a spinster just for you, just so you can say, "Look, I made a woman into a man". And don't wave your stick at me, I'm eighteen now and I can do as I please.'

'You cheeky young bugger, you!'

'And shouldn't you be down the betting shop? They'll be shutting the doors without your custom.'

'Enough! Is it any wonder I've taken to the horses? With you coming in like a bloody rainbow and your mother going through one of her "silence is golden" phases? Look at you! Just look at the state of yourself! What the hell have you been up to at all?'

'I've been painting ducks.'

He nodded sagely. 'I hope the park keeper never caught you.'

'Pictures of ducks. Not the actual birds.'

'Oh, I thought they'd happen struggled and covered

you in something or other. And what's me-lad-o been up to while you've been painting ducks?'

'Trees. He's been experimenting with greens.'

'Very nice. I hope it stays fine for you.'

She sucked in her cheeks, then exhaled loudly. 'Have you finished? May I go to my room now and get ready for the dance?'

'What dance is that?'

'The Thornleigh and Mount leavers. They've booked the Palais for the fifth and sixth years.'

'What about the paint? Are you going covered in that?'

'No. I'm going to the slipper baths, if you'll excuse me. I agree, I need a good scrub.'

They looked at one another without speaking for several seconds, then she went upstairs to fetch her bath bundle. The man was impossible, he really was! And he looked so . . . so ill. No wonder, she thought as she slipped towels and soap into her brown paper carrier. He drank enough for ten men, gambled away the change. Poor Mam.

Downstairs, Peter Murray pulled on his coat and walked out of the house, leaning heavily on his stick as he made for the betting shop. With a bit of luck, he could catch a bet for tonight's dogs, and to hell with Katherine and her cavorting. But oh God! If only he could say . . . if only he could find the words. What words? I love you? Would she believe him after all this time? Could she be made to realize that he'd loved her since the day of the rope and the lamp-post? Aye, to hell with her. Her and all bloody women.

At the baths, Katherine paid her pennies, refused the bar of coarse soap and the rough towel that came free with the service, then locked herself gratefully into a cubicle. Although splashings and singings could be heard from adjoining baths, this was one of the few places where she could feel alone. She filled the bath as far as it would go without spilling into the overflow, poured in some salts, stripped off her disreputable clothes and sank beneath hot soothing water. It was bliss. Heaven, she had long ago decided, was a hot bath with taps, a soft towel and a jug to rinse her hair with afterwards. Simple. Life could be so simple.

It would be simple with Mike. Mike had already left school and had done his national service in the Air Force. So now they would go to college together, get engaged, be married as soon as the last term was over, then live happily ever after in a cottage with roses round the door. In the evenings, they would paint, together and separately. One day, one of them would become famous. One day, there'd be a Wray hanging in some London gallery and all the snobs would gather to say that they simply had to have a Wray. It didn't matter which one of them became famous – the other would stay at home to mind children and prune roses. Happy. Simple. A perfect life, a life without parents.

She worried about Mam, though. It seemed cruel, leaving her alone with Dad the way he was. It was obvious that he'd never really forgiven life and Mam for not giving him a son. Still. There was nothing she could do about any of it, was there? And it was OK to be happy. Yes, it was OK.

That evening found Kate standing on the corner outside the Palais de Danse. She knew she looked nice. From Auntie Vera, who was always generous with her clothes, she had borrowed a newish cotton dress in pale cream with a pattern of large gently blue cornflowers. The same aunt had lent her some dyed blue high-heeled shoes and an off-white stole full of holes, as light as a spider's web, it was. Her burnished hair had curled properly for once, and it reached just to her shoulders, softening the startlingly clean lines of her face.

Mike was late. It wasn't like him to be late. A few of the lads whistled as they passed her, while one or two asked her to go in with them, but she remained where she was, faithful as always. Then he came round the corner with a girl on his arm and a fixed smile on his face. The shock sent her reeling, so that she literally fell against the building.

'Kate!' He sounded breathless. 'This is Josianne, our Pamela's French penfriend. My naughty little sister had other plans for tonight, so I brought poor Josianne as my guest. She has very little English.'

'Allo?' The pretty gamin face was creased by a frown. She looked gorgeous, all swathed in a red silky-satiny material with a daring halter neck. Her eyes and hair were dark, and the mouth was generous, too generous for Katherine's liking. 'How old is she?'

'J'ai seize ans!'

'Ah.' Sixteen! She looked older than Kate did! And suddenly the cornflower dress was dowdy, just a borrowed frock with no glamour, no panache. 'Shall we go in, then?' Katherine's tone was cool.

Inside, a few Brothers and lay-teachers from the girls' school were getting politely inebriated at the bar. Mike left the two girls together while he went for pineapple juices and a glass of beer for himself. Josianne's eyes swept over the room with an air of contempt. '*Il n'y a quelquechose à manger?*'

'I don't speak French.'

'Oh. There is not the professeur of French at your *lycée*?'

'Yes, there is the professeur of French. I don't like French, can't do it.'

'*C'est la même chose pour moi.* For me the same. I not like English, so my father is send me here.'

Katherine ground her teeth noiselessly. Mike's French was flawless – he spoke it like a native! But when he returned to the table, Josianne had been whisked away by the first in a long queue of potential partners.

He sipped at the beer, his eyes following the French girl's every move.

'Well? How long is she staying?'

'Till the end of the dance, I suppose. Though perhaps I should take her home early, she is only sixteen . . .'

'In England. How long is she in England?'

He shrugged, rather too carelessly for Katherine's liking. 'A month – six weeks – I'm not sure.'

'And you'll have to look after her because Pamela's French is appalling.'

'I expect so.'

'What a terrible chore.'

He looked at her for what seemed like the first time since they had come into the hall. 'Katie, are you jealous?'

'Of course not. It's just going to be such a nuisance. It will cut into our art time.'

'Yes.'

She sighed. 'Ah well. Never mind. In a few weeks, we'll be off to Manchester. I hope there's something to paint in Manchester.'

He hesitated, then took another swig of Dutch courage. 'Katie?'

'It's Kate, or Katherine. You know I don't like Katie.'

'OK. Sorry. Look, I didn't want to tell you this tonight, but I'm not . . . I mean . . . I won't be going to Didsbury. My parents weren't happy in spite of the fact that the college had a decent art department. They want me to get a Catholic certificate. I'm going to De La Salle, staying with the Brothers.'

'Oh.' What else could she say? All those plans, all those years . . . 'Oh' somehow summed it all up, didn't it?

'We can meet some weekends.'

'Yes.'

He swallowed another mouthful of ale. 'And we should really mix with other people. I mean, we've only ever been out with one another, haven't we?'

'True. But that was fine with me.'

'Me too!' he said hastily. 'We can get together again,

when college is over. It's not the end, Katie – I mean Kate. But we may be cramping one another's painting style. And you're so much better than me,' he added generously.

'Yes. Yes, I know I am.'

'Pardon?' His jaw dropped for a moment.

'Your style is too flat and lifeless. Perhaps you will do better away from me.'

He stared hard at her. She wasn't talking just about painting, was she? No. The yellow lights in her eyes were flashing like some awful warning of shipwreck or earthquake. 'Do you want to dance?' he asked quietly.

'No. I think you should go and rescue your little French girl before something interesting happens to her. After all, she's only half dressed.'

'Katie!' But she had left him, the table and the pineapple juice before the second syllable of this unwelcome name had left his lips.

She learned several things that night. The first was that she couldn't depend on Mike. The second came to her after several dances; Katherine sounded too saintly and it was better to introduce herself as Kate. Kate from *The Taming of the Shrew*? She half-smiled as some clumsy sixth-former put her through a painful square tango. The last lesson was quite an interesting one. Although she was completely covered by the dress, it was without sleeves, and if she let the stole slip to reveal a shoulder, she got more dances than the girls in low-necked frocks. The introductory stages of sex were no longer a mystery. Men were malleable and women were clever.

Mike didn't get much of a look-in with his French partner. In fact, he seemed to sit out most dances. Almost every time Kate waltzed or quick-stepped by, he was nursing his beer at the same table. Hard cheese, she thought viciously. He came across at one point to where she stood with several girls from school, his face flushing deeply as he asked for a dance. She refused, pleading a sore foot, only to sweep past him seconds later in the arms of a very popular house captain.

The last waltz loomed dangerously near. He wouldn't get a look-in with Josianne, Kate realized that well enough. She glanced round frantically, hoping that some handsome chap would claim her before she became a midnight wallflower. Or cornflower, she mused grimly as she dropped the stole an inch more. She was not heartbroken, refused to be, surely didn't deserve to be heartbroken? Why this great leaden lump in her throat, then?

She swivelled on her heel and faced a blank wall, remembering, seeing in her mind's eye, almost tasting the days that she and Mike had spent together. Eight years, nine years, how long had it been? A hairslide, a new paintbrush, a dirty hanky dipped in the pond to soothe a scraped shin.

It had all been planned, hadn't it? Marriage, children, painting, roses round a cottage door. She was going to cry. She must not cry! For pride's sake, she must hold herself together until the end of this nightmarish dance. Or could she leave now? Could she cross this vast room full of sweating bodies and escape to cleaner and fresher air? Could she?

'Good evening.'

With a supreme effort of will, she pulled herself together and turned to see a man by her side, a real grown-up man, very dashing and good-looking. 'Where did you come from?'

'I gatecrashed.'

'Thought so. How old are you?'

'That's a rude question.'

'And gatecrashing's a rude business.'

'OK. Let's just say I've turned thirty, shall we?'

'Oh. How far over the hill are you?'

'Two years. Will you dance with me?'

She studied him while he led her expertly through a

foxtrot. He had dark hair, eyes that were nearly black, a fresh complexion and thick dark eyebrows. When he closed his eyes, the lashes curled up on his cheeks. It was quite a good face, she decided. Spoiled slightly by a weakish chin, yet saved by a strong nose. Nice. Comfortable. She felt right in his arms. Yes, they fitted together. Mike would be furious, wouldn't he? She looked round and caught no sight of her boyfriend; nor could she see his little French girl. Ah well. Mike was gone, possibly forever. A cold fist seemed to close around her stomach, and she shivered in spite of the intense heat.

'They've gone,' he said into her hair. 'He wasn't good enough for you anyway. I've been watching you for the past hour. Near to tears, weren't you?'

She nodded.

'Not worth it, me dearie. He's a mere child, and here you are dancing with a man. That's why he left. He stormed out with that awful girl in the red dress as soon as he saw us talking.'

'Oh.' She liked him. Especially if he thought Josianne was awful. 'What's your name?'

'Geoff. Geoff Saunders.'

'Kate Murray. Are you married?'

'No. I'm going to marry you.'

She gulped back another 'oh'.

'Knew as soon as I saw you. I'm middle-management with Transglobe Plastics, good prospects, not a bad looker . . .'

'Hang on. I'm only eighteen!'

'So what?'

'I've got to get through college.'

'I can wait.' The music stopped and the last waltz was announced. Without asking, he folded her in his arms and led her round the floor. 'You dance quite well for a young one,' he commented. 'What'll you do at college?'

'Art main, History and English subsids.'

'Teaching?'

'Yes.'

They danced the rest of the waltz in silence, then, after Kate had been to tidy herself in the ladies' room, he took her out into a clear moonlit night and walked her down to his car. 'I'll drive you home.'

'I've not to get in cars with strange men.'

With great ceremony and much flourish, he extracted a card from his wallet. 'At your service, ma'am. Geoffrey Saunders BSc, ARCS.'

'Are you a surgeon or something?'

'No. College of Science, Royal, Associate of. Ma'am!' He clicked his heels and held open the door. 'I don't bite, I change my socks every day and my mother is well looked after. Yes, I am interested in you both body and mind, but I shall not rape you at the traffic lights. Not tonight, anyway.'

She began to giggle. 'You're hopeless, Mr Saunders. And you're only seven years younger than my mother! My dad will go mad if he hears I've been out with an older man.'

'I shan't tell him if you don't.'

'OK. But drop me on Derby Street.'

When he stopped the car at the bottom of View Street, she didn't know what to expect. He was a grown man after all, an adult, probably with experience too. Yes, he was too handsome to be inexperienced. She decided to go for the gauche tack. Perhaps if she came over all innocent, he would like her better. 'What do we do now?' she asked sweetly.

He smiled. 'Well, I ask if I can see you again and you say no.'

'OK. We'll take that bit as read. What then?'

'I find out your address, send flowers and chocolates – oh, and a Valentine's card . . .'

'My mother will kill me!'

'Then I beat down your door, knock out your father,

pick you up on my white horse and we ride off together into . . .'

'An orange sunset with a touch of burnt umber,' she concluded for him, thinking of her father. 'Right. I'll see you again.'

'Tomorrow?'

She shook her head. 'I'd play my hand closer to my chest if I were you. You've already proposed, which I felt was a bit premature and immature . . .'

'Well, hush my mouth!' This was said in a perfect Southern drawl.

'Next week. I'll see you next week. Pick me up here on Friday at seven-thirty.'

'Fine. Now, I kiss you.'

'Is that obligatory?'

'Absolutely compulsory. I cannot allow you to leave these premises without being kissed. It's something to do with car tax.'

'And insurance?'

'Naturally.'

And it was natural, too. It created in Kate the first real sexual feelings she had ever had in her young life. She was confused. Somewhere inside, a knife still twisted in the raw wound left by Mike. But she was young, desirable, wanted by this stranger. That heartbreak could turn to bliss in such a short space of time was a source of great wonderment to her. She wanted more, more kisses and more than kisses. He smelled good, felt good, tasted right and held her properly.

He released her and pushed her towards the passenger door. 'You'd better go. I knew as soon as I saw you . . . You'd better go, Kate.'

'Why?'

'You know why. I'll have to be careful. I've never been with anyone so much younger than myself.'

'But I want . . .'

'To get through college.'

73

'Yes. But I think I could . . . learn to like you. Only I'm all mixed up about Mike and that girl and everything.'

'OK. See me next Friday, then.'

'Bye.'

'Bye, darling.'

She stood on the pavement while the car made a big circle and drove away. No-one had ever called her darling before; darling was something out of the films. The whole thing was like a fairy story. Her legs were suddenly turned to jelly and she leaned against a nearby wall for a bit of support. Mike? God, who the hell had he been? She had a man, a real man, one of her own. And she couldn't tell anybody about him!

She ran into the house, unaware that her cheeks were glowing, that her step was lighter. 'What's up with you?' growled her father who had lost ten bob on a bent dog. 'Been at the beer, have you?'

Rachel looked at her daughter and shivered slightly. She recognized that expression. She remembered it reflected in a mirror years ago when she'd been in love. When she'd thought she was in love. 'Nice time, lass?'

'Great.'

Rachel glanced at Peter. 'Was . . . was Mike there?'

'Eh? Oh Mike, yes, he was there. With his new girlfriend.'

Peter threw his fag-end into the fire. 'Oh heck,' he said with false sadness. 'There's love's young dream gone for a running jump, eh?'

'Pardon?' Kate glanced at him uncomprehendingly. 'Oh, him. Yes. Running jump, I'm afraid.'

'You'll not be getting married straight after college after all, then?' Was that a gleam of hope in his eye?

'I might,' she said defiantly.

She wept that night, soaking her pillow with bitter tears as she mourned her lost love. Yet hope lingered in her bruised heart, hope for a future that had to become

74

a different dream now. Perhaps Geoff would be in the dream, perhaps he wouldn't. But the pain lingered till morning and for many days to come, because the pain was bigger than the pleasure.

At college, Kate was treated as very special because she had two men. There was the young one who used to come over from Cheshire on the bus, a fine-looking blond chap, he was, quite muscular yet sensitive. Everyone knew Mike was sensitive because he carried a portfolio. So in this one boy, Kate had just about everything. Who could need more than brawn and sensitivity?

But then there was her other chap, the one who sent roses on exam days, he who turned up in a car with bouquets and chocolates and lovely manners. Many of the girls were smitten with Geoff, but opinion was divided more or less fifty-fifty. Half the girls felt she should settle for someone her own age, while the rest thought Geoff Saunders too great a chance to pass up. He had money, a car, a good job, superb clothes and, as Kate reminded them jovially, excellent taste in women.

But Mike haunted her, often missing lectures just to come over and see her. 'That bloody French girl!' he cursed more than once. 'I could murder our Pamela. If she'd looked after her penfriend, you would never have gone off with this Geoff chap. Is there nothing I can do? Nothing I can say? Remember our grand plan, Kate. How we were going to get married after college and work together on our painting. He's a pleb. You can't leave me for a pleb!'

She stared hard at him. The hurt he had dealt her had remained raw for many months. Geoff had been the balm, the booster of her ego, the answer to her pain and sorrow. 'I haven't left anyone for anyone. He's just a good laugh . . .'

But he was more than a good laugh. Geoff was her lover, had been her lover for a few weeks now. And she had given herself so freely once he'd explained about keeping her safe from babies. Now, she could scarcely manage to be in the same room as him without touching and caressing him. Sex was addictive. Sometimes she made up her mind to leave it alone, to resist temptation, yet she quite frequently made the first move. But it was easy to leave Mike alone, because sex with Mike would have meant total commitment – he was that kind of boy. Geoff wasn't a boy, and that was the difference. If she tired of him, he wouldn't make a song and dance about it. Not that she would tire. No, he would never become boring. Though his mother was something of a trial.

Then, when Kate was exactly halfway through college, the unthinkable happened. More to the point, something which ought to have happened didn't, and she found herself in a terrible tear. Two girls had already left college because of being pregnant, and Kate looked like being the third.

They sat in his car outside the main gate. 'We'll just have to get married rather earlier than planned,' he said reasonably. 'Pity about your finals, but I'm afraid the child will be born before you ever get into the exam room.'

She twisted her skirt between her fingers. 'Mam's already upset because I didn't go to university like Judith. As for my father – he'll blow his top!'

'Leave them to me.'

'But they don't even know you exist! And I want to finish college, I really do!'

'I'm sorry. What else can I say, Kate? I took every precaution, but these things are not always a hundred per cent reliable. Get this term over, then we'll go for a licence.'

'Oh God!'

'What?'

'They'll want it to be Catholic.'

'No can do, old girl. My mother would not be seen

dead in a papist church. We'll have to settle for the registry.'

'That will be like living in sin as far as my family's concerned.'

'The details will sort themselves out, my darling. The main thing is to make sure that our baby is born in wedlock.'

'Yes. Yes, I suppose so.'

'There's no "suppose so" about it. We're going to get married anyway, aren't we?'

'Yes.' Her voice was small and far away.

'You're not still seeing that Mike fellow, are you?'

She shook her head. 'He's given up the ghost, found himself another girl.' No, she didn't feel any regret or jealousy. She didn't. And anyway, she was in no position . . .

'In about six weeks, then?'

'Pardon?'

'Our wedding. Six or seven weeks.'

'Oh, right.'

A fortnight later, she arrived home for the weekend sporting a large diamond twist on the third finger of her left hand.

'Who?' Rachel's eyes were huge with surprise. 'Geoff who? And what will your father say?'

'Saunders. His name's Geoff Saunders and it doesn't particularly matter what anyone says. We're getting married . . . soon. He's older than me, quite a bit older. I met him last year at the leavers' dance.'

Rachel folded her arms and put her head on one side. 'And what does he do for a living?'

'He's a manager with Transglobe Plastics in Trafford Park.'

'You'll finish your course first, though?'

Rachel got no answer, because Peter chose this moment to put in an appearance. He was in a jovial mood, having won several pounds which he had used to improve his demeanour by drinking a few double whiskies. 'Ah, you're here, then.'

Kate inhaled deeply. 'Yes, I'm here. And I'm engaged.'

'What?' He stumbled against the sideboard, righting himself immediately with the aid of his cane. 'To that soft Mike lad? Him with the paintbrush and easel?'

'No. Someone else. Mam will tell you. I'm off to bed.'

'Oh no you're not, young lady! You can stop here and explain yourself. Do you think your mam and I have gone without all these years so that you could get wed before twenty? Judith's not getting wed, is she? Oh, no. She'll stop on and do her Masters – likely one of them doctorates too. But you've got to go and get mixed up with a man, haven't you?'

'Yes. Yes, I have!'

'Why? Just tell me why the bloody hell . . .'

'To get away from you.' Her tone was even. 'I'm not stopping in this house a minute longer than I have to.'

The silence that followed was deafening. Rachel broke it by fiddling with the fire, poking the ashes through the basket and piling on some fresh coals. 'Cold for June,' she muttered lamely.

Peter staggered across to his usual chair. 'This is all the thanks we get,' he said to no-one in particular.

'In life, people tend to get what they deserve,' said Kate. 'You have never given me anything except a feeling of inadequacy because I was born female. And as for you, Mam, you've supported him by not sticking up for me. I know you're a spirited woman – I've seen you happy and angry – I know you're capable of normal emotions. But you've let him rule you just for the sake of peace. Your attitude to him is almost apologetic . . .'

'Enough of that!' snapped Rachel. 'I've done me best, which is more than can be said for some here. You could have been something great, but oh no, you went off to be an ordinary teacher. So don't be telling me what I

78

should have done. We all know what you should have done, Katherine Murray!'

Peter said nothing. He simply stared at Kate with such hatred that she turned and ran from the room, pounding up the stairs until she reached the relative safety of her bedroom. It was then, as she lay on the bed, that the pain came and she realized that she was no longer pregnant – if indeed she ever had been pregnant. And for some reason she could not explain to herself, she began to cry, sobbing and howling a mixture of sadness and relief. But she clung to Geoff's ring all the same as she rolled around the bed with the familiar agony of female cramps. Whatever happened, she would marry him after college. No way would she stay in this house of misery.

Dora Saunders' pale blue eyes were narrowed with shock as she studied Kate's engagement ring. 'So, when's it to be, then?'

'As soon as she finishes college.' Geoff's tone was conciliatory. 'We shan't be too far away, Mum. It's not as if you're being abandoned to the elements. Not emigrating to China, are we?' He hugged his fiancée, then pulled his mother into the crook of his other arm. 'We'll be a family, a real family.'

Kate and Dora stared at one another, the younger woman feeling a brief shiver of fear as she caught the animosity in Dora's face. The woman hated her. God, what was she coming into at all?

Dora, meanwhile, was fighting with very mixed emotions. He was getting married, so at least that proved he was normal. There'd been a few snide comments in the Co-op over the years, remarks about lads staying with their mothers longer than was good for them, loud conversations about 'nancy-boys' and the like. This would stop the wagging tongues. But he was leaving her. And she'd three bedrooms, there was plenty of space here for them. She repeated her plea, trying not to sound too desperate in front of 'that girl'. 'You know you're welcome here. Stop here till you find somewhere decent.'

'We've a year to do that.' Geoff patted his mother's shoulder. 'And I've plenty for a deposit. We'll come and see you often, won't we, Kate?'

'Yes.' She looked hard at the woman who would be her mother-in-law. In her own way, this old biddy was nearly as bad as Kate's father! Kate wanted a life of her own, a life without parents in it. She wanted a cottage with roses . . . no. Mike Wray was gone, gone forever. This was a different kind of love, real love, she told herself stubbornly.

In later years, Kate would look back at this moment, seeing herself, Geoff and Dora caught up, frozen in a sliver of time. Because, somehow, this particular instant summed up everything that was wrong with Kate's life. It all came down to lack of communication. If there had only been honesty. If Dora could have said, 'I'm scared of losing him', if Geoff had said, 'I can never really leave my mother'. Better still, if the man could have admitted there and then that he knew as little of love as Kate herself did.

And in other areas, too. If Kate had only opened up to her mother, 'I must marry him, I almost had his child and he needs me'. Or to her father, 'Dad, I know you started loving me in your own way, I know that way is limited'. But no-one ever said anything. Rachel never expressed her love for her younger daughter; Kate herself seldom gave out any positive emotion. But should she blame herself? Should she? After all, in the summers of '53 and '54, she had been so young . . .

In July 1954, Kate and Geoff were married at the registry office in Bolton. Rachel wore a blue suit and an air of great hurt because her daughter's marriage was not a 'proper' one. Dora wept copious tears into a scrap of lace while Judith, down from Oxford for the summer, looked gorgeous in pink. Peter, still drunk from the night before, kept a reasonably low profile as the couple walked in together – there was none of the traditional giving away in this brief ceremony.

Afterwards, the reception was held in the semi Geoff had bought with his dead father's legacy. One or two of Kate's old friends from school were present, but the majority of the guests were Geoff's, colleagues from work who took an abundant interest in plumbing, new windows and the greenhouse at the bottom of the back garden. Kate, who looked stunning in a princess line dress of cream satin, felt everyone's loneliness during the catered buffet meal. The hired servants seemed to have a better time than anyone – Kate caught them sipping furtively in the kitchen. Her poor mother looked so bereft and solitary seated in a corner, yet every time Kate went near her she was admonished, 'See to your guests, never mind us.'

So Kate found herself alone in the spare back bedroom, no-one to talk to, no-one to empathize with. Till Judith came in.

'What's up?' asked the beautiful Oxford graduate.

'Crazy. I feel lonely.'

'Not surprised, stuck up here on your own. Where's your husband?'

'Down the garden showing off his raspberry canes. Have I made a mistake?'

'Yes. All marriage is a mistake. Just do the best you can.'

'We've . . . we've never been close, you and I, Judy. Do you think we ever will be?'

Judith shrugged. 'Hard to say. I'll probably buzz around the world soon, exchanges and so on. I'm trying to get into Russia – that's a fabulous language, Kate.'

'I know. Is that the one you learned in three months?'

'Don't be silly, that was Swedish.'

Kate stared down on to the top of her husband's head as he bent to display some strawberries. 'He's got a bald spot,' she said to herself. 'It isn't getting in that will be a problem. It's getting out.'

Judith smiled grimly. 'Do you mean marriage or Russia or both?'

'I'm not sure. I do love him, Ju. I really do love him.'

'Then why do you have to keep saying it? Look, like I said before, just make the best of things. He's not an ogre, though his mother does a fair imitation. With any luck, she'll perish soon of one of her illnesses – that's quite a list she was reading out downstairs. Did you know she has them all written out in capital letters? Just settle down, have a couple of kids.'

'I'm probably already pregnant. No show at all this month.'

'Great. Then he made an honest woman of you just in time.'

Kate turned from the window and studied her beautiful sister. 'Will you ever get married?'

Judith tossed the long black curls. 'No. I have lovers. Don't look so shocked, it's purely biological. I've had one Harley Street abortion already. No man is going to stand between me and the United Nations, Kate. A translator I am and a translator I intend to be. No nappies for me, love.' In a rare display of affection, Judith threw an arm across her younger sister's shoulder. 'Terrified, aren't you?'

'A bit. It all seems so . . . so final.'

'No such thing, my dear. Marriage is like a handkerchief; once it gets too stained, you throw it away. Divorce is quite common these days, you know. Mind, it does seem strange to be talking of separation with you standing here in your wedding dress. It's only the change in lifestyle that's frightening you. Look. What are we used to, eh? A squashed-up little house in the thinnest of thin streets. And see what you've got now? Awesome, isn't it? When I went home last hols with Liz Beresford-Smythe, I was completely overcome. There they were with stables and servants, a grand big mansion in the middle of Hampshire. Out of my depth, I was. And that's where you are now. You'll get used to it.'

'Will I?'

'Yes. Didn't you always say that heaven was a proper bathroom with taps? And here you are with a full dining room suite and a real kitchen – what more do you want?'

Kate sucked in her cheeks before replying, 'I always wanted roses round the door. A little country cottage . . .'

'And Mike?'

'Dear God! How did you know about that?'

'You talk in your sleep.'

'Do I? Oh heck, I'll have to stay awake all night.'

Judith's grip tightened. 'So, it's just been sex with Geoff, has it? And you felt you had to marry him because he'd deflowered you. Oh, Kate! What am I going to do with you at all?'

'It isn't just sex. I love him. And . . . and I didn't want to live at home. It was all right for you, you were forgiven for being a girl. And you didn't ruin my mother's chances of giving him a son, did you? But me? I've been treated like a dishrag all along . . .'

'Dear God, Kate! Dad loves you more than anything in this world. I can tell from the way he looks at you . . .'

'Rubbish.' Kate pulled herself away from her sister's arm. 'You were the pretty one. You were the one with the nice clothes and the Sunday outings.'

'I was a doll. A doll for dressing up. I wasn't expected to have a brain. He thought I'd get married and have all his grandsons. But here we are, both arse over tip, eh? And you are the one with the brains, Kate. That's always annoyed both of them, that you never tried at school. If I'd done as little work as you did, I'd have finished up spinning cotton. Cheer up, though. This is supposed to be the happiest day of your life. And on Monday, you're off to London and Paris – plenty to look forward to.'

Kate nodded grimly. 'Including morning sickness and no job.'

'Stop it! Stop it this minute! There's no point in going into any situation with an attitude that's less than positive. If you want to run, run now.'

'Where to?'

'What a terrible reason for staying. What a terrible reason to get married in the first place. Won't you ever grow up, Kate?'

The younger girl's chin jutted forward fiercely. 'I expect I shall. In my own time. It has to be in my own time.'

Judith sighed. 'Your own time is over, for a while, at least.'

'I shall make my own time, when I'm ready . . .'

The honeymoon was a hilarious mixture of success and disaster. After London, they stayed at the Henri Quatre, a small hotel in the middle of Paris. Kate didn't like crossing the Channel, French food, French wine, French people or the French language. Geoff hated the lumpy bed, the view from their window – which consisted of a high brick wall and a row of dustbins – and the food. They ate copious amounts of croissants in bed, thereby creating more lumps and crumbs, and drank expensive cups of coffee in the cafés along the Champs-Elysées.

But they both loved Paris. Because of currency restrictions, they had to do everything on the cheap, yet Kate was drawn repeatedly to the Latin Quarter and the Left Bank. Once she had spent most of their allowance on paintings, she had to concede that they must, in future, visit places that were virtually free. So they strolled daily down the Champs to the Eiffel Tower, saw a lot of Napoleon's famous Arc, and even found a back-street church where lay a glass tomb enclosing a perfectly preserved but very dead nun who awaited canonization.

Towards the end of their fortnight, Kate began to get sick in the mornings, thereby confirming the suspicion she had expressed only to her sister. 'I'm sick,' she told him one breakfast time.

'Homesick?'

'No. Pregnant-sick.'

He paused fractionally. 'Good. Proves we can get something right, eh?'

She turned and looked at his head on the pillow next to hers. He seemed complacent, and it suddenly struck her that she was just a part of his plan – no kiss, no cuddle, no 'thanks for being the bearer of such news'. 'Shouldn't we sing the "Marseillaise" or something?' she asked.

He yawned and stretched. 'No, "Land of Hope and Glory". That's no French citizen, is it?'

'Conceived about six weeks ago, I'd say. On the floorboards of our new house.'

'English, then. Fancy a croissant?'

'Stop it!'

'Mind if I pop out for something to eat, then?'

'Not at all.'

She lay there while he performed his fussy toilet. He was a fussy man, an old man . . . Swiftly, she jumped from the bed and vomited noisily into the washbasin, rinsing away the stains in the bowl immediately.

After that, he didn't touch her until long after they were home. That she should vomit and spoil his breakfast was a shame; that she should continue sick for a further four months was an absolute nuisance.

Melanie was born in the spring of 1955. Right from the start, she was a screamer and Kate seemed to have little say in her upbringing. Dora became an almost permanent fixture at the house, declaring herself to be indispensable now that Kate had the little one as well as the house to look after.

The young mother found herself spending a great deal of time with Rachel, going up to Maybank Street whenever the opportunity presented itself. Peter accepted Melanie well enough, though Kate felt that he was merely trying to disguise yet another generation of disappointment. It was during the first year of Melanie's life that Kate really began to know her own mother, to see the character behind the two-dimensional figure that had occupied her life thus far.

'It's not easy, Katherine. There's nowt easy about being a mother. For a kick-off, that child is your guilt from now on; it should be printed on nappies and bottles, "Beware of the guilt". If she cries, it's your fault. If she doesn't walk and talk when she should, then that's your fault and all. And if she turns out a monkey for toilet training, your failure will be at the front of your mind. So ignore it all. Ignore that blessed Dora woman for a start, don't let her tell you how to bring Melanie up.'

'That's not easy. She's like one of the house fittings, and Geoff seems to like having her there.'

Rachel nodded wisely. 'Aye, best of both worlds, eh? Wife and mother, everybody there to run after him. You want to get rid of her before she digs her heels in.'

'How?'

'Just tell her to go. Better still, tell her when she can come. Ask her to tea Wednesdays and Saturdays, go out other days.'

'I do go out. My legs are worn out with pram pushing. And there's no-one to visit. You're at work most of the time . . .'

'Where are your friends?'

Kate laughed mirthlessly. 'Friends? They're all Geoff's friends. We play bridge, that's all. I've no-one from childhood because . . . well . . . I never brought anybody home, did I? Not with Dad's moods. The college lot are all over the country. No. There's only Geoff's crowd.'

'Then get to work. Give Dora a full-time job – that's what she wants any road. Do your probationary year and let Dora mind the kiddy. After that, you could happen go to university and do a degree.'

'No. I'm a mother now. No time for study.'

'What about the teaching?'

'I'll think about it.'

4

The discussions were endless.

Sometimes Dora pretended to see Kate's viewpoint – or perhaps the woman was simply planning her way into the house. Because if Kate went to work, then Dora would be required on a more or less permanent basis. 'Look, son,' she would say in something that imitated a reasonable tone, 'Kate's had her training, she should perhaps get some experience.'

'No.' His face always went purple during these arguments. 'She doesn't need to work.'

'That's true.' Dora's eyes would settle on her daughter-in-law. 'There's no shortage of money, dear. Let's have another cup of tea, then we can talk about it . . .'

'The 'talking about it' went on forever.

In the brief privacy of their bedroom, Kate tackled her husband. 'If I have to stay here for one more day with your mother, I think I shall go mad. She's taken over everything, including our daughter. I'm no more than an ornament, might as well be working and doing something useful at least.'

'Look.' His voice held that patient note, a note she found difficult to tolerate. 'I'm general manager now. Whoever heard of a top man's wife working? There'll be a seat on the board for me eventually. I tell you now, Kate, that I will be managing director in Trafford Park before long. How will it look if my wife's out doing a job?'

'Intelligent,' she snapped viciously. 'How would it look if your wife left you?'

'What?' Though the voice was quiet, his eyes bulged

ominously and a large vein throbbed in his neck. 'Are you threatening . . . ?'

'Yes. Yes I bloody well am! This is no life for me, Geoff. At least if I do my probationary year, I'll know whether or not I'm going to make a teacher. And another thing, look how much older than me you are. If you died, how would I support my daughter?'

'On insurance,' he snarled. 'So, you either teach or you leave me. Is that it?'

'Quite possibly.'

He sighed heavily. 'If I tell Mother to stay away, will you . . . ?'

'No. It won't make any difference. I am twenty-two years old and I have never worked in my life. Anyway, your mother would die if she couldn't come here, she lives for you. I may dislike the woman, but I should hate to take responsibility for her early demise.'

He flung himself on to the bed, the soft lower lip thrust out petulantly. 'I want you to see a psychiatrist.'

'What? Bloody what?'

'You need help, Kate. There's a theory now that new mothers are often a bit . . . well . . . unhinged for a while. If this post-natal thing is left untreated, it can go on for years.'

She sank down on to the dressing stool. 'Good God! If anyone needs a mind doctor, it's that mother of yours. Try two for the price of one, Geoff, because you'll need help for your Oedipus complex. I have never known a man cling so fiercely to his mam. I suppose it's all her fault, somewhere back in the dim and distant past. But never mind all that. Kate's the one dancing to a different drummer, eh? Kate's the one not doing as she's told.'

'I've booked you an appointment,' he went on smoothly. 'Next Monday afternoon. Private, of course.'

'Of course. Well, I'll keep that appointment. I'll ask the doctor how he'd go on if he had to live with a hypochondriac and a mother's boy who's thirty-five years old. Yes, I'll keep your bloody appointment for you. And on Tuesday, I have an interview. Try to stop me going for it and I'll be out of this house before you can shout "Mother". I'm going to be my own woman with my own job. Even if I hate the work, I'll damned well stick to it. And don't be thinking you can lumber me with any more babies – I've seen our family doctor about that, there are things women can use now, you know.'

'See?' He raised arms and shoulders in an 'I told you so' gesture. 'You're all worked up again. That's why I want you to see a psychiatrist, because you're always getting worked up. There is no shame in requiring this type of treatment, Kate.'

She jumped up and hurled a pot of face-cream at him, narrowly missing the side of his head with the large white jar. It smashed on the headboard, spreading glass and contents all over pillows and cover. 'Bastard!' she screamed as she sank back on to the stool. 'Why did I marry you? Why?'

He was already out of the bed and tidying up the mess.

'Look at you, Geoff. You don't care about anything real. I don't think you've ever once looked at a sunset or at a bird's feather and wondered about beauty. No music moves you, no sound, no sight! All you care about is winning the rubber and keeping up with the rest of the management team. I have married a very old man. Fourteen years between us? It might as well be forty. Look at you. LOOK AT YOURSELF!'

'And you look at yourself, screaming like a Fleetwood fishwife. You are not normal, Kate. This is not your fault . . .'

'Stop being so patient with me. Stop treating me like a child. I got away from home so that I could stop being a child!'

'Then there's your answer.' He wiped the wall with a soiled pillowcase. 'That's why you married me. To escape

90

from your father. To get away from him, you would have married anyone who offered security.'

The silence was filled only by the sound of her laboured breathing. He changed the bed swiftly, taking clean linen from the ottoman at the foot of the bed. 'Right,' he said finally. 'You can get in now.'

'No.'

'Then where will you sleep?'

'In the spare room. Where your mother usually sleeps.'

'You will sleep here in your own bed!' At last, some sign of anger.

'Make me! Go on, make me! Force me to go to bed with a man who comes home smelling of another woman's perfume. What's the matter? Didn't you think I knew? I've always known, it's in your chin, Geoff. Anyone with a chin as weak as that will never resist temptation. And there's always been a rather seamy side to your nature, hasn't there?' She shrugged her shoulders. 'I will have my own way, Geoff. Perhaps this makes me an un-nice person, but for the first time in my life, I will have my way.'

'Go to hell, then.' He got into bed and switched off the lights.

Kate turned and sat for a long time staring at her dim reflection in the dressing table mirror. When at last she spoke, it was almost in a whisper. 'Our marriage was a mistake, Geoff. Almost from the first day, I knew that. It's not your fault, love. I was young and stupid and I got sex all mixed up with real affection, didn't know the difference. And I'm changing, changing all the time. When we got married, I wasn't grown-up. I'm still not an adult, not a fully-fledged one. I think women get more growing years than men do. Even people of the same age have trouble because the woman carries on altering. I remember reading about this in a psychology book at college. On her wedding day, a woman sees what she's getting. A man doesn't. It's not that we're cleverer –

nothing as easy as that. It's because we never stop changing. A man doesn't see what he's getting. That's why there's truth in that old adage, look at her mother if you want to see how she'll turn out. I'm sorry. I am so very, very sorry . . .'

'Don't. Don't leave me. Get your job, but don't leave me.' His voice was muffled by the bedcovers. 'I could not stand to be left.'

She resisted the urge to run and comfort him, to be his mother again. Two mothers he had, two mothers he obviously needed. Except that Kate's brand of comfort inevitably culminated in sex, and although she herself needed such consolation, she would not go to him on this night. 'It will end some day, Geoff.'

'Doesn't everything? But not yet. Please – not yet.'

'All right.' She crept from the room and lay between Dora's lavender-scented sheets, tossing and turning as she planned a new beginning for herself. Her life in this house was not over, for she had not the courage to carry out her threat. But she would find some release. Release, freedom and peace. Yes, her idea of heaven had changed already. And she knew that it would carry on altering for many years to come.

Daubhill Junior Mixed and Infants was a hideous school, a Victorian monstrosity of the worst kind, draughty in winter and boiling in summer, flagged floors in the basement where Kate was to teach, the luxury of boards to higher floors. Although she had studied for junior teaching, the real shortages existed with nursery and infant classes, so she was condemned to the depths with forty-eight five-year-olds. But they were an easy generation, a group of triers and workers whose parents were keen for good results, so the task was not a difficult one.

The real difficulty lay in the staffroom, where Kate was to learn quickly that she was the lowest in a very rigid pecking order. First, there was Mr Partridge, deputy-head and teacher of the scholarship class. He held forth from the top of the long table. To his right sat Miss Gibbons, head of infants, while various other teachers were graded according to responsibility, leaving Kate's chair right at the other end, away from any 'real business'. The friendliest was Maureen Carter, who had taught at Daubhill School through two pregnancies, abandoning her children to her own mother as soon as they were born. With Maureen, Kate felt a degree of empathy, because the tiny blonde had fought her accountant husband to the last ditch in order to retain some independence.

At the other side of some lockers and filing cabinets there was another long table where sat the staff from the senior school which took up the third level of the building. No-one from the junior mixed and infants ever spoke to the senior staff except for the odd 'good morning'. Kate could not understand this. 'Why?' she asked her new friend. 'Why don't we all sit together?'

'They're higher than us,' whispered Maureen. 'They teach subjects and they blame us when the kids can't read. It's a sort of armed truce, I suppose.'

'That's ridiculous! There should be some kind of liaison – after all, they get all Mr Partridge's eleven-year-olds who fail the scholarship exam. I know they have elevens to fifteens up there, and I realize that everyone upstairs ought to be able to read, but don't they ever ask us for a scheme of work for an illiterate child?'

'You must be joking.'

'I'm not joking. Anyway, I shall speak to them. I'm not working in the same building as another crowd of adults without trying to be civilized.'

'You'll get no answers. Fortunately, only the lunch-times coincide completely. The playtimes are staggered, so we don't see a great deal of the enemy.'

'They shouldn't be the enemy. We're supposed to be here to educate children, not to fight among ourselves!' Her voice had risen and eight pairs of eyes were suddenly fixed on her. Boldly, she addressed Mr Partridge himself. 'Why can't we all work together? Some of the seniors might benefit from repeating a year and no-one needs to know; they could do their work upstairs in a remedial department.'

Mr Partridge sighed, shook his grizzled head, then looked knowingly at his near colleagues and allies. 'It doesn't work that way, Mrs Saunders.'

'Why not?'

He tapped the table with an irritated hand. 'Because I've forty-three in my class. I can't be running up and down stairs doing that lot's job for them. We get enough flak without new members of staff telling us how to run the school. Probationers!' He took a noisy sip of coffee. 'Always know it all, don't they?'

Miss Gibbons nodded sagely.

Maureen dug Kate in the ribs. 'Shut up,' she mumbled.

But Kate did not shut up. 'It's a very narrow viewpoint, Mr Partridge. The idea should be to produce as extended a child as possible. Obviously, the system is wrong.'

'And there speaks a future Min of Ed if ever I heard one.' His tone was sarcastic. 'Get through the first year, child. If and when you've done that, perhaps you'll see things differently.'

She rose from the table. 'I've a class to teach, Mr Partridge. But if I can help any boy or girl upstairs – even in my lunch hour – then I shall. That won't change. I'm here to educate children, not to drink coffee.' With this final statement, she flounced from the room.

Maureen caught up with her in the infant hall. 'Be careful. He writes a crit for your assessment.'

'I'd love to write one for his. Don't worry, I'll pass. In the next few weeks, I shall turn this hall into an Aladdin's cave with my artwork.'

'Good. I'll help. A nice display does wonders when the

examiner comes round. There's an epidiascope in the projector room, we can copy some fairy tales . . .'

'No need. I work freehand, then collage the kids' work on top of mine.'

'You can draw?'

'I can.'

Maureen giggled. 'What with your drawing and my piano playing, we shall have Miss Gibbons redundant. They're . . . having an affair, you know.'

'What? The Gibbon and old Partridge? Can you imagine it? Where do they do it? Is it Partridge in a pear tree or Gibbon in a monkey puzzle?'

'They stay behind and lurk in stock-cupboards.'

'No!'

'There have been rumours about certain stains on gym mats . . .'

'Oh, Maureen! Shut up! That's awful.'

'Isn't it? Then he goes home to his insipid little wife and acts the big man.'

'Does Miss Ashe know?'

'Our dear headmistress knows everything, my dear. Do not be taken in by that injured spaniel look. I'm just waiting for her to catch them actually at it in her office.'

That afternoon at dismissal assembly, Kate had a terrible job keeping a straight face. Gibbons and Partridge exchanged several meaningful glances across the heads of four hundred children, while Maureen kept turning from the piano to wink at Kate. In the end, poor Mrs Saunders simply developed a 'bad cough' and left them all to get on with it while she hid in the cloakroom. Miss Gibbons found her there after all the children had gone. 'Are you all right, Mrs Saunders?'

'Much better, thanks.'

'You may go home now if you wish. Mr Partridge and I will hand over to the caretaker. Of course, Miss Ashe has already left to see to her mother – on her own all day, dear old soul.'

'Yes.'

'Are you sure you're all right?'

'Yes.' Oh, if only she would go away! Kate was plagued by pictures in her mind, vivid images of Partridge and Gibbons in the most impossible of poses; across the head teacher's desk, swinging from the ropes in the junior hall, behind the projection screen, in the caretaker's mop cupboard. A laugh rumbled ominously near to the surface and she changed it to a cough.

'Honey and lemon,' said Miss Gibbons sweetly. 'And an inhalation of menthol. Anyway, I must go and help poor Mr Partridge. Good afternoon, dear.' She left, only to be replaced almost immediately by Maureen.

'I'll kill you!' gasped Kate. 'You've no idea what I've been through this last few minutes!'

Maureen grinned. 'Where do you live?'

'Crompton Way.'

'I hail from Edgeford. It's on my way, come on.'

'You have a car?'

'Of course. You don't think I do this job for fun, do you? I do it for extras. I'll pick you up every day if you like.'

'OK. But I'm still going to kill you . . .'

From that day on, they were firm friends.

Most lunchtimes, Kate went home to see her mother who was doing just mornings at the mill now. The school was almost at the bottom of View Street, so it was only a few strides from classroom to fireside. She found Rachel very quiet these days, withdrawn to the point of near-silence. Drawing her out was hard work, but Kate was of a persistent nature. 'What is it, Mother?' she asked for days on end.

'Nowt much. Just a bit on the tired side, that's all.' The reply would vary slightly, but on the whole, Rachel stuck to her tale of exhaustion. One April noon, Kate decided that enough was enough. 'Tell me. Tell me or I'll stay here all day.'

'You'll lose your job.'

'So? Tell me what's on your mind.'

Rachel drew a hand across her brow. 'You've enough of your own, Katherine. What with him not liking you working and that there mother of his creating all the while. It's not fair for me to burden you.'

'The biggest burden is not knowing. Or knowing that there's something wrong and not knowing what the something is. So you'd better tell me before I start losing sleep. You see, I didn't know you till lately, Mam. He was the noisy one, he was the one I noticed. You've been just . . .'

'A shadow?'

'Something like that. Till I grew up, anyway. Only now, we've an idea of each other, haven't we? A bit of one, at least. Can't you tell me what's on your mind?'

'It's . . . it's him. Your dad.'

'Oh.'

'I don't pretend to understand him completely, lass, but I do know when there's summat up. Same as you know now with me, I suppose. I think . . . Oh God! I think, no I know, we're losing him, love.'

Kate swallowed hard. 'He's . . . dying?'

Rachel nodded quickly. 'The doctor told me it's more than likely. Peter knows nowt for definite, and don't you be telling him either. It's cancer. I don't know how I shall cope when it comes to the finish.'

The younger woman reached out and gripped her mother's hand. 'Without him, you mean?'

'No. The going. When he knows, when he realizes that there's no hope. See, it's not too bad yet. He still gets into work and goes for a drink, still manages to get his bets on. But when he had them there X-rays down the infirmary, they knew there was no hope. And the doctor decided to tell me instead of your dad. He looks at me,

97

Katie. I'll swear he knows something. Not all of it. He just knows he's not right. He must have lost two stone these last weeks. What'll I do? When the real pain comes? Eh?'

'Get help. Nurses, doctors, the hospital . . .'

'No! He had enough of that in the Army. It'll have to be here. It's the last thing I'll ever do for him and I don't even know how to do that right. I feel so guilty!'

'So do I. I've never liked him, but I don't want him dead.'

They held hands tightly, each staring silently into the grate. After a few moments, Rachel pulled away to dry her eyes. 'I did love him once, you know.'

'Yes.'

'And he loves you, our Katherine. He loves you more than anything in this world.'

'I know. He loves me and hates me. I feel the same way about him. Do you want me to come home for a while?'

'No. He'd guess right away, wouldn't he? But . . . well . . . I'd be grateful if you'd . . . you know . . .'

'Be here at the end?'

'Aye, lass. When he realizes. When he takes to his bed.'

'I will. I'll be here, Mam.'

Rachel looked at her favourite daughter and smiled sadly. 'I thought my heart would break when you married yon feller. He's not right for you, girl, and I should know better than most. But we stick with it, don't we? We go on like blinking carthorses, head down, pull the load even when the cobbles are icy. One step forward and two back it was for me. Most days, any road. He . . . he wanted a lad. He sets store by education, see, and he wanted a lad. We can't blame him for that, can we?'

'He shouldn't have blamed us.'

'No. No, he shouldn't. But I mind the times he's sat up in bed talking about you. "She's different," he said. "She could be a lawyer or summat," stuff like that. I agreed with him. They told me at school that you were gifted . . .'

'I'm talented, Mam. It's all in my hands and in my head. It's not something I can improve with books.'

'What'll you do with it? Can you tell him, before he . . . he goes?'

'No. I don't even know myself what I'll do with whatever it is.'

'Don't hate him, Katherine. Please?'

'Even I can't hate the dying, Mam. Now put the kettle on or I'll be back at school without a drink.'

Rachel went through to the kitchen while Kate sat and stared through the small window. Her mother's life had been so awful, so narrowed by a difficult husband. Would her own be the same? Would she carry on like that carthorse? And Dad, poor Dad . . . No! She must not think of him, even now. Thinking of him in the past had only led to confusion and anger . . . 'Mam?'

'Hello?'

'Would you marry again if you knew what was in store for you?'

'Yes.' The broken voice floated though the two small rooms. 'I got my daughters out of it, didn't I?'

'What else did you get?'

The only reply was the clink of cup on saucer, the hollow rattle of a spoon against the sides of the tin teapot. Kate sighed. There was no other answer. Often, actions did speak louder than words.

'He's dying. I have to go. I can carry on teaching, it's only round the corner. But I have to sleep there, Geoff. She's up all hours of the day and night with him, so I'll try to get some unpaid compassionate leave.'

'Are you sure about this?' His voice was strained.

'Sure about what?'

'That your nerves will stand it. Remember what the doctor said about getting tired.'

'Oh, stop it! If my mother can cope, then so can I.'

'It's not that.' He dropped his head and stared into his coffee cup. 'I'm scared.'

'What of? Cancer's not catching.'

'You . . . you may never come back.'

'Pardon?'

'This may be your first step towards leaving me. Kate, I don't want you to leave.'

She raised her eyes to heaven. 'Good God! I'm going to stay with my mother until my father dies – did I say anything about leaving? Do you think I'd go off and abandon a fourteen-month-old baby? Look. You'll be well looked after. Dora will stay here, see to the baby, make your meals . . .'

'And I'll sleep alone.'

She bit her tongue; this was not the moment to bring up his extra-curricular activities. 'You'll manage. How do you think I manage when you go away on business? Can't you be the fixture for a change? Do I have to provide the permanence in the house all the time? Be fair, Geoff.'

'I'm trying to be fair. It just doesn't seem right for you to go off and leave Melanie while you nurse a man who never treated you properly.'

'He's my father. More to the point, she's my mother. Now, just settle down and accept it. I'll be back before you know I'm gone.'

But it didn't work out that way. Peter Murray lingered for months, his temper shortened even further by the realization that he was not long for this world. He took it out on Kate, on Rachel, on doctors and nurses – he even turned on Judith when she paid a brief visit before setting off for Moscow. 'Bloody Commie,' he spat viciously. 'Anybody who'll visit that country has to be a stinking Red.'

Judith glanced across the bed to where her sister sat knitting. 'Is he always like this?'

Kate changed needles. 'Except when he's asleep.'

'You don't give a damn, either of you. Neither does your flaming mother. Look at this one!' He waved a thin hand towards his elder daughter. 'She knows I'm dying, she knows she'll never see me again. And all she can go on about is getting her blinking visa for foreign parts!'

'Calm yourself.' Judith, as always, seemed very unruffled. 'I'm only going for three months.'

'Aye, and I'll not be here when you get back.' He glanced at Kate. 'Look at her. She's like one of them that sat by the guillotine while heads got cut off. I suppose she never put my bet on today.'

'I did!' Kate struggled with a dropped stitch. 'Sparkling Sam in the three thirty. I put it on in my lunch hour and I hope none of the parents saw me. I called back after school to see if you'd won, but they all laughed and said the horse was still running. That's another five shillings down the plug hole. Do you want a drink?'

'No. I want to go out.'

The sisters glanced at one another. 'Where to?' asked Judith eventually.

'I want to go to the memorial.'

'Middle of Bolton?' Kate's eyebrows shot upward. 'Whatever for?'

'To say a last ta-ra to my mates. Do you know how many Lancashire Fusiliers never came back? Bloody thousands. Well, I want to say ta-ra in this world before I say hello in the next. Tomorrow, you can shove me down in that there wheelchair.'

Judith scratched her head. 'It's not the pushing you down, Dad. That'll be easy enough. But it's uphill all the way back . . .'

'You're strong enough, the pair of you. Is it too much to ask for you to respect the wish of a dying man? And don't start with all that stuff about chronic bronchitis, Katherine. I know what I've got.'

Rachel came in with his bowl of broth. 'Shall I feed

you?' she asked, her voice trembling slightly at the sight of the three of them together. This was how it should have been all their lives, not just now. Not just at the end, when one life was almost over.

'Judith can give it me,' he said breathlessly. 'She's the only one of you that can get the spoon in my gob without spilling half down the bed.'

Rachel and Kate left the room together. 'Nothing changes,' muttered the latter. 'She got the Sunday out- ings and the best coat, now she's given the praise.'

'Stop it. He's got days, that's what the doctor said. Just a few days now.'

'If he'd take the morphine . . . ah . . . I don't know . . .' Kate's words tailed away to nothing.

'If he took the morphine, he'd be no trouble.'

'He'd have less pain. He wants us to wheel him out tomorrow.'

'Then do it. It'll be his last time.'

They took him. First one, then the other pushed the wheelchair down Derby Street and through the town centre till they reached the cenotaph. He sat quietly, medals pinned to his chest, sunken eyes glued to the statues. 'We can't stand here forever,' whispered Judith after a while. 'I'll just nip across to the library and look at the languages section.' She turned and fled towards the civic buildings, leaving Kate to stand between her father and the passing shoppers.

'Rachel?' The voice cracked through parched lips.

'It's Kate.'

'Oh. Should have been a lad.'

'I know.'

'Where's Judith?'

'In the library looking for a Russian book.'

He sighed, sputum rattling in his chest. 'God, it hurts.'

'There's no need. You could have the medicine.'

'No. The pain reminds me that I'm alive. The pain's all I have left now. Is that our Katherine?'

'Yes, it's me. You should be home in your bed.'

'We called a gun after you. All the lads put names in a hat and Katherine came out. A big cannon, it was. Mad Katie, they called her. She was an angry gun. Like you. Angry.'

'Oh.' She didn't know what to say to this stranger who had occupied her whole life.

He looked up at her, his eyes brimming with tears. 'It's time, lass. Just thee and me and my time's come. Use it, Katherine. That cleverness. Use it.'

'I will.'

'Like we used Mad Katie.'

'More constructively, I hope. Do you want to go home now? We can pass the library and collect Judith.'

'I am home.' He stared briefly at the words on the monument, shivered, then dropped his head.

Instantly, Kate fell to her knees. 'Dad?' She touched his shoulder and he slid sideways, hanging like a doll over the side of the wheelchair. With an agility that belied her state of mind, she jumped up and straightened her father's body, closing his eyes with the pads of her thumbs.

For an interminable and very shaky half-hour, she stood with the corpse and waited for her sister. At last Judith arrived, a large volume clutched to her chest. 'Right. Let's get him home, shall we?'

'He's dead.'

'What? Don't be silly, he's just asleep.'

'He came out here to die and that's what he's done. Hold him steady while I push.'

Judith stood, mouth agape, precious book still folded in her arms.

'He died while you were in the library,' said Kate softly. 'The least you can do is help me to get him home.'

'But . . . but . . .'

'Are you practising to be a goldfish? Pull yourself together, Judith Murray.' Although she herself felt far from 'together', one of them needed to display a bit of commonsense.

'Shouldn't we tell somebody? We can't take a dead man through the streets without telling somebody.'

'Why not? He's been dead for weeks anyway, only hung on till you came home. This is how he wanted it. We take him back, put him in bed and say he died there. He is not to be taken to any hospital – you know how he feels about hospitals.'

They stared at one another. 'You're not crying,' said Judith at last.

'Neither are you. Do you think Mam will cry?'

'Yes. She'll cry because she wasn't with him. He gave her one hell of a life, Kate.'

'I know.' They began to push their burden which seemed heavier now in its inert state. 'He always made Mam feel so guilty,' Kate continued. 'Me too for being a girl. He messed up my mind, Judith. But, oh God, I'm sorry he's dead. He was waiting for us, expecting us to do great things, waiting for grandsons.'

Judith took over the pushing. 'Everything seems so unimportant now. Russian, Swedish, German, all I've worked for. When you see a life snuffed out like this . . . What's it all about, Kate?'

'Strangely enough, it's about staying alive. So stick to your books and your plans. It's what he would have wanted.'

'And you?'

'What about me?'

'He expected a lot from you, Kate. He thought you'd end up running the country or something like that. Are you going to carry on with that silly marriage?'

Kate pushed her sister to one side. 'I don't know. Let me take the chair for a while. I'll do what I have to do. When the time comes. I just wish . . .'

'What?'

'That I could trust and love somebody for a while.'

Judith glanced down at the dead man. 'He took a lot away from you, Kate.'

'Yes, well, he probably couldn't help it. Now, let's get home and explain all this to Mam. We'll have to make all the arrangements for her. Strange how she always stood by him in life. Now he's dead, she'll probably be absolutely useless.'

But Rachel proved far from useless. Once she recovered from the initial and very brutal shock, she set to with funeral arrangements and insurance policies, bought herself a nice navy-blue suit – 'it'll be more useful than black' – and shoo-ed her daughters out of the house as soon as her husband was buried.

'But, Mam!' protested Kate. 'You'll be on your own for the first time ever!'

'Then I'd best get used to it, eh?'

Judith was busy with her packing, but even she looked astonished when she understood her mother's intention. 'Let Kate stay a while. I can't, unfortunately. I've to see my professor before I set off for Russia. Don't be on your own, not just yet.'

'Stop talking as if I'm ill!' Rachel pushed a damp curl from her forehead, then carried on cleaning the grate. 'I shall manage. In fact, I've plenty of thinking to do and you two only get in the road.'

'What's there to think about?' asked Kate.

'Me job for a start. I've a widow's pension now, plus a few bob a week from some policy of your dad's. If I'm not careful, I shall lose me pension in tax. So happen I'll do a bit of cleaning, cash in hand. Or get a job that doesn't pay enough for me to be penalized. Makes you think, doesn't it? Years he struggled on with his bad leg and never a penny for all that pain from the war. Then there's the war widows, treated like muck, they are. Their husbands went out and died for England, but what do the women get? Nowt. A fistful of pennies every week, that's all. So if you ever have lads and they start on about defending Queen and country, tell them to hang on a bit, 'cos it's not worth it.'

Kate and Judith stared at one another. This was the longest speech their mother had ever made within their hearing. 'So you'll give up the mill?' asked Judith.

'I will that, and never a backward glance. I've got you two through now, and that's what it was about. Do you think I'd have stuck all them years without a darned good reason? No. I've finished with spinning.'

'There was no need. He earned enough . . .'

'Shut up, Katherine!' Rachel's face glowed in the light from the fire. 'I know what he was. There's no need for you to be telling me what he was and him hardly cold in the grave. If he hadn't gambled, if he hadn't been a drinker. Yes, he was a weak man. Your father was a hurt man, and don't you ever forget that.'

'He never let any of us forget it, did he?'

Rachel rose from the floor and slapped the cleaning cloth on to the table. 'He's dead, lass. There's no need for revenge now. You can't hurt him past dead, can you?'

'I never set out to hurt anyone!'

'Aye, but you never forgave him for his mistakes, did you? He wasn't lovable, I know that. But he was a human being, our Katie, a human being with feelings the same as the rest of us. He loved you and Judith in his way.'

'In his way.' There was a steely edge to Kate's voice. 'And I loved him in my way, the way he showed me. So don't blame me for my dad's failure.'

'I'm not blaming you. I'm just asking you to accept the way he was. Accept it and get on with your lives, both of you. I'm going to get on with mine, and it'll be easier without two grown women under me feet all day. You'd best get back to your job, Katherine, or they'll be finding somebody else. And our Judith has to finish her education. I'll be all right. I don't need anybody with me.'

'Are you sure? Shall we have a phone put in?' It

occurred to Kate that this would be the first time ever that Rachel had been truly alone. As a child she had been surrounded by brothers and sisters; even during the war she had had company. 'A phone would be useful.'

'I'm not having one of them things! Jessie Turnbull's daughter had one put in for her, and she keeps it in a cupboard so she can't hear it.'

'Why?'

'Because she feels right daft talking to somebody who's not there. Embarrassed, like. Mind, she always was three sheets in the wind, was Jessie Turnbull. Did I tell you she's got a new dog? Fierce, it is. It'll let anybody in the house, but it won't let them out. It took five men to get him from the Wesleyan and General through the back door last week. Still, he should be well-insured being as he's the insurance man. Now. Where did I put me brass polish? I'll just give that plaque another once-over . . .'

Judith and Kate stared at their mother. She was different, voluble, amusing. Although saddened by her husband's death, she seemed to be breaking free from some invisible bond that had held her shackled for many years. 'She doesn't need us,' said Kate to her sister. Her mother apparently had all she needed for now. And the chief ingredient seemed to be freedom.

Kate's own freedom was confined to school. At home, Dora was well dug in by this time; in fact, she seemed to resent Kate's going back to Crompton Way after her father's death. 'You should have stayed with your mother, dear. We can manage here perfectly well.' Yes, Dora had all she wanted. Her son, a lovely home and a baby to care for.

Little Melanie's relationship with her mother was a difficult one. As a toddler, she began to discover that she needed only to run to Dora or Geoff and her own way could be had instantly. But Kate was not so easy, not so malleable. Kate did not believe in giving in to children, but in the face of the other two adults in the house, there was little she could do to prevent the spoiling of her daughter. In the end, she took what she later realized to be the easy route, the lazy way out. Dora brought up Melanie while Kate went to work. At the weekends, she tried to instil some discipline into the child, but all her good work was ruined by Monday morning when Dora took over.

Kate tackled her mother-in-law just once. 'There are too many tantrums,' she said. 'Melanie is growing up believing she'll get her own way just by screaming. You give in to her too easily.'

Dora bridled. 'She's just a baby. How can it be possible to spoil a baby? It's only a few sweets . . .'

'And she'll have no teeth left.'

'Milk teeth!' snapped Dora. 'You've only to worry when the second lot comes.'

'That's not true. The longer she keeps her milk teeth, the better her others will be.'

Dora slammed the bag of sweets on to the table. 'I see. So you know more about bringing up children than I do, eh?'

'She's my child!'

'And I'm the one who looks after her while you go out all day!'

Kate marched to the table and slammed down her bag next to the packet of sweets. 'That can soon be altered, Dora. If you object to coming, I'll get a nanny in . . .'

'No need.' The woman's expression was suddenly frantic. 'Nannies are too expensive. And anyway, Geoffrey likes to see me every day. He wouldn't hear of it.'

'No. No, I'm sure he wouldn't. And I won't hear of my child being ruined to the point where I can't handle her. She thinks she's only to run to Granny and everything will be just the way she wants it. I don't like spoiled brats, Dora.'

'I see.' The arms were folded beneath the pendulous

bosom. 'I never spoiled Geoffrey. I brought him up on my own after my poor husband died. There's nothing spoiled about him, is there? Well? Is there?'

Kate stared at the woman and knew that it was pointless. If she came out with all of it, if she stood her ground and said all that needed saying, then she would destroy what little peace there was. Geoff was a spoiled brat and would continue so for the rest of his life. But what would be the virtue in telling this woman, 'you did it all wrong'? Anyway, who the hell ever got it all right, this child-rearing business? Was Kate doing a good job, had Rachel done her best, was any mother perfect? So she simply sighed and said, 'No. He's not spoiled. But please stop giving in to Melanie. I don't like her so petulant.' To ease the pain she added, in a kinder tone, 'And thanks for the date scones, Geoff will enjoy one of those later.'

With a heavy heart, Kate left her daughter in hands that were deemed capable and went off to the bedroom. There was an unreal quality to her life here, as if it were temporary, as if she knew that she would not be staying. At times, she felt like a guest in her own home, because that was how Dora made her feel. The best hours were spent at school where, in spite of the fact that she disliked the system and most teachers, she could at least make a contribution she knew to be valuable. The self-starters had begun to read, and among them Kate had found little teachers, children who re-learned while educating others. Thus, in a way other teachers might have derided, Kate had a smooth-running class full of good learners and potential successes. If she could just have her own school. If she could just escape a system apparently comprised of the deliberately blinded led by the totally inept.

Melanie tottered in followed closely by Dora. 'Mummy doing?' asked the child.

'Mummy's thinking,' said Dora gently. 'Mummy's got

all her work to do for school, then she has to change for when Daddy gets home. Come along now . . .'

'Leave her,' said Kate quietly. 'Let her stay here for a while.'

'Oh but it's time for her supper.' Dora's tone remained sweet as she led the infant away towards the stairs. 'Granny's mashed you a lovely banana for afters. Come on, leave Mummy to get on.'

The door closed.

Kate leaned forward and stared at herself in the dressing table mirror. Who am I? she seemed to be asking herself. I'm not a wife, I'm hardly a mother. Who then? What then? A teacher? Is that all I'm going to be, a teacher in circumstances that almost make me puke? Partridge and Gibbons, am I like them? Surely not. What the hell am I going to do with the rest of my life?

She tore off her clothes, pulled on a robe and went into the bathroom. Where were the roses round the door? Where were her brushes and paints, easels and charcoal? Her hands turned taps and sprinkled salts into water as she studied the long tapering fingers. These hands used to have talent, these hands were once going to change the world.

What had happened to all that ambition? Had it disappeared with Mike, did she need a man to prop her up, give her a sense of direction? She sank gratefully into the hot tub, remembering her old idea of heaven. No, it hadn't really changed, had it? Not basically. In the slipper baths, Kate had felt alone. Perhaps her idea of heaven all along had been aloneness. Did she love Geoff? Or Melanie? Was she capable of loving anyone – even herself?

But oh Lord! A teacher? Forever? No!

5

At twenty-six years of age, Kate Saunders was approaching her best. Although she had always been thin, there was at last a little flesh on her bones, a fine layer of firm texture that covered the sharp angles of her face and lent them some softness. Her body, too, was rounder with maturity and her hair had settled into a soft billowing mass of red-blonde waves that framed her features perfectly.

She would never be a real beauty – she knew that well enough – but she attracted attention as she shopped in town, drew male glances and the odd wolf-whistle which improved her self-image no end. And it needed improving too. Geoff treated her as if she were an old habit, something he could pick up or discard as the mood took him. His frequent visits abroad gave him the opportunity to indulge his need for other women; it was as if he required a whole harem to support an ego that was receding along with his hairline.

Dora continued in frequent attendance even though Melanie was now at infant school, and life had taken on the sort of humdrum normality that was supposed to soothe. It did not soothe Kate, though. She found herself longing for things she couldn't even name, intangible things that were probably connected with a freedom she did not dare to steal. If she left Geoff, she would be universally condemned, and she had not yet reached the stage of maturity – or would it be desperation? – that might lead her to dissolve her lifeless marriage.

School became the only place where she felt real and required. In her class, there were several children of great promise, infants whose parents, like her own mother, had slaved for years in factories just to give their offspring 'a decent start'. Kate's progress in Class One did not go unnoticed, and when Mr Partridge suffered a stroke which left him unable to teach, she was invited to apply for his position. No-one else in the school seemed to be interested in the deputy-headship, so the job was hers after an interview at which she was the sole applicant. Miss Ashe shook her hand firmly. 'We shall do very well, you and I, Mrs Saunders. Your ideas are progressive and you will keep me on my toes.'

'Thank you. For the chance and for having faith in me.'

'You're a good teacher. How do you think you'll like the change from infants to juniors?'

Kate smiled sadly. 'Funnily enough, I'll miss the little ones. Strange, because I'm not very good with my own five-year-old.'

'Typical, I'm afraid. Good teachers do not necessarily make good mothers. My own life has been childless, of course, so I don't know how I would have coped with motherhood.'

'I don't get the chance. My mother-in-law is there at weekends, too, now. And Geoff is talking about buying a new house in Edgeford, a house with a bit of land for his mother to have a separate flat on our property.'

'Oh, dear. Will that be a very sore trial?'

'It will indeed.'

'Hmm.' Miss Ashe tapped a toe against the rug in front of her desk. 'Get rid of her, my dear.'

'Easier said than done. My husband is very attached to his mother.'

The headmistress inhaled deeply. 'Listen to me. There comes a time for all these things to be put into perspective. You are his wife, Mrs Saunders. Your wellbeing should be of paramount importance to him. From little things you've said over the years, I gather that the senior

Mrs Saunders is a bad influence on your daughter. Explain this to . . . what's his name?'

'Geoff.'

'Explain it to him. Surely he will see reason?'

'No. No, he won't.'

'Too late for him, is it? Oh dear, when I think of my own poor mother . . .' her voice tailed away to a whisper.

'Pardon?'

'She used to say to me, "Leave me, Celia. Leave me before it's too late, before you turn into a Cinderella", the number of times she said that. She was a truly unselfish woman. Always matchmaking, always looking for a man for me to marry. She didn't want me fastened to her, you see. That's a proper mother.'

'But you stayed.'

'Because I never met the right man. And because I loved her. I still miss her dreadfully.'

'Are you lonely, Miss Ashe?'

The older woman stared unseeing through the window, her eyes misting with unshed tears. 'Mrs Saunders, we are all lonely in the final analysis. We come into the world alone and we leave it in the same condition. I am no lonelier than you are, my dear.'

Kate looked at the sad spinster she had known for over five years. A funny old thing, everyone thought. Not quite the full shilling because she'd never married. Who could know about life without being married? She was strange to look at, yes. She still wore her hair shoulder-length like a young girl, still moved as if she were in her twenties or thirties. But Miss Ashe was the full shilling, Kate knew that now. 'In the final analysis, we are all alone.' Kate would remember this woman's words for the rest of her life.

'Back to business,' snapped Miss Ashe, as if deliberately pulling herself together. 'You will take responsibility for playtime rotas, dinner registers, teachers' signing in and out book, the nurses' visits and any dinner time supervision that might be required. Timetables and schemes of work will be organized by both of us in conjunction with each separate member of staff. You'll get some ribbing because of your position and your youth. Get that staffroom sorted out. Now that the . . . the liaison between . . . well . . .' She coughed. 'The barrier to progress has been removed, Mrs Saunders. I know that you are simply dying to help upstairs with the less able, and there is now nothing to stop you offering such assistance. Persevere. Against all adversity.'

'I shall.'

'I know that. Why do you think I persuaded the board not to advertise? I knew I wanted you right from the start, since poor Mr Partridge became ill. So, onward ever onward, eh?'

'That's right, Miss Ashe.'

'And don't be a stranger. Any problems – familial or educational – just come to me. And I'd love you to visit me some evening or weekend. We can do a lot of planning once we get into a pair of comfortable chairs with a sherry in our hands.'

Kate grinned broadly. 'Sounds just my cup of tea.'

'You prefer tea?'

'Not really.'

'Good. A sherry or a fine port blurs the edges of a grim day, Mrs Saunders. Goodbye now. I'll see you to-morrow.'

Maureen was waiting by her car in the street. 'Hello, boss.'

'Don't start.'

'Can I open the door for you, boss?'

'I'll batter you in a minute.'

'Isn't life going to be hard now? You'll be closeted with old Spaniel face every other day, staying behind for meetings and looking into her soulful doggy eyes.'

'She's OK.'

'And can we still be friends? I mean, how are you going

to tell me off if I don't do a good job? You'll laugh.'

'I won't. And anyway, you do a good job. Get in the car and drive.'

'Yes, ma'am.'

As Maureen climbed into the car, Kate noticed a young man hovering by the side door of the school. There was something familiar about him, she had seen him at parents' evenings, hadn't she? He looked so sad and lost, while his clothes appeared to have been thrown on in haphazard fashion – coat unbuttoned, tie hanging loose from a creased collar, shoes scuffed and unpolished. He was an attractive man with gentle blue eyes and soft light brown hair. She took a step towards him as his name suddenly dropped into her mind. 'Mr Collins?'

He stared at her as if from a great distance. 'Pardon?'

'You're Mr Collins, aren't you?'

'Yes. Yes, I am. Are you Rosie's new teacher?'

'That's right. I took over from Mr Partridge yesterday. Did you want to see me? Is there a problem?'

He shuffled about for a moment or two, eyes downcast, head shaking slowly from side to side. 'She's . . . in hospital.'

Kate waited for a while, but no more was forthcoming. 'Is it anything serious?' she asked.

He cleared his throat. 'It's . . . er . . . something to do with her blood.'

'I see.' She waited again. 'Are you her father?'

He drew a grubby hand across his eyes. 'Our parents are dead. I'm her brother. She'll . . . she'll be back at school, Mrs . . . er . . .'

'Saunders. Kate Saunders.'

'Right. Yes.' Sad eyes were slowly raised until they met Kate's questioning gaze. 'Look after her.'

'Pardon?'

'Don't tell any of the other teachers. I want her life to be as normal as possible. She . . . isn't going to make it.

She'll get better for a while, but she's got . . . it's leukaemia, I think. Be kind to her. Just be kind to my little Rosie.'

Her breath was caught in her dry throat. 'I will. I most certainly will. And I won't tell anyone. Wait! Please? Is there anything I can . . . ?'

But he was already walking away, leaving Kate staring at his sloping back. He stumbled along like an old man, though he was obviously only in his twenties.

Kate climbed into the car.

'What did he want?' asked Maureen.

'Not much. Just asking about Rosie's progress.'

'Hmmph. He looked a mess. He's a teacher, you know. Usually very smart and up to the minute.'

'Let's go home.'

In spite of Kate's disquiet about Rosie, they drove in comfortable silence down to Bolton and through its heart. This friendship had become valuable to both women over the years. Each now knew the other's hopes and fears; there were few secrets between them. One of the few was Rosie . . . 'How's it going in there?' asked Maureen as they stopped outside Kate's house.

Kate shrugged. 'The only bit of French I remember is "plus ça change, plus c'est la meme chose". It's true. Things change while remaining the same.' Except for Rosie Collins. Things could only get worse for that poor kiddy.

'You're the one that's changing, love. Silly old Geoffrey can't see what he's got. I was saying to Phil only the other night that neither man is grateful for a wife who works in a good profession. He's no different to yours, I'm taken for granted too. He's glad we can afford to renovate the bathroom, but doesn't notice that it's my money we're using. Not all of it. I keep some to one side. What do you do with yours?'

'I save most.'

'Oh, what for? Holidays?'

'I really don't know what for, Maureen. Against a day that will be more than rainy, I suppose.'

'What? You'll leave him?'

'I don't know the answer to that, either. Perhaps I intend to invest in myself some day – do something other than teaching. At first, I wanted my own school, but, as I say, things change all the time. Not in there, though. Everything's still the same in there. He can't see it, won't see it. Now she often takes Mel back to her house for weekends. When I complain to Geoff, he just says she's lonely. The child is becoming an old woman herself.'

'Then do something about it!'

'Oh, Maureen, even you don't truly understand. I can't alter the situation. I've tried. If I say anything, it's because I'm unstable. You see, when I talk about things, about Dora's interference and Geoff's indifference, I get upset. When I get upset, he makes another appointment with the psychiatrist. The psychiatrist is also a man, so he shares Geoff's viewpoint. I'm doing too much, don't need to work full-time, should invest my meagre store of energy into making a home. If I did finish working, Dora would still be here almost every day. I've told the psycho all this, he knows I work just to get away from home. But he says I'm running and that I'll have to stop some time. If I gave up teaching, then I'd probably run in a different way, a more dramatic way. At school, I see some sanity and order. I can even have a say in its creation now. Here . . .' She waved a hand towards the house, 'I have to be a good girl, say nothing and do little. As long as I look the part and hold my corner in a bridge game, then all's well. You and Phil are the only pair of friends discovered by me. Everyone else is positively geriatric.'

'Oh Lord! I can see big trouble ahead for you, Kate. Why don't you get it over and done with? Why don't you cite one of his floozies?'

Kate shrugged slightly. 'In the first place, I don't know who they are. Even the letters have no addresses on them.

Secondly, I can't seem to care enough. Also, I'm not ready yet. Perhaps the doctor is right, perhaps I can only do one thing at a time. Then there's Mel. What would I do about her? The child doesn't know me – if I took her away, she'd scream blue bloody murder. But if I were to leave her with Geoff and Dora while she's so young, then what would become of her? There are too many things to consider, Mo. One day, though. One day . . .'

Geoff's face seemed to cloud over that evening when she told him the news about her job. Dora, who had stayed again for supper, mumbled something about a little brother or sister for Melanie, and Kate foolishly latched on to this. 'I'm not here simply to breed, Dora. There are other important things in life, you know.'

'But Melanie's a big girl now.' Dora drew in her third chin. 'It's a very big gap you're leaving.'

Kate nodded her head towards her husband. 'Geoff had no brothers or sisters.'

'His father died!'

'When Geoff was ten. Mel's nowhere near that age. I really think you should mind your own business, Dora. When it comes to producing children, our life is no concern of yours.'

'Kate!' barked Geoff. 'Enough of that, now.'

She turned on him, her temper snapping in spite of the rein she was trying so hard to apply. 'I am sick to death of your mother's interference. Every time I come home, she's here. Every time the school day ends, I've got her to put up with!'

'I bring Melanie home from school,' wailed Dora. 'Do you want me to leave her here alone?'

'I want you to leave me alone,' screamed Kate.

Dora burst into tears. 'Thank goodness the child is in bed,' she sobbed.

Geoff rushed to his mother's side. 'This is no time for one of your tantrums, Kate.' He hugged Dora closely.

'They're not tantrums! I am stating the plain and

simple fact that I don't like your mother being here all the time. Do you know of any other marriage like this one? Do any of your friends' wives have to tolerate another woman in the house all the time? And she's turning our daughter into a grabbing, scheming little bitch. What's the matter, Dora? Are you having a tantrum? I'm not allowed to cry like that, so just enjoy the luxury of indulging yourself. As for you, Geoff, you are not a man. You never were and you never will be. She made sure of that!' Kate pointed an accusing finger at the weeping woman, then flounced out of the room, slamming the door in her wake.

In the bedroom, her own tears came, quickly soaking into the pillow she used to smother her sobs. She had a new job, a good job and no-one in the house was even slightly impressed or interested. As a person, she didn't count here. But why had she suddenly opened up tonight? After being so good for so long? Was it because of her conversation with Maureen, or was it because of her unnoticed and uncared about promotion? And why was Mr Collins' face in her mind all the time? Poor Rosie! Dear God, poor Rosie!

It was yet another lesson for Kate. From this day on, she showed little emotion at home, was even less of a wife and mother than she had been previously. An armed truce existed between herself and Dora, who continued to haunt the house as if it were her own. There was little in life for Kate. Her only solace was school, where she was slowly breaking down the barriers between uppers and lowers, where schemes of work for poor achievers were now sent upstairs to a sensible if not quite enthusiastic reception.

It was in the middle of this very dead period that she met Mike Wray again. She was in the Central Art Gallery with a party of six from the scholarship class when he turned up similarly surrounded, though by older children.

As soon as he saw her, his handsome face lit up. 'Kate,' he yelled across a dozen heads.

She stopped dead in her tracks and stared at him. He hadn't changed, not much anyway. Wavy blond hair was pushed back carelessly from a fair-skinned strong face, while his bearing was still youthful in spite of the dark grey suit he wore. 'Mike! How are you?'

'Buried in work.' He negotiated his way round the children and came to join her. 'Still painting?'

'No. Married with one child.'

'Ditto. Did you marry that Geoff chap?'

'Yes.'

'I married a nurse. Susan, she's called.' He collared a passing youth of about fourteen. 'Marshall! No trouble in here or it's double detention. Right?'

'Right, sir.'

'Sir.' She giggled quietly. 'And I'm deputy-head now.'

'Honestly? Well done.'

'Only because nobody else wanted it. The school's a mausoleum, looks like a derelict workhouse from the outside, and inside's not much better.'

'Which school is that?'

'Daubhill.'

'Really? I'm at Thornleigh, as you can see from these dreadful uniformed urchins. Got a degree in art, finally. Stayed on and went to Manchester University. So I'm second in command of the art department. Mind, there are only two of us, so second in command is bottom rank.'

They watched their charges for a few minutes, each suddenly shy and unsure of what to say to the other.

'Roses round the door, eh?' he finally whispered from a corner of his mouth.

'And painting on summer evenings.'

'Are you . . . are you happy?'

'No.' Her voice was low.

'Neither am I.' He raised his tone. 'Marshall! Do not touch anything. For goodness sake, boy, go down into the aquarium where you can do no damage.' He turned and looked at her again. 'I shall serve time for Marshall. One day, I'll be put inside for what I'm going to do to that silly lad. You've turned out pretty, just as I always knew you would. Why aren't you happy?'

'I don't know. Too many reasons.'

'Meet me by the duck pond on Saturday? Please?'

'What if someone sees us? That's silly, Mike. We're both married. Meeting will only bring trouble for us.'

'Sue doesn't give a damn where I go or what I do. She's too busy midwifing to care about me. What's wrong with two old friends meeting? Is there a babysitting problem?'

'No. My daughter goes to Geoff's mother most weekends. The problem is with me, Mike, I don't know what I want from life. Please don't complicate matters any further. And if Geoff found out, he would go mad. It's all right for him to play away from home, but . . .'

'Does he?'

'Yes.'

'Then why worry?'

'Because I have my own standards. I'm a married woman. Perhaps I won't always be married . . . Look. These kids are getting out of hand. I'm going, fine art is obviously not their forte.' She dragged herself away with reluctance, but he pursued her.

'Saturday. Two o'clock,' he whispered.

When Saturday came, she went to the duck pond, just as she had always known that she would. It was drizzling and they huddled together beneath Mike's large black umbrella. 'Why didn't we wait for one another?' he moaned softly. 'Why did you have to marry that bloody man?'

'I loved him. It seemed right at the time. Only it's turned out to be a stinking rotten bore. I am not right for marriage, Mike.'

'All because of Josianne Hedouin.'

'Who? Ah, yes. The French girl in the daring red dress. I wonder what became of her?'

'My parents sent her packing after a fortnight – she was always trying to get into my bed. And there were boys hanging round the house at all hours of the day and night. She's probably running a thriving business in the Quartier Latin.'

'Did she take your virginity?'

'Don't be silly. I lost that in the Air Force.'

'I see. I lost mine to Geoff. The ducks are still here, I notice. Remember how I used to try to paint them? So many different colours in their feathers.'

They gazed together at a past that was gone and, beyond that, at a future they had denied themselves. Each could feel the other's misery soaking deeper than the wetting fine rain. 'What do we do?' he asked at last. 'Can we see one another?'

'I think,' she said carefully, 'that I would like to have a lover. Someone who thinks I'm special, someone all to myself. But a married lover isn't the answer. We could not communicate when we needed or wanted to, could not meet whenever or wherever we pleased. Apart from which, it would be totally dishonest. I scream at him for knocking about with other women and I enjoy the virtuous stand I am able to take. The guilt would weigh me down.'

'That's daft.'

She turned slightly and studied his profile. 'What about you and Susan? Surely you would feel some guilt, too?'

He gripped her arm. 'We get one life, Kate. This isn't a rehearsal, you know. There is no second chance, so why don't we take some pleasure while we can? And the relationship need not be physical.'

'Rubbish!'

He inhaled deeply, then blew out his breath in a noisy fashion. 'Damn and blast everything! You just walked out of my life when I made one mistake – why? Now I'm married to a woman who's married to her job, while you live with a man who bores you senseless. Let's run away.'

She began to giggle. 'Away? There is no away, Mike. Life is all around us, it's part of us, inside us. We can't run from what we are, which is basically a decent pair of people. OK, we've dealt ourselves a bad hand, but we chose our own cards, remember that. Through selfishness and bad management, we've made a muck of our lives. Now, we just have to grin and bear it. Susan and your child would really miss you. And I can't let them pay for the roses round my door.'

He grabbed her to him and kissed her fiercely on the lips. In spite of the rain, she could feel the heat coursing through her body, a heat she had felt years ago with Geoff. Sex. It was only sex. She pushed him away. 'No! Please, I am not very strong just now. It would be unfair of you to take advantage of my unhappiness. There can't be a relationship. Two children, Mike . . .'

'We'll take them with us!'

She thought of Dora, giggled again as she pictured herself trying to grab a screaming Melanie from the cozy fireside at home. 'No. I can't take my daughter anywhere. She's been raised by Geoff's mother. There is nowhere I can go, Mike, nothing I can do.'

But he kissed her again and she knew that she was lost, that she would grab this small island of happiness and keep it close for this one day at least.

He drove her to his parents' house where they made gloriously uncomfortable love halfway up the stairs. 'They won't be back till tomorrow,' he moaned into her hair. 'I'm supposed to look after the cat.'

'Where is it?' she managed while he caressed her naked thighs. 'Where's the poor cat?'

'Bugger the cat!'

They heated soup in the kitchen, then made beans on toast to assuage a hunger that had arisen out of their joining. After eating greedily, they talked about the old days, days of bullies and house-making on the bombsite, days of dreaming about a home in the country and children and art galleries. Kate found herself laughing, really laughing in a way she hadn't laughed for years. 'Remember Froggie-Boggie Dawson?' she screamed. 'How he used to bring all sorts of creatures to school?'

'Worms in the teacher's desk,' he said. 'Caterpillars in her paper-clip box. But the frog in the bog was the best, especially when the nun came out with her skirts held high. And then there was that other lad in your class, the one with the speech impediment. He always said "shit" instead of "sit" and the nuns didn't know where to look. Good old days, eh? I wish, oh God, how I wish Pamela hadn't gone in for that French exchange bit. It did her no good. She's a clerk in some office in town, not an O'level to her name. You look delicious after making love. Shall we do it again?'

She was suddenly sober. 'I have to go home. I will always have to go home. So will you.'

'No!'

'Yes! That's why it could never have worked for us, Mike. You're an incurable romantic and I've always existed on a less elevated plane. It's lovely to see you again, but it can't go on. We'd fall in love, then we'd both be miserable. If we became long-term lovers, we'd get all screwed up about when we'd see one another, worried in case one of us might be making love to wife or husband. And if we ran off together, that would set off a chain of endless unhappiness for everyone. Nothing built on sand can last, love. Second marriages are not joyful if they're started off by abandoning dependants. See? I told you I was sensible. Let's just keep today with our other memories.'

'It's not enough, Kate! Now that I've found you again, I absolutely refuse to let you go. Can't we meet sometimes? Just a few times a year? Once a month, eh? Four weeks from today by the duck pond at two o'clock. Think about it. Please?'

He drove her to the centre of town where she could catch a bus home. She promised to think about a second meeting, but her emotions were so churned that she would have said just about anything to get away from him, to escape to a place where she might think.

For over an hour she wandered aimlessly around the shops, not buying, not even noticing the items on display. That she was so upset amazed her greatly. After all, she'd only done what Geoff had been doing almost from the start of their marriage. But Mike had touched her – not just physically. He was one of the few good things she remembered from her childhood. Good, clean and whole-some Mike Wray.

Could she go home now and act as if nothing had happened? And how would she explain such a long absence? With a total lack of real interest, she marched into Timpson's and bought the first pair of shoes that fitted. They were ugly shoes, teacher's shoes and she would never wear them. Their hideous heaviness re-minded her of what she had done, of the enormity of the step she had taken on this very day. Shoes. Steps. Walking into things, running away from things. The shoes were somehow symbolic and she would keep them in her wardrobe as a reminder of her folly.

Geoff was in jovial mood when she reached home. A fine buffet supper had been prepared by Dora and a good bridge pair would be arriving in a couple of hours. 'Had a good day?' he asked.

'Excellent,' she replied curtly, hoping her cheeks did not look as hot as they felt.

'Buy anything?'

'Just a pair of sturdy shoes for school.'

'Ah.'

'I'll . . . er . . . I'll just pop upstairs for a bath.'

'Yes. You seem a bit flushed. Not coming down with anything, are you?'

'No.' Nothing that would spoil his rubber, nothing important.

She ran upstairs to wash away her sin. But the glow remained with her all night and she played brilliantly. Perhaps adultery was a good idea after all? It might even save her marriage. She shuddered. Did she want it saving? Ah yes. Back to the burning question once more . . .

'What are you up to, lady?' Rachel Murray leaned across the table and stared hard at her daughter. 'There's devilment in you, I can smell it from here.'

'Don't talk so daft, Mam.' But Kate knew she was blushing. Three times she had seen Mike now; three times they had made love in odd places. First there had been his mother's stairs, then the back seat of his Morris, last of all behind a derelict barn. It couldn't go on, it really would have to stop.

'I can always tell when you're up to something, madam! Is it a man?'

'What?'

'You heard. I asked you if you were seeing a man.'

'Oh, Mother! Why on earth would I be seeing a man? And when? I've no time for anything these days . . .'

'Why? You ask me why you would be seeing a man? Why does any woman see a man, eh? As for the when, determination always finds its way. I don't like your husband, Katherine, but you know how I feel about the sanctity of marriage – even a registry office job deserves some respect. Then there's little Melanie to consider . . .'

'Shut up, will you? I come here to see you in my lunch hour when I should be doing the requisition forms and what do I get? Bloody insults and innuendos.'

Rachel swallowed the last of her sandwich, then drained her pint mug. 'All I know is this. You've no appetite, you glow like the sun and there's that secretive look about you, the look you used to wear when you'd dipped your grubby little fingers in the condensed milk. You'd best pull yourself together, or yon feller will be on your tail.'

'I don't know what you mean.'

'Neither do I. If I knew what I was on about, I'd tackle you proper. Just frame yourself. Whatever you're up to shows, and I won't be the only one to notice.'

Rachel went through to the kitchen to wash the pots while Kate stared into the fire. This was a right pickle as her mother would have said if she had known the full truth. Mike was on the verge of telling his wife, was pressing Kate to tell Geoff. He had this vision of what he called 'life after death' and he wanted to ride off into a sunset whose colour he would no doubt choose. All along, Kate had had Mike's measure, right from the time when they had been young. Mike was not one for dalliance; he now expected Kate to make an honest man of him. Yes, he wanted the relationship to be verified, made permanent, glorified by a marriage certificate.

And what did Kate want? Not that. No, she didn't want Mike. He was a good lover, had been an excellent friend and companion during the past few weeks, but she didn't want another marriage. Was there something wrong with her? How could she sit here and coldly analyse her feelings, his motives, the possible outcome of their joint folly? Was she a cold-hearted bitch?

Rachel bustled in with a package of scones. 'Give Dotty Dora one of these,' she said in an acid tone. 'Happen she'll lighten her own once she's tasted a proper scone. And don't be taking any more nonsense from that daughter of yours. She created something shocking when you left her here last Saturday. Wanted sweeties, she said. Always gets sweeties from Granny Dora, she said. If she'd been my own, I'd have tanned her backside for her.'

'It's Mike,' said Kate suddenly. 'From school. The one who looked after me at Peter and Paul's. He's . . . turned up again.'

'I see.' Rachel sank into a fireside chair. 'Thanks for telling me, love. Thanks for trusting me enough. You're not the first – I had me own moments, I can tell you that now. But you have to weigh up what's right, lass. I mean, what does he want?'

Kate studied her hands for a second or two. 'He wants me,' she said simply.

'For permanent, like?'

Kate nodded.

'And what do you want?'

'Oh, Mother! I don't know. I can give you a long list of what I don't want, but I can't think of one item on the positive side. I'm unhappy at home, you already know that. Geoff treats me like a cross between an ornament and a skivvy, Dora drives me mad, my child infuriates me. He – I mean Mike – wants us to go away together. I can't do it. Not because of any sense of loyalty to my husband – and I know that must sound awful – but because I don't seem to want anybody. And now Mike's pushing me to tell Geoff and to make the break. Huh. A clean break, he calls it. What would be clean about it, Mam?'

'Nowt. You'd leave a pile of dirt behind, especially with Melanie so young. Dora would go mad if you took the child away.'

'I know.'

Rachel jumped up and grabbed her daughter's hands. 'Finish with him, Katherine. Bad enough giving up all you've got for something you really want. But to spoil your life for a man you're not sure of . . .'

'I need . . . something. Something of my own.'

'Then use your brain! Get something out of that God-given talent we all know you have! Paint pictures, write stories, go back to college. But don't throw any more of yourself away, love.'

Kate blinked back the threatening tears and hugged her mother tightly. 'You're not a bad old bat, are you? I'll sort it out, Mam. But I'm going to miss him. He was like a ray of sunshine in a very dark world.'

'But he's not for you?'

'No. There's something missing. Like Geoff, he's a weak man. It's a different sort of weakness, but I couldn't put up with him for long.'

'I'll pray for you, Katherine. Find the strength. Please.'

'I will. Next time I see him.'

Steve Collins hovered in the doorway. The class of boisterous eleven-year-olds had just been dismissed, and Kate was packing her bag for home. He knocked on the open door. 'Mrs Saunders?'

'Yes?' She turned and stared at him. 'What is it? Please come in.'

He staggered into the room and sat on a front row desk. 'Excuse me,' he mumbled. 'But I haven't slept since . . . oh, I don't know when. I've come all the way from Townley's Hospital.' His voice was quiet and tired. 'Rosie's asking for you.'

'Oh.' She sank on to her chair. 'Is it . . . ? I mean, is she . . . ?'

He nodded dumbly.

'Oh, my dear God!' Her head dropped to her hands as she thought of the pretty bright child whose life was ebbing away at this very moment. 'Me?' she asked eventually. 'She wants me?'

'You've been good to her. And you never told anyone. I know you never told anyone, and I'm terribly grateful. Please come. Please say you'll come.'

She pulled herself together and gathered up her bag. 'Hang on. I have to tell Maureen Carter to go on without me, she can give a message to my family. Just two minutes. Stay there. I'll be back directly.'

They sped through the town in his battered wreck of

a car, he white-faced and weeping, she clinging to the edge of her seat as the car flew along at a speed that did not match its obvious age. Outside the hospital, the vehicle shuddered to a halt and the man immediately reached for her hand. 'It's not easy, Mrs Saunders. Seeing a child die, I mean. I wouldn't have left her, but she was crying for you. She . . . hasn't had a mother for years.'

Kate shook her head, knowing that she was no proper mother to anyone. 'I understand,' she said softly. 'Please don't cry. Don't let Rosie see you crying.'

He scrubbed at red-rimmed eyes with the heel of his hand. 'Better?'

'You'll do. Come on, we must go in.'

Rosie Collins lay in a single ward, her face as white as the linen pillowcase on which incongruously healthy hair lay fanned out like the display of some exotic bird.

Kate crept to the bed. 'Rosie?'

'You came.' The child opened her sunken eyes. 'She came,' she said to her brother. 'Give it to her. Give my work to Mrs Saunders.'

He bent to the locker and pulled out several sheets of paper. 'It's her homework.' His voice was cracking. 'She's done special pictures of flowers for you, Mrs Saunders.'

The little girl's face brightened momentarily as she watched her teacher poring over the work.

'Ten out of ten, Rosie. I'd give you eleven out of ten, but that would be silly, wouldn't it?'

'Yes. I don't feel very well. I couldn't come to school.'

Steve Collins sniffed. 'That's OK, Rosie. School has come to you.'

Kate placed the child's work in her bag. 'I see you got all our cards.' She pointed to the display hung on a string over the bed. 'And thank you for doing your homework.'

The child suddenly stiffened, her whole body seeming to go rigid as a spasm racked her depleted form. Kate averted her gaze. The girl was bleeding to death before their very eyes. There was no sign of blood, because the haemorrhages were probably internal, but the situation was clear from the colour of her skin. Couldn't they do anything? Couldn't they do something to ease the agony?

Steve read her thoughts. 'She's had her quota,' he whispered.

They sat by the bed, each holding a hand while the little girl dozed, then woke, then dozed again.

A nurse brought tea and biscuits, then a doctor came in to feel Rosie's pulse. The man looked meaningfully at Steve. 'I'd stay if I were you.'

Kate grabbed the doctor's sleeve. 'Is there nothing . . . ?'

'No, nothing more. I'd give my right arm to find something more.'

Endless night turned reluctantly to morning. There was more tea, this time with toast, and another visit from the sad doctor. Rosie had now been unconscious for many hours.

Steve stood by the window with his cup and saucer. 'She's all I have,' he said brokenly.

Kate watched the grey face on the pillow. He wouldn't have her for much longer, would he? She swallowed her tears. Everything seemed so unimportant now – school, Mike Wray, Geoff, Dora – all of them paled into insignificance next to the sight of this poor dying child.

She reached out and stroked Rosie's hair, and the child's eyes opened. For an instant, there was a terrible fear there, an awful and unbearable knowledge, then this was replaced by serenity as Steve and Kate clutched at skeletal hands.

'Steve,' breathed the child with difficulty.

'I'm here.'

'And Mrs Saunders.'

'Yes.'

She looked from one to the other, sighed happily, then gave up her tiny spirit.

Kate watched as if from a distance while Steve Collins stroked his dead sister's hand. It was terrible. This was definitely the worst moment of Kate's life thus far. Terrible because she could do nothing to mend it. She was useless, useless and utterly stupid.

'Don't cry,' he said simply.

'I didn't know I was crying.'

'Well, you are. Rosie's OK now. Nobody can hurt my little Rosie ever again. Alive, she made me weep. But now she's at peace, I just feel relieved. No doubt the tears will arrive later.'

Kate dabbed at her eyes with a totally inadequate scrap of handkerchief. 'She's so . . . so pretty.'

'Yes. She looks like a little wax doll. I don't know what I'll do without her. But I have to go on, haven't I?'

'Yes.'

They had to go on, both of them. Each stared at the other across the still figure in the hospital bed.

'She's taught me something,' said Kate. 'She's taught me that I'm lovable. This little sister of yours loved me. That means something. It will help me to sort out my life.'

'Go home,' he said wearily. 'Phone the school, then take the day off. I have to get on with my own sorting out. Thanks for coming. You're a good woman.'

She glanced at him again. 'Want any help?'

He shrugged. 'There is no help, not for me.'

'Pardon?'

'Never mind. Perhaps I'll tell you all about it one day – when you're old enough to hear it.'

Kate phoned for a taxi cab, then waited in the hospital foyer for it to arrive. Little Rosie would stay in her mind for many a year to come. And so would the girl's troubled brother.

*

Mike was furious.

She distanced herself from him deliberately and carefully, leaving several inches of space between himself and her on 'their' bench in the park.

'I've told her,' he said sulkily. 'She knows there's someone else now. Kate, you are not a giver. Do you realize that I am prepared to put my job on the line for you? I'd never survive in a Catholic school as a divorced man. It's OK for you, isn't it? No-one would mind if Mrs Deputy-Head left her husband. It will get back to the Brothers in the end. And what am I left with? Just "cheerio, Mike, it's been good to know you"!'

'I'm sorry.' This sounded lame, but she could say little else.

'Sorry? That's hardly enough!'

She sighed deeply. 'I told you right from the start that there was no future in it.'

'Huh! You didn't say that when you were moaning in my arms, did you?'

'That's unfair.'

'Unfair? Who are you to talk about unfairness? You threw me over once before for an old man, now you tell me I'm still not good enough for you! What sort of a future will you have with him?'

'A poor one.'

'But you don't want me instead?'

'It wouldn't work.'

He stood up and began to march up and down between bench and pond, arms waving wildly as his temper got the better of him. 'I'll tell him!' he cried now.

'Don't be silly. That's a woman's trick.'

'I want you with me. I always wanted you with me! We were going to paint, remember?'

'I remember.'

'What chance is there now? For either of us? She doesn't support me, he doesn't support you. How the hell will either of us become a painter now?'

'Perhaps we don't need support. Talent will out, if it's there.'

'Ah yes,' he said viciously. 'How smug you are, Kate. You always knew you were better than me. But when did you last paint a picture, eh? When did you last sit by a pond and paint your ducks? I haven't put brush to canvas since I got married . . .'

'That's hardly my fault.'

'IT IS YOUR FAULT!' Several passers-by glanced towards the small area of excitement they were creating.

'Shut up and be your age,' she snapped between clenched teeth. 'Stop drawing attention to yourself.'

'I will not shut up.'

'Then I shall go home.' She rose from the bench, but he crossed the small distance and pushed her back into a sitting position. 'Don't ever do that again,' she said quietly. 'Lay one more finger on me and I'll have every policeman in Bolton running to Queen's Park.'

He clenched his fists, groaned loudly, then threw himself on to the bench beside her. 'Sorry,' he mumbled.

'Like all men, you are no better than a spoiled child. Go home, Mike. It's not worth this, nothing is worth this.'

They sat in grim silence for several minutes, each staring at the pond and its surrounding bushes.

'Hello.' The cold voice greeted them from Kate's side, and she looked up to see a small dark-haired woman standing next to her. 'I'm Susan Wray,' announced the pretty stranger. 'I followed my husband, I'm afraid. So you are the famous Kate he's always going on about.'

Kate swallowed hard and painfully. 'Yes. I'm Kate Saunders.'

'I wish I could say that I was pleased to meet you.'

'So do I.'

Mike edged away from both women, his fear-filled eyes fixed on his wife's angry face. She sat down on the bench beside Kate. 'Well,' she began. 'What are we going to do about all this? I've a two-year-old son at home, and he and I would dearly like to know where we stand.'

'It's over,' said Kate. 'We were just finishing it.'

'Is that right?' Sue asked her cowering husband.

'Yes.' His voice sounded small and hurt.

She angled herself so that she could study Kate's face. 'You're not the raving beauty I expected.' There was a nasty edge to her words. 'I thought he was about to run off with some golden-haired princess. Not that you're bad-looking. I daresay you're all right with a happier expression on your face. Why did you try to steal my husband?'

'I didn't.'

'But you've had an affair with him?'

'Yes.'

Mike placed his elbows on his knees, then doubled over to bury his face in his hands.

'He has reverted to the foetal position,' said Sue. 'The man is a coward.'

He jumped up, mumbled a few curses that were practically inaudible, then set off down the path as if the devil were at his heels.

'There he goes,' sighed Sue dramatically. 'He never could face the music. So, where do we go from here?'

'Home. Back to normal, I suppose.'

'Not for me. Nothing can ever be normal for me now, Kate. I trusted him. I know he's attractive, but he's never strayed before. How can I believe in him now?'

'I suppose you'll just have to do your best. Look, Sue, I've known Mike since we were children. He's not the unfaithful type. This was just a . . . an aberration. We were very close many years ago, and I suppose we were trying to recapture our youth. I'm sorry. What more can I say to you? Or to him?'

'He still wants to run off with you, then?'

Kate dropped her head in shame. 'He thinks he does.

But it would never work. Like all artists, we are both selfish people. You may not realize this now, but he needs you more than he ever did. I've hurt his pride – he'll get over that. I could only inflict a shallow wound, Sue. But if you leave him because of this silly little affair, then he'll never mend. I think he loves you.'

Hope sprang into the sad brown eyes. 'Does he?'

'Yes. He has a lot of respect for you. Don't give up on him, please! I couldn't bear to think I'd broken up your marriage. For me, it was just physical with Mike. There are no real feelings on my part.'

Sue studied her adversary. 'What about your husband? Does he know about this?'

'No.'

Sue got up, drew herself to full height and clutched her handbag to her chest as if using it as a barrier. 'Right. So you've got away with it this time. Well, let me tell you now, Kate Saunders, that if you ever go near my husband again, I'll be round to your house in two shakes of a lamb's tail. Let's see what your husband makes of this if it carries on. Let's see you suffering while your world crumbles about your ears. If you want a new man, find one who's not already spoken for. All right?'

Kate nodded slowly.

'I'll do it,' said the small dark woman. 'I will!'

'I know. But there'll be no need. I won't be seeing Mike again.'

'Better not. Because after I've told your husband, I'll take you apart limb from limb. OK?'

'You love him.' This was not a question.

'Of course I bloody love him! Do you think I'd have humiliated myself by following him if I didn't love him? He's a good father and a damned good teacher. I can't let a slut like you ruin his life, can I?'

'No.'

The furious little woman paused for a second. 'Only you're not a slut, are you? This is your first time, isn't it? You'd be less dangerous if you were a slut. Oh God, I wish you were . . .'

'Don't be afraid of me. You're prettier than I am, more sensible too. And you have his son. He won't stray again, believe me.'

'He'd better not!' She swivelled on her heel and marched away. As soon as she had disappeared, Mike crept out of a clump of bushes.

With cold deliberation, Kate drew her Thunderer from her bag, placed it between her lips and let forth a blast that would have reached the deafest ears. Sue returned immediately to see what was going on. 'I think you've forgotten something,' said Kate, waving a hand towards Mike. Sue ran across the path, grabbed her husband's arm and pushed him towards the nearest gate. 'Thanks' she threw over her shoulder.

'Don't mention it,' said Kate to herself.

She sat for a long time in the park, drawing her coat around her as the air grew chill. It hadn't been worth it. Adultery might be the answer for some people, but it wasn't for her. What would happen to Mike now and should she feel guilty about his trouble?

Strangely, she didn't really feel much at all. Since the death of little Rosie, she had felt little but grief at the sight of the child's empty chair in her classroom, and at the memory of Steve Collins' troubled face.

With a heavy heart, she jumped on to the Daubhill bus and then ran to her mother's house. 'I've done it,' she announced as soon as she got through the door.

'Good. I should think so and all, our Katherine. You shouldn't go messing about in the fire unless you've got asbestos fingers.'

'I'm cold.'

'Right, I'll put the kettle on.'

'Not that sort of cold, Mam. I'm lonely.'

'Lonely? What's lonely got to do with anything? I've been lonely all me life, but I never went chasing other folks' men. They might have chased me but . . . anyway, that's another story. Lonely's no excuse.'

'I know. His wife came.'

'She what? She followed him, you mean?'

Kate nodded. 'She's a really nice girl, probably too good for him. That's what gets me about men, you know. They're supposed to be the big guys, but it's the women who keep life in order. You should have seen her, Mam. She laid into me, then dragged him out of the park like a little kid. I felt really proud of her.'

'Eeh, God in heaven!' Rachel dragged a hand through her hair. 'What's life coming to at all? You'll have to settle down, love, make the best of what you've got. Just imagine what old Dotty would have made of this, eh? It would have been served up breakfast, dinner and tea for the next ten years. Good job your husband never found out.'

Kate placed herself in a chair and held out her hands to the fire. 'I think I'll start painting again. It's no use saying I've no time. Writers and artists never have any time, most of them do other jobs as well. But I've got to have something of my own, Mam, something that's nothing to do with anybody else. Is that selfish?'

'Nay, lass. That's talent. Do you think John Milton thought about other folk when he was writing *Paradise Lost*? Did he hell as like. Somebody as starts stuff from scratch needs to be that bit selfish. So, do you want me to pose for you? Come on, cheer up.'

Kate shook her head. 'Not that kind of art, Mother. I'm not sure yet. Maybe illustrating children's books if I can find an author or a story. Or cartoons. I've always liked cartoons and comic strips. I'd like to write a set of reading books that look like comics, but I'm not so sure about the script. Perhaps I'll meet another teacher with ideas. It'll come to me.'

'It will, love. I've always known that, and so did your dad.'

'Did he?'

'Oh yes.'

'I'd like to have been sure of that. Years ago. I'd like to have been sure.'

6

Edgeford, Bolton, 1968

It was a nice enough place, she thought while she wiped
the dishes. It could be a lot worse. Many people must
have tedious lives in surroundings far inferior to these.
Like her own mother. Poor Rachel Murray had never
lived in a place like this, had she? There was a fourteenth-
century church, a little village hall where the drama
society and the brownies vied for time and space, four
pubs named after several animals of various colours, a
park complete with putting green, and a strange mix of
old and new housing.

Kate had lived here now for five of the fourteen years
of her marriage. Theirs was a modern detached house, a
largish property with a long garden to the rear and, at
the front, part ownership of a brook where nested noisy
ducks and small furry animals whose names she could
never master. This was happiness? This was supposed to
be bliss. She swished the dishcloth around the bowl for
à while, then dabbed in desultory fashion at a few stains
on the Formica worktop. Housework had never been her
forte. Perhaps her darker suspicions of herself were true,
perhaps she had no forte, no strength, no particular
talent.

Jemima, who had been sitting silently on the grass
beneath the kitchen window, suddenly quacked and
flapped her snowy wings, demanding and expecting
immediate attention. The white duck was out of place
among all the mallards, mused Kate as she threw some

bread through an open pane. Jemima mated with the wild ones, reared some beautiful mixed-up ducklings, yet remained tame and domesticated, often training her young to come right into the house during spells of frost. Kate grinned broadly. 'You're out of step, Jemmy,' she called. Then, to herself she said, 'Like me. We've both got it wrong, old duck.'

She glanced out towards the cream slatted fence at the bottom of the garden. It was a tidy area, neat-edged and unimaginative, with a path of pink and white flags stretching its whole length beneath a plastic-coated washing line. Happiness. The fence wanted painting again. She looked down at her watch, dear God! she wanted painting too. He'd be in in a minute, briefcase and deep frown, Italian suit, Italian shoes, Italian martini clutched to his chest almost before he got through the door. Geoff. If Kate were to write a list of her mistakes, poor Geoff would be at the top. At the top in large letters and with a thick black border. Why did she think of him as 'poor' Geoff? He was a womanizer, a mother's boy, a big soft lad. Why then? Because it wasn't his fault? Because it was his mother's fault? Were all the faults in the world women's mistakes, then?

None of it bore thinking about, especially now after what she had just been through. The last few days had left her drained; never, as long as she lived, would she care to make a decision so important again.

Pristine waved cheerfully from next door and Kate plastered an obedient smile across her recently down-turned mouth. Blinking Pristine. Of course, the girl's real name was Christine, but Kate had renamed her on a particularly venomous day. Because Christine Halls always got it right. Not only did she get it right, she achieved her level of unmatchable sainthood in a manner that seldom left her ruffled. If it rained, Pristine's washing was already in and dry. Pristine's carpets never showed fluff, while her furniture seemed to nestle in some air-free bubble where dust never landed.

'Shut up,' she said aloud to her disobedient mind, but still it wandered among Pristine's shag-pile. Dust was ninety per cent human skin, and Pris probably didn't shed like everyone else. Perhaps she was a robot, something that had been beamed down from another dimension, a thing that got serviced along with Derek's car, Derek's lawnmower and Derek's precious bloody pedal bike. He was skinless too. Skinless, gutless and spineless. 'Stop it,' Kate yelled into the empty room. 'You are a bitch, Kate Saunders,' she muttered. 'Just because you're useless at housework, you pull down someone who's good at it. And just because you're unhappy, just because you've been through a bad few days, you tear at those around you. You are a bitter woman with a warped imagination. Derek and Pris must shed skin. We all do. What you need, madam, is a timetable and a better Hoover.'

She practised smiling as she ascended the blue-carpeted stairs to wash, change her frock and apply her evening face. Nothing must show. Whatever had happened these past days, she must keep it to herself for as long as possible. Geoff would be angry if and when he found out that she had been making decisions for herself. Poor Geoff, she thought again. There were worse people than him, she had to admit grudgingly. There were the Dereks of this world. Living with Geoff and Dora was almost impossible, but the man next door would surely have been worse. Lugubrious Derek Halls was probably the most tedious creature ever to have crawled, no, slow-pedalled from a mother's womb. He was an amateur racing cyclist. That, thought Kate as she pulled on the white and gold trouser suit, very likely said it all. Why, oh why was she suddenly so vitriolic? She'd always been sharp, but this was getting beyond a joke now.

With her new face on, she suddenly indulged the

irresistible urge to grip the handle of her husband's wardrobe, flinging back the door to reveal the expensive and obsessively ordered contents. Unused to such rough handling, the teak panel groaned against a dry hinge.

She stepped back, one hand supporting the opposite elbow, a finger and thumb stroking her newly painted mouth. Brown items were hung to the left, grey in the centre, blue on the right. Her fingers itched with the unreasoning need to take the whole lot and dump it in the brook. But they'd warned her, hadn't they? 'Stay calm' and 'keep your blood pressure steady', it was like a litany now. But the damned man annoyed her! He even folded his dirty socks! What man in his right mind folded dirty socks? Was she really the crazy one? Every night, before placing soiled linen in the wicker basket, he carefully examined, studied, assessed and folded each item. It was enough to drive the sanest person crackers. Shoes were all on trees in the bottom of the cupboard, rich leathers gleaming with many applications of polish, laces removed, ironed, then hung on the tie rack, everything sorted again according to colour. She had drawn the line at ironing laces; he had had to learn to do his own. Till the granny flat had neared completion and Dotty Dora's frequent appearances had started up again. Oh Jesus!

She didn't need to open her own wardrobe, she knew about the mess. The mess was her mess, her special and private disorder, a mess she had created and nurtured lovingly over the years, the only chaos she was allowed to own. And the hidden things were there too, things she could talk about only to her best friend.

'Darling?' This enquiry floated up the stairs. He had a nice voice, dark brown like his eyes. Though, beneath the velvet, there echoed a faintly disgruntled tone on this particular occasion.

'Coming,' she responded obediently. Yes, she would be good. Right to the end, whatever the end might be, she would be an outwardly perfect wife, if she could keep her temper. The image in the glass stared back at her. Who the hell are you? asked a frightened inner voice. And how the dickens are you going to get out of this one? Talk about another fine mess, Stanley, this is ridiculous! Katherine Saunders, nee Murray, would it be right for you to get out? Right for you, for him, for them? Oh, stop conjugating. Was it conjugating? Where was the verb? And, of course, there was Melanie to consider. Awful name, Melanie. It made her think of shelving and kitchen surfaces.

Melanie. Oh, Melanie! Over at the stables with her friends, all those up-market brats with silly un-Bolton, high-pitched voices and hard hats. Hearts to match the hats too, no doubt. Melanie. Doing all the nice girly things that Kate herself had never got to do.

She pursed her lips tightly. Kate Saunders. You really are the lowest of the low. Do you resent your own daughter?

'Kate?' Imperious now. 'I need to talk to you.' Managing director tone, bring your notebook and sit pretty, sit on my knee, what lovely limbs you have, my dear. Oh shit! 'You're not pretty,' she mouthed at the mirror. 'You're quite ordinary, really. Without the paint, there'd be nothing much to write home about.' Reddish hair, freckled skin, unremarkable green eyes.

'Kate! Do you hear me?'

'I hear,' she spat silently. 'I always bloody hear.'

She walked into the living room, a large and beautiful area that ran the full depth of the house. He was seated in a chair by the fireplace, briefcase placed correctly on the bureau, a dry martini poured and standing to adequate attention on an occasional table, his ankles crossed in what was supposed to be a friendly and conversational fashion.

'One for you, dear?' he asked predictably.

'No. No thanks.'

'Given up?'

She ground her teeth noiselessly. No, I'm thinking of taking it up full time actually, darling. Aloud, 'Yes. Probably.' She must be good. If ever she needed wits about her, then this was the time!

'So.' He sipped his drink slowly. 'I saw Phil Carter today.'

This promised to be rivetingly interesting. 'Did you now?'

'Yes.' The glass was twisting round in his fingers, a sure sign of inner agitation. 'Bit confusing for both of us, actually.'

'Why? Has one of you had plastic surgery?'

'Pardon?'

'I just wondered why you should be so confused – we've known Maureen and Phil Carter for years.'

He coughed in that irritating way, the way he had developed of signalling that something of importance was about to be pronounced. 'You were the cause of our confusion, Kate.'

'Oh.' A warning bell sounded clearly in her head.

'He was on business last week, up in Scotland?'

'Yes.' Her voice seemed to come from far away.

'And you stayed with Maureen because she's been nervous about all the burglaries on Higher Lane?'

'That's right.' Bump, bump, lurch. Her heart was all over the place. Not now! Surely she'd covered her tracks.

'That's not right and you know it! Phil's sister arrived unexpectedly, she's still staying with them. And you were never at the Carters', not at all! I felt such a damn fool about the whole thing, had to make an elaborate excuse about dates and names being mixed. What the hell are you up to?'

She paused for a frantic think. She wasn't going to be good, was she? It would be impossible to be good now. 'I was . . . having a break.'

'Having a break? Having a bloody break? From what?'

145

Her temper teetered on the brink of being lost. She must hang on, she had to. 'From school, from the house, you, Melanie . . .' She managed, just, not to mention his mother on this occasion.

'I see.' His foot tapped silently against the carpet. 'With whom?'

She ran her eyes over him. So bloody smarmy, he was, so correct. So . . . so . . . yes, there was that familiar adjective again, predictable. And dull and uninteresting and all the things she'd married him for not being. How blind she had been! Though he hadn't changed, oh, no, he was still the same. The difference was in herself, she had mislaid the rose-tinted glasses somewhere along the road.

Everything he did annoyed her, every last damned thing. The way he spooned his soup away from himself, the sniffs of disapproval when she dipped in her spoon and simply scooped up the liquid. The way he touched the end of his nose after shifting into fifth gear in that bloody precious Rover – the item she privately called his penis extension. He got on her nerves, ruined her nerves, reduced her to wreckage at times. It was as if he were shouting to the world, 'Look at me, I'm a big boy now with five gears'. Dora Saunders had a lot to answer for.

Kate turned her head and stared into the grate. He might have five gears, but his wife had never had an orgasm. Not from him, never from him. This was 1968! She was thirty-four and entitled to some pleasure.

'Where were you?' So controlled, that voice. He might have been chiding a secretary, or even the office lad.

There was no point in trying any longer, because there was no place where she might hide. The truth had to come out. Where had she been? Yes, she would tell him where she had been. 'I . . . I was in a Rodney Street clinic.' She knew her shoulders were sagging.

'Rodney Street? Liverpool? Whatever for?'

'I don't need to tell you,' she said quietly. 'Matters

medical are private, even my doctor can't talk about why I was there. In fact, he especially can't say anything. I needed treatment. Isn't that enough for you to know? And I paid for it myself.'

He began to tap rhythmically on the chair arm, his fingers beating out a fast and furious pattern that he knew she would not tolerate for long. 'Tell me,' he said. 'I shall have no rest until you do. Are you ill?'

She laughed mirthlessly. 'Of course I'm ill. You're always telling me I'm ill. Aren't I crazy? Isn't this mad lady second in command in one of the biggest schools in Bolton? Aren't you and your mother the ones who diagnosed me as manic? I am sick, sick of . . . of you!'

'Don't start that again. It's all my fault or my mother's fault, though God knows we have set out to make your life as easy as possible. If you are ill, then I have a right to know about it.'

'You don't own me!' she yelled. Her patience, never her strongest point, suddenly snapped. 'I was having an abortion,' she screamed now. 'A termination, a good clear-out with a vacuum cleaner attachment. Is that plain enough for you or shall I draw a picture?'

His glass bounced on the fireside rug. For the first time within memory, be made no immediate move towards the kitchen for cleaning materials. 'Why?' The jaw, hanging low and loose, looked weaker than ever. 'What the hell for? And why wasn't I . . . ? I mean, I didn't even know you were . . . Was there something wrong with it?' The tone was accusatory now. Anything wrong with 'it' would have been her fault; from his loins, there could have been nothing short of perfection.

She breathed deeply. 'As far as I knew, there was nothing wrong. Nothing specific, anyway. It was a bit early to tell, though, I was only weeks pregnant when I went to the clinic.'

He glanced down at the pool of fluid that was slowly soaking into the long-piled rug. 'I'll . . . I'll get a cloth,' he muttered quietly, though she could tell by the set of his spine as he left the room that he was angry. Not to say furious. Fury might be a bit strong for Geoff, but perhaps this time he might at last show some real feeling about something other than himself.

He mopped up the mess. 'Does Maureen know? Was she in on the secret?'

'Yes. We were hoping . . .'

'That I'd never find out. Of course, it's fine for your best friend to know our business. I, of course, am the last to come out of the dark. If it hadn't been for Phil's sister . . .'

'Exactly.'

'Why?' he asked as he straightened from his task. 'Just tell me why.'

Kate pondered for a second. 'I'm . . . not ready for a baby, not right for one.'

'Oh, I see.' He placed the cloth on his neatly folded copy of the *Guardian*. 'It goes without saying that you would never consider consulting me. Have you not thought that I might have wanted the child?'

'No. You don't seem terribly interested in children.' He didn't seem terribly interested in much, come to that. Himself, his mother, bridge, golf, Melanie when she came up to scratch. But his interest in people was minimal.

His thick lower lip quivered slightly. 'That's a fine attitude, I must say! You flush my son down the toilet and it doesn't even dawn on you that . . .'

'Might have been a daughter!' she snapped. 'Another Melanie for your mother to ruin.'

'Leave Mother out of this!' His cheeks, always florid, were purplish now. 'At least she's normal. You're not. Do you hear me? You're not normal, Kate. No maternal instinct, no need for anyone, no feelings for what you have done to this family.'

'What I've done?' she yelled. 'And what have you done? You've ignored me, you've had women all over the place, you've allowed your mother to rule in my kitchen. It's a good job Mel has a bit of sense, otherwise she'd be as bad as you are.'

'Stop it! Stop this now!'

'No! It's my body. I'm the one who gets the swollen ankles and morning sickness. I'm the one who blows up like a wretched barrage balloon!' Kate stood feet apart, hands on hips, her eyes bravely meeting his at last. Why should she apologize to a man who had worn her away over the years, someone who had dripped like water on to a rock that had finally cracked? 'Would you have carried it for nine months, then worked for several terrible hours to push the little darling into an unfit world? Would you? Or how about a spell of two a.m. feeds? That would soon put a stop to your caperings in Amsterdam and Brussels.'

He took a step back, obviously unprepared for the force of her anger. 'What am I supposed to say? That I'm sorry for not thinking? Look, you should have mentioned it, informed me at least. Bloody high-handed. This is not a decision for you to take alone.'

'Why?'

'Why? Because you're my wife! You should . . .'

'You should, you should,' she mimicked viciously. 'How many times do I have to tell you that you don't own me? No-one owns me. And stop saying what I should have done. The doctor decided that I was unfit.'

'Ah. An unfit mother.' There was a hint of triumph in his narrowed eyes.

'Yes.' She paused fractionally. 'But not unfit because I can't cope mentally. You're the one who wants me to believe that. It gives you a feeling of superiority, doesn't it? But I'm sorry to disappoint you, Geoff. I was declared unfit because I am diabetic.'

This silenced him, but only momentarily. 'Diabetic?' he roared. 'Bloody diabetic? How the hell long have you been a diabetic?'

She took a slow, deep breath. 'I was diagnosed last year.' Her tone was quiet, almost mournful. 'I became tired and extremely thirsty and . . . well . . . there we have it. There is no way I would have had an abortion for a frivolous reason. It would have to be for physical problems. Although in one sense, I . . .' She shrugged inpatiently. 'If you don't believe me, you'll find my equipment in the top of my wardrobe and most of the insulin in Maureen Carter's fridge behind the butter. I inject myself at her house each morning before she drives me to school. That's why I visit Maureen every day, including weekends and holidays. Until your mother began to live here off and on, I used to hide it in my own fridge.' But there was no hiding anything from Eagle Eye, was there?

'Well!' He swivelled abruptly on his heel and stared through the large rear window. 'And you never told me. You never tell me anything. But this? Something as important as this? You never told me,' he repeated lamely.

'No.'

'Why not?' He stared at her over his shoulder. 'Why ever not?'

Kate took a deep and shuddering breath. 'I'm already a freak. You and your mother have made that plain enough in the past. So I forbade the doctor to tell you unless I became comatose or seriously ill. The termination was judged to be necessary, believe me.' Her shoulders were suddenly straighter. 'Though I might have wanted it anyway.'

He took a step in her direction. 'You would have wanted the baby?'

'No. The abortion. I know it's wrong, and I probably couldn't have gone through with it. But for once, I was grateful for my inadequate pancreas.' Endlessly slow seconds ticked away. 'I'm not happy, Geoff. I don't seem to want anything any more. No more children, nothing to fasten me . . .' Just in time, she bit off 'to you'. 'Sometimes, I've even thought of taking myself off somewhere, leaving the insulin behind, just . . . oh . . . I don't know . . .'

'Suicide?' There was shock and what sounded like real concern in his tone.

'Not quite. Just to see what would happen, let nature take its course, as they say.' She checked herself. She had seldom confided in him, never since those first few happier years. Confiding in him was confiding in Dora, who had a communication system that might have put the daily press to shame.

'Kate! You must not think like that. It's stupid and dangerous.'

'This is what's stupid and dangerous.' She swept an arm across the room. 'We shouldn't be together. You're not happy either. My misery is ruining everybody's life here.'

He ran to her and clutched at her hands. 'Stop this now! I've told you before that I will not listen to such talk. Things will get better. Mother's going to move into the flat soon, and she'll take over the lighter housework. I'll get a woman in for the heavy stuff. And there is no need for you to teach. Why, with a serious illness like diabetes, do you insist on continuing to do that taxing job? Why?'

She pulled away from him. 'That's it, treat me like a freak again. Good old Kate, she can't help it, have you heard she's diabetic? And poor Geoff, what a brick, having to live with such a sick and difficult woman. No! I won't have it! And bring your mother here by all means, but don't expect me to put up with her!'

'The flat's separate.'

'Separate? Her house is separate now – five miles separate – but she still haunts me. What about my poor mother, eh? Don't you think she'd like a flat on the edge of the countryside? But the difference between my mother and yours is greed. My mam is not a greedy woman, she expects little and gets nothing. Your old girl grabs and I cannot stand the woman!'

'Stop this! Stop! You're becoming hysterical again. Mother needs us. Her heart isn't good and she needs a reason to . . .'

'There's nothing wrong with her heart. Her heart is about as healthy as a brand new pneumatic drill. I will not have her fussing around me. You know how morbid she gets about illness, how fascinated she is by everybody's symptoms. You mustn't tell her about my insulin.'

'All right, calm down. Now. When did you last see Dr Coakley?'

'I've given him up along with the gin, he was becoming just another bad habit.'

He swallowed. 'That's a damned good man, highly recommended for managers with stress . . .'

'I'm not having a shrink, Geoff. He digs about in my head with a pick and shovel, trying to find out what I had for breakfast on a certain Monday in 1942, asking me stupid questions about my difficult relationship with my father. And not content with that, he wanted to plug me into the mains like a bloody kettle! I was fine till you sent me to him. Just because I don't dance to your tune, a tune invented by your wretched mother, I'm mad. You don't give a damn about me, Geoff Saunders. Only my performance. What am I? One of Pavlov's dogs?'

'Where are your Valium?' He was suddenly pale with fear.

'Down the toilet with your son!' Her voice cracked, so she deliberately took some deep breaths. 'Listen to me. This one last time, listen.' She walked away and sat down on a chair by the front window. 'We talked. During what I decided was to be my final appointment with him, we really talked. He knew I wouldn't take the electroconvulsive therapy, wasn't really sure anyway of how it might affect my diabetes, so he had to resort to treating me like a human being. Not a woman, a person this time. At the end of our talk, he was quite surprised. Perhaps he's actually read some books at last, maybe he realized that you've wasted your money all along. "Mrs Saunders," he said, "I have watched you now for thirty-five minutes. Your blink rate is correct and you make bloody good sense. You are certainly not psychotic," he said. It's taken him twelve years to find that out! Then he decided that I wasn't even terribly neurotic. Don't you see? He told me to go home and look at my life, analyse it, treat myself, much as I treat my physical illness. And I've done just that – I can handle my own therapy. There's nothing wrong with me. It's . . . it's . . .'

'Me? Is it me? I'm too old for you, is that it?'

'No! Please don't think that, Geoff! I won't have you thinking that! It's us. It's you and me together. Like some chemicals, we simply don't mix.'

He sank on to the sofa. 'I see. Then what are we going to do about it?'

' "We" don't do anything. I work it out. I'm the one with the problem. You haven't changed, love. You're still the man I married. It's me – I'm changing all the time, don't know what I want, don't know where the hell I'm going. But that's not insanity. It's female maturation and I can't help it.'

'So . . . so none of it's my fault?'

'Oh, I wouldn't absolve you completely. You haven't exactly improved my lot, nor has your mother. Always putting me down, forever undermining my confidence. Of course she does it because she has to be top dog at any price, needs all the attention she can get. She's stupid. But you, well, I'd say you're afraid of me.'

'What?' He laughed mirthlessly. 'Afraid of you?'

'Yes.' She nodded cautiously. After years of deliberately sitting on all of this, of holding it tight to herself, the whole thing had taken on the massive proportions of a long-dormant volcano. She must not go too far; she must not let things get right out of hand. A worm should turn quietly, not to the accompaniment of thunder and lightning! 'I don't do your bidding,' she said softly. 'I'm not a servant like your mother was and I don't fit in with your Victorian concept of womanhood. It's probably not all your fault, it's more likely to be hers. Your mother has been to women's liberation what the iceberg was to the *Titanic*. I cannot be like her. And you have been wrong in trying to mould me.' She folded her arms and leaned back in an attitude of great calm. 'You're afraid because I'm a professional woman with a degree of ability. That is a challenge to your supreme masculinity.'

'What absolute rot!'

'You don't want me working. You know I have a good chance of a headship, so you want me here, trapped and ordinary. Geoff, you really ought to have married someone like Pristine. She's good with a feather duster and doesn't know her Cartland from her Trollope. It would have suited you to have a wife who could scarcely read and write, because you have an inferiority complex. In order to prop yourself up, you need the reassurance of a so-called lesser being. Well, I'm not a lesser being and I've no intention of becoming one.'

He sighed loudly. 'I suppose there's no point in arguing, though I never heard so much rubbish in my life.' He paused. 'Are you . . . are you going to leave me?'

'I don't know,' she lied. Because she had to lie now, just as she had to leave.

'What about Melanie?'

'Again, I don't know. Unlike you, I don't pretend to have the answers. There is nothing positive here for me, and there's much that's negative. Your mother in permanent residence will be the icing . . .'

'Then I'll keep her away!'

'No point. Nothing can make matters worse, and you know damned well that she won't stay away for two days together. No. Life's bad. I had to make a terrible decision the other day, a decision that involved a poor little unborn soul. After that fiasco, your mother is easy meat. I can't stand the woman, but she can't hurt me. Not now. Nothing can hurt me now. Because, you see, I've already gone away in the truest sense. Now that you know everything about how I feel, well, it's rather like being divorced already.'

He cleared his throat. 'Is there nothing we can do?'

'Nothing at all.'

His head was bowed now as he spoke. 'I don't know how I feel about you any more, Kate. You've changed so much . . .' His voice tailed away as if he were lost in some private memory. 'Can't we keep it going?' he asked then. 'On the surface at least?'

'Why? To save face, to stop you appearing a failure? Look, I know you have other women. Go off with one of them and make it look like your decision. It won't bother me. As my mother always taught me, pride won't pay the rent.'

'Bloody hell,' he cursed quietly. 'Poor Melanie.'

Kate watched Jemima waddling across the road to the brook. Jemima looked after her ducklings, just as Kate had, whenever Dora had allowed it, seen to Melanie's physical requirements. But Kate didn't always like Melanie. Obliquely, she found herself wondering whether or no the duck always liked her offspring.

'Are you listening to me, Kate?'

'What? Sorry . . .'

'I said you can't take Melanie with you if you go.'

'No.'

'And even your daughter cannot hold you here?'

'Stop trying to blackmail me! She's thirteen now. It's too late for me to put right the ruination performed by your mother. In fact, Melanie is so much like Dora at times that I almost dislike her too.'

'I see.' His voice held an icy tone. 'So none of us is

required by you, is that it? And we're to sit here in the pending tray until you decide whether we're incoming or outgoing?'

'Shut up.'

'You always were a selfish and arrogant bitch, Kate. Too good for Ladies' Circle, too good to support me at Round Table. I was actually relieved to turn forty! And for the last eight years, you've shown no interest in my Rotary work. Even my job is a bloody joke to you, isn't it? All those remarks about American companies and how you hoped they're better run than the war was. These things are noticed. Your sense of so-called humour is twisted to the point of being dangerous, Kate. What makes you so different? What sets you apart from all the other wives?'

She gazed at him steadily. 'I don't know. I really don't know. But I sure as hell am going to find out!'

She spent the rest of the evening with Maureen, Phil having taken his sister to meet some remote cousin up in Rochdale.

'I can't go on,' wailed Kate. 'I'm sick of men. My father was useless and made me feel useless, Geoff treats me almost as badly.'

'Stop feeling so bloody sorry for yourself. You got yourself pregnant by him, didn't you? How the hell can you get pregnant by a man you loathe? I couldn't sleep with Phil if I didn't love him.'

Kate half-smiled. 'You're so naive, Mo. I pretend he's somebody else. Most women pretend their husbands are somebody else, don't they?'

'Eh?' Maureen's eyes were round with shock. 'I don't. I've only ever needed Phil. Who do you pretend about?'

'Someone I used to know. Another spineless bastard, but at least he was gifted at something.'

'Good God!'

They stared into the fire, each lost in her own private thoughts. Maureen was worried, Kate sensed that. And it was nothing to do with the abortion or with the topic of conversation tonight. Whatever it was, Maureen was not yet ready to open up. When she did become ready, Kate would be the first to hear about the trouble.

But what was she going to do about her own mess? Where could she go, who would take her in? Rachel? Oh, Rachel would never turn her back, not completely, not on her own daughter. But Kate had the need for a completely fresh start in a place of her own, yet she had not the money to buy a house. It would have to be rented. Where? Where would she go?

Maureen broke into this glum reverie. 'What do you do when he's unfaithful?'

'Why? Is Phil at it now?'

'No!' The denial was rather swift and emphatic.

Kate raised her shoulders and arms in a hopeless gesture. 'What can I do? What could I ever have done about it? Of course, I blamed myself at first. I wasn't a good wife, wasn't lively enough in bed, couldn't keep him interested. It took a long time for me to realize that I didn't count, except as an image of a wife. No matter who he'd married, Geoff would have been unfaithful. It's in his nature, it's his personal weakness. So I've tended to ignore it.'

'How? How can you ignore such an enormous problem?'

'By stopping caring. It was an act of will, Mo. Funnily enough, it had precious little to do with my emotions. I just decided not to worry when he was away. Now, I don't even think about it except when I need to throw it in his face. Of course, I never speak of it in front of his mother, she simply wouldn't believe me. It would be nutty old Kate all over again, imagining things, getting it all wrong.'

Maureen sighed. 'You've had a hard life, love, what with your father and all.'

'Yes, but I'm still here. I do have some faith in myself,

you know. Somewhere, buried under piles of rubbish in my brain, there's a lot of personal ambition and drive. It won't be long now, Mo. The tide of my life is shifting. As Macmillan said just a few months ago, there's a wind of change.'

'What the hell are you up to now, Kate? Wasn't the abortion enough?'

'The abortion was just the beginning.'

Kate refused a lift from Maureen, choosing to walk the half mile or so that separated their two houses. Beside the brook, she stopped and searched the twilight for Jemima. 'Where do you go at night,' she whispered. 'And is there room for me?'

7

Maureen Carter ran past the *Golden Lion*, her bright bleached hair streaming behind her like the wake of a boat. For once, she took no leisurely joy from her surroundings, didn't care to study the Victorian village hall, the beautiful church spire, the rows of ancient gravestones. She paused for breath beside St Peter's boundary wall, a hand straying along grey stones as she fought for breath and composure. Across the way, the top of a familiar reddish head was just visible in the doorway of the supermarket, the rest of her friend's body being obscured by a gaggle of gossiping females in the shop's broad entrance. It must be Kate, had to be Kate! And she had better be coming out, not going in to start on the week's list. 'Kate!' she yelled, her tone wavering, 'Kate, it's me, over here!'

Kate crossed the narrow road carefully, shoulders dragged down by her newly acquired burdens. 'Glad to see you, these bags must weigh about a ton. Have you brought the Mini?'

Maureen nodded, too winded for speech.

'You'll have to cut out the fags, flower. You sound like an old puffer steaming its way into Trinity Street. Hey, what's up with you at all?' She looked hard into the older woman's haggard face. Maureen Carter was still pretty, fortyish, very dainty and always extremely well-groomed. But the hair was limp and tangled, the nails chipped and half-covered in flaking fuchsia-coloured polish, while the usual ornaments – bangles, beads and earrings – were remarkable by their absence. 'Come on now, Mo. This'll never do, will it? I'm not used to seeing you looking so

159

down in the mouth.' Kate dropped her shopping into a careless heap and placed an arm about trembling shoulders. 'Is it the end of the world, or what?'

'It's near the end. We can't talk here.' Maureen snatched up one of the bags and marched ahead, leaving Kate to tag along behind with the rest of the parcels. At a half-run, they passed the wallpaper shop, the fruit and veg, the newsagent, finally coming to an abrupt halt outside the National Westminster where Maureen's small red car was slewed at an angle that barred the entrance to the bank's parking lot.

An angry motorist jumped out of his Jag and approached the two women. 'What sort of parking do you call that?' he barked, his lip curled into a sneer.

'Imaginative,' snapped Kate with a strength she didn't feel. Maureen said nothing; she simply began to hurl parcels into the Mini's back seat.

'Bloody women drivers!' shouted the Jag man. 'Pathetic. No idea, no idea at all.'

Maureen straightened, a hand resting on the roof of her car. 'I've got plenty of ideas,' she said coldly. 'For a start, you can take that thing . . .' she pointed to the rampant cat that decorated his bonnet. 'You can take it and shove it right up your . . .'

'Maureen!' yelled Kate. She knew her own eyes were wide with surprise, while her lower jaw seemed to have dropped by several inches. She had never seen this side of Maureen before. Such a sensible girl, such a sweet-natured person. What was going on? It was as if Mo had changed overnight. 'Maureen,' she repeated. 'We've got to move. The bank manager's trying to get out of the carpark.'

Maureen immediately leapt to the gate. 'Just the man,' she muttered almost inaudibly. She rolled up her sleeves, then placed her hands on the bank manager's car as if to hold back its progress. Though there was no need, because her own car was very much in the way. 'Listen you!' she yelled. 'That was my money. Mine!' She beat her breast with a closed fist. 'Fourteen years I've taught the unteachable for that money. Fourteen bloody years!' She turned to the Jag driver. 'Why don't you go to the Midland, sonny-boy? It might save you a bob or two. I parked here for a reason, you understand. See him? The bloody bank bloody manager? He's given all my money away . . .'

Kate began to chew her fingernails, something she had not done for thirty years, ever since her mother had dipped them in bitter aloes. She had to stop Mo making this awful scene, she must. But how?

The bank official wound down his window. 'Mrs Carter, calm yourself, please. It was a joint account, either signature would do.'

'You could have warned me!'

'Warning you was not part of our agreement, Mrs Carter . . .'

Maureen's hands shaped themselves into talons. 'Putting a brick through your windscreen isn't in our contract either, but I'm considering it. You could have warned me. You should have . . .'

Kate took a few deep breaths. This wasn't Maureen, this wasn't her dear friend. How could she cope with or talk to someone she didn't even know? It would be like tackling a wild animal! And the ice-cream would be melting soon, she thought irrelevantly. It would probably drip all over the sausages.

An inquisitive crowd was gathering, and Kate thanked the stars that both she and Maureen worked on the other side of Bolton. The parents would have soaked this up like water in a sponge.

'The agreement,' the manager was saying now. 'Both you and Mr Carter were cognisant of . . .' He checked himself as the pavement filled with people. 'This is neither the time nor the place,' he muttered.

Maureen jumped on to the bonnet of his car, folding

her arms as she claimed this very strange piece of seating. 'I'm waiting here for my housekeeping,' she pronounced clearly.

'I'll give you some,' whispered Kate in desperation. She could feel those icy fingers creeping round her stomach. If this went on much longer, she would have a full-blown panic attack. 'Come on, for goodness sake. Look, the bin men are trying to get through and there's a coal lorry too. The police will be along soon . . .'

'I don't care!' Maureen tossed her head and Kate was suddenly touched deeply, partly because she knew that Maureen did care, but mostly because she glimpsed a good half inch of dark roots near her friend's scalp. Oh God, this was so sad. Here was Maureen's vulnerability on show for all the world, well, for all of Edgeford to see. 'I want my money, I want my money!' This chant was turning the situation into an even bigger farce.

'I'll give you some,' repeated Kate. 'Anything you want, just clear the road.' She glanced at the tailback which stretched now from the church to the bottom of Cross Pit Lane. 'Move the Jag,' she hissed imperiously at the increasingly angry motorist.

'What?' The man's face was contorted with passion. 'I'm trying to get into the bank.'

'You're stopping the traffic,' said Kate with a degree of confidence that belied her terrible nervousness. 'Move the Jag, I'll move the Mini. Then you can get in and Mr Shaw . . .' She jerked a thumb in the direction of the red-faced bank manager, 'can get out.'

'You can't drive,' announced Maureen to the world in general.

'I know. I've never been allowed. But give me the keys anyway.'

'Not till I get some money.'

Kate walked to the open window of the large blue Ford. 'Give me some money,' she ordered wearily. He pushed a five-pound note at her.

'Not enough!' screamed Maureen. After assimilating the steely stare that occupied the face of his bonnet squatter, the manager pushed two further notes into Kate's hands. 'I'll pay you back tomorrow,' mouthed the shamefaced recipient of this bounty.

'That will have to do, I suppose.' Maureen jumped down, leapt into the Mini, screaming off in reverse almost before Kate had time to close the passenger door behind herself. 'Dear Lord, you'll hit the Jag!'

'Good.'

'Maureen, behave yourself!' Kate shouted as they sped forward past the newsagent, the fruit and veg, the wallpaper shop. 'You'll have us both dead.'

'Sorry.' The car screeched to a halt opposite the church, its weeping driver burying her face in her hands. 'Oh God,' she sobbed, 'where did I go wrong? Where?'

'I don't know. It's a mystery to me. Why are you so upset? I've never seen you like this before. Come on, calm down. Whatever it is, it's not worth making yourself ill, is it?'

The tiny woman leaned back in the seat, her face wrinkled as she struggled with tears and thoughts that were obviously unsavoury. 'When you said the other day – when you were talking about imagining other men – I was shocked, Kate. He's always been enough for me. I've loved him ever since the first time I set eyes on him. But I felt a bit guilty when we were having that chat, because I have fancied other men. Just in passing, nothing serious.'

'That's all right. It's perfectly normal.'

'Like the young Reverend . . .' she waved an arm towards the church. 'And the dentist. Then last New Year at Beryl's party, there was that young policeman. I dreamt about him for days. This is probably my punishment for being mentally unfaithful.'

'What are you on about at all?'

'Men. I'm on about men.'

163

'I see. Life's great confusion, eh?' Kate grabbed her companion's arm. 'Now that you've calmed down a bit, you can tell me what this is all about. If you don't, I shall get out and walk. Because you are driving me nowhere except stark raving bonkers.'

'Oh, am I? Sorry.'

'It's like a flaming detective novel. I don't know whodunnit, or what they done, or who they dunnit to.'

Maureen shifted in her seat and gazed at Kate, her eyes hollow, empty and enormous in the small pale face. 'No. You don't know, do you? Though after what you went through with the abortion and all, you must have some idea of pain. Tell me, is shock bad for diabetes? Can it shove you over into a coma?'

Kate shrugged as lightly as she could. 'Not sure. But I suppose we'll soon find out, eh?'

Maureen shivered. 'I can't say it. Saying it will make it more real. I can show you, but I can't talk about it. Perhaps I'll be able to talk after you've seen it.'

'Seen what? Bloody what?'

'The kids were in a bit of a state, so I took them to my mother's.'

'Oh heck. You . . . you haven't . . . killed anyone, have you?'

'Not yet. But in view of my terrible behaviour just now, I wouldn't put anything past me. Maybe I'm working up to that one. Slowly.'

Kate's head dropped as she spoke. 'Actually, it's not a complete mystery. I gather that Phil has cleaned out the joint bank account and left you penniless?'

The answer arrived in the form of a swift nod.

'You have nothing at all?'

'I've got . . . I've got . . .' The voice was choked by a hysterical giggle. 'Just my running-away money. It was my mother, you see. She always told me to have running-away money, it's in a building society down town.' Again, a muffled sob. 'Only I'm not the one who ran . . .'

'Then . . . then what is there for me to see?'

The car jerked forward. 'Wait. Don't say any more.'

They drove in silence to Maureen's house. She and Phil lived at the top end of Edgeford, while Kate's house was lower down the moor. They stopped on Higher Lane, giving Maureen time to compose herself slightly before pulling into the drive of number 117.

Like a pair of thieves, they crept in at the back door, Kate afraid because she didn't know what to expect, Maureen shaking because she had already had a good view of the devastation.

'Christ!' Kate paddled her way through two inches of water that covered the kitchen floor. A note, which had been screwed up then flattened out again, lay in the centre of the table:

Dear Mo,

I'm taking half of everything to set myself up in a flat. The house will be sold when the solicitors have come to terms. I've emptied the bank account pro tem. I understand you have some money in a BS account. Sorry.

Phil.

'That's all you get, Kate. After years of love and care. A roomful of H_2O, a missing washing machine and a note you wouldn't send to the milkman. The living room is great; he's ripped down the front curtains, rail and all, he took the sofa and left me the chairs, it's a wonder he didn't saw the dining table into two equal halves. The kids are demented. I told them we'd had the burglars, but Tommy isn't fooled, not at his age.'

The icy fingers were back again, creeping around Kate's middle and holding her like some hungry carnivorous plant. But it wasn't a panic attack this time. Oh, no. This was anger, a real fury. That a wonderful wife and mother could be treated so shabbily.

'Well?' she cried eventually. 'Well?'

'Well what?'

'Are you going to let him get away with this? Are you going to sit here, or swim here, while he makes off with everything you've worked for?'

'I don't know what to do.'

'I do.'

'Oh.'

'You want your furniture back?'

'I want him back! I don't care what he's done, I'll forgive him anything, anything at all.'

Kate tutted impatiently. 'I can't get him back, but I sure as sixpence will try to get the furniture. So. You can either have no him and no furniture, or no him and some furniture. Which is it to be?'

'What does it matter?' yelled Maureen. 'Nothing matters now, not without Phil.'

'The kids matter. Normality matters. Now, what's it to be?'

Maureen dabbed at her eyes with an ineffectual and very damp handkerchief. 'Something to sit on, I suppose. Amanda was screaming, Kate, screaming past herself. We were on our way to Bury market for shoes and some bits of new uniform for next week. Then I turned back because I'd forgotten my chequebook. That's a laugh, isn't it? Some bloody good my cheques are now. The van was just disappearing down Rookery Lane – I'll swear I even saw our gardener driving it. And everyone can see right in at the front because there are no curtains. I bet they all saw it happening.' She dissolved into a new flood of tears.

'Stop this. There's enough water in here already without you adding to the mess.' Where was this strength coming from? From anger? Or was it because this wasn't her own problem? 'This is a day for you to remember, love. And I'm going to turn it into a day Phil will never forget either.'

'What . . . what are you going to do?' Maureen blew her pink nose. 'I love that man right to his bones, Kate, but I can tell you now that he's clever. Clever and extremely dangerous. He's an accountant, a professional cheat and liar of the highest order. Only lawyers get away with more. Be careful. Oh, by the way, he's taken the fridge and left me the chest freezer in the garage. But he pulled the stuff off the shelves, so your insulin is in the larder.'

'It's OK. I've told Geoff everything.'

'No!' The tears cleared miraculously. 'Not . . . not everything? The abortion and how you feel about him and . . . oh, my God!'

'Exactly. He knows enough. Listen, Mo, all our lives are going to change. Now, I'll have to leave you with this mess, save what you can of my shopping, will you? I'll pop back for it later. But there are one or two things I have to do. He had no right, you know. No-one less than a judge can empty a house, I know that much. Will you manage for a few hours? Only if I leave the legal situation as it is, time may not be on our side.'

'Let me come! I don't want to stay here on my own. You've only seen the kitchen, I can't bear to look at the rest of the house again.'

'You won't want to be where I'm going. It will be humiliating for you, and certainly for him. Sorry, pet. This is one time I really do have to go when you need me most. Get on the phone, ruin his reputation with everyone you know . . .'

'I can't do that. I still love him. I want him back . . .'

'Then talk to your mother or to his mother. Just talk to somebody. And for God's sake, cheer up. There's a lot worse off at sea.'

'Is there? We're standing in the bloody Atlantic. How will I cope? What shall I do? He's mine. He's my husband and I thought he loved me and I know I love him.'

'Don't start all that again. We can all love the unlovable till we view them from a distance. This is your chance for a bit of space. And believe me, Maureen Carter, he'll sell this house over both our dead bodies. You've a twelve-year-old and another who's only ten. He'll not get custody, and the house stays with the kids.'

Kate left the little woman pouring her grief and hurt into the phone, then ran the downhill distance to her own house.

Three o'clock found her alighting from a taxi outside Woolworth's on Deansgate. She crossed the road and walked slowly along Mealhouse Lane, a large plastic portfolio clutched to her right side. The offices of Willow and Carter, chartered accountants, were a few doors away from the *Bolton Evening News*, and she smiled grimly to herself as she passed the doorway that led to the *News*. This paper would be her biggest bluff, her heaviest weapon. Bolton was the largest town in England, the readership was vast.

'Have you an appointment?' asked the pretty young thing behind the Willows and Carter desk. Kate stared at her with a degree of enmity. Perhaps this was the one Phil was about to make off with. 'No. It's an emergency involving a lot of cash and property. I want to see Mr Carter, I believe he's very good. There's an urgent need for a sensible tax consultant and I understand that he's the best in the north west.'

The girl preened herself on her employer's behalf, and Kate's hatred grew hotter. 'What name shall I say?' Red lips parted in a smile that displayed perfect teeth. Too perfect, thought Kate, praying hard that the teeth were a job for Steradent. 'Mrs Hardcastle,' she replied with all the sweetness she could dredge up.

He was seated at an immaculately tidy desk, no papers, no books, just a few pens and pencils lined up parallel to the top of a huge clean blotter. His face changed colour when 'Mrs Hardcastle' was ushered in, and it did not settle to a proper shade until the pretty receptionist had left.

'Well, Kate,' he finally managed.

'Lovely office,' she said slyly. 'Not a bit damp, no water in here. And a good chair for you to sit on. Never mind *well*, Phil Carter! Your children are in a terrible state of hysteria. What sort of a nutcase makes off with a plumbed-in washing machine without turning it off at the hoses? And did you never learn to take down curtains by removing the hooks from the eyes? Then there's the legal aspect. You must know some law, Phil, goodness knows you've helped in enough division of property cases.'

'This is nothing to do with you.'

'Isn't it? It'll be something to do with you, though. Especially when my husband tells all his Rotary friends to take their business elsewhere.' She paused for effect, amazed at her own strength. That a woman with 'bad nerves' could stand here and tackle an important man . . . No. She mustn't think of it. 'Then there's the publicity.' Her heart was pounding loudly in her ears, but she ignored it. 'Publicity can damage a man.'

'What publicity? I only took what I considered to be fair, and who's going to be interested in a marriage break-up these days? Stop bluffing, Kate, and mind your own bloody business.'

'What you considered to be fair? You?' Her voice rose. 'Let's see what the people of Bolton think after they've seen the photos. Oh, there'll be no mention of your name, Maureen can't afford to defend a trumped-up libel action. But people will know it's you.'

'Which photos?'

She stood up and placed the portfolio on the desk, slowly unzipping it while her eyes remained riveted to his face. 'Posters. I've done a lot more, so you can keep these as samples. The *Evening News* is interested in this kind of social issue. After all, leaving two kiddies in a half-furnished house with a flooded kitchen is bad news. Good for the paper, though. I've done one large poster for each of the rooms you . . . er . . . altered.' She smiled sadly. 'Two doors away, I've a photographer waiting. So call my bluff, eh?'

'You always were a devious bitch, Kate.'

'Yes. And loyal to my friends.' She sighed with heavy drama. 'Maureen's angry. I had to sit on her so that she wouldn't go straight for an injunction. The injunction would give you seven days to restore your children's home to order. I'll give you seven hours. If that furniture isn't back, if that house isn't spotless by half past ten tonight, you'll get all the glory you need.' She rose to leave. 'Is that the tart, the one in the outer office?'

'Get out!'

She snatched up her portfolio. 'Ten thirty. That's all the time you have. You've just lost a damned good wife, two lovely kids and all your goods and chattels. We're going to take you for every penny, Phil. And you'd better play fair, or you'll lose more than clients.'

'Is that a threat? Are you daring to threaten me?' He jumped up from his chair and she noticed as he moved how bald he had become lately. 'They do some quite good toupées these days, Phil. And get a bit of that weight off; if you're running with the fillies again, you'll never keep up.' She shuddered inwardly. Was this to be her forte then, her lot in life? Was she going to become one of those awful masculine women who went round ruining men, men who had neither sense nor guts to defend themselves? Surely not! She didn't like what she was doing, but it had to be done; someone had to help poor Maureen.

As she closed the door, the word 'bitch' was thrown, together with some weightier object, against the frame. The girl sat round-eyed at the idle phone, her colour betraying that she had heard every word. And suddenly Kate knew that this was the one, that young madam here had hitched her carriage to a passing star, an older and obviously affluent bloke. Was it the men, then, who caused such problems? Or was it scheming females who left children homeless, wives suicidal, hearts bleeding and bank accounts dry?

'Want your picture in the paper, sweetheart?' asked Kate airily before marching out into fresher air.

On Deansgate, she paced up and down past the shops for a while until the shaking subsided. What she had just done was amazing, unbelievable. She would never be able to do that sort of thing for herself. Had she enjoyed it just a little bit? After all, she was the unloved child of a loveless marriage – no. Rachel did love her, she did! But was Kate paying back the world, particularly the men, for her own unhappy childhood? It suddenly struck her as she passed Marks and Spencers for the fourth time that she was incapable of loving. There was something missing, something deep inside her. It probably wasn't Geoff's fault, any of it. Even Dora might have been tolerated by someone kinder. Was it her dead father's fault, then? And if it was, for how long could a person blame the dead for her own short-comings?

She phoned Maureen from outside the Post Office. 'Your furniture will be back tonight. Leave the children at your mother's.'

'What did he say? Is he all right? And if I leave the kids at Mum's, I'll be alone.'

'He said several things, he's fine, and no you won't be alone. I would not leave you at a time like this.'

A muffled sob came over the line. 'Thanks, Kate. But after that abortion thing, will Geoff believe you're here with me?'

'Doesn't matter. Anyway, I'd scarcely be needing another operation just yet. We'll go to the *Black Bull*, it's quiz night. Then we can sit in the car and eat chips out of the *News Of The World*, see if there are any juicy bits of gossip in the paper. It'll all be over by the time you get home.'

'I want to see him.'

'No you don't.'

'Kate, I'm getting angry. I think I want to scratch his eyes out.'

'That's why you don't want to see him. Anyway, I've already altered the shape of his face for the foreseeable future.'

'Eh? What have you done? Did you hit him? You haven't hurt him . . . ?'

'Don't be daft, Mo. The size of him and the size of me, well, it would be like setting a tiddler to attack Moby Dick. No, I was speaking metaphorically.'

'Come back, Kate. This is awful. I've always known where he was, always been sure. Now it's like . . . like somebody's cut off my right arm. I'm furious and sad and all churned up like butter. Will he come back, Kate? Will he?'

'I don't know, love. But I'm coming back, that will have to do for now.'

'Hurry up!'

'I'm hurrying, I'm hurrying . . .'

They sat outside Kate's house eating fish and chips rich with brown malt vinegar. Beech Gardens had houses on one side only, so they enjoyed a dim view across the brook and into a vast barley field. 'Daft quiz, that,' mumbled Kate through a mouthful of cod. 'They didn't ask any good questions.'

'Watch your carbohydrates,' came the quiet answer. 'And the quiz was daft because you didn't know any of the answers. Will he be there now? In the house? What time will he be gone?'

'Don't think about it. Look at the stars.' Kate licked her greasy fingers and screwed the remaining chips into a ball of newspaper. 'Wouldn't it be lovely if I could eat without counting bloody diabetic points? I'd have cream cakes and trifles and . . .'

'Let's go and see him. If I talk to him, I might change his mind.'

'Not tonight, Mo. If you're going to change his mind, it won't be tonight. He'll be fixing the fridge and the washing machine, you know how ill-tempered he is around anything mechanical. Listen, I've got a good question.'

Maureen sighed loudly. 'All right, go on.'

'Ready?'

'Hmm.'

'Right. What's the difference between a duck?'

'Eh? Between a duck and what?'

'And nothing. What's the difference between a duck?'

'That's crazy.' Maureen fingered the cooling food without interest. 'OK. What is the difference between a duck?'

Kate giggled. 'One of its legs is both the same.'

'Pardon?'

'You heard. I think it's hilarious. It's one of Mel's.'

'Huh. That's not a question, it's not even a joke! There is some of you in Mel after all, then.'

'Yes.' Kate fixed her eyes on the silent bank with its border of tall rushes. 'Jemima's a different duck. So am I. So's Boothroyd, but he's a drake and a figment of my imagination.'

'Boothroyd?'

'I draw cartoons of him sometimes.' Lord, how was she going to keep Maureen occupied for the next fifteen minutes? She had to make sure that she and Phil did not come together tonight while all the wounds were still raw. Any coming together would have to take place some other time, after they had both had the chance to calm down.

'Mo?'

'What?'

'I can't stand any more. I have reached the end of my

tolerance. As old Winston used to say in his heyday, up with more I cannot put.'

'Neither can I. What will I do without him? Phil made all the decisions, paid all the bills. I never had to worry once during my whole married life . . .'

'Let's talk about me. I'm leaving Geoff.'

'That's old news.'

'I'm leaving him now-ish. Within weeks, I'd say.'

'Weeks? I'd give anything for weeks. This is happening to me now, tonight. At this very minute, Phil is in my house and you won't let me go anywhere near him.'

'I can't stop you, not ultimately. You're the driver.'

'I know. But you're very good at putting me off.'

'A talent at last!'

'Shut up! You're the best teacher in Bolton.'

'Let's walk a bit.'

They linked arms after getting out of the car and strolled across the tiny bridge that spanned the brook between Beech Gardens and Harper's Farm. The water rippled and gurgled over stones and through small channels, sending up the scents of a lovely spring night as it hurried along to find a larger river.

'Water is so free,' sighed Kate. 'If I come back again as something elemental, I shall be water.'

'You should have been born under Aquarius.'

'Aquarius is an air sign, Mo.'

'Daft.'

'Yes.' She leaned over the rusted iron rail. 'I think I shall be water.'

Maureen shrugged listless shoulders. 'Then you'll get consumed one way or another. Some bugger will drink you, or flush you down the lav. Probably both. Or you might stagnate then evaporate.'

'And come down again as rain. The eternal cycle.'

'Whatever, you'd get consumed, Kate.'

'We're all consumed.'

'Even the men?'

'Especially the men. They are so infantile and devoid of instinct.'

They left the bridge and continued along the rough path. 'What about Melanie?' asked Maureen suddenly.

'Melanie stays with Daddy and Dotty Dora.'

'You what?' The smaller woman stopped and gripped her companion's arm. 'Your child? You will leave your child?'

'Of course. She'd never forgive me if I took her. God knows where I'll finish up living, it certainly won't be Edgeford. A separation between her and that pony would be worse than any divorce.'

'I . . . I don't understand you at all. My best friend and I don't understand you. Nothing could ever take me away from my kids. If I had to choose between them and Phil . . . You don't love her, do you?'

Kate thought about this. 'I love her. I'd fight to the death on her behalf. But I can't always seem to like who she is. There is no law that says we have to like our children all the time, is there? My mother has never particularly liked me. And my father hated me. In fact, he probably created the screwed-up mess I am today.'

'Rubbish! You're old enough to be what you want now. And your mother's very fond of you, even a blind man could see that.'

'OK, let's just say I was a disappointment. After Judith and her string of degrees, I'm just an ordinary worker ant. And I suppose Melanie disappoints me. I didn't even choose her name, Mo! Dora and Geoff made me call her Melanie, I was too weak to care at the time. Right from the start, she was theirs to cosset and spoil. I've been an intruder in their little lives. I can't take her away with me, I simply can't.'

'Then you'll have to stay, won't you? No woman leaves her kids, Kate. No woman worth her salt, anyway. I mean, look at the animal kingdom. Right from bunny rabbits up to tigers, the females guard their young until they're independent.'

'And the males stalk off to impregnate some other passing cat. No, this is humanity we're talking about. We're the ones who stood on our hind legs, we're the ones who invented murder and all the other niceties, we're different, terrifying and powerful. And because we're different, a man can make just as good a mother as a woman. How do you think widowers carry on? They've no choice.'

'But you have, Kate! I never thought you'd leave your daughter. I always assumed . . .' Her voice tailed away.

'Don't assume, love. Assumption is the greatest form of self-deception. In particular, don't assume about me.'

'Where will you go, then?'

'Don't know. Not sure at all, not sure of anything.'

Maureen gripped her friend's hand tightly. 'You can stand it for another five years, surely? Until she's eighteen or so?'

'No, it has to be soon. For long enough I've been trapped by a situation just because it existed. Well, I exist too, Mo. I have to go, I must.'

'Why? There must be a real reason, Kate. No-one just floats away into nothing. What are you going towards?'

The taller woman shrugged, and in the dim light from the farmhouse, Maureen could see that the eyes were wide and moist. 'I'm going towards something big. Something really wonderful. A new life, a light at the end of a long tunnel.'

'Good God! You're not . . . not . . . ?'

Kate laughed. 'No, I'm not dying. But there's . . . oh . . . I wish I knew.'

'It's all about proving yourself as good as Judith, like when you were kids.'

'No, it's my own thing, is this, there'll be no tar in my hair this time. I suppose I'm going off to find my talent. Or my destiny. Perhaps I'm a misplaced flower-person, someone who ought to put on a back-pack and head for San Francisco.'

'What a load of compost.'

'Yes.'

They turned and headed back towards the bridge. Kate tried to look at her watch, but it was too dark to see the dial. Oh, she hoped that Phil and Maureen would not come face to face tonight. If anything could save the marriage, it would involve a separation for a little while.

They reached a street lamp. 'Will Phil have finished putting the stuff back now, Kate? Can we go home?'

Kate glanced at the time, the safety zone had been reached at last. 'I think so. Yes, let's go home.'

8

Dora Saunders had been dying for as long as anyone could remember. Now in her seventies, she was probably nearer than most to the grim reaper, yet few listened to her recitals. These litanies were endless; complaints about doctors and their inadequacies, moans about the side-effects of the twenty-odd tablets she was forced to take each day 'just to stay alive', laments referring to her actual and imaginary illnesses. According to Kate, Dotty Dora had made a career out of two things. The first was being in charge of everything and everybody; the second was being sicker than the next man, even if the next man had terminal carcinoma.

But Dora's main goal in life had been to make sure that all mortals recognized her dear son's superiority. Geoffrey had been to Bolton School, Geoffrey was clever. Not only that, he was a gentleman. Never once had he required punishment, never once had he come home from football or cricket in a state. At Imperial College, he had shone forth like some great star, leading the debating team, running the union, planning all rags and functions. Now, at the infantile age of forty-eight, Geoffrey was managing director of a leading American plastics company. And, naturally, Americans only hired the best.

Kate was not good enough for Dora's Geoffrey. She was a Catholic, which was always a bad thing, of course, especially in 'better circles'; Dora went on a great deal about better circles. Kate did not have a degree, Kate was only a teacher, and everyone knew how stupid teachers were. Teachers did not move in better circles, and they held back partners who might otherwise have risen to heights too dizzy even for Dora's colourful language.

Yet what Dora would really have chosen for her darling Geoffrey was a manageable wife like Christine Halls. No qualifications, no ambition, just a 'jolly good little cook and housekeeper'. Kate was good for next to nothing. She earned too paltry a sum to justify her frequent absences from home, yet was slightly too bright to stay in, knit sweaters and listen to her mother-in-law.

Dora could not handle Kate, so she simply disliked her. After all, Geoffrey had been quite happy at home till he was almost thirty-four. Then along had come madam with all that false and shallow charm. Dora could have told her son – in fact she had tried to warn him – that the girl was odd. But no. For that one and only time, young Geoffrey had not listened to Mother. And now he was reaping the benefits. The house was unhappy, even Dora could sense that. It never occurred to her that the couple might have stood a better chance if she had kept a sensible distance.

Kate sat now at the kitchen table, a pile of arithmetic books by her elbow. Dora wiped an onion-induced tear from her eye and cast a glance in her daughter-in-law's direction. 'Where's Melanie?'

'Out on her pony.'

'Hmm. Have you got any nutmeg?'

'Don't know.' Kate waved a vague pencil towards a row of cupboards. 'In there somewhere, if there is any.'

'Hmmph. When did you last shop?'

'Can't remember. Look, if you're going to talk, Dora, I'll take my work into the sitting room.'

'Pardon me, I'm sure. Just trying to cook a meal for everyone, that's all . . .'

'I see.' Kate slashed a red pen through a page of what looked like ant droppings. 'This kid can't see, though. Must make sure he gets an eye test. What a mess.'

Dora clattered a few pans for effect. 'Good job I'm

moving into the flat, then. If your school work takes all night as well as all day, you'll be needing a house-keeper.'

Kate looked up and fixed a steely stare on Dora Saunders' plump rear. 'I won't be needing a housekeeper at all, Dora. But if you consider yourself needed, then move in by all means.'

The woman turned slowly and caught the malice in Kate's expression. 'You'd rather I stayed away al-together, wouldn't you? You'd rather I lived all alone and . . .'

'Don't start all that again. My mother lives alone . . .'

'She's only fifty-five! I'm seventy-two in November.'

November. Scorpio. Many mass murderers and rapists were Scorpios. Though this one didn't keep its sting in its tail; this one was all sting. 'Dora, whatever you do is no concern of mine.'

The older woman bridled. 'I see. And what's that supposed to mean?'

'It means I don't care. That dinner would have got cooked by me eventually, but as you seem to derive so much pleasure from the culinary arts . . .'

'Pleasure?' This word was shouted. 'It's not pleasure, it's duty. My arthritis doesn't allow me any pleasure. I just like to see things done right and at the proper time. Geoffrey enjoys his food . . .'

'And that's where your pleasure comes in. Now, if you don't mind, I really must get on.'

Dora, calmer now, decided to go for a truce. She sidled slowly towards the table. 'Sorry to hear about your bit of trouble,' she mouthed almost soundlessly. 'Of course, they can do wonders now, can't they?'

'Pardon?'

'For sugar. I was just saying, they can cure sugar.'

Kate's jaw fell. 'Who the hell told you?'

'Why, Geoffrey did. Of course he did. I have a right to know – after all, there's your diet to consider . . .'

'I can look after my own diet, thanks. Stupid man. I told him not to tell anyone.'

Dora smiled triumphantly. It wasn't often she managed to rile Kate, and this time she'd done it without even trying! 'Geoffrey is not stupid, far from it. And he is concerned about you, very worried. Never keeps anything from me, dear. You should know that by now. Tell me.' She licked her lips salaciously. 'What are your symptoms?'

Kate eyed her adversary for a second or two. 'Thirst, loss of weight, frisky kidneys and anger with people who ask personal and unnecessary questions while I'm marking . . .'

'Oh dear.' Dora, who had chosen to hear just the early part of Kate's sentence, sank into the opposite chair, a tea towel twisted about her hands. 'Thirst? You say thirst is a symptom? I've got a mouth so dry I couldn't even begin to describe it. And as for kidneys, well, if I've to get out of bed once for the bathroom, that's a good night. Mostly, it's six or seven times – can't remember a full night's sleep. Do you think I've got it?'

'Probably. You seem to have everything else.' The irony in Kate's tone passed unnoticed. 'And it can come on with obesity in older people. It's very dangerous, of course. If it's uncontrolled, it can strip your insides within a fortnight.'

'Ooh. Ooh, I say! Whatever shall I do?'

'See the doctor. Take him a urine sample, a very large one, about a pint, I'd say.' She tried not to grin as she pictured Dora struggling to surgery with a huge bottle. 'He'll soon analyse it for you.'

Dora's face was white. 'Is it dangerous?'

'It's a killer. Heart attacks, strokes, blindness, gangrene, kidney failure . . .'

'Ooh. Ooh my goodness.'

Kate leaned forward with a conspiratorial air. 'My life is suspended by a very slender thread, Dora. Positively dangling, it is, hanging on by the skin of its front teeth. I could go just like that.' She snapped her fingers before the mesmerized face and Dora blinked rapidly. 'What with hypers and hypos, it's all very confusing. Just a whiff of a boiled sweet could throw me straight into a coma. Or a drop too much of insulin. I depend totally on my needle, you know. It's an awful business, sterilizing, tapping the bottle to get rid of air, disinfecting my skin. The tiniest bit of dirt, the smallest air bubble, these things could finish me off quick as lightning. And, of course, I'm like a pincushion. It's difficult to find a new site every day. And so unpleasant when I hit a vein. Blood everywhere, gallons of it.'

'Ooh. Ooh my!'

Kate nodded solemnly. 'An unboiled needle could give me septicaemia, there's so much worry, isn't there?'

'Ooh yes. I think I'll go and have a lie down. Can you finish the dinner? And have you got a big bottle for my . . . you know . . . for my sample?'

'There's a lemonade bottle in Mel's room. Rinse it well, there's sugar in pop, you know.'

Dora fled from the room to indulge her latest 'illness'. Although she had thoroughly enjoyed tormenting her tormentor, Kate remained furious and she continued to mark her books in angry haste. For fourteen years she had tolerated this. For fourteen years Dora had been around, always moaning, always demanding and getting attention. Well, it wouldn't go on for much longer, Kate intended to make sure of that. She'd been a target for long enough, first for her own father, then for Dora and Geoff. A sickness rose in her gorge and she breathed deeply through her mouth. Dora must not get to her! She should not allow a creature like Dora to upset her like this!

Dr Coakley's voice echoed in her brain. 'Have your panic attacks happily, my dear girl. They are a sign of energy and intelligence, a sign that you are truly alive.

When the feeling comes, tell yourself it's just a surge of adrenalin that will soon disperse in your bloodstream, that it will pass in minutes. Your main enemy is tiredness, so never overplay your hand. And take a close look at your life, identify the triggers. You say you don't know what frightens you, but I can assure you that your subconscious is in touch with these triggers.'

Dora was a trigger. So was Geoff. Even poor Melanie. She threw the red pen across the kitchen. If it were not for Maureen, Kate Saunders would probably be a strait-jacket case, sitting and rocking in some dark hospital corner, nails chewed to hell and back, eyes glazed by sedative drugs. Strange how school never brought on an attack, though. Kate hated her job. Not the children, there was nothing wrong with them. It was the system she disliked. The system, the protocol and other teachers whose bitterness at poor pay and conditions often showed in their faces and in their work. She had used to wonder why they didn't go for other jobs, better jobs. But she knew better now than to wonder that. Most were fit for nothing else, just as she was fit only to teach.

She would go tonight. But she wouldn't go to Maureen; poor old Mo had enough on her plate without getting Geoff at the door every five minutes. Where then? And first, she must have a talk with Mel. She grinned in spite of her misgivings. The talk with Melanie was not the source of her amusement; no, she was thinking about Dora's absolute conviction that Geoff told her every-thing. He hadn't told her about the widening rift, had he? Oh no, she would have remarked on that. Nor had he mentioned the abortion. If Dora had known about that, she would have demanded a blow by blow account. Operations were fascinating, after all . . .

Melanie, as if conjured up by her mother's recent thoughts, burst in at the back door, jodhpurs muddied by yet another fall. The child was a cruel rider, cruel to the animal, hard on herself. Like Geoff, she was ambitious and spoilt, just half an inch away from being a thorough brat. Though of late Kate had noticed the odd sign of improvement in her daughter, as if she were finally making some of her own judgements. Yes, she was getting too big to hide behind Granny Dora's skirts now. Was there, after all, the promise of a fine young woman here?

Without a word to Kate, Melanie made for the door to the dining room.

'Hang on, lady. I want a quick word if you can fit me into your incredibly crowded social calendar.'

The girl ground to a halt. 'Very funny, ha-ha. I need to change, Mum.'

Into what? A human being? 'Sit.' Kate waved a hand at the chair where Dora had sat a few minutes previously.

With all the grace of a stranded whale, Melanie flung herself into a sitting position. 'Well?' Mum was in an odd mood again, that was plain from the look in her eyes. Melanie had been reared to know that her mother was mentally frail, that she must take any problems to Daddy or to Granny Dora, that Mum must be left to 'get on with things'.

'I want a serious talk, Mel.'

'I don't like Mel. My name's Melanie.'

'Yes. It was not of my choosing. And, as your mother, I shall call you whatever I damned well please.'

Melanie slid an inch or two down in the chair. A dictatorial mood this time.

'You're as plump as a puppy,' continued Kate. 'Watch your diet, you'll be having spots. Thirteen is a great age for spots. And if you get any fatter, you'll be breaking that poor animal's spine.'

'OK, OK! Keep your shirt on.'

'I've always been liberal with you, Mel. My own upbringing was so . . . so unpredictable. I never knew when my father was going to pounce on me for some crime or other. I didn't know where I was most days.

184

My father was one of the strangest men I've ever known. You're a lucky girl, very lucky with your daddy.'

Melanie raised green eyes to heaven. What was all this about? Had Mum truly flipped at last?

'But not so lucky with your mother, eh?'

'I never said . . .'

'No, I said it. I was not cut out for motherhood. This is not my fault, and it most certainly isn't yours. You're growing up now, dear, old enough to understand what I am about to tell you. This is going to be a secret for now, just between you and me. OK?'

'OK.' Greedy eyes glistened. Melanie liked having things to herself; a secret was nearly as good as an unshared creamcake. 'What is it, Mum?'

Kate took a deep breath. 'I'm . . . going away.'

'Oh.' The disappointment was plain, nothing world-shattering in this confidence, was there? 'On holiday? How long for?'

'Not on holiday.'

The creased young brow slackened as if a mist had lifted. 'I see. Going in hospital with your nerves?'

Kate groaned and gripped the edge of the table. 'There's nothing wrong with my nerves, love.' What was it Dr Coakley had said at the end of that talk? 'We treat depressives as sick, Mrs Saunders. Sometimes, they're just realistic like yourself. You refused to wear the tinted glasses, that's all. Has it never occurred to you that you might have it right? That the rest of us are deprived of an extra sense, the sense to worry about the world and its self-destructiveness? We, the blind ones, have the temerity to treat the sighted . . .'

'Mum?'

'Sorry. Where was I?'

'Going away.'

I've already gone. 'I need to live somewhere else. Now, the choice is yours. You can come with me, or you can stay here with Daddy and Granny Dora.'

'Oh.' Long seconds ticked away. 'Are you going abroad? Anywhere exciting?'

'No. I'll probably stay with Granny Rachel for a while.'

Melanie pursed her lips. 'Ugh. She's got no bathroom. I'm not going there.'

'There's a bath in the kitchen, a proper bath under that table-top thing. She manages.'

'And the toilet's in the yard.'

'Yes. Don't screw your nose up like that, Mel. The wind might change and you'll stick like that forever.'

'Don't be silly, Mum. Granny Rachel keeps a thing under her bed.'

'That's because the toilet's down the yard.' She paused for a moment. 'So you'll be staying here?'

'Yes.' Melanie's brow was furrowed again. 'But . . . but all the girls at school will find out you've gone. They'll feel sorry for me like they did for Jenny Blake when her father died. I'll get pointed at. You can't just go off like that. People will think you don't like me.'

'I'm sorry.'

'I mean, Jenny Blake's dad had no choice, did he? He got a heart attack in the night and never woke up. But if you choose to leave me . . . I haven't a lot of friends, Mum. People don't like me because I'm a bit fat. This will just make everything worse for me.'

'I've said I'm sorry, dear.' She reached across the table, then recoiled as her daughter's hand snatched itself out of what was meant to be a friendly grip. 'There's something I have to do, love, something I have to try. It's a big secret, even from myself.'

'How can you have a secret from yourself? That's silly. You're just being silly again.'

'Then allow me to be silly. You must try to understand. All my life I have never had the chance to consider myself. When I was a child, well, there's no need to burden you with all that. But after leaving college, I got married, had a baby. I didn't even do my probationary year until after you were born. Melanie, it's hard for you now, but when you're twenty, you'll understand. I have to go off and find out what I am, who I am.'

'You're a teacher. You're Daddy's wife and my mother.'

'Exactly. I can only see myself as part of other people; Standard Four's dragon, a mother, a wife. You are far too young for this, Mel, and again I say I'm sorry. But I need a life of my own, I need to find out what I can do.'

'That's selfish.'

'And you should know all about selfishness. I am going off to have the teenage years I never got as a kid, the years you're having now. After a while, I shall probably stop being a teacher and become something entirely different.'

'Such as?' The lip curled into a sneer. 'What else can you do?'

'I can draw!' There, it was out. The thing she had never dared say aloud even in an empty room. 'I can do cartoons, birthday cards, cereal packets, anything I turn my mind to. This means I am going to live a very odd life. People with jobs like that lead a strange existence. I shall be travelling about with my portfolio, trying to sell myself to advertising firms and newspapers and comics.'

Melanie stared at her mother. 'Will you be famous?'

'I doubt it. I shan't use my own name anyway. But I can't do it here, Mel. Not with Granny and you and Daddy around. I need lots of space and privacy.'

'Rich? Will you get rich?'

Kate heaved a great sigh, sad because her daughter could measure success only in pounds, shillings and pence. 'I hope to become rich in spirit.'

'Oh. And that's what's important to you?'

'At the moment, yes.'

'But . . . why can't you stay for a few more years, just until I've left school then it won't matter as much?'

187

Kate swept a hand around the neat kitchen. 'Can you see me spread out here with ink and paint? Can you? Boothroyd is now, Mel.'

'Boothroyd?'

'He's a duck, well, a drake. I can make him look like anyone. He makes comments about the political situation, funny remarks about the government. Then there's Boothroyd Junior, he's for children's comics. I must get on with it, Mel.'

'Oh.' The voice was tiny and hurt. 'Don't you . . . don't you love me, Mum?'

Kate hesitated, but only for a moment, remembering her own childhood and a parent who had never shown her love. When she spoke, she knew she was talking from the very depths of her soul, that she was dredging up truth from beneath all the confusion.

'I love you. Even when I don't like you, I love you. In fact, I probably love you most when you're at your terrible tricks. You remind me of myself. There's something about you, Mel, something that you won't grow into until you've got past the spots and the puppy fat. Like me, you're independent and stubborn. Like me, you would have been a self-made aristocrat whatever your beginnings. You have an awful pride and I am proud of that pride. Never let anyone put you down, child. Never let anyone tell you what you might have been, what you should or could have been. And keep a distance from Granny Dora, because she'll tell you you're better than you are – better in her way, at least. Don't let them turn you into what you are not, keep going with what you are. I shall stay in touch with you . . .'

'Oh, Mum!' Tears welled in the large emerald orbs. 'Don't leave me. Please don't leave me!'

'I shall never leave you, Mel. Wherever I am, you will be with me, and vice versa. And you'll always be able to find me when I'm needed . . .'

The child jumped up and fled from the room.

Kate sat very still, tears pouring silently down her cheeks. She had not expected it to be so hard; she had not known her own feelings for this daughter. Exactly! She pushed the sleeve of her cardigan against the end of her nose. Everything was clouded here; she couldn't know anything here. Not with him and his shoe-trees, not with Dora and her pills. Away. She had to get away. Tonight.

But Kate didn't go anywhere that night, because this was the night when Christine Halls' world fell apart. The reverberations of this were to echo down many future years, but no-one saw past the immediate and terrifying shock for a long time.

They were seated in the dining room, Kate, Geoff and Melanie, the latter pair struggling to finish off Dora's delicious apple crumble. Dora did not take kindly to remaindered food; she saw it as an insult, a blot on the landscape of her considerable culinary skill. Dora had taken herself off to the granny flat where, in spite of uncompleted decorations, she was no doubt in residence and working on her sample for tomorrow morning's surgery. She had already consumed three gins and an unusual amount of dinner wine, and had made off through the front door towards her own entrance with a large jug of mineral water.

Geoff expressed his concern. 'I think Mother's a bit tiddley. Why on earth is she drinking so much?'

Kate choked on a mouthful of cream cracker.

'Mother's never been a drinker, except of tea. Stop fidgeting with that good food, Melanie. Granny will not be pleased if you leave it.'

Kate recovered her composure. 'Mel needs to lose weight. If your mother carries on producing such gargantuan meals, our daughter will be the size of the *Queen Mary*. She can leave it if she wants to.'

Disgruntled but unwilling to argue, Geoff returned to the original subject. 'I should hate Mother to become alcohol dependent.'

'She isn't,' said Kate. 'She's just trying to increase her flow.'

'Flow of what?'

'Micturation.'

'Pardon?'

'She needs to pee.'

His face darkened. 'No need for that at the table, Kate.'

'She isn't doing it at the table. She's got that blue plastic jug in her bathroom. Her bathroom that used to be my garage. My garage for the car I never got.'

He tapped his fingers on the table. 'You'll get your car, don't worry. But why does Mother need to . . . make water in a jug?'

'For a sample. For the doctor.'

'Really?'

'She's decided to have diabetes.' After darting a meaningful look at Melanie, Kate continued, 'She must have heard of someone with a sugar problem, so she's cashing in on the act, another illness for her list. Though I daresay the doctor will find her urine to be clear, apart from alcohol. At this rate, she'll be producing pickling vinegar.'

'That's enough, Kate.'

'I hope so. God knows she's filling a big enough bottle.'

Melanie pushed her dish away. 'Can't eat any more, I'm stuffed.'

'The language at this table!' cried Geoff. 'It's obvious that you get all this from your mother, Melanie. It is unladylike and very unbecoming.'

'Be yourself, Mel,' said Kate, immediately sorry because she was using the child as a buffer between herself and Geoff. 'Remember what I said earlier . . .'

'Did I miss something?' His eyes were fear-filled, as if he'd failed to meet a deadline at his precious work.

'You missed the bus, darling. Years ago. Your mother's probably holding your ticket in her handbag.'

'Stop this! What's got into you lately?'

She shrugged, glancing at Melanie and wishing with all her heart that the child would leave the table. 'Just getting my own back for past put-downs, that's all.'

'What put-downs? Where and when?'

Fortunately, she gave herself time to think and breathe, time to prevent herself from launching into a long diatribe that might have caused mayhem. It all sat on the tip of her tongue, but she bit it back fiercely. She could have told him where and when – probably would have told him if Mel had not been sitting there. Works' parties, in the car when he was trying to stop her learning to drive, at her mother's house, even on open days at her school he had crushed her in front of others. She nodded. Yes, she was always clumsy and her dress sense was often wrong. No, she shouldn't drink cider, she shouldn't drink pints. And yes, her hair sometimes had all the delicate texture of dried straw. All spiteful, petty and mean in spirit.

Dora crept in, rather the worse for wear, her walk unsteady, the greyish white hair tumbling over one eye. 'Ooh Lord,' she groaned. 'It's full. I managed to fill it. Are you quarrelling?' Even in her present condition, she missed little.

'Yes,' said Kate.

'No,' pronounced Geoff simultaneously.

'Yes they are!' yelled Melanie. 'And Mum's leaving us. She is! Don't look at me like that, Granny! She told me before, and it's supposed to be a secret, only I think it's too bad and I don't care about splitting on her.'

Dora Saunders belched not very discreetly, her hand straying along the sideboard for support. 'I don't feel very well,' she moaned sadly.

Melanie flew out of the room.

'I had to tell her,' said Kate lamely. 'She's my daughter. I couldn't just dash off without explaining . . .'

'Dash off?' shouted Geoff. 'There's no need for you to dash off anywhere.'

'I'm going to be sick.' Dora followed her granddaughter with a speed that was miraculous in one supposedly riddled with osteoarthritis.

'You can't leave,' he said now. 'One foot out that door, lady, and you don't get back in.'

'Fine. But I want a lump sum, compensation for fourteen years of penal bloody servitude. And take that look off your face – perhaps it wasn't quite fourteen years.' She nodded thoughtfully. 'The first year or so wasn't too bad. I thought you were so dashing, so elegant. What you were, what you are, is a big fraud. You're a flaming nancy-boy. Huh. Ironed laces? Whoever heard of a real man with ironed laces? And I don't want to sleep with you any more. I cannot compete with your army of women.'

'Women?' His face coloured deeply. 'Which women?'

'The women you have receipts for! I've seen them, bills for Chanel and Je Reviens. Well, don't bother "reviening" for me, I've had enough of your returns. Has it occurred to you that I am now the age you were when we married? While you're like a man in his dotage?' Oh God, she hadn't meant it to be like this! Not with all this bitterness. Hadn't she decided that it was no-one's fault, that she would go quietly and gracefully? Yet still the words tumbled out of a mouth over which she seemed to have lost control. 'I've had enough of you, your house, your job, your Rotary Club and your blinking mother. So I'm off to find a better life, even if it's a life without comfort and apple bloody crumble.'

He covered his face with his hands, and she was just on the verge of forcing herself to apologize for her tone when the back door flew open.

'Geoff! Kate! Please, somebody, help me!'

Pristine! Kate clenched jaw and fists. 'In the dining room,' she called eventually.

Christine arrived in the doorway between dining room and kitchen, her face whitening, legs obviously buckling as she clung to the door jamb.

'Catch her,' yelled Kate, but she was too late. Poor old Pris lay flat out, head on the carpet, feet on the kitchen tiles. Even this had been done tidily, thought Kate as she and Geoff struggled through the house with the dead weight of their neighbour.

They placed her on a sofa, where she came to after several seconds. 'Where am I?' she groaned. 'Where's Derek? Oh Derek, Derek, no . . . no . . . NO!'

Geoff knelt on the floor and rubbed Pristine's hands. Kate knew he'd seen this done in an old black-and-white Bette Davis film, so she didn't expect it to have much effect. Rubbing people's hands and burning feathers under their noses only worked in movies. 'Here.' She thrust a cup of brandy between the woman's lips as soon as there came a more positive sign of life. 'Here. Take a sip.' She glanced at Geoff. 'Better a cup than a glass. She might bite through a glass, poor soul. She must tell us what the matter is, she looks awful.'

The brandy went down in one huge noisy gulp, then there followed a severe attack of coughing during which Geoff patted Pristine's back and looked meaningfully at his wife. His eyes said 'you shouldn't have given her the brandy', but Kate wasn't taking him on. Her attention was given completely to Pris, who looked as if she'd been clobbered with a sledge hammer.

'He's dead.' This pronouncement arrived once the throat was cleared. 'He died at the top of Deane during a race. And he was winning, too, he had the yellow shirt . . .' The word 'shirt' was elongated into a high-pitched wail.

Kate swallowed deeply. This was dreadful. She would not call Christine Pris any more. Any woman who had lost a husband so cherished was deserving of respect and good treatment. 'Dear God, Chris. I am so sorry. So very, very sorry . . .' And so inadequate. What could one say to a woman who had been the butt of jokes for so long? How might one comfort a person whose malapropisms could cause hilarious laughter at any second? Not with Geoff, though. Geoff never laughed at Christine's gaffes, didn't notice half the time.

'It was one of those artickerlated lorries,' said Chris now. 'It just folded up, sort of, oh . . . oh . . .'

'Jackknifed?' suggested Geoff.

'That's it. And Derek got killed under the load.'

'What was it carrying?' asked Geoff irrelevantly.

'Potatoes.'

Kate turned away. She would never look a bag of chips in the eyes again. Trust old Derek to end up mashed. And who ever heard of an articulated lorry carrying vegetables?

'We never even had a baby,' moaned Chris now. 'It was my fault, not Derek's. My filipine tubes are blocked, but there was nothing wrong with my Derek. He was . . . he was . . . the vocal point of my whole life.'

Kate told herself sharply that she was not a nice person. Noticing Christine's vocabulary at a time like this was a very un-nice thing to do.

'I've got nobody,' wailed the voice from the sofa. 'No family for the funeral, nobody to come and care about him. Or about me.'

'We'll come. Kate and I will come. Won't we?' He threw this last short question over his shoulder.

'Of course we will.' Kate faced the prostrate figure of her 'perfect' neighbour. 'Make her some cocoa, Geoff,' she whispered. 'I daresay she needs a woman just now.' When they were alone, Kate fetched a footstool and sat by Chris's side, almost wincing as the grief-stricken woman gripped her hands with a strength that was near to iron. 'Talk to me,' said Kate gently. 'Tell me anything or everything, whatever you feel like.'

'You know the most ridicerlous thing, Kate?'

'What?'

'Well, it's the thing he enjoyed most except for bikes.'

'No, love. You tell me about it.'

'Jacketed potatoes with creamed mush-erooms. When we went out on the tandem, we always had to stop at some cafeteera and ask if they did creamed mush-erooms in jacketed potatoes. That was because they never served things like that at the orphanage.'

'Dear Lord,' breathed Kate. 'Which orphanage?'

'Where we met, where we fell in love. I was eight and he was nearly nine. We used to touch hands over the fence. Boys and girls were separated except on Sundays. We did this pledge, Derek and I. He would teach me to read on a Sunday afternoon if I would marry him and look after him.'

Tears pricked Kate's lids. 'And . . . you both stuck to it, eh?'

'Oh yes. I used to draw a picture every week, of a house with a nice garden and a hedge and a gate. On Sundays, I gave him the pictures. The curtains were always nice bright colours. We like colours. In the orphanage, everything was green and cream and brown. I made him a nice house, Kate.'

'You did. You certainly did.'

Christine sighed and turned her face away. 'It was hard pretending to be like the rest of you. We made relations up, said we were going visiting mums and dads. That's why Derek was so quiet with everybody. He didn't want you asking why nobody ever visited.'

Kate blinked rapidly. She knew what it was like to be unloved, didn't she? Oh yes, she'd had a father, but . . . Her heart went out to the woman on the sofa. 'We never guessed, Chris.'

'Didn't you?' She faced Kate again now. 'Did we seem normal?'

'Of course you were normal, you still are. In fact, I'd say you're quite extraordinary in the best sense of the word. There is no shame in being an orphan, none at all.'

'There is. Some days, there weren't enough knickers to go round, so we had to wear yesterday's. I have sixty pairs now, Kate, all different colours. I love colours. And it was so hard for Derek getting qualified, winning scholarships to Thornleigh, trying to pretend he was just like the other boys. He came out top in his electrical engineer class at the technical college, nothing he didn't know about electrics. He was so strong and so good. What'll I do, Kate? What'll I do?'

It was like Maureen all over again, only grimmer, more final – and certainly more desolate. 'Do you have friends?'

'Just who Derek worked with, and we don't want them knowing too much. There's you and Geoff. And you don't like me much, do you?'

Kate's heart felt as if it were filled to bursting point. A great pity welled up inside her chest and she hugged the trembling woman tightly. 'I like you, Chris. I understand you now. Try not to be afraid . . .'

'I don't know anything about funerals and monumentals. I want him to have a nice one with a bike on it. Bikes were his freedom. He never had a bike till he was twenty.'

'Geoff will see to everything.'

'We're Catholics.'

'That's OK, so am I. Not that I practise, but I know the rudiments. We'll sort it all out for you.'

'I can't go home, Kate. Derek's not there. I can't go to sleep in that bed without my cuddle. We loved cuddles, both of us. Neither of us got cuddles till we married one another.'

It was all too much for Kate. Great sobs racked her body as she poured out her grief for Chris, for her own desolate childhood, for Derek whom she'd never troubled to understand, for Maureen and her children. Last, but never least, she cried for her baby, the baby Chris would have deserved and loved. So when Geoff returned with the cocoa, he found the situation greatly altered, for it was Chris who now did the comforting.

'Come on, Kate,' he said tightly. 'That's not helping Christine.'

'Oh yes it is.' Chris smiled through her own tears. 'It's lovely to know someone else cared about my Derek. This puts a different complexity on everything, as my Derek would have said. There may be only three of us, but we can give him a good send-off, God bless him.'

'There'll be more than three,' sobbed Kate. 'I can promise you that. Every biker in Bolton will come out for him.'

'Yes,' said Chris, calmer now. 'I'd forgotten about the clubs. Let's hope it stays fine, eh?'

It didn't stay fine. But the riders of Bolton lined up, each man holding his bike to attention while Derek Halls was carried to his last rest. Kate felt sorry for the bikers, because they had opted to wear their various 'uniforms', just thin shirts and nylon shorts, not a single umbrella between them. Chris had chosen a tasteful headstone, though this item would not be on show until the following week. In white Italian marble, it was a simple slab that stated the bare facts, then, under the carving of a racing bike, the words 'ON HIS WAY TO FREEDOM'. As the only confidante of Chris, Kate felt truly moved by such restraint, because she knew how many years, how much feeling lay behind these five stark words.

After the funeral, they all returned to Chris's house where Dora presided over a feast of enormous proportions. There were vol-au-vents and sausage plaits, cheese straws and quiches, hot and cold drinks and a wide selection of puddings. But there were no 'mush-erooms' or 'jacketed potatoes'. Kate had considered making this delicacy of Derek's, but had finally decided that it would be wrong to include it. For one thing, it might have underlined Derek's absence; for another, the poor man had been killed by his two favourite things, bikes and spuds.

She wandered with her glass of mulled wine into the empty kitchen. Kate didn't particularly like herself these days, and she was learning that not liking herself was one of the causes of her depressive phases. But she had many reasons to question herself just now, many attitudes to analyse.

There was the 'Pristine' thing for a start. She had condemned poor old Chris without ever giving her a chance. Derek too. Skinless, gutless, spineless and boring . . . She slammed her glass on to the surface by the cooker. If she was going to be a cartoonist, a commentator and critic of her times, then she had better put a stop to this horribly superior way of assessing people. People, like diamonds, were multi-faceted, rare, unique, very special.

Then there was the way she treated Dora, sending her off to the doctor's with a bottle big enough to fill her shopping bag. Not a nice thing to do to anyone, and sad old Dotty couldn't help her hypochondria. Dora's 'ill-nesses' were probably an illness in themselves. And Melanie weeping for a mother she'd scarcely had, and Geoff being treated like a whipped dog. By God, how she had set about him lately, what a harridan she was becoming! After all those years of passivity, why had she suddenly turned? Was this the proverbial worm, was she justified?

She sank on to Chris's pine bench. What a bloody mess, eh? Everyone seemed to be losing a husband. Maureen's had gone off, Chris's had been wiped out. Those two women would probably give an arm and a leg for what Kate had now. Security, a home, a man. Yet Kate Saunders, with all her airs and graces, was just going to turn and walk away! When, though? Melanie wasn't accepting the situation. Chris wasn't fit to be left, Maureen was still running round like a headless chicken,

Geoff wore an air of great hurt, while Dora was feeling decidedly put upon. Running Kate's home on a voluntary basis was one thing; to be forced into it would be another matter altogether. And there'd be no Kate to preside over, no-one to punish, no inferior wife to . . .

Stop it! She beat her hands against the table. It was happening again. In her mind, she was destroying people. It was like cutting up caterpillars or taking the wings off flies, it was not a fair fight. Dora was Dora, Geoff was Geoff, Mel was Mel. A leaden sky hung over the window and Kate stared at it as if searching for a ray of light. Yes! That was it! She must accept them as they were, but she must also accept herself. The main thing was accepting herself. This was how she was made, she had her faults and her good points just like everyone else. Taking the wings off and making judgements was probably a part of what she had to do, the thing she was moving towards.

Her head was in her hands when the door opened. 'What am I going to do, Kate?' The eternal cry now, and in that tiny little-girlish voice. 'They're all quite happy in there, plenty of refresh-erments. What'll I do? There's nothing I can do, Kate.'

Kate straightened. 'Sit down, love.' She waited until Chris's earnest face was level with hers. 'How has he left you? Financially, I mean?'

'Oh. Yes. He had one of those mortgage pertection policies. The house is mine and he was well-insured. There's no money worry. But . . . it's all day and all night, isn't it? Every day and every night. I think Father Costigan's drunk,' she added irrelevantly.

'Priests always get drunk at funerals. It's a perk of the job.'

'What'll I do with my life?'

Kate smiled and reached across to pat a rigid hand. 'You'll free some women, pet.'

'Eh? Free some women? Me?'

'Yes, you. Stop putting yourself down, Christine Halls, before I give you a good smacking. You love children, don't you?'

'Oh yes. Only I couldn't have any. My o-verries are all right, but it's these filipine . . .'

'Yes, I know, Chris. Damned nuisance, blocked Fallopian tubes.'

After a small pause, Chris shrugged and said, 'See? I can't even talk properly. I've got my accent better, Derek said so. Only I can't do big words. So how do I free women when I can't do big words?'

'Margaret Liptrot on Rookery Lane would give her right arm for a lady like you. She needs to work. Hubby's gone back to do his Ph.D., so they're living on fresh air. A qualified nurse like Margaret could work if someone would mind the kids.'

'Oh.'

'You could take a couple of under-fives, then pick a few up after school, keep them till the mums finish work.'

'Like one of them creeches?'

'Yes, like a crèche. You would be doing a tremendous thing for this community, Chris.'

'Would I?'

'Of course.'

'And you'll help me? To set it up?'

'Initially, yes. But you'll soon get the hang of it.'

Chris smiled weakly. 'There'll be nappies on my line after all. Nappies and little coatees and bibs. I can pretend they're mine . . .'

'Don't get too close. I find at school that it's important to keep a distance. Otherwise, some of the little beggars would have my heart wrung dry.' She thought briefly about little Rosie Collins and her tormented brother, was momentarily back in that awful hospital with the sweet dying child. Yes, a heart could be broken, couldn't it? She shook herself visibly.

'Kate?'

'What?'

'Are you really like that, you know, all cold and hard? I know I shouldn't say this, but sometimes you seem . . . well . . . cruel. Derek thought you were a hard woman. He was terrified of you ever finding out about us not being wanted by our mothers.'

Kate's head dropped. 'Chris. I wasn't wanted either. By my father. All his life he made sure I knew I wasn't wanted.'

'Ooh! Ooh, how awful for you. I never guessed, never thought. Perhaps that's why you seem to have no patience. Derek said you were very . . . what was the word . . . ? judgemical. As if you're better than everyone else. Poor Kate. Like us, you had something to hide.'

Kate drew a hand across her brow. 'I'm not nice, Chris. I was just thinking before you came in that I'm not nice. Dora and Geoff both drive me to distraction, but it's my fault, not theirs. I get very depressed.'

'I know. Dora said. And I'm sorry.'

'I have to accept their faults, stop laughing at them and getting angry. But at the same time, I have to understand my own limitations. Being judgemental is part of my character, it's deep in here.' She placed a hand against her breast. 'I must learn to like myself, Chris. The depressions are because I don't trust me, don't want to love myself.'

The pine-framed clock ticked. 'Did you laugh at me and Derek? Did you?'

'Sometimes.'

'I don't mind. Not now. You're my friend now, aren't you?'

'And you're mine. Hey! This is the first time I've seen crumbs on your carpets.' She inclined her head towards the living room. 'Crumbs and paper napkins and fag-ash.'

'This is the first time I haven't cared. But with kiddies coming, I'll have to start caring again, won't I?'

Kate smiled. 'That's right. I'll put the word out and I'll place some adverts in the local shops. We'll have you run off your feet in no time.'

'That's what I want, isn't it? Oh, I shall miss him, though. Daft way to die, wasn't it? Under a pile of spuds?'

'It was unusual. But his mates loved him, Chris. That wasn't just rain on the bikers' faces. Those were real tears.'

'I haven't cried today. Am I getting better? Am I?'

'Another door will open. Perhaps you'll find another relationship in time.'

'No. He'd have to be an orphan. Only an orphan can understand.'

'I understand.'

Chris gazed at her neighbour thoughtfully. With a perspicacity Kate would never have suspected, the young widow said, 'Yes. But in your heart, you're an orphan too, Kate. It's as if you were brought up like me and Derek, sort of different. I always knew you were different, but lately I've realized that you are one of the loneliest people I ever knew. I can't understand why you're lonely, not with Geoff and Melanie and Geoff's mum popping in all the time. But I think you're . . . iserlated.'

And the tears came for both of them, so they sat and wept, hands gripped together across the pine table. A door had opened for each of them and they stepped into the light of an odd friendship, a friendship that would become odder with the years. But its strength would never be diminished.

9

Kate wandered along Deansgate in the centre of Bolton, a brown carrier containing Melanie's new blazer dangling from her left hand. It was a short walk from Henry Barrie's along to her favourite shop, Preston's of Bolton, and she lingered in the doorway indulging her passion for diamonds. This was a splendid display, undoubtedly the best for many a mile, thousands of pounds worth of precious gems beautifully displayed on royal blue velvet cushions.

The staff knew her well. Here she had bought her small collection of jewellery, including her engagement and wedding rings, the former being an expensive twist of two large clear whites set in yellow gold. Here they had become used to her over the years, because she would pop in at Christmas and birthdays to buy a charm for Melanie's gold bracelet, and she would linger every time to study stones and to learn about flaws and deposits and carat values. There was much to know about diamonds, because each had its own character, its very own essential personality. There were blues and yellows, pure clear whites – some even had a hint of pink about them.

She sighed greedily as she studied a small but perfect tear-drop set to dangle free inside a hollow gold heart. On its fine chain, it made a wonderful necklace, and she had coveted this item for weeks. No hope now. No hope of any fripperies once she had fled the nest.

'Splendid, isn't it?'

She turned to look at the man by her side. 'Oh. It's you. Strange place for you, isn't it? Or are you looking for something for your floozie?'

Phil Carter grinned sheepishly. 'How's Maureen?'

'Coping. Just about. That interim maintenance buys the catfood, don't worry. Everyone else in the house has learned to exist on faith, hope and fresh air . . .'

'Kate!'

'Don't "Kate" me! You make me sick. Those poor children are crying themselves to sleep.' Would Melanie cry? Should she really stay for Melanie's sake? Oh, what good was she to Melanie? 'And your wife's a shadow of her former self.' Thin, but suddenly having the time of her life, was Maureen. Grief had given way to the undeniable urge to get out and do something useful. So Maureen, when she could get babysitters, attended no less than three evening classes and was becoming proficient in spoken French, modern dance and the art of throwing pots.

'Come for a drink?'

'No thanks. I've still to get to Woolworth's for Mel's hair ribbons. Then I'm going for a quick dash round the market, see if they've any decent towels that don't cost an arm and a leg.' For my flat, Phil. God, if he only knew!

'Please?'

She studied him for a moment or two. He had the air of a man who was carrying the world on his shoulders. 'OK. We'll nip into the *Man and Scythe*, that's the nearest.'

He held her arm as they crossed Bank Street to the opposite corner where stood the oldest pub in Bolton. Inside it was dark, filled with the atmosphere of stale tobacco, fresh ale and long-dead ghosts. He found a table, then went off to buy a half of dry cider for Kate and a pint of bitter for himself. She watched him. He seemed ill at ease, uncomfortable with himself. The usual cloak of self-assurance had slipped, for once. And a hole in his sock showed in the slight gap between trouser and shoe as he lifted his foot against the low bar-rail.

He did not beat about the bush. After taking a swallow

that left his glass half-empty, he said quietly, 'I want to go home. I've had enough of this lark to last me a lifetime.'

She fingered a cardboard beer mat. It was probably all to do with undarned socks and badly cooked meals. His complexion was grey; she envisaged him living on a diet of shop-bought chips and meat puddings, all suet and dripping. 'Why tell me?' she asked. 'Just go home.'

'Things have got out of hand.' His chin dropped and he was blushing right to the top of his bare scalp. 'These bloody lawyers have turned the whole thing into a slanging match. Talk to her, Kate.' He looked so vulnerable and lost, she could have wept on the spot for him.

She laughed grimly, determined to hide her pity. 'Why me? Why the bloody hell does it always have to be me? I'm the one with bad nerves, remember? What do you think I am? Some kind of winged messenger? They should have built a statue to me up some pole in a London circus. Send her a letter, sack your solicitor . . .'

'She might knock me back. I want to know where I stand.' He pushed a hand across his mouth to remove a small moustache of beer foam. 'I've gone through something, Kate. Something I don't understand. All of a sudden, I was scared of getting old without anything ever happening. I think it's had a lot to do with fear of death. Death or senility.'

Kate inhaled deeply. She understood; after all, wasn't she 'going through something', too? 'Male menopause,' she pronounced. 'It does exist. Look, lad, there's nothing wrong with admitting a mistake. Just go and see Mo. It's not my job to patch things up between you. If I'm not a messenger, I certainly can't be a puncture kit. Oh, Phil!' Her tone expressed frustration. 'My own life's about as straight as a pan of soggy spaghetti.'

'She's . . . going out at nights, isn't she? Having a whale of a time . . .'

'Well, she certainly hasn't taken the veil. But I think

you'll find most of Maureen's expeditions to be educational. She's doing pottery and stuff like that. There's no man.'

'Are you sure?'

'I'd be the first to know.'

He emptied his glass, then sat staring into it as if it were a crystal ball with all the answers contained in its depths. He was a man without hope, an angler who had lost the biggest catch ever without getting it weighed in.

'OK,' she mumbled. 'Got your car? We'll go now. Come on, hop to it.'

'Now? Right now?'

'Strike before the iron cools. Not chicken, are you? Faint heart never won fair lady.'

He hesitated. 'What about the market and Melanie's hair ribbons?'

'Thursday will do. It's still half-term.'

He blinked rapidly behind the tortoise-shell-framed spectacles. 'Christ, Kate, I'm scared. Is it the right thing to do?'

She suddenly felt more than sorry for him, because she understood his dilemma perfectly in that instant. Hadn't she been wondering for weeks about the 'right thing' for herself? 'I don't know, Phil. But it's worth a try. Just follow your instincts.'

He hung his head. 'I still love her, you see. I had to leave to know that.'

'What about your . . . flatmate?'

'Bit of a kid. I suppose we were both flattered, she because I was the big boss, I because she was so young and lovely. Too young. Young and boring. We both expected too much. She wanted pearls in her oysters, and I just needed the damned oysters to keep up with her!'

Kate picked up her bags. 'You know, Phil, I think I like you. Let's go and face the music, shall we? Don't look so worried, it may not be Wagner. Just cross your fingers and think of a nice Chopin nocturne.'

After the drive to Edgeford, Phil stayed out in the lane while Kate went in to prepare her friend. She found Maureen seated on the sofa, legs raised at impossible angles while she struggled to paint her toenails. 'I need a magnifying glass,' groaned the tiny woman. 'Can't even see the littlest one. Here, you do it.'

Kate grabbed the brush and applied lacquer with a hand that was far from steady. 'Sorry. You've a Poppy Red toe now. Perhaps you'll start a new trend. By the way, Phil's outside.'

'What?' Beautification of the extremities was suddenly forgotten as she ran barefoot towards the front window. 'Where? Where is he? Do I look all right?' She straightened her short spine and pushed a hand through her hair. 'I don't want him to see me all untidy.' She bustled about for a few moments, fiddling with makeup and comb, then suddenly the anger arrived, just as Kate had known it would. 'Hey. Hang on. I'll ram that last letter down his throat. Ten pounds a week for each child? I'll show him ten pounds' worth . . .'

'Hang on, Mo. Don't do anything hasty.'

'Where are my slippers? No, my shoes, I want to look good. Lipstick . . . lipstick . . .' She painted her mouth quickly. 'I'm off to Manchester tonight, going to the trad jazz club with a group from the modern dancing class. Is my hair all right? And my solicitor says there's no way I can be forced to sell the house till Amanda's eighteen. I'll show him! I'll show that bloody so-called husband. Thank God the kids are out . . .'

'Maureen!'

'No tights. I can't go out on the lane without tights. Be a love and run upstairs, will you? Top right-hand drawer of the dressing table . . .'

'Shut up, Mo.'

'Eh?'

'He wants to come back.'

'Oh.' There followed a long pause.

'Isn't that what you want?'

'What?'

'Wake up, woman! I said, isn't that what you want?'

'Yes. I mean . . . yes. Of course. But . . .'

'You've had a taste of freedom and poverty, eh? Well, the man's got his pride, sunshine. He's not going to ask twice, is he?'

'No.'

'Well?'

'Well, I'm having such a good time, aren't I? I've never had so much fun for years. Through the night classes, I've found out there's a lot more to life than washing and ironing. Will he let me carry on with my pottery and my dancing? Will he?'

Kate sat down on the carpet beside Maureen's chair. 'Look, love. You can go out to lessons for years and never learn anything better than what you and Phil had together. He might not object . . .'

'Perhaps I don't want what I had before. Perhaps I've changed.'

'So, at fifty, you'll be alone. No kids, no husband, just a few nice vases decorating your lonely kitchen.'

'Oh, I never thought of it like that.'

'And you still love him.'

'I hate his bloody guts!'

'Yes, that's because you still love him. Give him a chance, Mo. Just have a trial run, see how it goes for a month or two.'

'He flooded my kitchen!'

'Yes.'

'And drained my bank account.'

'I know. Give him a chance, eh?'

'Do you really think I should?'

Kate raised her arms in a questioning gesture. 'I think you should do what you want to do. But I also think you might regret not giving him an opportunity to prove himself.'

Maureen sighed her confusion. 'OK. Wheel him in.'

'Oh, no. This is where I make my exit, flower. I'll send him in, but the rest is your business, yours and his.'

'I'm scared to death!'

'So is he.'

Kate walked out and summoned Phil to the gate. He locked his car doors, then walked with a degree of reluctance towards the pathway of number 117. 'How did she take it? Will I live?'

'I'm not sure, she's confused.'

'That makes two of us.'

'Three.'

'What? Oh, yes, sorry. Thanks, Kate.'

He took a deep breath, then, with rounded shoulders, followed the pathway up to the front door. Just before he knocked, Kate called out to him, 'Good luck, lad. Good luck and God bless.'

That night, she discovered a small parcel behind the front door at 50 Beech Gardens. When she tore off the wrapper, she found a necklace in a Preston's box. It was a gold heart with a diamond teardrop suspended from its centre. With this three hundred pounds' worth of treasure there was a simple card. 'Thanks. Good luck and God bless. From both of us'.

It would have to be done in words of no more than two syllables, in language Chris would understand. This was going to be harder than Melanie. Kate fingered the handle of her delicate china teacup. No wonder Chris always had everything so nice, she thought. After such a grey childhood, the need for beauty and symmetry around her was completely natural. 'So the Liptrots are settled, then?' she asked.

'Starting Monday. Such sweet little boys, they are. Ooh, I do hope they like me.'

'They'll like you.' She cast a quick glance round the room. 'But they'll ruin your lovely home.'

'That's OK. A house should be a home once children come, That's what Derek always said.'

Derek had assumed the proportions of a long-dead martyr by now. He was mentioned and referred to by his widow in every other breath. But at least some of the life had come back into her; at first, she had looked like another candidate for the cemetery. Enthusiastically, she went on, 'And I've had special permission to attend the evening baby-care class at the village hall. It's really for expectant mothers, but everyone is being so kind and understanding. And I do want to be good at my job.'

'You'll be good, you're a natural.'

'Thanks.' There followed a short pause while Chris studied her neighbour covertly. 'Is something wrong? Only I've found you a bit . . . er . . . let me see . . . a bit preoccerpied just lately. As if there's something on your mind.'

'There is.'

'Oh.' Unlike Maureen, Chris would never get close enough, would never gain the confidence to demand and dig for gossip or truth.

'Remember how you felt at the orphanage, Chris?'

'Yes. Oh, yes, I'll not forget that in a hurry.'

'Remember how you felt lonely even though you were surrounded by people all the time?'

Chris hesitated. 'You're . . . you're going to say . . . well . . . that's how you are.'

'Yes.'

'Still lonely in a crowd.'

'That's right. There isn't even a Derek whose fingers I can touch over a wall. Marriage isn't right for some people. I'm one of those people.'

'Oh. What'll you do if you stop being married? It's not easy, stopping being married. I didn't have any say in it, but I certainly wouldn't have chosen to be on my own. Don't you love Geoff? And what about Melanie and Dora?'

210

'I don't seem to have a lot of love for anyone.'

'You've been good to me, Kate. I'd never have got through these awful weeks without you. There must be some love in a person who gives so much time to helping a neighbour.'

'That kind of love, yes. But the sort of love that's required to live peaceably in a house with others, that close, day to day love, I don't appear to be very good at it. That's why I get depressed, because in my present position I can only be a failure. I have to find somewhere I can win.'

'What about school? Don't you win at school? Maureen says you're very good at teaching.'

'I don't like teaching.'

'Oh.'

During the ensuing long pause, Chris fidgeted with the fringe on the cloth that covered her tea trolley.

'I have to go away, Chris. If I stay, I very much fear that I shall go insane. The panics are less frequent, but I have this awful feeling of being an observer in my own house. And it's nothing to do with Dora or Geoff – I'm just a fish out of water. There'll be trouble, love. Dora isn't talking to me at all since she found out what I intend to do, and poor old Geoff's sulking like a baby. My main problem, though, is Melanie. I can't take her with me. You will have to look after her.'

'Me?'

'Geoff's at work and Dora's bad for her. Mel doesn't want to come with me.'

'You'll be alone? Assolutely alone?'

Kate grinned. 'Assolutely.'

'I meant absolutely, Kate. Stop laughing at me.'

'Sorry. Just keep an eye on my daughter, will you?'

Chris poured more tea, a hand straying to wipe a tear from the corner of her eye.

'I know it's not fair,' whispered Kate. 'You lose a husband you wanted and loved, I walk away from a child while you could never have one. I must seem so bloody arrogant to you. But we only get one life, this isn't a practice run. There's no chance for an encore, Chris, and no point in looking back at sixty and saying "if only". This may be the biggest mistake I ever make, yet I must be allowed to make it. If I stayed, I would make all their lives a catalogue of misery. Perhaps I'll be unhappy after I've gone away, but at least they will recover.' She jerked a thumb in the direction of next door. 'I'm cutting out their cancer, they'll thank me in time.'

'You're not cancer!' The tone was angry and distorted by tears. 'You're pretty and clever and all the things I can never be. Look at me! Short and plump, stragg-erly black hair with some grey already, and I'm only thirty-two! You keep telling me not to . . . to . . . denigrate myself. That's what you're doing. Cancer, indeed!'

'Don't cry. Please don't cry.'

'Well, I'll miss you.' Her face suddenly brightened. 'I've just had a thought! You could move in here!'

'Too close. I'm going back to Daubhill initially.'

'Have you told your mother?'

'No. It's best to present my mother with a *fait accompli*.'

The strained smile still remained on Chris's face. 'Never mind, eh? Perhaps you'll be like Maureen and Phil. Perhaps you just need a few weeks apart.'

'No, it won't be anything like Maureen and Phil.'

'How do you know?'

'I just do, love. I'm going for good. But I'll phone you and we can meet up sometimes – you could bring Melanie.' Her heart shuddered as she heard herself speaking these lies. She would have too much to hide, too many reasons not to meet people once she'd left. 'We can shop together,' she said lamely.

'Won't be the same.' The mouth pouted childishly.

'Nothing will ever be the same again, Chris. You, above all people, should know that.'

Later in the day, Kate wandered along the bank towards the Harper's Farm bridge, Jemima waddling hopefully in her wake and quacking for bread. Kate threw a handful of crusts, then squatted among the rushes and watched ripples of activity where fishes and voles gallivanted in the secrecy of water. It was going to be hard, so much harder than she'd imagined. Even Chris was pulling at her heartstrings, while the atmosphere of hopelessness in her own household was devastating.

'Mum?'

She looked up. 'Ah. I never heard you coming.'

'Why are you crying?' The girl looked embarrassed. 'People will see if you cry here.'

'I didn't know I was crying. Perhaps it's a bit of hay fever.'

Melanie joined her mother on the grass. 'I'm not a nice girl, am I? And I'm sorry for what I did.'

'Why? What did you do, where did you do it, and will it cost much?'

The youngster grinned ruefully. 'I meant for telling your big secret. Not about drawing cartoons and pictures, I never told them that. But about you going – I shouldn't have. Oh, it's awful in there now, isn't it? I hate being in the house. Everything's been such a muddle, I haven't known what to think. But I'm trying hard to be good. Sorry.'

Kate remembered her own time of 'being good', when she'd felt responsible for everything up to and including the Second World War. Life was so unfair, especially to young people. 'It's pretty rough at home, yes. But don't be apologetic, it's not your fault.'

Melanie pulled up a handful of rye grass and sucked at the pale roots. 'You'd better go, Mum. Before it gets any worse. If you stay, you'll be ill. I wouldn't like to think I'd made you stay and made you ill.'

Shocked and stunned, Kate turned and stared at the figure by her side. 'Did I hear you right, Mel?'

The girl's head sank to her knees, and she hugged her calves, rocking slightly back and forth as she spoke in muffled tone. 'I can't bear you unhappy, Mum. I'd sooner you were happy away from me than unhappy with me. I don't want to lose you, but . . . It's your turn to be selfish now. I've had my chance.'

Dear God in heaven, when had this child grown up? Any why hadn't she, her mother, noticed it? 'I . . . I don't know what to say to you, Mel. Except thanks. And you won't be losing me, you'll never lose me. When I get settled, you might come and stay for weekends.' Oh dear. Would that really be possible? Taking into account the true size of Kate's plan . . .

'He wouldn't like it. Daddy would probably make a big stink. But we can meet and write, and I can phone you when you get a number.'

'Mel?'

She lifted her head and looked into the sad face of her mother. 'What?'

'I love you.'

'And I love you too, and I've always known that you care about me. It's hard for you. I know about that, because it's hard for me too sometimes. We're alike, aren't we?'

'Yes, very much so.'

'Granny Dora has spoiled me. But I'm not really like her, Mum, honest. I'll probably turn out OK, just like you always said. Granny Dora hasn't got a lot of influence over me. I've heard you say that I'm her all over again, but I'm not. It's just . . . well . . . I act up when she's around so I'll get my own way. But I don't want you to think I'm like her.'

'All right.'

'Then there's the other thing, you and your nerves. Dad and Gran have always treated you as if you'd a few bits missing, and I copied them. But I'm thirteen now and I know you're not crazy. There are times when you need staying away from, but you're not crackers.'

'That's one of the nicest things you've ever said to me.'

'Are you being sarcastic?'

'No. If you realized how many times I've doubted my sanity . . .'

'You're OK. I bet we'll be good friends when I'm grown up.'

'You're already grown up, pet. I don't know when it happened – it must have been terribly sudden – but you've certainly shot up in my estimation. What did I miss? What's changed you?'

Melanie shrugged. 'All kinds of things, really. Watching in the house, seeing how Gran and Dad treat you. Then there's biology at school; we were learning about women's bodies and what I have to go through, what you've been through having me. I thought about everybody going on about your nerves when it's probably those hormones Mrs Wright was teaching us about. Then Rita Smythe's dad upped and left last week, and that was no big deal. If men can move on, why can't women?' She raised her head and studied the sky. 'Women have it rough, Mum.'

'So do men. They usually have to do a horrible job from fifteen till sixty-five, no time off for having babies. Try not to be unfair, Mel. I'm unfair and I don't like it in myself.' She reached out her arms and enfolded this child, this person she had never known, the one creature in the world she should have known above all others. 'I gave birth to you,' she whispered, 'and I seem to have had post-natal depression ever since.' This caused a loud guffaw from both parties. 'Not possible, Mum!' screamed Mel.

'How would you know?'

'Stands to reason, you must have plenty of oestrogen, you're only thirty-four. Hormone levels do settle.'

'Clever clogs!'

'Well, I'm going to be a doctor. Or a nurse. That's my

secret, in case I don't make it. You know what those two are like.' She inclined her head towards the house. 'And if Gran knew my ambition, she'd have me looking at her illnesses day and night.'

'That's true. So, we have reached an agreement at last?'

'I suppose so. I'll miss you something awful, though.'

'And I'll miss you. But we'll be together in the way that counts.'

'Yes.' Mel pulled away and jumped to her feet. 'By the way, I've cleared a wall in my room.'

'What for?'

'For your pictures, Mum. For all my mother's pictures.'

While Melanie seemed to grow fast towards maturity, Geoff evened matters out by apparently regressing into a youth that had never been misspent. He stayed out late, returning with a gleam in his eye that could only be called triumphant. On several occasions, he was drunk to the point of disorderly, and once he had to be fetched home by a taxi driver who declared his passenger to be 'on the rigid side of dead'. Dora, who never saw her son at his worst, forgave him his trespasses because a man whose wife was so inadequate deserved forgiveness and a bit of leeway.

Kate continued with her preparations. She borrowed several suitcases from Maureen so that Geoff could not accuse her of making off with his property. The house had four bedrooms, and she moved herself and her belongings into the guest room, leaving the smallest bedroom to hold her packing. She hadn't realized how many clothes she possessed, having always held more or less rigidly to the school of the 'good suit' and the 'little black dress', but her accessories were manifold. Also, her predilection for trousers, jeans and lumpy sweaters took up a fair amount of room, as did her love for shoes.

She had intended to leave with a whimper rather than

with a bang, to summon a taxi in the dead of night or on a weekend afternoon when everyone was out, but the size of her move was increasing by the day. Boxes, plastic bags and suitcases were soon piled high in the small back bedroom, and each day she came across something else that required packing. And where would all this go in her mother's two-bedroomed cottage? Not that she intended to stay there for long, but this particular stepping-stone was necessary. After all, she couldn't just leave home without telling Rachel Murray of her intention, and that alone would take several days of argument.

In the end, she had to settle on a compromise. Through a teacher at school, she heard of a flat at the bottom of Chorley New Road and, after viewing the accommodation and paying a month's rent in advance, she decided to move most of her things there, saving just a night bag for the statutory stop at Mother's. As she packaged her belongings, she found herself smiling because of her adherence to working-class protocol. She had educated herself and married herself into the middle class, yet she knew in her bones that she must still return to base before altering the course of her existence in any way. Rachel Murray and others of her cult and generation represented a power whose tentacles reached out to touch offspring whatever their ages or wherever they went.

It was Sunday. Kate stood in the kitchen ironing Melanie's school blouses for what would probably be the last time. She felt fairly safe. Geoff was out at the golf club, more than likely at the nineteenth propping up the bar and working hard to achieve a state of numbness and paralysis. Dora had popped out to play afternoon whist with some cronies on Eagle Crescent, while Mel was at the riding school having a dressage lesson.

When Maureen arrived at four o'clock with the hired van, the two women set to, carrying a seemingly endless pile of parcels out to the vehicle. Except for Jemima, they would have got away in time, but Kate insisted on saying goodbye to her favourite duck. It was as she was feeding this special feathered friend that Dora put in an unscheduled appearance. Her stomach was bad. She hoped it was her stomach, only it was on the left side and might be her heart. And what was this dreadful van doing on the driveway and did Kate know where the antacid tablets were?

It was several moments before Dora assessed the situation. She stood on the front lawn, handbag placed at her feet, arms akimbo, face ablaze with anger, and possibly with dyspepsia too.

'I see, sneaking off, are you?'

'I've said my goodbyes.'

'Oh yes? To your daughter? And what about your husband, the poor man who has fed, clothed and sheltered you all these years?'

'Melanie knows I'm going today and she chose not to be here. As for your son, he has probably reached that happy stage of oblivion where nothing matters except his next drink.'

'And who drove him to that?' barked the furious woman. 'Who made his life such a misery? Answer me that one, lady.'

'You did.' Kate's tone was icy.

'I did? What do you mean by that? I'm not the one who's abandoning him. I'm not the one who . . .'

'I have nothing to say to you, Dora, nothing at all. I have to go, and that's the end of it. Please don't force me to say things we'll both regret.'

'How dare you?' Dora Saunders' face was now an interesting shade of purple. 'I looked after my son, which is more than you've done for my granddaughter. He had a normal upbringing in a proper home. Even after his dear father died, I made sure that Geoffrey was cared for.'

'Yes.' Kate turned away. She must keep her mouth firmly closed, because if she were to start now, if she were to air her feelings, then the whole of Edgeford would probably come out to witness the humiliation. 'Don't tempt me, Dora,' she muttered, her jaw stiffening from the effort of holding back a tirade of abuse. 'And stop making a scene.'

'A scene?' screamed the older woman. 'Me make a scene? You're the one who does that sort of thing. You're the one who's needed medical help for nerves all these years. You can't go! If you go, it will damage Geoffrey.' She straightened her spine to show that she meant business. 'I have never done anything to hurt anyone, especially my own son. So don't tell me about making scenes. You're the one that's showing us all up, taking off in the middle of a Sunday afternoon.'

This almost proved too much for Kate. Quietly, and with her head bowed slightly, she spoke to her mother-in-law. 'I married the wrong man. It probably isn't his fault and it probably isn't mine. These things happen in life, Dora. Get used to it. I've had enough, so I'm going away to save myself. You'll all be better off without me. It's what you've always wanted, isn't it? Geoff and Melanie to yourself? Be satisfied. For once, just be satisfied with your lot.'

Maureen coughed into the heavy silence. 'Time we were off, Kate.'

Dora sagged against a cherry blossom tree whose frailty threatened to snap under her not inconsiderable weight. 'No-one,' she gasped, 'no-one has ever treated me like this before. You're implying that it's all my fault, aren't you? I have never been so insulted in all my life!'

'Hang around, there's more.' Kate's voice was still quiet. 'You have abused me verbally and emotionally for fourteen years. I have listened to your criticisms and throw-away caustic comments almost every day since I got married. There is no nastier person on this earth, Dora Saunders. You sicken me. Showing me up by washing the walls and leaving a dirty corner so that everyone could see my filth measured against your virtue. Washing clothes I'd already laundered, rearranging my cupboards to prove how unmethodical I am. You're the failure. Only failures wash walls and have long discussions across fences about the merits of soap powders. Only failures turn out sons who iron shoelaces.'

'He's a good clean boy . . .'

'He's forty-bloody-eight! He doesn't need you any more. With a different mother, he might have had a better marriage.'

'You're going too far now,' warned Maureen. 'She'll have a stroke in a minute.'

But Dora didn't get time to have a stroke. Just as the old woman reached out to grab Kate's hair, Melanie dashed round the corner on her pony. 'Here comes the cavalry,' muttered Maureen.

Mel jumped down from the saddle, whip tapping gently against her boot, eyes blazing with tears and anger. 'Don't you dare touch my mother,' she said, her tone low and restrained.

'Mother? That's not a mother, it's a walking nervous breakdown!' Dora was screaming now, yelling like a fishwife. 'She's blaming everything on me, Melanie! She says it's all my fault.'

'Go in the house, Gran.'

'But I . . .'

'I SAID GO IN THE HOUSE!' This change in volume proved most effective. Dora staggered towards the front door, not even stopping to pick up her bag.

Melanie turned to her mother. 'I think you should get away now,' she said coldly. 'This is a very untidy way to leave. I thought you might have had some consideration for the rest of us. We have to carry on living here, you know.' Then she climbed on her pony and rode away.

Maureen and Kate got into the van. 'That daughter of yours,' said Maureen as she started the engine, 'is quite remarkable. Doesn't give a damn about you, does she?'

Kate grinned. 'That's right. She doesn't give a damn.'

They stopped the van at the bottom end of Church Road so that Kate might make her farewell to Edgeford. 'Anyone would think you were taking off for the bloody moon,' grumbled Maureen. 'You're only going a few miles.'

'I'll miss it. The Co-op and the lychgate, that air-raid siren on top of the village hall, the stocks, the graveyard . . .'

'Oh, shut up! You'd miss toothache if you had it long enough. The trouble with you is you're an incurable romantic who doesn't even recognize her own disorder. Speaking of disorders, can you have a square of Fry's Chocolate Cream? Have you had your injection?'

Kate nodded mutely and they sat for a while sucking at the delicious mint filling.

'I'll always associate goodbyes with chocolate now, chocolate's such a rare treat for me. My, I gave old Dora some stick, didn't I? I didn't mean to. I'd no intention of saying a word, but she pushed me too far. All those years I held it back, then whoosh! It was like firing a machine-gun, I simply couldn't manage to run out of ammunition.'

'I wasn't proud of you today, our kid.'

'Neither was I. It just happened.'

'She's an old woman, and you've put up with her for centuries. Why couldn't you manage just one more afternoon?'

Kate shook her head. 'Revenge. I suppose I wanted my pound of flesh.'

'Revenge is a dish best served cold. You were about as cold as a gas oven on nine. And there was no need to pick her bones. Mind, I suppose you were justified in a sense. No way would I have put up with that dragon in my house. Marriage is hard enough without added irritations.'

Kate glanced sideways at the perfectly painted face. 'You and Phil OK now?'

'Fine. Jogging along quite nicely, in fact. I'm grateful to whoever she was, she certainly put the spark back. But I'll watch him in future. And, of course, I've got my safeguard now.'

'Safeguard?'

'He's signed the house over to me. If he leaves while the children are young, I get everything.'

'Hell's bells!'

'Those were Phil's words. Yet he never blinked an eyelash when he signed the cheque for your present at Preston's. All misty, he was, that first day. "Good old Kate", he kept saying. At the finish, I was sick of the sound of your name. Mind, he's gone off you now. Thinks you're giving me a bad example. He keeps muttering on about how we'll have girls' nights out and he'll never know what I'm up to.'

Kate laughed heartily. 'Does he want his teardrop back?'

'He's not getting it, is he?'

'Not on your nelly, missus!'

A car screeched to a halt outside the church and Kate held her breath as she identified its driver.

'Good grief!' exclaimed Maureen 'What the hell do I do now?'

'I don't know. He must be drunk, the car's halfway up that lamp-post. We could drive off, I suppose, but he'd only follow and cause a crash.'

Geoff wended his unsteady way across the road, and Kate was suddenly touched as she noticed how unkempt he looked. Almost human, she thought.

'Is that you?' he shouted.

Maureen wound down her window. 'No. It's the Avon lady.'

'Mother phoned the club.' He belched loudly. 'And told me that you and Kate had taken off. She was most

222

upset, very distressed.' He wandered round the front of the van and stood swaying slightly beside the passenger door. 'Get out,' he ordered uncertainly.

Kate opened her door slightly. 'No. I'm staying exactly where I am.'

'Really? Going to camp out here on Church Road? You're on your way to some flat, aren't you? Some bloody love-nest for you and your boyfriend.'

'That's right.'

'Eh?'

'I'm just agreeing with everything you say. That's what you always wanted, for me to be agreeable. Think what you like, it's of no importance to me.'

'You are a cruel, heartless bitch.'

'And you're a drunken old bum, so go away and leave me to get on with my life.'

It was then that he started to cry. Kate stared at him in stunned silence for several seconds, then she leaned over to Maureen. 'Nip out and pinch his keys, he'll have left them in the ignition.'

'But he won't be able to drive!'

'Exactly. He won't be able to kill himself or anyone else. He can walk home, and you can drop the keys through the letterbox tonight. Go on. Be quick before he notices.'

She kept him occupied while Maureen slipped away to carry out her secret mission. 'Look at you blubbering like a baby! Alcohol tears, that's all they are. It's not the end of the world, is it? You know how things are between us, I'm not going to hang around being a complete failure for the rest of my days. Don't you see? This is your chance, too, your chance to find somebody decent and competent, a suitable wife for a man in your position.'

'I still love you!' His mouth was distorted with a fair imitation of grief.

'You said you didn't. Only weeks ago, you said . . .'

'I didn't mean it. I like you odd and difficult.'

'Yes, it makes you feel superior. Sorry, I didn't intend to say that. You don't love me; you love a memory. There were good times, Geoff, some very good times.'

'Yes.' He blew his nose noisily. 'Remember Paris?'

'I remember.'

'And London in the rain?'

'Yes.' Maureen was back. 'I remember all of it, love. And it's not all your fault, but I'm not going to take full responsibility for it either. It's just one of those things.' Out of the corner of her mouth, she whispered, 'Got the keys?'

'Yes.'

Kate slammed her door. 'Then drive. For God's sake, get me away from him.' As the van started up, she covered her face with her hands. 'It wasn't all me,' she moaned, 'but I feel so guilty. Why must I always feel so bloody guilty?'

Maureen sniffed loudly. 'Because you're a woman, lass. Because you're just a flaming woman.'

The house was in the centre of a large and still opulent terrace at the bottom of Chorley New Road, just a few doors away from the Royal Infirmary's nurses' quarters. This row of rather splendid old homes would not have looked out of place in Kensington or Mayfair, and Kate knew she had been lucky to find such a lovely place in which to start her single life. She had never been alone. There had always been Mother and Dad and Judith, then the crowds at college, and soon after college had come marriage to Geoff. And Dora. Yes, she'd married the pair of them, hadn't she?

The Misses Helen and Sarah Brandon lived an impoverished but elegant life in the house bequeathed to them by a long-dead father, who had been a doctor, and now they rented out all the upper storey, plus the rear half of the downstairs where Kate was about to make her home. Everyone had a key to the main door, but she was luckier than the other tenants, having a back door all to herself. Her life could now, therefore, be as detached as she chose to make it.

There were two rooms. The first, a large living room, had a bed covered in scatter cushions, three comfortable chairs, fitted cupboards to one side of the chimney breast, and a door to the kitchen at the other side of the fireplace. It was spacious and airy in spite of several trolleys and occasional tables, but Kate's favourite spot was a little alcove with a window overlooking the back yard where ivy and honeysuckle grew in sweet abundance.

The second room was a kitchen-cum-diner, with an old porcelain sink, a geriatric gas cooker and some servants' stairs leading out of the back corner. There was a massive Victorian dresser, a meatsafe, a group of ancient dining chairs, and a table covered by a cloth of heavy dark green cotton.

'A bit on the antique side,' commented Maureen who, like Kate, was used to all the niceties of modern living. 'Look! You have to put money in the meters for gas and electricity.'

'Never mind. I've been given a place for coal, so I'm going to take out that electric fire in the living room and have a proper fire.'

'What? You're going to burn coal? In this day and age?'

'Yes. Coal and candles. Remember, I've rent to pay now.'

'Let Geoff pay it.'

'Why should he? Oh, I made the usual noises about wanting a lump sum for compensation, but this is my decision, Mo. He didn't throw me out of the house. This could be the beginning of the most colossal mistake in history.'

'And you look radiantly happy about it. Where's the bathroom?'

'It's shared. I get it Tuesday and Friday evenings.'

'But . . .' Maureen looked flabbergasted. 'What do you do on other days? Walk about smelling like a navvy?'

'I wash here, in the sink.'

'In the sink where you do the dishes?'

Kate grunted her exasperation. 'I'll get a bowl. I've lived in conditions far worse, I can tell you. The Misses are really nice. They're keeping my insulin in their fridge until I buy my own. Very understanding, they are. And it's only three pounds fifteen a week.'

'Daylight robbery. I'd rather you than me, sweetheart.'

Kate fiddled with the stiff drawers of the dresser, averting her face and keeping her tone light as she said, 'I'll be leaving school at the end of the summer term.'

There followed a long and uncomfortable silence.

'Did you hear me, Maureen?'

'I heard. Damned stupidity! How are you going to keep yourself? Giving up a deputy's job just like that? I can't believe it! Perhaps you do need a psychiatrist after all.'

'I have to leave.'

'Why? Bloody why? Now of all times?'

Kate shrugged. 'There's something I have to do.'

'Something? What, though? Who's going to feed you while you do your "something"? Who's going to pay the rent if you don't go for some sort of settlement with Geoff?'

Kate rounded on her friend. 'Yes, I'd rather me than you, too. This is what I want. Absorb it, come to terms. I never asked for automatic washers and food mixers. I can work here, I can sit at that table in the alcove and . . .'

'And what?'

'Well, until summer I can mark books and plan lessons.'

'Riveting. And what do you do when Standard Four's had all its marking done? Will you get a telly?'

'Might.'

'What about your social life? You can't stop in here vegetating.'

Kate said nothing.

'It's this thing of yours, isn't it? This whatever-it-is, this grand bloody project you're mapping out. Well? Do I have to crawl about on this kitchen floor and beg? What are you up to, Kate Saunders? Are you working on a formula to change water to oil? Or is it sculpture? Writing?' She stamped an impatient foot as Kate shook her head. 'Well what the hell is it, then? Come on, we've been friends ever since you started at Daubhill School, surely you can tell me?'

Kate sighed. 'Only Melanie knows. Even then, I didn't intend . . . Oh, Maureen! Remember when Phil left you and you couldn't talk about the mess? When you said that talking about it would make it more real? I feel that talking about my ambition will make it less real. I don't want to tempt fate.'

Maureen coughed and lit a cigarette. 'I showed you my kitchen, didn't I? I showed you mine, now you show me yours.'

'This is my kitchen. You are standing in my kitchen.'

Maureen flounced into the other room and flung herself into an armchair. 'You can fetch your own bloody stuff from the van, then.'

Kate followed and seated herself opposite her friend. 'Stop sulking. If a child at school carried on like this, I'd put him in a corner on his own. Behave yourself.'

'Shan't.'

Maureen studied her nail polish and flicked cigarette ash on to the hearth rug, while Kate tapped the leather arm of her chair. 'I'm doing cartoons,' she said finally. 'I've already started a strip in a boys' comic, and I'm trying to break into newspapers. My adult character's called Boothroyd; he's a drake but I can make him look like anyone, so I hope to do a bit of political stuff. My children's character is Boothroyd

Junior, he's a drake too and he goes to school and causes mayhem . . .'

'Great!' Maureen's face was almost split by the width of her grin. 'And I knew it was something like that, anyway. I've watched you scribbling in corners, girl. You'll be a household name. I'll be able to say "I knew her when she had to put shillings in the gas meter"!'

'Rubbish.' But Kate knew that her own face registered pleasure. 'It's only a beginning, Mo. But it's a thing I have to try.'

'You'll do it. I know you will. When I think of the way you transformed the school with your pictures. This is it, then? This is your reason for giving up your job and your marriage?'

'Yes.' The lie was getting easier now. Though it wasn't a complete untruth, was it? *Boys' Laughs* had taken her work, and the editor had promised to put some of her adult stuff under a few of the 'right' noses.

'Just wait till I tell Phil . . .'

'That's just it, you mustn't! I'm sick of failing, Mo. Sick of being a bad wife and a poor mother – I was even judged an unfit daughter, just because I wasn't a son! Let me keep my secret. Let me shock them all. Please? God's honour?'

'OK, kid. They'll have to pull out all my lovely fingernails before I squeal.'

'And your toenails too?'

'It's a deal.'

They brought in the van's contents and distributed them throughout Kate's new home. Then, when everything was tidily put away, Kate packed a bag for a week, school dress, suit and blouses, shoes, toiletries, nightdress and some items of underwear. They sat side by side on the bed.

'Are you ready for it?' asked Maureen, her tone quiet but amused.

'Ready? I've never been ready for my mother, not for thirty-four years. For the first twenty, I didn't even know what she was thinking! Now she's . . . well . . . strong.' She straightened her shoulders. 'But I'm stronger. The question is, Mo, is my mother ready for me?'

IO

Cleaning the education offices was not much fun, but it was the best that Rachel Murray could expect at the age of fifty-five. Having been forced by circumstances to leave school at just turned thirteen, she had spent her life being pushed from pillar to post in the cotton mills, so she now turned to cleaning for a rest. It meant being up and about before five o'clock every weekday morning; it also meant shoving a mop and bucket round empty marble halls for a couple of hours in splendid isolation, but it was better than the noise.

Noise had always got to Rachel; the clatter of the spinning mule had never held much appeal, while the raised voices of workmates, who usually seemed to celebrate their evening release by screaming all the way to heaven, had driven her to distraction. And home hadn't been a peaceful place, not until he had died. When she thought of him dying, she always blessed herself. Not so much in prayer for his salvation but more to assuage the guilt because of her relief. It wasn't right feeling glad about being a widow; it wasn't right to celebrate anyone's demise. But every year when a certain date came round, she bought fish and chips and a pint of stout, then had a quiet little party all to herself in the back kitchen.

Rachel gave the impression of being a hard woman. Most of the neighbours from the 'good old days' had moved on or died, and the replacements found her unapproachable because she wouldn't linger on the corner for a good old gossip; nor was she given to borrowing a cup of sugar or half a block of marg. Number 39's window and sill were always wiped before she set off for work, and nobody could have a chat with someone who cleaned her outside at half past four in a morning. Then there was her step; she had been the first to get it painted red so that it only needed cardinal once a week. Many in Maybank Street still used donkeystones, and during the daily ritual of step-cleaning much social intercourse took place. But number 39's combed and varnished door always remained closed during such exchanges.

She had done her best with the tiny weaver's cottage. In bygone days, Maybank Street had used to be slightly up-market, a place where the higher earners had dwelt, but it now teetered on the brink of slumdom. There were two rooms down and two up, just a living room and kitchen to the ground floor and a couple of dampish bedrooms up the stairs. But Rachel had installed a bath in her kitchen, a proper plumbed-in bath with taps and a drain. This treasure was kept hidden under a wooden bench which she had covered with a custom-made mattress and some colourful cushions. Here Melanie had slept in younger and more carefree years when it had been 'fun' to snuggle down in a kitchen. But it wasn't good enough for Melanie any more. It wasn't good enough for Rachel, and she intended to get out at the earliest opportunity. Not like Dora Saunders, though. Oh, no, she wasn't going to climb out of the gutter by stepping on her child's back. Rachel had a plan, a plan no-one knew about. And the longer she kept it to herself, the better.

On the built-in sideboard to the right of the fireplace stood all her photographs. Judith was in the middle, dark-eyed, dark-haired and beautiful, Judith in her gown and mortar-board, a ribbon-tied scroll hugged tightly to her breast. This centrepiece was flanked by Katherine's wedding photos, then smaller pictures of Melanie in a sand-pit, on a donkey at Blackpool, on a proper pony at one of the many shows where she had taken rosettes.

Rachel sat on her green moquette sofa, a mug of strong

tea in one hand, a ginger biscuit in the other. It was Sunday. She liked Sundays. All her housework had been completed the day before, everything shone and glistened with polish, each tuft on the rug stood to attention after yesterday's beating. The clock ticked and the large Baird television that Kate rented for her stood silent in a corner. Peace. No-one ever came on Sundays. During a term week, Kate visited each lunchtime because her school was just round the corner, and although Rachel was always glad to see her daughter, she looked forward to a weekend's silence.

Kate. Oh Katherine! What had the teachers said? 'Judith is clever, but Katherine is brilliant'. Huh. And what had she done with her brilliance? Like the man in the Bible, Rachel's younger daughter had squandered her talents, or buried them beneath an early marriage and a diploma that was hardly worth the paper it was printed on.

It was wrong to have a favourite, and Rachel knew that. But ever since the red-haired mite had been delivered into her hands, Rachel's heart had been lost forever. Blinking kids! They never did what you wanted them to do, never listened. How many times had she warned them, 'don't get married young, look at me, I was nineteen when I had my first baby, and not twenty-one when I had my second.'

The older girl had taken Mam's advice all right. Judith was now in Washington, doing translations for senators and president's aides, using her talent for languages in a way that kept her away from England, away from her mother and, it seemed, away from marriage.

But Katherine was another kettle altogether. Head-strong, stupid, deaf to advice . . . Rachel sipped her tea and sucked on the dipped biscuit. Katherine should never have married Dora Saunders' precious lad; Katherine should never have married at all. Really, everything was the wrong way round. If Judith hadn't been such a hard worker at her books, she would have been married by now, married with a few children and a smile happier than the strained expression that showed in recent photographs. Judith was very likely built for marriage and motherhood. She was placid, kind, gentle, too good to be terribly interesting. Though there was a coldness in Judith, a quiet strength that sometimes made Rachel wonder. Did Judith get up to no good on the sly? Was she as virtuous as she seemed? Rachel shook herself sharply, tut-tutting as she just managed to save her tea from spilling. She settled herself again. Aye, compared to the older girl, Katherine was a coiled spring, all wound up and ready to jump. Where the hell could she jump to? Nowhere. Nowhere at all. So she hopped about between Edgeford and Daubhill, happy in neither place, discontented with marriage, unfulfilled as a teacher.

'I could shake her. I could. She might be going on thirty-five, but I still feel like giving her a darned good hiding.' This was said to Puddy-Tat, the large striped monster who was Rachel's sole live-in companion. 'I told her how she'd finish up. Don't you dare claw at that chair, I'll have them blinking feet of yours surgically removed one of these days! Where was I? Oh yes, our Katherine. There's summat brewing, Puddy. I could see it in her face on Friday. Right from a kiddy, she's shown in her face when she's been up to no good. And I'll be in it, just you wait and see. When she topples over, it'll be me she runs to. Psychiatrists!' She spat this large word as if it were poison. 'She needs a psychiatrist like I need haemorrhoids!'

The cat gave a small yowl then rolled over to expose his underside, paws coming up to beg for a scratch on the belly, but Rachel was too engrossed in her monologue. 'Big girl's blouse, he is.' Rachel had a penchant for Hylda Baker's phraseology. 'He's not a husband, him. More of a liability. Oh, I told her, Puddy, time and again, I told her. But would she listen? Did she ever listen? So

I had a word with St Jude during mass, well, I've tried everybody else, and he's supposed to be favourite for hopeless cases. If she'd just pack her job in and go back to university – it's never too late for learning. And that daft barmpot could afford to send her. She could be a lawyer or summat of that nature, summat to keep her occupied. Aye, she's made her bed, but she doesn't need to lie in it all the while, does she?'

The cat said nothing and, in that special way known only to cats, it said nothing loudly. Slanted yellow eyes were fixed on Rachel's face as he purred enormously and performed an impossible twist into a more sensible position.

'Nay, I'm dafter than you, I am. Talking to a blessed cat! At least you've the sense not to try and talk back, eh? She'll be round to see us tomorrow, our little Katie. With them sad green eyes that make me think it's all my fault. It weren't my fault, Puddy, honest.'

She placed her mug on the floor. 'Then there's the other matter. I don't know whether it'll be the right thing for me, not after what I've been through. But he seems nice enough, never makes demands. And it's a lovely house, Puddy-Tat. Stuck on the back of his shop, it is. I think I shall ask him to tea next week, see how you two get on. Eeh, just think. I've never even been out for a drink with him, yet he's proposed. I mean, we've got talking, like, many a time, and I've never given it a second think. Then he starts asking me in for a cuppa every time I'm on me way home from work. And that's all it is, just a cup of tea. Don't look at me like that, you miserable old cat, there's been no messing. Only after Peter . . . well, you wonder, don't you?'

Rachel Murray retreated into her reverie. Married at seventeen to escape a house filled by siblings, she had truly fallen into the fire. Peter had been a gambler, a drinker, a man whose vocabulary did not carry the word 'forgiveness'. Yet only once had she failed to stand by him, because in her younger days, she had believed loyalty to be a wife's prime debt. The strain of standing by him had left its mark on herself, probably on Judith – though only to a minor degree – and most particularly on Katherine, who had felt the brunt of her father's wrath on too many occasions. So, like her mother, young Katie had fled prematurely, retreating from the frying pan and into an inferno that was plainly too hot to handle. Judith hadn't needed to run; Judith, who was Peter's double except for round the nose, had never been chastised, had been possessed anyway of an other-worldliness into which she could somehow escape from reality.

Rachel exhaled loudly and wondered what would be on telly tonight. She'd done her crossword and her bit of Sunday reading, and was hoping there'd be a good play on BBC. Just as she reached for the television page, a key turned in the lock and Kate stepped into the house.

'Hello, Mum.'

Rachel stared for a moment at her daughter, taking in quickly the whitened face, the small suitcase, the clenched free fist. 'Well, I never expected you, lass, not on a Sunday.'

'No.'

'Well? Shut that door, you'll have the street in. Whatever are you doing wandering about Daubhill today? Started working Sundays, have you?'

'Maureen brought me. And no, we're not teaching at weekends.'

'I see.' Rachel glanced at the bag. 'So what's in there? A picnic? Or has he got you selling door to door to make ends meet?'

'No need for sarcasm, Mother. These are clothes.'

'Ah. I see. Picked me out some nice jumble, have you?' Kate often commandeered a coat or a skirt for her mother whenever the school held a rummage sale.

'They're . . . my clothes.'

235

Rachel's jaw was clenched tightly for a moment. 'Right. You'd best sit yourself down, hadn't you? Tell me what it's all about. I suppose there is a tale to it, I can tell from the set of your mouth.'

Kate placed her case on the floor, picked up Puddy-Tat and sat with him close to her chest as if using him as a shield. 'I've left home,' she said baldly. The kitchen cuckoo clock sang the hour, seeming to underline Kate's foolishness.

'Oh.' Rachel smoothed her navy skirt and brushed a few non-existent crumbs from its pleats. 'Well, I can't say I'm surprised. The only thing that surprises me is that you've put up with Geoffrey and Fanny Fannacker-pants for this length of time without making some sort of a stand. Mind, it is only a stand, isn't it? I mean, you will go back?'

'No.'

Rachel's lower lip sagged for a fraction of a second. 'What do you mean, "no"? You don't just walk out on a marriage, girl. Marriage is sacred, even if the ceremony was performed in a Proddy church or a registry. Have you no sense at all? Dora Saunders is getting exactly what she wants, her son back all to herself.'

'She can have him and welcome.'

'But . . . but what about your daughter? You can't just leave Melanie.'

'Yes I can. I can, I will and I have done. Don't you start, Mother. I know what it's like being brought up in an atmosphere . . .'

'Atmosphere? Atmosphere? And what do you mean by that, my girl? You and your sister had the best education we could afford. We went without so that you and Judith . . .'

'No, Mam. You went without. He never did.'

'I suppose "he" is your father, God rest him?'

'Yes, "he" was my father. If he had five bob in his pocket, it went on a horse while we got clothes and shoes

236

for a shilling a week in the pound. He was a drunken slob . . .'

'Don't you dare!'

'Stop treating me like a child. Stop telling me what to think and feel and say.' The cat jumped down, eager to get away from such ill-concealed anger. 'Don't tell me you weren't relieved when he died. I saw your bruises, Mam, I saw you having an all-over wash before we got the bath; I watched you wincing while you bathed the black and blue bits. I hated him. I still hate him now!'

Rachel crossed herself hurriedly.

'That's right, Mother, bless yourself against those thoughts, those awful memories. Ask God to forgive you for being content now. But don't ever tell me to be grateful to a man who tried to crush my spirit.'

'Katherine! Stop this!'

'My daughter is being brought up in that same atmosphere.'

There followed a long pause. 'What?' asked Rachel eventually, her tone quiet. 'He . . . he actually hits you?'

'He daren't. Only once did he hit me. I waited till he was asleep and then I clobbered him with his tennis racquet. After that, he seemed to go off physical violence. Now, it's just verbal. And it's not really violence, Geoff hasn't the emotional energy for that. And he's not really a bad man, he's just weak and under his mother's thumb. But he undermines me all the time, belittles me in front of our daughter. Well, I've started to fight back and that's not good for Melanie. It wasn't good for her when I used to sit there and take it, but now . . .'

'Katherine, you cannot leave that poor girl to him and his mother. Think how she'll turn out.'

'She'll turn out fine. Anyway, I couldn't stay. That's all there is to it.'

Rachel sucked on her teeth before speaking again. 'That house is worth a fortune but you'll get not one penny . . .'

'I know.'

'No security, lass. Can you really come back and live here? No bathroom, the lav down the yard . . .'

'I'm not coming back. I've taken a flat on Chorley New Road. Don't look at me like that, Mam. I have never been able to stand the way you look at me.'

'Why? What do you mean by that, eh? I look at you the same road as I look at everybody else. I'm not cross-eyed, am I? What's the matter with the way I look at you?'

Kate hung her head. 'It's as if you don't like me, as if I'm some sort of great disappointment.'

'Well.' Rachel's feet shuffled against the lino. 'If you want the truth, I was disappointed in you at one time. I thought you'd have made some sort of a mark in the world. But I don't feel like that now, not any more. You're a beautiful young woman and a fine person . . .'

'And a stupid one. How do you think I felt as a child? "You should work hard like Judith, you should stay clean like Judith". I got Judith rammed down my throat until I almost hated my own sister. I am me . . . me . . . ME!' She beat her breast harshly. 'And I'm sick of being compared to perfection and coming out less than second best.'

'Well. Well, I never thought . . .'

'Never thought I cared? Well, I did care. I wasn't going to turn myself into a doctor or a lawyer just to please him. I never did a stroke of work at school, that was my way of paying him back. I wanted out of here, Mam. The two-year course at training college meant a year less than university, a year less with this as my permanent address. Getting away from him was my prime ambition since I reached the age of reason. We tried to love one another, he and I. But we never managed it, not quite. His love had too many conditions attached to it, it was not the instinctive love of parent for child. And all you could say was "you never got a degree" and "look at Judith with her doctorate". A failure. All my life, I was a failure. So I ran. And I ran to the wrong place. Just like you did, Mother.'

Rachel shivered and folded her arms across a suddenly chilled body. 'I know. I know. There's no need for you to rub it in.' The shoulders drooped heavily. 'I watched you, love. Like me all over again, you were. It broke my heart to see it. Because, Katherine, I loved you more than . . . more than I should have done. And when they told me at Peter and Paul's that you had this high intelligence quotient thing, I hoped you'd ride out on your own star, lass. You didn't need anybody, because you had it all in your head. There was no need for you to escape as a pillion passenger, no need for you to sit in the shadow of a man. As I told you at the time, he was all wrong . . .'

'And I didn't listen.'

'Huh! If you'd listened, it would have been for the first time. But I did warn you never to trust a man whose eyebrows meet in the middle . . .'

'Or a man in a pink shirt.'

'Exactly. And he was always too well turned out for my liking, never a hair out of place. He wasn't good enough for you, Katherine. But you still have to go back.' Rachel's mouth set itself into a stubborn straight line.

'No.'

'Then you'll get no blessing from me, Katherine Murray.'

'Saunders.'

'Aye, that's the nail on the head, isn't it? You're Saunders now, and you've been Saunders for fourteen years. Perhaps you should never have married him, but you know me, Katherine, I'm straight as a die when it comes to marriage. Yes, I know I left your dad for a while, but I did go back. I was teaching him a lesson. It's all right to teach folk a lesson. But once wed, always wed till death you do part. And it's not just my religion.

It's other things like commonsense. I mean, you get married, set up a home, put time and money and effort in – you can't just throw all that away! It's like investing in a failing bank! Then there's kiddies to consider. Children need two parents . . .'

'I needed my father like I needed a hole in the head. Without him, we might have been happy, Mam. Judith would possibly have stayed in England – where do you think she got her wanderlust, eh? She was quiet, I know, but he got on her nerves and that's what made her decide to leave the country the first time. And I might have taken time over my decisions if I hadn't had him breathing down my neck all the time. All it needed was for you to do what I've done, you should have got out while Judith and I were young.'

Rachel glowered. 'Ah, yes, but I would have taken you with me, wouldn't I? The one time I did clear out for a while, I took you with me to my dad's. And after he'd died, where could we go except into poverty? And what good would that have done? I notice you've not fetched your daughter away from her home, so why preach to me?'

'She chose to stay. Melanie's thirteen. At thirteen, a child should have a say in its own future. She wants her horses and her friends.'

'Aye, and that's one of the reasons why I stayed here. Because you two had school and friends. So you should do what I did, stay with your daughter.'

They glared at one another for several seconds, then Rachel stood up and walked out to the kitchen. At the stove, she paused, a hand on the kettle's handle. She suddenly realized that she loved and understood her little girl more in this moment – much more – than she had ever done in the past. Katherine was breaking out, emerging at last from that whited sepulchre of a marriage. And what was a sepulchre after all? A fancy blinking coffin, that was what! And should she, Rachel Murray, ry to force her own child back into a place of decay and mouldering? 'Katherine?' Her voice was unsteady.

'Yes?' A similar shaky tone.

'Cup of tea?'

'Please. No sugar.'

'Aye, I know. I know, love.'

Rachel scooped tea from the Coronation caddy into a brown teapot. 'I love you, child.' It was easier from in here, easier not face to face. 'It's always been a terrible burden for me, knowing I loved you . . . differently from the way I love our Judith. You must never tell her, not as long as you live! That's why I was so hard on you, because I needed it not to show.'

'Oh, Mam!'

'Stop where you are! Don't you be coming in here and watching me crying into the Black and Green's. When you were born, we couldn't open your hands. It was like you'd come into the world for a terrible big fight. Twelve months you screamed when you were awake, then you learned a few words and started telling us what was what. You were always special. Then when . . . when he treated you different and you went all quiet, I could have . . . oh God . . . I could have murdered him. All inside yourself, you went, as if you'd no idea of your own worth. I know what he did. I know what I let him do. May God find it in His heart to forgive me, because your childhood must have been awful, lass. But to me, you were the most special thing in all the world.' She dabbed at her eyes before scalding the tea.

'You never told me.' The voice from the front room was small.

'Didn't want you big-headed, didn't want our Judith feeling out of place with me. Two wrongs would not have made a right. Because I love my other daughter too, always have and always will.'

'Yes.'

Rachel took a long, deep breath. 'I'm going to show

you now how much I really care for you. I'm going to swallow all my principles, everything I believe in, and I'm going to . . . to wish you luck.'

'Eh?'

'I'm standing by you, princess.'

'Thanks. Thanks, Mam.' This was fractured by tears.

'You're right, I never loved him. Not after he started taking his frustrations out on my kids. I was a loyal wife, loyal to the point of stubborn. When you told me he was dead, my first thought was, "well, he can't hurt our Katie no more". Even though you were wed, I was still scared of him lashing out at you. Aye, and I was scared of you hitting him back, because I'd seen temper in your eyes when you looked at him. I know you came to the funeral just for my sake. Even our Judith never shed a tear and she was always his little doll.' She paused to blow her nose. 'Do what you have to do, my girl. You were never what they call conventional. Happen this is your way for a new start. I'm . . . I'm behind you. I just want you to know that no matter what my own beliefs are, I am on your side.'

'Oh, Mother!'

Rachel sniffed impatiently. 'Don't you be "oh mothering" me now. This tea will be iced lollies before we've even got to it. Drag yourself in here and butter these two scones. Can you have a scone? How many points is a scone? And before you come in, knock that cat off my chair, I know he's on it, I can feel his eyes boring through the wall. And take your coat off unless you're not stopping. I hope you've walked nothing in, lady, I was an hour doing that floor yesterday. You can switch the telly on if you want, there might be some nice hymns on. We've got some new neighbours, Santosh Mathur and his wife Hamida. Nobody else bothers with them, 'cos they're from India or some such fancy place, but I like them, they're blinking hard workers. She wears them fancy frocks and a red mark on her head, very pretty.

Have you read about all that fighting in Paris? It's in the paper, all knocking spots off one another round that Latin Quarter. You went there, didn't you? I remember you telling me about the street women and all them funny underclothes in the shops . . .'

Kate relaxed. All this chatter was just to hide emotion, to bring things back to 'normal'. She looked at her watch. It hadn't taken a week to argue it out; it had taken all of fifteen minutes. And there was a new warmth in her breast, a feeling of comfort and deep security. She didn't yet recognize it as her mother's love.

So you married her and she married you without either of you knowing the other?' Rachel's eyes were round with amazement. 'Sounds like a flipping raffle to me. How did you know what sort of prize you'd get, if any?'

Santosh Mathur's white teeth glistened in his coffee-coloured face. 'We knew nothing, but our parents knew everything. This is the way in my country.' He glanced lovingly at his shy young wife. 'The fathers and mothers think about suitability. Much is taken into account; education, upbringing, temperament. I saw Hamida only twice before our wedding, never with the two of us alone.'

'Oh, I see.' Rachel glanced from one to the other, mischief plain in her eyes. 'Did you like her?'

Hamida giggled as she stirred the pot on the fire. 'He was told to like me.'

'Hang on, hang on.' Rachel lowered herself on to the brightly coloured couch. 'This is daft, this is. Suppose you'd hated one another? Suppose you'd got wed, then found out that he snores or that she can't cook.'

'This does not happen, Mrs Murray,' smiled Santosh.

'Don't talk so wet. Stands to reason, folk is folk no matter which side of the world they come from. There's all the little things in life like talking with your mouth full and cutting toenails all over the bedroom. Them things on their own can ruin a marriage.'

'We do not allow anything to spoil our marriage, Mr Murray.'

'Rachel. I've told you to call me Rachel. If I can get my mouth round your names, you can have a go at mine, so stop all this "Mrs Murraying", if you please. Anyroad, how come you're working in the mill? Didn't you say you had a job doing accountancy back home?'

'My qualifications are not recognized here, Rachel. I have to learn all over again.'

'Why? Numbers is numbers.'

'I need English examinations.'

'Oh aye? Well, I'll see what our Katherine can do about that. She has this friend called Maureen and her husband's a money man, accounts and suchlike. Happen a new face would brighten up their office, eh?'

Santosh spread long delicate fingers towards Rachel. 'Please, do not trouble on my behalf. Remember, I am Indian, a coloured man.'

'Eh? What's that got to do with the price of eggs?'

'I am sorry, but I do not understand.'

'Just a saying, lad. Now listen to me, you big soft thing, what's this about being coloured? I'm coloured, look, I'm covered in freckles. One of the lesser-spotted, I am, quite rare. So don't you be setting off with a chip on your shoulder. You're as good as any man in this street and a darned sight better educated too.'

'I am of an ethnic minority.'

'Oh yes? We had one of them, but the wheel fell off. Another joke, son. Don't talk to me about minorities. My mam and dad were both Irish, School Hill scum, they were. You should have seen the way we were treated. We had to take it in turns to go to school, one pair of clogs between two. There wasn't enough plates, so we shared and it was a race to see who could eat most and quickest. And they used to come round with their charities, bits of food and a couple of shirts for my brothers. They gave us boots, and it didn't matter if they weren't a pair as long as you could squeeze both feet in. I used to get clouted by the nuns because I was dirty, only there wasn't no soap for a wash. We were covered in fleabites, and we smelled like only those from bug-infested houses can smell. I remember our Nellie blackleading her legs so's the holes in her black stockings wouldn't show and I've seen my mam cry for lack of bread to feed her kiddies. We had nowt till me dad got a better job and moved us all to View Street, but me mam didn't live to enjoy that. So don't talk to me about being different, Santosh Mathur, else I'll clock you one with me clog-iron.'

He bowed slightly. 'I am sorry. Very sorry for your poverty in childhood. No offence against your good person was intended.'

Hamida pushed a wooden spoon under Rachel's nose. 'Here, taste, it is not all hot.'

Rachel allowed a hesitant tongue to stray along the spoon. 'Hey! That's lovely, that is. You'll have to get me some of that there garry marsala . . . what are you laughing at? I can't master Indian in a flaming fortnight! And I'll have one of them thingies, them poppy-dums when you've made some.'

Hamida retreated, head shaking with mirth.

'And as for you,' Rachel glared at Santosh. 'Stop acting like a fairy cake, get the good suit out and go for a proper job.'

'I will try.' The black eyes were solemn now. 'For a woman, you are very strong in personality.'

'Hey, get away with your bother! I might be a woman, but I've got me head screwed on the right way round. Mind, it used to be cross-threaded, but it seems to have sorted itself out since he died.'

'Pardon?'

She paused, deep in thought. 'Mind you, there might be summat in what you say about marriage. If I could have arranged my daughter's, she'd have finished up with something a bit better than what she's got.'

'Precisely.'

'Aye, precisely and exactly. Anyroad, come round Wednesday for a proper English meal, and don't worry, I know your meat rules. But if I can eat your poppy-wotsernames, then you two can get your chops round a Yorkshire pud even if I have to serve it with rice or what have you. And don't take any notice to this lot round here. There's not one of them worth the paper they'd be written on even if they did have birth certificates. And get that front step painted red, it'll look better.'

She left them to get on with their meal. In his own language, Santosh said, 'There is much strength and joy in the little woman.'

And Hamida replied, 'There is also much of her god. We have a fine English friend and I love her.'

'So do I.' He grinned broadly, then, in a fair imitation of Rachel's Boltonese, he said, 'Don't forget her poppy-dum!'

Arthur Bottomley stared at his pretty fiancée. It was still unofficial, because she wouldn't yet allow him to buy her a ring, but he was getting near to pressing her for a fixed date. At least, he had been getting near. But now . . . 'Do they have to come?' he asked hesitantly.

'Course they're coming. They're my friends, best neighbours I ever had. I mean, look at me with that chest cold. Hamida was in and out like I don't know what, fetching me potions and poultices. She cured me, didn't she? If I get married, they'll be there.'

He shook his large head. 'In all that fancy palaver they wear? Whatever will the priest think?'

'He can think what he wants, look at the soft frock he has to put on! I mean, would it be the same if Santosh and Hamida were Jewish? Would you still want them kept away? Or wouldn't it matter because Jews are not particularly visible? Come on, Arthur, I never thought I was considering marrying a man with prejudices.' She folded her tiny hands and looked hard at him. 'They're my friends,' she repeated stubbornly.

'Oh Rachel!' She was under his skin and she knew it! And he knew that she knew it! Lovely red hair streaked with silver that was near to platinum, large grey-green eyes, skin that had defied time . . . 'Have it your own way, then,' he sighed finally.

'I'm not so sure that I shall have it any way, Arthur Bottomley. This has come as a great shock to me.'

'Well, look at it from my point of view. There'll be Chamber of Trade there, happen the odd councillor – I am a man of standing. You don't run the biggest iron-monger's in Bolton without becoming a man of standing.'

'I dare say. And I'm a woman of standing too, and I'm standing my ground. I want Santosh and Hamida there; if she wasn't a Hindu or whatever they call it, I'd ask her to be my matron of honour. Still, that would be pushing Katherine's nose out, wouldn't it?'

'Have you told that daughter of yours yet?'

She sniffed in a significant way. 'No, I haven't, 'cos there's nowt to tell. And there won't be either if you carry on about Indians at my wedding. I am very bigoted against bigots, Arthur. You might not be the right man for me after all.' He was, but she didn't need to let him know that. This piece of small-mindedness was just a tiny flaw; he was generous of spirit in spite of his concern about what people might think. 'Happen you should marry someone nearer your first wife, somebody who does as she's told.'

His head dropped. 'My Emily never did as she was told, Rachel. If she had, she wouldn't have died so young, she'd have looked after herself proper. Aye, and I might have had a son to carry on in the business after me.'

'I'm sorry.'

He smiled at her. 'Nay, I'm the one that's sorry, lass. Poor little devil, you are, marrying a crusty old crab like me. I'm set in me ways, see? And there's all this talk about immigrants . . .' He raised his shoulders in a gesture of despair.

'What talk?'

'Well, they're getting pitches on Bolton market, selling stockings with no feet in them, making a bad name for other traders.'

'Really? Well, you just listen to me, Mr Bottomley. If you want me helping on your market stall, don't you be talking like that. It's not that long since we had a war, and there was a million black marketeers selling bad stuff, every last one of them an Englishman. So put that with your Virginia and smoke it. I will not be told who to like. And stop tarring everybody with the same brush. And while we're on about it, you can see to getting Santosh a proper job, summat away from the mill.'

'But I . . .'

'Never mind "but I". Just do it. Get him set up as a clerk or one of them others as works in an accounting shop, same as an apprentice. He'll not be mithered if they treat him as a starter, there's no false pride in him. I want him out of that factory. Sharpish!'

'Yes, miss. You should have been the teacher, not your daughter.'

'I know that. But education was a luxury in our day and age, as you well know. So, are we having this wedding, or what?'

'We're having it.'

'And Hamida can come in her sari?'

'Course she can, you daft duck.'

'Right, then. Give us a kiss, then put that kettle on, I'm fair clemmed. Then I'll have to go and see our Katherine. I won't do nothing without her blessing, even if she is a mess herself at the moment.'

'OK, OK, keep your shirt on.'

'Don't you worry, I will. I shan't even take me coat off, not till I've got me wedding ring!'

*

Kate opened her back door a fraction 'Who is it?'

'It's me, you daft bat! Let me in, I'm fair witchered.' Rachel dragged her dripping umbrella into the kitchen and stood it in the sink.

'I've been thinking about "witchered",' mused Kate as she cast an eye over her bedraggled mother. 'That and a few other Boltonisms. Witchered probably comes from "wet shod". If you say wet shod quickly, it comes out as witchered.'

'It'll come out as a case of double blinking pneumonia if you don't shape, girl. What's got into you at all?' She glanced round. 'Not a bad kitchen, but hardly up to Beech Gardens' standards, eh? What's up them stairs?'

'Another flat, I'm not allowed up there. This side of the house was servants' quarters – see the bell discs over the door? When the gentry rang for service, a little marker dropped to show the maids which room. Come through, I'll switch the fire on.'

Rachel steamed gently in front of the electric elements while Kate made coffee. It was a lovely room, and Kate had added little touches of her own; pictures, posters, a Paisley shawl draped across a worn chair. On the wall over the bed hung a huge collage made up of photographs of Melanie, some taken recently, others going right back to babyhood.

In the alcove below the window stood a table on which rested a large pad of art paper, ink, pens and brushes. A completed cartoon of Boothroyd in all his colourful glory was propped against a table leg. 'What's that for?' asked Rachel.

'What's what for?'

'All this here paper and stuff.'

Kate shrugged. 'Oh, that, it's KAZ at work, I suppose. KAZ is my cartoon name, the name I draw under. It's Katherine Anne Saunders, only I changed the S to a Z. The duck, or rather the drake, is called Boothroyd. His son puts in an appearance in *Boys' Laughs* from time to time.'

Rachel swallowed a mouthful of hot coffee. 'You've been . . . published?'

'Well . . . yes. I've been doing it for a year or so now.'

'I see.' The short spine straightened in indignation. 'And you never bothered to tell me, of course.'

'Oh, Mother! I didn't want to tell anyone. I mean, who's going to brag about having a strip in a comic? I didn't want to say anything until Boothroyd Senior got off the ground, and that hasn't happened yet. There's a new national starting up soon, the *Mercury*, and the editor's interested in a daily cartoon. Political stuff. No words, or very few words. Just Boothroyd being the government or whoever. I've sent some samples in and I'm waiting . . .'

'Well! Aren't I always the last to find out? Now I'll have to order *Boys' Laughs* every week just to see what my daughter's up to.'

'Mother!'

'What?'

'Shut up!'

'That's very nice, I must say. Here I am, taking a normal interest in your doings and you tell me to shut up.'

'Well.' Kate bowed her head. 'I don't want any interference or advice. I'm streamlining my life.'

'I can see that. No washing machine, no fridge . . .'

'I manage.'

'Aye, I suppose you do. Any problems? Has he found you yet?'

'Not that I've noticed. Anyway, he knows where I work. If there's a problem with Melanie, he can always phone school, or he can contact me through you.'

Rachel placed her cup on a small table and studied her daughter covertly. She seemed slightly ill at ease, as if she had something on her mind. But then she probably did have more than enough to think about. Leaving home was not an easy thing to do, Rachel knew all about that. 'Do you worry about her?'

'Silly question, Mam. Of course I worry about her. You don't give birth to someone without fretting over them forever.'

'Ooh! Listen who's talking! To use my own mother's words, you have had the heart scalded out of me every minute since the day you were born. Not that it finishes there, mind. You still get a lot of worry over grand-children. I hope that blinking Dora isn't turning our Melanie as potty as herself.'

'Mel has a lot of good sense in her head.'

'She's spoiled rotten.'

'I know. But brains will out in the end.' Kate lowered herself into the Paisley-shawled chair. 'Well? What brings you out at half past four on a wet Wednesday? Are you on your way to somewhere?'

'Yes. I'm on my way to here. Anything in for tea?'

'Bacon, eggs, I can rustle up a few chips if I'm pressed.'

'You're pressed – I'm stopping.' As if to emphasize this intention, Rachel slipped off her damp shoes. 'Wet shod, witchered, you're likely right. You always were right when it came to English. Remember all the prizes? And the letters in the Bolton *Evening News*? Happen you should have been one of them reporters, going round mithering folk for their life history. You were like that as a small child, very embarrassing. Always asking questions, you were: "Why has that lady got feathers on her hat?" and "why does that man walk funny, has he got a war wound like Grandad?" Murder, it was, especially when you asked them to their faces. We were on the Daubhill bus once, and this woman was sitting opposite next to the door. You kept staring at her 'cos she had a skenning eye. Then when we came to our stop and we stood up to get off, you told her she was very clever and asked her how she'd learned to look both ways at once.

I could have died on the spot! We flew out of that bus, couldn't get away quick enough. In fact, a few of us got stuck in the doorway fighting to get off, because there wasn't a straight face to be seen. Except for the poor skenning woman, of course.'

'How awful for you.'

'Aye. And, of course, I couldn't tell your . . . couldn't tell anybody about it.'

'You couldn't tell my father.' This came out as statement rather than as question.

Rachel sighed heavily. 'I never told him anything.'

'You used to hide the housekeeping in a tin under the bedroom floorboards.'

The older woman's jaw sagged for a fraction of a second. 'Eh? Well, I'll eat my hat. How did you know about that?'

'There was nothing in that house I didn't know about. Nothing at all.'

'Oh.'

'I knew you were frightened of having any more children even though the doctor had said it wasn't likely.'

'Katherine!'

'And that's why he beat you. And raped you. More than once, too.'

Rachel's hand strayed to her face. 'Dear Lord!'

'Well, you can't live in a two-bedroomed house without knowing these things. Mind, Judith managed to sleep through everything including the Second World War.' Kate paused, her head nodding slightly. 'My father was a fool of a man. He didn't realize what he had in you, or in his children. I hated him, Mam. I was glad when he died, because I didn't like you being alone with him.'

Rachel's hand covered her eyes now as she said, 'We are terrible people, you and I, Katherine. Because – oh Lord in heaven have mercy on my sinful soul – I was glad when he left us too. Mind, if he hadn't died, I did have some ideas. I thought once I was sure that you and Judith were settled . . .'

'We were settled. You could have left him.'

'Aye.' She ran her fingers through her hair. 'But he was ill, wasn't he? It's all very well meaning to go off and leave a man once your children are independent, but I couldn't leave a dog with what he had. It was all through him at the finish. There wasn't one part of him healthy.'

'Rotten to the core, Mam.'

'More ways than one.' This was almost whispered. 'Isn't it funny how close we're getting since you left yon queer feller? It's like having a friend as well as a daughter. So, friend and daughter, I've got something to tell you.'

'All right, spit it out.'

Rachel giggled girlishly. 'It's not summat as will come out easy. Happen a drop of sherry would hasten it up a bit?'

Kate walked to the drinks trolley and Rachel noticed how much more relaxed her daughter's movements sometimes were, how pretty she looked these days. There was a new bloom to her skin, a bright sheen in her hair, lightness in her step. Yes, in spite of some misgivings and worries, Kate was better off.

They sipped their Harvey's slowly until Kate, on the edge of her seat, could bear the suspense no longer. 'Well?' she cried. 'Will it take a scotch and a crowbar?'

'Eh?'

'Don't you come the innocent with me, Mother. These things work both ways, you know. Just as you can always tell when I'm up to something, I know when you've a weight on your mind. Unload! Immediately, if not sooner!'

Rachel hesitated, then drained her glass in one gulp. 'Right,' she gasped. 'I've met a bloke, a nice bloke. He wants to marry me.'

Kate's face was a picture of surprise. 'Really?'

'Yes, really. I'm not that bad a catch, you know. He's

a man of substance too, a dealer in hardware goods. Arthur Bottomley.'

'What? Bottomley's big shop down Derby Street? That one with two fronts? Bottomley's off the market too?'

'That's him. He's a good chap, a bit on the big side, heavy like but ooh, he is good-hearted and pleasant company. A bit of a change from . . . from anybody I've known before. His wife died and they never had a kiddy, so he's lonely.'

Kate pondered for a while. 'Why?'

'Why is he lonely? Because he's stuck on his own all the while.'

'No, I mean why are you getting married?'

Rachel raised her shoulders in a gesture of exasperation. 'Because I like him. Because he asked me, and he's Catholic . . .'

'Are you running, Mam? From a house with no bathroom, from your own loneliness?'

'Eeh, well.' Rachel leaned back in her chair. 'I wouldn't say I'm running, not like some folk I could mention. No. Arthur's like an old friend. Like a glove I might have lost years back, and it turns up still a good fit. We're a matching pair, him and me. He likes crosswords and reading, a nice ride out in the country. And he loves cats. I have to sign a paper about cats.'

'Oh? What paper's that?'

'It might be called a dis-claimer or summat of that sort. Anyroad, it boils down to this: if he dies before I do, I've to sell up and give half to stray cats. He's got nobody to leave it all to anyway. Except a nephew who's usually half-cut, up to his ears in beer every other day. So I agreed to sign.'

Kate tapped the base of her glass against the chair arm. 'All a bit sudden, isn't it?'

'No more sudden than you were, lady.'

'And look where it got me. I don't want you suffering, Mother. In fact, I won't have it.'

'Ah.' Rachel grinned very broadly. 'The shoe's on a different foot now, isn't it? What did I say to you when you brought soft lad home? "You'll regret it," I said. But now you're trying to stop me and you haven't even met Arthur . . .'

'Oh, Mother!'

'It's true enough though, isn't it?'

'I suppose so. Yes, yes, it's true. A mother threatening to get married is as frightening to a daughter as vice versa must be to a mother. I mean, what if he's not good to you? What if you've only seen his best side?'

Rachel giggled. 'Arthur hasn't got a best side. In fact, there's no side at all to Arthur Bottomley. He smokes a pipe, breeds Persian cats and sells paraffin heaters and firewood.'

'And pots and pans and shovels.'

'Exactly. With Arthur, you get what you see, no more and no less.'

Kate thought for a moment. 'Does he drink?'

'He likes a pint, but not every day. Don't be thinking of the past. And he never goes near the greyhound track, never haunts the betting shop. He's a good lad.'

'How old?'

'Fifty-nine. And he'll be here in ten minutes, so get cracking with the eggs and bacon.'

'Oh, Mother!'

'If you say "oh mother" again, Katherine, I'll belt you one. I asked him to come because I know you'll like him. And because I trust you too. There's no side to you either, our Katherine, never was and never will be. If you were the sort that needed advance warning of a visitor, you'd be no daughter of mine.'

Kate's mouth hung open for a second or two. 'But, there's only three eggs,' she declared finally.

'One each. Shut your gob, there's a tram coming. Look at you! Your mouth is hanging as wide as the Mersey tunnel. Stop fretting.'

The younger woman pulled herself as near together as she could manage. "Hang on a minute. I think I've a couple of slices of gammon left. And I can do a bit of cauliflower cheese. Does he like cauliflower? Shall I go out and get some beer? And just look at my hair, Mam. Ooh, I could kill you, really I could.'

'Get away with your bother! We can just as soon send Arthur out for fish and chips, he'll have his car or the van. And there's nowt wrong with your hair – shove a comb through it and spray some of that glue you're so fond of.'

Kate rushed off to the kitchen to search her sparse cupboards. Just as she was debating about whether or no to add tinned tomatoes to her proposed gourmet feast, the back door was pushed open.

'Hello? I've got no hands. Anybody in?' Arthur Bottomley's beaming round face gazed benignly upon her. 'I'm loaded up with curry and chips three times, your mother seems keen on Indian cooking. You're Katherine, I take it?'

'Kate.'

'Oh.' He juggled with his parcels and removed a flat check cap. 'I'm Arthur, the intended. Though what she intends to do about me, well, I really couldn't say. Get some plates, love.'

Rachel stayed where she was, an ear cocked towards the next room.

'They're not warmed,' muttered Kate lamely as she took three plates from a rack above the cooker.

'Never mind, this here stuff has its own central heating. Ever had curry?'

'Yes. Oh, you brought some rice too. I'm fond of boiled rice.'

'Good.'

They stood in awkward silence, each eyeing the other across the table. Kate liked what she saw. He was a tall man, large of build and with a smile that meant something, a smile that didn't reside on his face permanently. His hair was thinning and his cheeks were ruddy, while his clothes, though of good quality, were those of a working man. She smiled. 'Hiya, Arthur.'

'Hiya, Kate.' They shook hands solemnly. 'I'm glad we've met at last, lass. She goes on about you something murderous, nothing bad, just endless chat about "my Katherine". Aye, she thinks a lot of you, does Rachel.'

'And I think a lot of her.'

'Oh, I see. Yes.' He flushed a darker colour and cleared his throat self-consciously. 'Well?'

'Well what?'

'Will I do? Do I come up to muster? Or shall I go out and come in again backwards?'

'No, you stay where you are, Mr Bottomley. I think you'll do very nicely for my mother. What's more, she'll do nicely for you. You're getting first prize with my mam, you know. I wouldn't let her go to any old bidder in the auction room.'

They turned simultaneously to see Rachel standing in the doorway. Kate stared at her mother and remembered the silent, cowed little woman Rachel had been, and her heart felt it would burst with joy, gratitude or some similar emotion as she watched the bustling new-born woman taking over the situation – just as Mother usually did these days. Women, Kate decided in that moment, were capable of changing almost indefinitely, for here stood the evidence, full of life where there had been none, full of love where little had been allowed to show in the past. Oh, Mother! No wonder Kate said those two words so often of late.

Rachel strode into the kitchen. 'What's up with you pair?' she barked with mock severity. 'Good food going cold, no kettle on, and this one . . .' She jerked a thumb towards Kate, 'due for her points. Diabetics has to have their points. Arthur, did you wipe your mucky feet? Has it given over raining? Katherine, take his coat. Has he got your seal of approval, then?'

Without waiting for any replies, Rachel carried on talking while distributing food on plates. 'Arthur Bottomley, you can put a few shelves up in the other room, somewhere for all her books. And see if you can come across a better cooker, this one hisses and spits like a cornered snake. Does everybody want a bit of rice? Is there any poppy-dums? Arthur, you should have got some. Right. Let's sit down and say grace like a proper family . . .'

They sat obediently while Rachel intoned the prayer, 'Bless us, O Lord, and these Thy gifts . . .' Arthur winked at Kate. Kate winked at Arthur. It was going to turn out all right after all.

11

The wedding took place at Saints Peter and Paul on Saturday 15 June 1968. Kate played a dual role. As matron of honour, she walked behind her mother and carried the bride's small posy throughout the service. And, because Rachel's father was dead, Kate gave her mother away. This had been debated for two or three weeks, Rachel uncertain about which of her three brothers she should invite to perform the task.

'See, our Jim's me favourite. He's awkward, is our Jim, funny sense of humour and always good for a laugh. But our John would feel left out. Then there's Joe. Poor Joe's forever been the also-ran on account of being youngest.' So Kate simply stepped in and said that if anyone were to give Rachel away, then it should be one of her own daughters. Judith had been sent an invitation, of course, but she was too busy looking after American statesmen and their translation problems, though she forwarded some pretty cotton sheets, her very best wishes and a lovely wedding card covered in white lace, the sort of card that was not available this side of the Atlantic.

Rachel looked a picture. She wore a beautiful dress and jacket in an odd shade of grey that somehow held a hint of pale violet in its floating folds. Arthur looked scrubbed, polished and pleased, while Kate had chosen a suit in a green that fell just short of emerald.

Outside the church, they lined up for photographs, uncles, aunts and cousins all squashed together in an attempt to get in on the act. Arthur's friends stayed slightly separate, their collective dignity marred only by a local butcher whose demeanour betrayed that he had imbibed rather too freely during the preceding night.

But everyone's thunder was suddenly stolen when a wonderfully elegant white horse trotted round the corner, its rider side-saddled to perfection and clothed in a hired Edwardian riding costume. Rachel and Kate ran forward. 'Melanie!' they screamed together.

The young woman slid down from her mount. Kate caught her breath, a hand to her throat. How long had it been? A month, six weeks? And here was a real lady, slim and elegant, all of five feet and five inches tall, hair scraped back beneath a hat of superb simplicity. 'Mel,' she groaned quietly. 'Dear God, you must have lost a stone.'

'Lost a shoe too.' Melanie pointed to the horse. 'Otherwise, I might have been on time.'

Rachel reached out her arms, tears of happiness threatening to ruin her discreet makeup. 'You came. You came, lass. Does your dad know you're here?'

'Yes. He was quite reasonable about the whole thing, actually. Though Granny Dora isn't pleased, she would have liked to be invited.'

'How's things?' Kate's voice betrayed a tension brought to the surface by the presence of her daughter. 'Everything OK?'

'Fair, thanks. He's off the booze,' replied Melanie with her customary bluntness. 'He's working on ideas to get you back, and he's told everyone you're staying with Granny Rachel because she's ill. Though why he should bother when Phil Carter has blabbed the truth all over Edgeford . . .'

'Has it affected you?' Kate lifted a hand and touched Melanie's arm. 'At school and so on, has it made a big difference?'

The girl shrugged lightly. 'Told them all you'd gone for sanity's sake and they understood – most of them do know Granny Dora. Those who didn't choose to understand, well, I advised them to mind their own business.'

'Good for you.' Rachel pulled her granddaughter to one side. 'Come and meet my . . . well . . . I suppose he's my husband now.'

Kate stood back and watched as Melanie shook hands with everyone. She was a brilliant girl, just simply brilliant! She stood out, yet she blended, could mix with anyone and everyone. All this had been coming, all this out of a spoiled and precocious brat. And Kate was missing it, had walked away from it.

Then a dim light dawned in Kate's brain, its luminosity increasing as she watched the young girl's very adult behaviour. Yes, it had been Kate's exit that had brought Melanie on. The child was now the only grown-up in the house, had therefore been forced to mature quickly. Which event might not have happened so becomingly if Kate had stayed. Because, underneath the facade of submissiveness, Kate's character had always been strong, perhaps too strong for the child to flourish in its shadow. Thus, out of a negative act, had come a positive change for the better. For both mother and daughter.

After the reception meal at the Swan Hotel, where Melanie had arranged feed and temporary stabling for her horse in a garage, the arresting young girl finally managed to corner Rachel and Kate. 'Listen,' she whispered. 'He's going to start on your school, Mum. Expect some phone calls. I think he's having your flat watched already.'

'For what? If he wants a divorce, he can plead desertion.'

'He's angry. You've hurt his pride, and I must say I do feel sorry for him. But he's pathetic at times. He seems to need you.'

'He can't have me.'

'I told him that.'

'Nothing else? You didn't tell him anything else?'

'Of course not.'

Rachel's ears pricked up. 'Why? What else is there to tell?'

Kate turned away as if to look for a drinks waiter. 'Oh Gran,' Melanie went on smoothly. 'We had a talk, Mum and I. It was little things, her reasons for leaving. Dad wouldn't want to realize that Mum had confided in me, would he?'

Kate breathed a heartfelt sigh of relief. There would be much for Melanie to hide in the coming weeks and months, and trust would be essential. She threw a grateful smile in the direction of her daughter. There had been no mention of drawings and cartoons, so would Mel be tough enough to hide the biggest secret, the one Kate didn't even think about most days? No. She could not impose on Melanie any more. After the event, after she had left her job at school, that would be the time for real explanations. But between July and November, Kate would be living in Bangor, in Maureen's caravan. The thought of this long separation from Mel saddened her, but it was an essential part of her plan.

For now, all was well. And she was grateful to Melanie for that.

Santosh Mathur loaded the last of Rachel's belongings on to Arthur's van. 'I am truly sorry that we could not attend your wedding, Mr Bottomley. My wife is not good with her first expected baby. It would not have been pleasant for any of us.'

'That's all right, lad. I'm sorry you couldn't come and all, she sets store by you, does my Rachel.' These last two words were spoken with an air of happy proprietorship. 'Now, just you listen here, my son. There's a few of us down the market could do with a good man. Casual basis at first, like, see how it goes. It's these damned tax laws. I reckon the Revenue owes us more than what we owe them. Have you studied British tax law?'

Santosh nodded. 'Oh yes, both in my country and also here as a refresher course. Really, I am looking for a permanent position in order to find a better house for my family. But a trial would be most agreeable, thank you.'

'That's settled, then.' Arthur spat on his palm and held it out to Santosh. 'Wet thy hand before shaking, eh? There's other rules here, daft ones. This is more of a market man's practice, don't you start doing it anywhere posh.'

Santosh spat and shook. 'You will make of me an Englishman yet.'

'Nay, I won't. You keep your traditions, lad, but learn ours. To live in Rome, you don't have to become a Roman. You just have to stay one step in front.'

'Rome?' Santosh's brow was furrowed.

'It's a saying. It means live here and mind what we do, but carry on being your own selves.'

'This I understand.' The serious face was clouded as he said, 'We shall miss our Rachel, Mr Bottomley.'

'Arthur! Call me Arthur! Nay, you don't need to miss her. Come down our house whenever you've a mind, fetch her some of them blessed poppy-thingies she's forever going on about. And bring the nipper when it's born.' Arthur studied Santosh closely. 'Don't be a stranger, else I'll send the missus up to flay you. I'm not having her saying I separated her from her best neighbours.' He shuffled about awkwardly. 'Er . . . look, I know you're different, man. I'd have to be blind not to see that you're different from me. You're a bloody sight healthier in colour for a kick-off – hey, don't you be telling her that I swear! She nags enough without that. But we're determined, Rachel and I, that you will get your rightful job back. She can't stand to see you coming home mucky from the mill when you should be in a collar and tie job. Right?'

Santosh nodded. 'Right. Everything is in the van now,

Mr . . . Arthur. You must go, or Rachel will be worried. When she is worried, she becomes quite angry.'

Arthur was just thinking how right this man was, when Hamida appeared carrying a large earthenware dish. 'This is a vegetable curry, Rachel's favourite dinner.'

'Ta, lass. Are you feeling mended?'

Hamida's cheeks dimpled as she fought a smile. 'Mended? I was not broken, simply sick.'

Santosh laughed. 'This barrier of language will always be with us, I fear.'

'Never mind,' replied Arthur. 'As long as we can pull a few of the other walls down, eh?'

But as he drove away, Arthur knew in his heart that the barriers would always be there. His country had survived a Roman invasion, a Norman conquest, plus several Germanic attempts to take over. But these brown and black people were visible, noticeable, resented. Hadn't he himself said a few negative things about them, wasn't he as guilty as the next man? Only education would help. Rachel had educated him, but who would take on the task for the rest of the Isles?

Perhaps, in the end, it would come down to inter-marriage. Perhaps everyone would have to get watered down so that folk would eventually look like peas out of a pod. Pity if it came to that, though. She was bonny, was Hamida. Bonny and different, with her liquid black eyes and that spot of colour stuck to her forehead, something to do with caste. Different and proud, she was. It was the pride that must always be remembered.

Rachel discovered that she liked being married. It gave her a sense of status, a new purpose to her life. Arthur was just a big soft lad at heart, happy as long as his belly was full and his slippers were warmed. And 'that side' hadn't turned out too bad either, because Arthur hadn't a lot of energy after ten hours in the shop, so once the first flush was over, most activity of an intimate nature was confined to Saturday nights.

Tuesdays, Thursdays and Saturdays found Rachel in the covered part of Bolton's outdoor market, where she sold all kinds of hardware goods from nine in the morning until six at night. It was here that she discovered her true vocation. With the help of Ernie, who was Arthur's right-hand man, she learned how to sell. It was no use standing there with a gob like cheese at fourpence; disposing of pots and pans meant believing in pots and pans, so she watched the other traders.

Within weeks, the rest of the market, particularly the hardware trade, realized that it had acquired a thorn in its side. This thorn took the form of a short reddish-haired lady with a voice that could have waged war against the Liverpool liners as they wailed their way up the Mersey.

Rachel believed in 'fronting' her stall for much of the time, which meant that she actually mingled with the buying public while Ernie remained behind the counter. Out among the throng, Rachel would yell, 'There's no cracks in my pots, missus! My head is where the cracks are! I'd have to be cracked to be giving stuff away at these prices! Ernie?' And Ernie would rise from his hide behind the stall. 'Show them, Ernie. Show them that cup and saucer for eighteen pence. Where would you get a china cup and saucer for one and six?' she would ask the nearest 'soft touch'. 'Get them genuine imitation Spode ladies out, lad. Show 'em how they can dress up their sideboard or their window sill for . . . no, not ten bob. No, not nine. For seven and six, madam. Seven and six for a beautiful Edwardian lady. All good stuff, this. All direct from Stoke-on-Trent . . .'

Rachel's world was further extended by buying trips. She and Ernie would set off on 'between' days – days when there was no market – and make for Stoke or Lancaster, coming home with large stocks of surplus goods, seconds, slightly damaged items. These were divided more or less equally between shop and stall, and Arthur quickly realized that he had acquired more than a wife; this little woman was an asset in every sense of the word. If he bought too many buckets or paintbrushes, she simply threw them into the van on market day and off-loaded them to people who had set out with no intention of buying buckets or brushes. It was this ability to persuade that made Rachel a star; also her acting talent, which had never found an outlet until now, was unleashed in all its glory for an unsuspecting world to enjoy.

On a Tuesday morning in late July, Rachel was arranging her stall, expertly mixing 'throwaways' with the good stuff, piling dinner services into attractive pyramids and dusting her bits of crystal. It was just on nine o'clock, so only the truly enthusiastic shoppers had arrived at the market. Early buyers usually had lists and a sense of purpose, these were not the types for dalliance. The real business of pot selling would not start until about tennish, when those with a few spare bob would arrive to indulge their hobby of spending money.

Ernie poked his comical face round the corner of the stall. 'Hey, Rachel.'

'What?' She turned to look at him, then doubled over with laughter. He was wearing on his head a particularly capacious and attractive chamber pot, roses round the rim and down the handle. 'Get it off, you big girl's blouse,' she shouted.

He removed the offending item and placed it out of sight. 'If Hylda Baker could hear you, Rachel, she'd likely sue you for breach of copyright. I've some Wedgwood plaques here, what do you want me to do with them?'

'Oh, pin them on your liberty bodice! And stop capering, this is supposed to be a serious business, Ernie Crawshaw.'

'Aye, it used to be and all. It were that bloody serious,

Arthur were thinking of closing it down. Till you arrived. Even Pot Bailey has a job to keep up with you.'

Rachel arranged a group of salt and pepper cruets. 'Nay, don't you be bracketing me with Pot Bailey. He could sell ice-cream to Eskimos, could that lad. I'm coming on. Let's just say I'm coming on . . .'

'Good morning.'

Rachel turned to find Dora Saunders standing back and sweeping a disdainful eye over the stall. 'Hello, Dora.'

'So.' This monosyllable was followed by a loud sniff. 'I wondered what you were up to these days. Now I know. What a pity. At our age, we should be taking our ease, shouldn't we? Still, I suppose it's better than cleaning. Though it must get chilly at times, and the smell from the fishmarket . . .' She waved a hand towards the other side where wet fish was sold. 'How do you do it?'

Rachel bridled, then fixed a grin on her face, a smile that failed to reach her angry eyes. 'Give over, Dora! I'm a good seventeen or eighteen years younger than you. And I do this because it's my own business. My husband has put my name on this stall.'

'How nice.' The tone was heavy with sarcasm.

'Yes, it is nice, very nice to have a husband who believes in me, someone who isn't afraid for me talents to develop.' She straightened her shoulders and puffed out her small chest. 'I'm responsible for all the buying when it comes to china and the like.'

Another sniff. 'Well, of course, I never had to work. My husband made sure I didn't need to go out. A woman's place is in the home.'

'In a home, more likely,' muttered Rachel to herself.

'Pardon?' The voice was edged with sugar now, though the sweet did not quite conceal the sour. 'Did you say something?'

'I said it was a good job you didn't work. After all, you've never been well, have you? And with no

267

qualifications, you would have had to do some kind of manual labour. But this . . .' she waved a hand across her merchandise, 'this is different. It's for myself – and for Arthur too. There's a definite dignity to this kind of work.'

'Is there?' Dora nodded thoughtfully. 'I wouldn't have said so. Not last week when I watched you and heard you screaming like a banshee.'

'Pardon?' Rachel's eyes flashed dangerously. 'What did you just say?'

'Well, it isn't very ladylike, is it? Shouting and bawling about pots and pans, grabbing people by the arm and being familiar. Most unpleasant, I should have thought.'

Rachel turned and shouted over her shoulder. 'Ernie?'

'Hello?'

'Fetch me that thing you had earlier. The one you were wearing on your head.'

Ernie approached with the chamber pot. 'There you are, missus,' screamed Rachel at the top of her voice. 'Shove this under your bed and never mind about being incontinent, it's nothing to be ashamed of, getting took short in the night. Comes to all of us, it does, specially at your age. And look, it's a nice big one, so it should hold plenty.'

A few passers-by stopped to watch this performance. 'And go down to Baxter's for a rubber sheet,' continued the furious Rachel, 'that should save your mattress from getting stained and smelly.'

Dora's face paled to a shade of grey. 'How dare you?' Her teeth were clenched. 'I can see where your daughter got her unpleasant ways from! Yes, indeed I can.'

'My daughter has no unpleasant ways!' Rachel waved the pot as if she intended to crown Dora with it. 'My daughter is the best . . .'

'Oh yes? The best, is she? Well, she walked out on a good husband and a lovely little girl. Broke their hearts, she did.'

'She walked out on you as well, you daft old bat. Who wants to be living with you and all your illnesses, eh? Who wants to live with a woman who still wipes her grown son's bottom for him? You ruined that man's life, positively ruined it. And you made my girl miserable by turning your own lad into a fairy-cake. It's your fault, yours!' She raised the chamber pot even higher, and Ernie crept up behind and snatched it from her threatening hand.

Dora staggered back, a hand pressed against where she imagined her heart to be. 'I am not used to . . . being spoken to in such a way. This is unforgivable.'

Shoe-ey Hughie stepped forward with a chair and pulled Dora into it, then ran off to continue taking slippers from a large box. Shoe-ey had a marked sense of the ridiculous, and was having trouble arranging his features. Dora sat in the centre aisle, legs splayed out any old way, skirt and coat riding up to display knee-length tea-rose directoire knickers. 'I shall tell Geoffrey about this,' she gasped.

'Oh aye? And what do you expect him to do, big soft gumboil that he is? Will he hit me? Or sue me? Nay, I shouldn't rely too closely on your Geoffrey if I were you. Keep giving him his nice chucky-eggs with soldiers, love, build him up a bit if he's going to come to grips with my Arthur. Because my Arthur will have him in a surgical corset before you can eat your next creamcake. Have you thought about dieting, by the way?'

The situation was getting too dangerous for Ernie's liking. He grabbed Rachel's arm none too gently. 'Listen,' he whispered. 'You'll have this stall lost if the bosses come round. Keep away from her. Look, go out to the van for those washleathers. I'll get rid of madam here.'

'That's a good idea.' Rachel's tone was a long way from quiet. 'I'll go and get the stuff. Keep that potty handy; if she's still here when I get back, I shall clock her one with it!'

Dora was looking like a Victorian painting entitled, 'Never Darken My Door Again', all hurt eyes and breathlessness. She was defeated, absolutely routed, so she summoned up what was left of her dwindling strength to make some sort of effort towards peace. 'Rachel,' she muttered.

'What?'

The large lady took a deep shuddering breath. 'I . . . I take it all back. Let us . . . not quarrel. This is . . . not . . . our fight.'

The little stallholder was immediately mollified by such an undignified apology. After all, the poor old lass looked so daft sitting there with her pantaloons and underskirt on show. Rachel shook her head slowly. 'All right. Don't over-fret yourself, Dora. We're all as the good Lord made us, can't help the half of it, I suppose. You stop here while I make you a brew.' She bent to rearrange Dora's coat into a more decorous state. 'You shouldn't fash yourself, woman. Don't get involved, keep clear of the blessed bullets. Them two'll sort their problems out without you and me shoving our noses in the cat litter.'

'Yes.' Dora was almost sobbing by this time. 'I feel so ill, Rachel.'

'I'm not surprised, missus! Take too much on yourself, you do. Credit where credit's due, you've always been a good little worker in the house. But you should have learned when to let go! No use worrying over Geoff the rest of his life . . .'

'He was all I had . . .'

'I know that. I do know that, love.' Any newly-arrived spectator would have taken these two for the best of friends – no-one would believe that they had so recently been at each other's throats. 'But you should have let go. If our Katherine and your Geoff had been left to get on with it, well, who knows? They might have made a go of it.'

'So. It's all my fault? All of it?'

'Did I say that? Did I? Nay, I always knew they weren't best suited. I don't like what's going on, no more than you do, but she's me daughter, lass, I have to side with her right or wrong. Just as you've got to side with her husband. As for Melanie, I reckon that young lady can make her own mind up about things.'

Dora wriggled miserably on the flimsy wooden seat. 'I . . . I miss Kate. There's nobody to talk to, Rachel. There's only the girl next door and she doesn't have Kate's . . . wit. Oh, I know we didn't always get on, but she used to be so kind. The change in her was unbelievably sudden. I am concerned for her mental health. After all, with her history . . .'

Rachel bit her tongue deliberately. 'Tea or coffee? Light that stove, Ernie. And watch out for the boss, he'll only start going on about fire hazards.'

Dora continued, almost to herself, 'My daughter-in-law used to listen to me. Until she turned like that. Why did she turn?'

'Could be her sugar diabetes. I know this much, Dora, there's nowt wrong with my lass's brain. Happen it's more emotional, this upset. Only to be honest, I've not seen our Katherine so contented for donkey's years. It's as if she's got her second wind or summat.'

'Oh. Oh dear. What shall we do, Rachel? I know that you agree with me, marriages are made in heaven. We never had divorce in my family before. Or abortion.'

Rachel's face paled as she staggered back against the stall. 'You what?'

'After Kate had left, Geoffrey told me that she had been forced to have an abortion. The doctors warned her that the baby might be born dead anyway, and that her own life could be at risk. As you say, it's probably the diabetes . . . Rachel? Are you all right?'

'But . . . but she never . . . that's against our religion! Abortion . . . it's not allowed. Not for any reason!'

Dora, for once, managed to lay her tongue on a bit of commonsense. 'You couldn't let her die, could you? Look, I'm sorry, I didn't realize that you hadn't been told. She might have died! You would have lost your daughter, forever!'

'I don't like it.' Rachel's face was still ashen. 'I don't hold with killing unborn kiddies.'

'Neither do I! Neither does my son! And I'm sure Kate had her reservations about the whole matter.'

Rachel bridled. 'Oh, I see. And why are you defending her now, eh? You'd enough to say about her before, why suddenly change your tune and start sticking up for her?'

Dora's chin dropped. 'Because . . . because since she left, I realize how much I liked her.'

'Right. Well, here comes Ernie with our cuppas. I'd best get back to me job, these here pots don't sell themselves. As you noticed last week, I have to get involved.'

Rachel stamped away angrily and left Dora sipping tea from a new china mug.

All that morning and for most of the afternoon, Rachel seethed. The seething helped put a lot of aggression into her selling, and profits that day topped all previous achievements. She didn't even notice Dora's exit, so engrossed was she in off-loading a heap of clay cookware.

That evening, she refused a lift from Arthur and set off on the bus to visit Kate. When the door was opened, Rachel bounced in like a rebounding rubber ball, cheeks ablaze, hands clenched with temper. 'How could you? How could you kill a little innocent child? In the same league as Herod, are you?'

Kate paused momentarily, feet apart, arms akimbo, eyes fixed on the sight of her furious tiny mother. Why couldn't she have been like this when it had really mattered, when Peter Murray had been alive?

'Well?' Rachel's eyes glowed with energy. 'Nowt to say for yourself?'

'Who told you? I thought I was in enough trouble already, didn't think he'd stoop so low . . .'

'What trouble?'

Kate shrugged. 'At school. He keeps mithering on the phone.'

'Mithering? I'll tell you about mithering, girl! That's murder, that is. Cold, calculated murder. It's a mortal sin. Did you talk to a priest or to one of Geoff's ministers before you did it?'

'No.'

'Who the heck did you talk to, then?'

'Nobody. I was supposed to go for counselling, but I didn't bother.'

Rachel threw her handbag across the room. 'Didn't bother? Didn't blessed well bother? How could you? And it might have been a boy. All my life I've wanted a boy in this family. Your dad wanted a boy, he was convinced you'd be a boy . . .'

'How disappointing for him! I suppose that's why I got clouted and left out so often, for being bloody female. And you expect me to breed just because you want a grandson? What sort of a reason would that be?'

Rachel waited a second before speaking again. 'I didn't mean that how it sounded.'

'Well I did!'

'Katherine!'

Kate inhaled slowly. 'Get out, Mother. Go on, out of my house!'

'But . . .'

'If you think I could do that easily, if you believe that I am capable of taking a life without caring . . . Go away!'

'Explain it to me! Just explain why . . .'

'No!' Kate's temper matched her mother's by this time. 'I owe no explanation about that to anyone! It was between myself, the doctors and my . . . my child. I used to lie with my hands on my belly, wondering what to do. And no, I don't even need to tell you that much, do I?

This is none of your business. The whole affair has been hard enough without . . . without . . . Go on! I mean it! I want you out of here!'

'I only need the truth. I only need . . .'

'You'll get what you deserve, and that's nothing. And until I receive a full apology in writing, you and I will have nothing to say to one another.' She picked up the handbag, tossed it into the back yard, then pushed her mother out through the doorway. Breathing heavily, Kate threw herself against the solid door, then twisted the huge key in its lock.

'Katherine! Open this door! At once!'

For answer, Kate moved into the bed-sitting room and turned on the radio, locking the internal door after a few moments' thought. Rachel, in her present mood, might well try to gain access via the main front door.

But she didn't. After a short while, the banging stopped and Kate sank into a heap on the floor by her bed. 'Oh, little one!' She hugged her belly and rocked back and forth. 'If they only knew! If they only knew what I've been through! Decisions . . . decisions . . .'

That night, Kate's dreams were terrible. A tiny dead boy was delivered into her hands, perfect but blood-streaked from the womb. 'Michael? Look at me, be alive! For God's sake, be alive!' She sat bolt upright in her sweat-soaked sheets. 'Jesus,' she moaned. Then, as she turned to face the wall, she cried out in a small voice, 'Oh, Mother!' before falling into another fitful sleep.

'I'm not apologizing to her!' Rachel's face was pink with righteous indignation. 'She should never have spoken to me like that, I am her mother when all's said and done. I was only sticking out for what I believe in, only speaking me mind . . .'

'So was she.' Arthur poked the fire and sucked loudly on his dead pipe. 'She's near thirty-five years old now, Rachel. You can't be throwing your weight about at this

274

stage in her life. Cast your mind back to Dora Saunders and what you've always thought of her . . .'

Rachel's spine was suddenly as straight as a ramrod. 'Eh? Are you comparing me to that great big soft powder puff? I'm nowt like her, nowt at all . . .'

He fingered his tobacco pouch nervously. 'She's interfered with that marriage all the time, dripping like water on stone. You're doing it now, just the once, but in a very big way. Stop shoving your nose in.'

'Arthur!'

'Well, you're forever going on about how Kate's marriage might have lasted without Dora and her messing. Just you take a look at yourself, love. You can't walk up to a young woman and tell her how to run her own life. It's not right. And I think you should apologize, else you will have lost your daughter.'

'I am not apologizing. I can't see that I've done owt wrong. I only said . . .'

'You only said that she ought to have risked her life so that you might have a grandson.'

'I never did. I never said no such thing, Arthur Bottomley. I just know what she's done is a sin. Our church believes in baby before mother, that's all. You're supposed to take your chances.'

'And you'd have let your girl die?'

She could not meet his penetrating gaze. 'Well, I would have hoped . . . with all the medical things that they've got now . . .'

He shook his head gravely. 'Could you have stood by and watched her struggling through a pregnancy that might have killed her? And the kiddy too? There's times when I'm not so sure of my faith, Rachel, and this is one of them times. If Kate were my daughter – and I wish she were – I'd give an arm and a leg to make sure she survived come what may.' He picked up a large Persian grey from the hearthrug. 'You'll get sunburnt there,' he said to the huge creature.

'She wasn't sure she'd die,' went on Rachel. 'And she'd talked about it to nobody, nobody at all.'

'Ah.' Arthur cleared his throat. 'Now we're getting down to it, right to the crux of the matter, as they say. What you can't stomach is the fact that the girl did something without telling you first. Even when she left home, she reported to base before making her move. So what's the difference between you and Dora Saunders, eh?'

'I never haunted them day and night, did I? I never told her how to do her washing, or that she was ironing his shirts all wrong. I didn't fall in the door every other day with some incurable illness. There's a mile of difference between me and Dotty Dora!'

'Is there?'

'Yes!' At last, she looked him in the face. 'Yes, there is.'

He lit his pipe slowly. 'Well, all I can say, Rachel, is that I've watched that poor girl looking at you. Worships you, she does . . .'

'Not as I've noticed. Specially today.'

'Shut up, Rachel! For once, bloody shut up and listen to somebody else for a change. At a guess, I'd say that Kate has spent her life looking for love and not finding it. From the little she's said, I gather that her father didn't love her, and I don't think she was so sure about you either. If you'd loved her, you would have protected her from him – that's how a child thinks. Now, them childhood feelings don't go. You can argue with yourself, tell yourself you're being stupid, but a kiddy that grows up feeling unloved becomes a grown-up what can't cope.'

'She can cope! Course she can cope!'

He nodded. 'Aye, happen she can on the surface. But what about all them years she put up with Geoff and his mother, never a word out of her, never a try to defend herself. That was because she didn't believe in herself, couldn't make no decisions. Well, happen her first big decision was not having the baby, and her second was getting away from them two leeches. This is just the beginning of who Kate is, she's never been herself before.'

'Rubbish!'

'Just you leave her alone, Rachel.'

'She's my daughter, not yours. Who are you to tell me what to do with her? And I shall leave her alone, never fear. My daughter's a murderer, and I'm not apologizing to no murderer. So there!'

He looked up to the ceiling as if seeking divine guidance. 'You'll regret this, lass. This will be with you all your life.' He sighed deeply. 'Well, as you said, it's nowt to do with me, none of my affair. So,' he stared hard at his wife, 'on your head be it. Aye, on your head and not on mine, thank God!'

12

The man in the white coat carried on hitting her. She wanted to sit up in the bed, needed to scream out, 'I'm not dead, I'm still here,' but he continued with the heart massage. And she didn't even feel detached or dizzy, so she couldn't understand why this great fight to save her life was going on.

How long had she been here? Years and years. And years. But here, in this extremely bright white room – how long? Was that her heart, beep, beep, hiccup and beep? Or was the other noise – that long drawn-out sound – was this the echo of a heart not beating at all? *I am alive! Look at me, you idiots, I am alive!*

'She's back, Sister. What's the BP?'

'Ninety over forty and rising.'

'Good. Let's hope she's strong enough for more treatment. We'll need to get her dialysed tomorrow if these kidneys don't pick themselves up of their own accord.'

Kate stared up at him. He had a silly moustache with some food stuck in it. She wanted to tell him about the food, only her mouth was on strike. *Am I paralysed? Did the operation turn out a mess? No! There is nothing wrong with my kidneys. I have been monitored weekly for centuries now. Prodded and poked and weighed and measured. Analysed, tested, catalogued, categorized, filed, disposed of! There is nothing wrong with my kidneys, you stupid ill-washed man.*

The sister bent over the bed. 'I wonder if she can hear us?'

Of course I can hear you. I can hear and see like everyone else. Your moustache is nearly as thick as his, though at

278

least you don't have your dinner stuck to it. What is the matter with this place? Is this an emergency room or a bloody pantomime?

The doctor coughed thickly and Kate wondered what she was going to catch in here. After joining the private medical scheme, too, posh Chorley New Road nursing home with operating facilities and television in every room. Bloody hospitals. Breeding grounds for germs, they were . . . If a person insisted on being ill, then he or she would be better staying away from hospitals altogether.

Another day. Another room. The whizzing and whirring of machinery.

They are cleaning my blood. My blood is being taken out of my body to be swished through a machine with knobs and dials on. There's probably bleach in there, some sort of sterilizing fluid. I shall finish up with Domestos in my veins. This will kill ninety-nine per cent of all household germs. What about the other one per cent? Should I worry about it? Dear God, let me not be a candidate for dialysis now!

She turned her head. No. There was just the one clear tube in her arm. Whatever the noise was, it was not connected with or to her. Above her head a saline drip. Drip-drop-dripping, drip-drop-dropping . . .

Hypnosis. Now they are trying to mesmerize me into submission. I shall fight the good fight. Why is my head such a mess, why can't I think in straight lines?

How many days now? They were talking again. Talking about why she could only think round corners. 'She's had so much to cope with . . . mumble, mumble.' Then later, 'The kidneys were clearing none of it, antibiotics . . . anaesthetic . . . mumble, mumble.' She wanted to scream at them, to tell them to speak up, but her mouth was dry. 'There will have been hallucinations, I should think. And, of course, she's diabetic.'

Yes. I am a freak. Bring in the spectators, eh? On with the show, the show must go on. It's pantomime time, folks!

279

Where's the magician? Perhaps if I try hard, I might become invisible. Though I must stay. There is a reason for staying. It is down a corridor somewhere. Boothroyd is going in the national press. Such a long way home . . .

'She's had only one visitor.' The nurse sounded sad.

Doctor Food-In-The-Moustache fiddled with his tie. He was something of a fiddler, always messing about with thermometers and gauges. There was one in every class at school. Two, sometimes. She didn't go to school any more, though. There had been a caravan, a cold caravan with just a paraffin heater. How long ago? He coughed again.

'Mrs Carter's been every day.'

Good old Mo! Why hadn't she been awake for Maureen?

'And it would seem that Mrs C's been instructed by this one not to tell us anything. It looks as if our Katie wants to be alone. Should have been a bloody film star!' Kate promised herself that she would get him later. Where it hurt, possibly in the cheque book.

'Well, she does have her rights, Doctor. If she doesn't want her family and friends fussing round the bed . . .'

'Hmm.' Phlegm rattled ominously yet again. Kate decided that he was a candidate for double pneumonia. 'Shame, though. She looks so lost and lonely.'

'Getting sentimental in your old age, Doc?'

'The girl's fighting for her life. Any worse, and she'll have to go to the district hospital. And I don't want to move her . . .'

'I . . . will . . . not . . . be moved,' managed Kate at last.

She caught them smiling as she slipped back into the endless dream.

Standing in Miss Ashe's office. 'These phone calls from your husband really must stop.'

'It's OK, I've got an injunction. If he phones me here or comes near my flat, he will be fined or put in prison.'

'But why are you resigning, Mrs Saunders? Are you going into another post?'

'No. I'm finishing with teaching.'

'Is it because of the phone calls? And how will you live?'

'It's nothing to do with phone calls. And I'll manage, Miss Ashe. There's more to life than teaching. A lot more.'

She knew it was a dream, because she was whisked now from Head Teacher's office to a strange place that was half caravan, half her flat on Chorley New Road. Maureen. Lipstick smudged across her two front teeth, hair escaping from a hurriedly donned scarf, eyes wide with shock and disbelief. 'You have to let me tell them! I can't go on saying you've moved to Manchester. Let me tell your mother, at least! Please let me send for Rachel, please? I'm taking you to the nursing home. Let me fetch your mother.'

'No.' The wind rattled a blind on the caravan window, yet Kate could reach out and touch the Paisley shawl on the old armchair by the big fireplace in her own living room.

Maureen was bouncing around in an agitated fashion. The caravan rocked. 'But you look so ill. What if you go into a coma all by yourself? Someone should know how ill you are.'

'The doctors know. Diabetes can be real fun, you should try it some time. I shall be in hospital soon. In and out, in and out . . .'

'Then Geoff must be informed.' Waves crashed against rocks, but that was silly, there were no waves on Chorley New Road . . . 'You must not carry on with this stupidity, Kate. Why? It's verging on lunacy! I'm taking you to hospital, then I'm getting Geoff . . .'

'Tell him, Maureen, and our friendship will be over.'

'BUT WHAT IF YOU DIE?'

Kate stirred in the hard hospital bed. *I am here. I am dying. But no, I shall not allow myself to die. There is a plan, and I have so much to live for now. There's . . . there's down the corridor and there's Boothroyd. I am KAZ and Boothroyd is mine. They are doing an offer of tea towels with Boothroyd on them. Did I do that picture? Yes. In the caravan. Yes, I did the cartoon for the tea towel. And seven weeks' advance work. I have to get out of here to keep my spot in the paper. The editor knows I'm here. He promised not to send flowers. Perhaps I am coming back now. Perhaps I can go down the corridor . . .*

'Good morning, Katie.'

Bloody nurses. Always so cheerful, they are. And so flaming false.

'I've brought your breakfast. The insulin and sugar levels are balanced and your kidneys have picked up fine. Isn't it wonderful? There we are now, just a wee bit of porridge . . .' Eat it up. Come on, mouth, open. There, she has gone. Nursie with her plastic smile is no longer with me.

Damn these dreams! *Where is he? Where is my son? Why have you taken him away from me? You had no right. Tell me where he is!*

Gone. Down the toilet with your hopes.

No! He is in Boothroyd Junior! He can't be in the toilet and in Junior! Look at Boys' Laughs! Junior is my son. He's not just a duck, he's my . . . All those months of hiding. Maureen bringing the shopping, the two Misses shooing Geoff from the door, Melanie on the phone, 'But when can I see you, Mum?' For what? Which is true? How do I find the truth?

A handsome stranger sitting on the edge of the bed, beautiful blue eyes and wavy brown hair. Sister will not be pleased; visitors must not sit on the edges of beds . . .

'Mrs Saunders. Remember me?'

Talk to him, you fool. Stop sulking. 'Yes. Just about. My faculties are not as sharp as they might be.' She remembered him now. Yes, she definitely remembered him.

He smiled tentatively. 'I teach at Lark Lane. You had my sister in your class until she . . .'

'Until she died.' Leukaemia. Pretty girl, dark hair and

impossible violet eyes. 'You were her guardian, weren't you?'

He nodded. 'Our parents were killed when Rosie was very small. I brought her up. You were so kind to her, Mrs Saunders. She loved you.'

Yes, she loved me. There were cards on a string above the bed. She had done her homework. Come back, Kate. Don't go into the nightmare again. Look at him – speak to him!

She raised her head. 'We all loved Rosie.' She stared at him. Was he trustworthy? He looked trustworthy. Strong face, broad shoulders, kind eyes. 'Don't tell anyone I'm here, will you? I'm supposed to have emigrated.'

'Where to?'

She smiled for the first time in weeks. 'Your guess is as good as mine. Timbuctoo. Or three, if you like. How did you find me?'

He hesitated a fraction. 'My . . . friend is a porter here.' Then, in stronger tone, 'I'm homosexual.'

'Are you? I'm Sagittarius.'

He laughed heartily. 'That has to be one of the most original reactions I ever had! How long have you been in here?'

'Most of my life. Have we had Christmas?'

'Few weeks to go yet. Can I do anything for you?'

Kate stared up at him. This was a crazy moment, or was it the beginning of a miracle, the start of her recovery, a first step towards life? Because she felt so close to him, as if the two of them had been joined for years, joined at the hip, inseparable, paired, twinned. Yes, this was crazy.

He was sad. In spite of all the surface frivolity, she could have almost reached out and touched the grief. It was raw and sore, just beneath the surface, just barely covered by a thin parchment of normality. Their eyes locked for several moments, as if each were reading the other's mind and soul.

They were coupled, the two of them, attached one to

the other by and through Rosie. Kate's thoughts were still somewhat dislocated, yet she recalled that awful long night so clearly. They had been strangers, yet because of his sister, they were now almost friends. No, more than friends. Perhaps people who sat together during a death were always united thereafter?

But she knew him. She knew him as well as she would ever know anyone. To this man she would and could talk; in this man she knew she might confide. It was madness, the whole thing was odd. She would never be able to explain it, yet her trust in him was suddenly and blindingly implicit.

'Can I do anything for you?' he repeated quietly.

She thought about this. 'Yes,' she said at last. 'You can go and see my son. He's in an incubator somewhere miles away. I wouldn't know him myself, but the name will be on the cot. He's Michael. Michael John Saunders. Only don't tell anyone about him because I had him aborted months ago.'

'Did you? How strange.'

Her grin widened. 'I had to have an abortion because of my diabetes. But I chickened out at the last minute and spent the night in a Liverpool hotel.'

The visitor chuckled. 'Alone?'

'No. I shared my bed with a bottle of champagne. It altered my perspective and buggered the insulin good and proper.' There! She was talking sensibly, coherently, even wittily!

His eyes widened. 'But how did you conceal the . . . ?' Words failed him as he marvelled at what she had done. Whatever her reasons, the task must have been a monumental one.

As if a dam had suddenly burst, words poured from a mouth that had been sealed for far too long. 'At first, I thought I might confide in my mother. But we had a big row about that abortion I pretended to have, so that left just Maureen. I quit school before the bulge became too obvious, told Maureen Carter the truth, and after that she looked after me. I lived in a caravan till Mo found me almost in a coma. And here I am, here I've been ever since. The only problem was my poor daughter. I still don't know what to do about her.'

He took hold of her hand and held it gently. 'What's . . . er . . . what's the basic problem? If you don't mind my asking?'

She shrugged and sighed heavily. 'I married the wrong man and he had the wrong mother. They were a bad influence on my first child, and I wasn't letting them sink their claws into a second.'

'They're sure to find out, though. Especially if you hang around in Bolton. Everything gets dug up in the end, which is why I'm moving jobs.'

'Because of your homosexuality?'

His eyes were clouded as he gripped her hand more tightly. 'Yes. There have been a few remarks, so I'm off to Liverpool. Not yet, though. And when Mark said there was a Mrs Kate Saunders in here, I simply had to come and see you. After all you did for Rosie . . .'

She swallowed. 'That was awful. Her dying like that.'

'Yes. Yes, it was. I still miss her. And I can't throw her clothes and dolls away. When I'm in a maudlin mood, I sit in her room and cry till Mark comes and finds me.'

'I'm sorry.' Although she didn't enjoy his misery, it helped somehow, made her own recent mess seem trivial in comparison. 'If I could bring her back for you . . . When are you going to Liverpool?'

'In a few months. After Easter.'

'And Mark?'

'He'll be a weekend visitor. I'm buying a semi-detached in Crosby.'

'The posh end.'

'That's right. Debtors' retreat, all fur coats and no knickers.' He stared at her for a long time. 'I like you. I actually do like a lot of women, you know. As friends.

285

You're . . . you're special. Why don't you come with me? Away from all the flak?'

'What?' Her breath was temporarily taken. 'But . . . sorry. I do wear knickers, might not fit in in Crosby. And you shouldn't make these offers on the spur of the moment, Mr Collins.'

'Steve.'

'I've got a flat for now, and I'll find somewhere safer as soon as the baby's strong. Don't worry your head over me.'

'What about money?'

'I've a bit saved. And I'll do some tutoring on a private basis. Then there's . . . well . . . I draw, for comics and newspapers. We'll manage. Go and see my baby.'

He turned and dragged a wheelchair across the ward. 'Good job you're in your own room,' he muttered furtively. 'Get out of bed.'

Her jaw dropped. 'I tend to fall. It was a Caesarian and I think it upset the old kidneys somewhat.'

'Stop being so bloody soft! You want to see your lad, don't you?'

'Of course I do.'

'Then shift yourself.' He dragged her from the bed, lifting her in strong arms and dumping her without ceremony into the chair. 'OK?'

She nodded. 'A bit dizzy. Still, at least I've had a conversation. This is the first time since the op that I've spoken sensibly, I think. You are a good influence on me, Mr Steve Collins.'

They crept silently down the corridor to the baby unit, only to be accosted at the door by Kate's favourite doctor, the one with the moustache.

'No food in it this time,' she commented.

'Pardon?'

'Your moustache. There's no soup in it. One day when you stood over me and talked as if I were already a corpse, you had tomato in your facial hair.'

He smiled. 'You're better. Get back to bed.'

Kate folded her arms. 'Shan't. Show me my son. Is he bigger now? Will he live?'

'Yes to both. But you can't go in without a mask.'

Kate glanced at Steve. 'Tonto,' she said fiercely. 'Bring Lone Ranger's mask.'

'Aye aye, Kemo whatever. I'm not too hot on Apache.'

They donned their masks. 'Hi-ho Silver, away,' shouted Kate as they approached the door of the baby unit.

'Shush,' ordered the doctor. 'There are sick babies in there. Is this Mr Saunders, by the way?'

Steve glanced down at the wheelchair. 'Yes,' he pronounced convincingly. 'We just had a bedside reunion, it was the most moving moment of my life.'

'Fool,' spat Kate beneath her breath.

The baby was beautiful, four pounds of humanity in a clear plastic case. He lay on his stomach, fists clenched into tight knots, a funny little bonnet on his head. A feed-tube, which ran to a stopper outside the crib, was fastened to the side of his face with paper tape.

'They're feeding him through his nose,' whispered Kate. 'Isn't he gorgeous? I want to take him home.'

'You wanted to take Rosie home, remember?'

Kate nodded. 'She needed a mother's love. So does Michael and so does my daughter. But you did well for Rosie, Steve. Better than I've done for Melanie. Rosie was well adjusted for a kid without parents.'

'Thanks.' He peered closely at the tiny infant. 'Handsome young devil. How the hell are you going to hide him?'

'I don't know. They make a lot of noise, do babies. As you say, I may have to come clean.'

'Does no-one suspect?'

'Only Maureen Carter, and she can be trusted. I don't want Geoff to have him, Steve!' Her tone was suddenly harsh. 'I don't want him or Dotty Dora getting hold of my boy. Can you imagine what they'd turn him into? Another like Geoff, another who'll need wet-nursing forever. I can't allow that.'

Steve whistled beneath his breath. 'Then you must come to Crosby with me. First though, you will have to explain yourself, to your daughter, at least. I mean, you can't just bugger off without a word, can you?'

'No. And I'm not so sure I'll come with you . . .'

'Where else would you go? How much money do you have?'

'How much is the house?'

'Three thousand.'

She studied him for a long moment. 'Right. I'll put a thousand down, can you match that?' He nodded. 'Then I'll take a mortgage for five hundred and you can do the same. I'll get a minder and teach part-time somewhere. This is crazy, isn't it?'

He grinned broadly. 'Naw. You'll be safe with me, flower. And I'm good with kids, so's Mark. We'll have to do it legal and proper, just in case it doesn't work out. Right?'

'Right.'

They gazed at the baby for a long time. 'That's the only thing I regret,' he said finally, 'that I'll never have a child.'

Kate glanced at her new-found friend. 'That's all right,' she said solemnly. 'You can borrow mine, old girl.' Then they both got thrown out for laughing.

Kate had spent four whole days cleaning up. There were only two rooms, but she was weak in body, so it was sheer determination that pushed her along with mops and wet cloths and dry cloths and polish. Anybody would think she was expecting Queen Elizabeth herself to drop in, she thought as she poked between fireplace tiles with a matchstick wrapped in cotton wool. This was for her child. No, it was for her children. One lay in hospital; the other was about to visit this very afternoon.

She sank into the Paisley-shawled chair. Melanie. Yes, this was make or break time. Either Melanie would keep the secret, or she would run home and tell Daddy and Dotty. Oh Lord! Her life would not be her own if the child decided on the latter course. And if Geoff were to find out that Kate intended to take the baby to live in a house with a member of a persecuted minority . . . Still. She couldn't hide a brother from Mel, wouldn't hide him from her. But what an enormous weight this was, a terrible burden for such a young back.

Yet Kate remained quietly confident. There was something about Mel, something that had only just begun to come out. She was a strong kid. Whatever Geoff and Dora had done in their spoiling, they had not taken away the strength.

She got up and straightened first the fire-brasses, then the photographs on the mantelpiece. Her favourite sat right in the middle, Melanie on horseback, her head held high beneath the lovely Edwardian hat. That had been taken on Mother's wedding day. Mother. Oh, Mother! What would she say if she knew . . . ?

To stop herself thinking about Rachel, Kate went through to the gleaming kitchen, put away her cleaning materials, washed her hands, then got on with her sandwich making. She had not seen Melanie for four months. The bulge had started getting too big, so she had taken herself off to Maureen's caravan. To protect the unborn, she had neglected her daughter ruthlessly. Would salmon sandwiches and a home-made cake really make up for that?

The table looked lovely. A dark red cloth with matching napkins, china cups, a gift from Arthur – no, she must not think about Rachel and Arthur – and a pretty posy of dried flowers as centrepiece. Next to Mel's plate was a beautifully wrapped gift, two pretty nightdresses covered in pale blue tissue. It was time. Any minute now. She looked at her watch. Panic peeped over the edge of sanity and she took some deep breaths, trying to empty her mind of all negative thought. It had to be done, must be done properly. If it failed, then she would have to fight them all.

A knock at the back door. Kate composed herself, opened the door and smiled. 'Come in.' She embraced her daughter. 'You're alone? No-one followed you?'

'They imagine I'm at school doing choir practice.' Melanie placed her bag on the dresser, a cursory eye sweeping over the prepared feast. 'I'm on a diet.'

'That's OK, you don't have to eat it.'

The girl swivelled on her heel and faced Kate. 'Oh, Mother! Why all the secrecy? Dad and the grans think you've moved. Where have you been? It's months since I saw you.'

'Sit down, Mel.'

Melanie placed herself in one of the straight-backed chairs while Kate marvelled at all this new poise and grace. 'You'd improved at the wedding, but now! Oh my goodness! What a beauty you are going to be.'

A loud sniff from the table was followed by, 'No need to flannel, Mum. Just tell me what this is all about. Months I've been trying to see you, months on end. Why? Why did you turn your back on me? Why did you tell the other people in this house to say you were no longer here?'

Kate shuffled from foot to foot. It was almost as if their situations had been reversed – she was the child, she was answerable to this young woman. 'I wasn't here. And I had a secret, something to hide.'

'Boothroyd. It's OK, everyone knows about that. Dad recognized your work in the paper.'

'More than Boothroyd.' Kate swallowed nervously. 'Look at me, Mel. You've . . . well . . . you've got a little brother. Michael John, he's called.'

'Oh.' There was shock behind the monosyllable. 'Where . . . where is he?'

'In hospital.'

'Oh.' Melanie chewed her lip. 'What's wrong with him?'

'He had to arrive on a prescribed date, so he was Caesarian and premature. Melanie! Look at me, love. Don't be jealous, please?'

'I'm . . . not jealous. Were you ill?'

Kate nodded. 'Very. And I didn't want you worried. I have diabetes. This means it is difficult for me to give birth to live children.'

Tissue paper rustled as Mel opened her gift and stared soundlessly at layers of pink and white chiffon. 'Is it . . . Dad's?' she managed at last.

'Of course it is.'

'Then why aren't you at home with us?' There was energy in the tone now. 'A baby needs a proper home, not just a bedsit with kitchen.'

This was going to be the difficult bit. 'I'm not staying here. Things are happening. There's talk of Boothroyd greetings cards and Boothroyd Junior plates and stuff for children. I shall be moving soon. And . . .' She inhaled deeply. 'And I don't want your father or Dora to have Michael.'

The paper crackled again as Melanie closed her parcel. 'I see. He's precious, then? It's OK for them to have me, but you won't let them near your son.'

'Stop that! Stop it right now! You can leave home and come to live with me and Michael whenever you wish.'

'I'm not living here.'

'Nor am I. I'm moving to Liverpool soon. And I've made enquiries; if you come up to scratch, they'll find a place for you at Merchant Taylors'. That's one of the best schools in England.'

'No.' The blonde head shook slowly. 'I can't leave him. He'd have nothing without me. And I think you'd better come home too, especially if you're diabetic. What if you get ill?'

Kate paused. 'I . . . won't be alone. I'm going with a friend.'

'A man?'

'Yes. But it's not like that. He's . . . he's not interested in women. He is not a boyfriend, Mel. Just a very good and caring person. We're buying a house.'

The young brow was deeply furrowed. 'All sorted out, then.' The chair scraped back a fraction. 'Dad will have to be told, of course . . .'

'No!'

Melanie half-smiled. 'Be your age, Mother. A man can't have a son without being told. He'll want to see him . . . buy him things . . .'

Kate watched while Melanie digested the idea of becoming second best and second class.

'And the two grannies ought to know, too. This quarrel with Granny Rachel has gone on for long enough, Mum.'

'Ah, yes. But what about Granny Dora?'

'What about her?'

'Melanie, she ruined your father. From birth he was mollycoddled and given in to, I don't want that for Michael. If you tell these people about the baby, then my life will not be worth living. Granny Rachel would be almost as bad – she's always wanted a boy in the family. Don't you see? It's not because I think Michael's special, that's not the reason for wanting to keep him to myself. It's because Michael is ordinary and I don't want him on a pedestal.' She paused. 'Your nose would be right out of joint, Mel.'

The girl whistled softly. 'That's not the problem. Anyway, I'm fourteen now, I've got my own interests.'

'Boyfriends?'

Melanie blushed. 'A few. Nothing serious.'

'I should hope not. Not yet, anyway.'

'Oh, Mother!' The exasperation was plain.

'What?'

'Well, how can I keep a thing this size to myself?'

'He's no size, he's only four and a half pounds . . .'

'You know what I mean. Don't start being silly. I can't carry on as if nothing's happened.'

Kate crossed the room and sat down opposite her daughter. 'Would you rather I had just disappeared without telling you about Michael? Should I have gone to Crosby and never a word to you?'

'No.'

'Then my future and that of your brother is in your keeping. I know it's a heavy burden for a girl your age, but if I didn't think your shoulders were broad enough, then I would not have piled it on to your back. Bear with me, sweetheart. There is a reason for what I am doing, believe me. I am sane at last, whole at last. Will you help me? Will you?'

Melanie sighed. 'You know I will. When can I see this brother of mine?'

'Now. Right away. He's only round the corner, and I've written a note so that you can identify yourself as his sister.'

'I see. All prepared, aren't you? What happened to my scatterbrained mother?' She waited a few moments, her eyes glued to Kate's face. 'Is he pretty?'

'All Caesarians are pretty. They don't get squashed on the way out.'

'Prettier than . . . than I was?'

Kate grinned. Here came the child again. 'No. You were utterly gorgeous. Look at all the pictures on my walls.'

The girl swallowed a little sob. 'I wish you would come home. Come home and live like a proper family.'

'I don't belong with a proper family.'

'But . . . but Michael does.'

Kate nodded wisely. 'Exactly what your father would say. In court, Mel. He will try to take my child away

293

from me. A baby needs its mother. You had me right up to this year, now it's Michael's turn.'

'OK.' The voice was very small and hurt. 'I'll go and see him, then.' She rose from the chair, clutching the gift of nightdresses to her chest as if it were something really special. 'I still think you're wrong, Mum.'

'I'm glad you have opinions, Mel. But let me stick to my beliefs. All right?'

They hugged one another tightly, then Kate stood at the door and watched the young back disappearing through the gateway. 'Please, Mel,' she whispered between gritted teeth. 'Don't let me down. For God's sake, don't let me down!'

The baby needed fresh air. All babies needed fresh air, and the back yard just wasn't big enough. Apart from which, Kate felt she had imposed enough on the two loyal Misses and on the upstairs tenants. Michael didn't often cry, but when he did, it was with feeling, volume and enthusiasm. He got plenty of outings at the weekends, when Steve and Mark would drive everyone out to the moors in their car, but weekdays were becoming a gigantic problem.

Then there was herself to consider. She wasn't getting enough sleep, food or exercise. The lack of sleep was Michael's fault, while food was no longer attractive. But the absence of exercise was due solely to her fear of discovery. Perhaps if she got some good walking in, she might enjoy her food. After all, daily points had to be balanced; a coma could well be achieved by too few calories measured against her insulin dose.

Kate was tense. Part of this anxiety was attributable to her concern for others in the building, particularly for the poor couple who lived up the servants' stairs. They had not complained, but they were certainly missing out on their full eight hours each night. Most of her tension, though, was caused by new motherhood and her very mixed feelings towards her young charge. Life was a constant round of drudgery; feed him, clean him, clean up after him; soak the nappies, wash the nappies, boil, hang out to drip; empty the bottle, wash the bottles sterilize, fill up again; scrub the teats, salt the teats, soak them in Milton.

She became a zombie after a while; the flat was her tomb and she walked around it like the living dead. A secondhand television was acquired by Steve, and she gazed upon this endlessly, sitting with the baby over her shoulder and staring at the picture until it shrivelled into a tiny dot at the end of each transmission. She knew nothing of what she had 'watched'. Things were rapidly approaching the stage where she might really need a Dr Coakley to look into what was left of her mind.

The flat was turning into a mess. There was a permanent look to the wooden airing maiden that surrounded the fireplace. Two lidded buckets in the kitchen were constantly filled by soiled linen and nappy cleanser. The baby's cot took up a lot of spare space by her bed, while his pram sat where Boothroyd had used to live, in the alcove by the window. Her work now covered the dining table in the kitchen, and although she had managed not to fall behind, she had little in hand for newspaper and comic strip.

Michael was dominating her life, taking away energy, personality, drive, ambition. She wanted nothing for herself, because she was no longer a person. Kate Saunders had been reduced to a mere appendage of this newborn man. How easy it was. Perhaps this would go on for years, perhaps this was how it had started with Dora.

Sometimes, Kate couldn't quite manage to like her son. He had Geoff's eyes for a start, very dark and oval in shape. He screamed and was always hungry, yet he never finished a feed properly. She did not know how to stop the screaming, especially that six o'clock knees-up-to-the-chest-I've-got-colic yelling. It was a six o'clock episode that finally made her snap. Although it was a winter evening, and in spite of all the warnings about premature babies and fog, she bundled him into a dozen layers, shoved him in the pram, then stalked out of the house.

After that, their relationship improved no end. She was up at five every morning, and by six-thirty, come rain, hail or snow, she and Michael were out on the road. By eight, both would be exhausted and hungry, so she would eat her points of toast and diabetic jam while he guzzled his bottle. When the washing was done, they shared the bed and slept until lunchtime. He thrived on this strange treatment. Once or twice, when the crying was really bad, she even pushed him out in the dead of night, whispering to him about stars and frost. In the pram, he was always good, but she would not take him out in proper daylight unless she was in Steve's car. If anyone saw her, the secret would be out before she achieved her escape to Liverpool.

Maureen still did the shopping, arriving almost every tea-time with fruit and veg, meat and bread, SMA baby milk and all the other necessities. She also undertook to drive Kate and Michael to evening surgeries, so that diabetes and infancy might be properly monitored. One evening a week, Maureen paid a proper social call, having told Phil that she was taking an evening class in Spanish. They sat by the coal fire, Maureen cooing over the baby as she gave him his bottle.

Kate leaned forward. 'What'll your husband say when he finds out you don't know any Spanish?'

'I'll tell him I was thick at it. He won't be surprised. But it's better than admitting I'm seeing you, isn't it? Geoff's convinced you've moved on now, especially after the Misses acted daft on your behalf and redirected that pile of mail to Edgeford.'

Kate nodded. 'They've been good friends, lying for me

like that. Amazing how much these so-called old maids understand about life.'

'Good sorts. I still think you're crazy, though. This little one could have his own nursery back in Edgeford.'

Kate sniffed loudly. 'And Dora crowing over him and turning him into a nancy.'

'Shut up!' There was anger in Maureen's tone. 'You're running off with one of those.'

'Steve's no nancy!' Kate's eyes were flashing ominously. 'If Geoff had been half the man Steve is . . . Oh, you wouldn't understand. Sexual preferences have little to do with true manhood, I can assure you.'

Maureen wiped the baby's chin and placed the bottle in the hearth. 'What about your mother?'

'What about her?'

'Aren't you going to tell her where you're going?'

'No.'

'That's cruel, Kate. I saw her on the market last week, and she looked worn to a shadow. Talk to her. Tell her about her grandson.'

'Her grandson was aborted,' whispered Kate.

'But . . .'

'Stop this, Maureen!' Kate jumped to her feet. 'It's hard enough being post-natal and alone without having my only visitor nagging at me once a week.'

'Sorry.'

'The only thing I know is that I can't go back. Michael and I don't belong there. I don't know much else and I'm not good for anything at the moment, but I'm not going back.'

Maureen placed the dozing infant over her shoulder and began to rub his back gently. 'OK. Calm down.'

'I've been close to giving in, I can tell you. Some nights, I've been an inch away from using the Misses' phone to call my mother. But I never gave in to the urge, no matter how lonely I felt. She cursed me for having an abortion that might have saved my life . . .'

297

'An abortion you never had anyway, and thank goodness, because he's lovely. Aren't you lovely?' She gazed at the baby now. 'And I never guessed you were coming, Michael, not till Mammy told me. And Mammy's going to have to do her own shopping for a while, 'cos Auntie Maureen's car's on its last wheels . . .'

'Oh dear,' interrupted Kate. 'What if I'm seen by anyone who knows me?'

'Wear dark glasses and a scarf.'

'Middle of winter? That would be enough to make anyone take a closer look. It'll have to be Steve. I'll get him to run out to the shops for me.'

Maureen paced up and down with Michael while Kate began to tackle the seemingly endless pile of ironing. 'Good boy,' crooned Maureen. 'Get that nasty wind up. Who's a clever little lad? Your daddy would have loved you, yes he would. Hey, Kate?'

'Hello?'

'Don't depend too much on this Steve Collins.'

Kate banged the iron on to its asbestos rest. 'Why not? He got me the interview, found me the bloody job. And he's arranged for the lady next door to mind Michael while I'm at school. Seems a very dependable sort to me.'

Maureen coughed quietly. 'But . . . but what if he wants his boyfriend to move in? Won't you feel de trop?'

'No more so than if I lived with a married couple. Your ideas are so quaint, Maureen. I must do a Boothroyd cartoon of you and Geoff, the original Victorian pair. Yes, you should have married my hushand.'

'I'm not Victorian! I like the men too much to be Victorian!'

Kate nodded. 'Ah, yes, but that's the essence of Victorianism. Sex mad, they were, but their minds were closed in public. Geoff's a dirty old man underneath all those folded shirts and starched hankies. And you're a manhunter, though you pretend to be respectable.'

Maureen's mouth fell open. 'Good God! Will all this

go in your cartoons? Depravity behind the doors of middle-class suburbia?'

'Abso-bloody-lutely.'

Maureen placed the sleeping infant in his cot. 'Well. There's my Spanish lesson over. I'm not hanging about to be analysed by you.' She kissed Kate's cheek hurriedly. 'I'll have to watch what I say in future.'

Kate laughed. 'Especially about the dentist and the young Reverend.'

'Eh?'

'Oh, never mind. Just something you let slip in a moment of stress.'

'Will it be taken down and used in evidence?'

'Depends.'

'What on?'

'Keep your gob shut!'

Michael had been a November baby; he therefore began to be interesting in about March of 1969. Until then, he had been something of a pudding, rather like a bowl of rice that soaked up milk however many times you tried to thin the mixture.

It was almost moving time; the Crosby house was now vacated and everyone had been over to have a look and to grab rooms. Michael was to have the smallest bedroom at the front, while Kate had been allocated the larger front bedroom. Steve – and Mark when he chose to visit – would sleep in the back bedroom next door to the bathroom.

It was a corner house, with large side and front gardens, then a triangular wedge of concrete at the back, so small that it would be necessary to have a rotary washing line. There were two living rooms, one for Steve, the other for Kate and Michael, though the relationship between these three was becoming so close that there promised to be little real segregation.

Kate was packing boxes while her son lolled against

pillows on the floor. 'You'll have to be good for Mrs Melia,' she said to him. 'Mrs Melia likes children, so don't start putting her off for life. Pardon? Oh, I see. Where am I going? I'm going to work, child. At a school in Kirkby, a special school for children with problems. What did you say? No, not that sort of problem, not your sort. They don't have difficult mothers, not all of them. They've illnesses that make them slower than you.' She leaned forward and twisted the mobile she had made out of coat hangers, ribbons and bells. 'Just be good while I'm out, that's all I ask.'

He giggled and slipped off the pillows, so she bent to pick him up. 'We have a serious dilemma here, Mike. I love you so much, I could burst. If we're not very careful, I shall turn out like Dotty Dora. I won't let the girls near you. I won't! I won't!' She tossed him into the air and he chuckled loudly.

It was then, as she played with her beloved child, that the back door opened. Kate stiffened and clutched the infant to her breast. 'Who . . . who is it?'

Rachel Bottomley stepped into the room, her eyes widening with shock and confusion as she took in all the paraphernalia; cot, pram, airing maiden. And finally, the child. 'Katherine?'

'Go . . . go away.'

'Katherine. I've brought it. The letter to say I'm sorry. I wrote it last night . . .'

'Leave it on top of the television. I'll read it later.'

Rachel hesitated for a fraction of a second. 'But . . . but we thought you were in Manchester. Miss Brandon said you'd moved to a school at Withington.'

'Then how did you find me?'

Rachel swallowed, her face a picture of disbelief and trauma. 'Arthur, he saw you putting your milk bottle on the front step last night. He'd been to a committee meeting at the Conservative club. So I . . . wrote the letter and here I am.'

'We can all see that.'

There followed a small silence, during which the older woman staggered forward several paces. 'But . . . but . . .'

'But what?'

'The baby . . . ?'

'I'm minding him for somebody. For a sick friend.'

Rachel's eyes swept over the room once more. Her voice wavered when she spoke again. 'She must have been ill a while, then.'

Kate sighed and raised her face to heaven. 'She's been sick for months. Months and months. The poor girl was teetering on the brink of coma when young Michael here was born.'

Rachel Bottomley seemed to shrink by several inches as the message finally took root in her brain. It couldn't be! Yet it had to be, must be! Sweet Jesus, what had Katherine done now? All by herself too, no help, no support either actual or moral. She cowered, cringing back from this new knowledge about her daughter's true strength of character. Did she know Katherine? Did she really know her own daugher? Who was Katherine if she could cope with such enormity while completely alone? 'He's yours!'

'Yes, of course he's mine,' snapped Kate. 'And I hope you and Arthur haven't been shouting your mouths off about my whereabouts.'

'Eh?'

'Watch my lips, Mother. I am not here. I have not been here for ages, got it?'

Rachel nodded mutely. 'Can I . . . can I hold him?'

Kate sprang forward and, without ceremony, pushed the small wriggling bundle into her mother's arms. 'Your grandson,' she whispered belligerently. 'But my son. Mine.'

'Yes, yes. Of course he's yours! Oh God, I think I'm going to cry!'

Kate's hands were trembling as she picked up a few

baby garments from a chair. 'Sit down, then. Sit and cry in comfort.'

The grandmother wept quietly but copiously into the infant's downy hair. 'How old is he?' she managed between sobs.

'Four months. He's Sagittarius, though. No more bloody scorpions in my life. I've had enough with old Dotty.'

'Does she know? Does Geoff know?'

'Absolutely not. There's just Melanie, and I'd trust that child with my life. Well, I would now. A year ago, things might have been different. We're moving away, Michael and I. Going to live over in Liverpool where we won't be found too easily. Of course, if Melanie tries to join us, Geoff will find out about this baby. Unless I lie about Michael's age, say he's someone else's.'

Rachel dried her eyes. 'My Lord! You are determined, aren't you? But why didn't you tell me that day? Why didn't you say that you hadn't had the abortion? Arthur and I could have helped you.'

Kate shook her head slowly. 'I was angry. Probably more angry than I've ever been. The doctors had warned me that I might die, that the baby probably would die. I was so confused! I had the medical people persuading me one way, my conscience pulling me in the opposite direction . . . But what hurt most of all was you. You didn't consider me.'

'I did. I cared about your soul. You would have been eternally damned . . .'

'Rubbish! Anyway, I had to be alone with my pregnancy. It was my decision, mine and no-one else's. I didn't want your praise or your condemnation. I didn't even want your opinion. And I'm not so sure that I want it now, Mother.'

'Oh.' Rachel stared down at the gurgling child. 'He's you all over again except for the eyes. He has your nose and your chin – even his hair has a little bit of red in it.'

'He is himself. I don't want him compared and I certainly won't have him sounding as if he's made up of other people's bits and pieces. But I will admit that he's a handsome enough child.'

'He seems bright.'

'Yes. I'm glad to announce that he appears to have a full set of chairs at home. Now, I think it would be best if you left and simply forgot about both of us.'

'What?' Rachel's jaw hung slack. 'What?'

'You heard me, Mam. Just go away and leave us alone.'

Rachel clung fiercely to her grandchild. 'I can't do that! I can't just walk away and forget my own daughter and her baby!'

'Well, you've been doing a fair imitation of that for a long while now.'

'But . . .'

'All it needed was an apology, an apology on time. Not a message that arrives later than the baby does.' She paused, her eyes straying over her mother's care-worn face. 'Whether I'd had an abortion or not, you should have stood by me. But you didn't. That's what the rift was about, you not standing by me. You have never stood by me, not when it counted. When I was a child, you let my father hit me. You knew he hit me, didn't you?'

Rachel bowed her head. 'I'm sorry, lass. I've muddled me way through life doing me best, only I've not always got it right. I made mistakes. We all make mistakes. Can't you forgive me?'

Kate sniffed meaningfully. 'I'm thinking about it. Anyway, what have you put in that daft letter?'

'Hey, shut up! It's a good letter, is that! All spelled proper and with capitals and full stops. I put . . .' She paused, her cheeks flushing. 'I put that I love you. Whatever you've done or not done, I do love you.'

'I . . . I love you too, Mam. I've missed you . . .'

'I know.' Rachel paused. 'Then what the blinking

heck's all this fuss about, eh? What are you doing stuck here by yourself, on your own—'

'With nobody,' interrupted Kate.

'Exactly. What sort of a performance do you call this, lady? And all out of pride.' She shook her head slowly. 'Eeh, but it must have taken some guts, our Katherine. Diabetic and pregnant and alone. You should have come to me before this.'

'You should have come to me, Mother.'

'Aye.' The older woman smiled. 'Pair of daft bats, aren't we? Anyroad, are we having that kettle on, or what? I'm as dry as Southport beach.'

Kate went into the kitchen to light the gas while Rachel played with the baby. Through the open door, Kate told her tale, the story of the 'abortion' she'd had at seven weeks, then the history of the rest of her pregnancy. 'Maureen found me almost in a coma at the end of September. So she threw me in the car and drove like the clappers up to the nursing home. I was in there weeks. Then, when Michael was ready, they did the section and I had to fight to stay alive. It wasn't much fun.'

'No, love.' Rachel fought her tears. 'I reckon it can't have been a laugh a minute.'

When Michael was safely in his pram, they sat by the fire and drank tea. 'I've missed you and all,' said Rachel eventually. 'Like having me right arm cut off, it was. I was wrong about you, Katherine. You're a good girl. I'm that proud, I feel like shouting from the rooftops.'

'Shouting what?'

'I don't know. I'll make it up as I go along . . .'

With this, they both burst into gales of laughter, each obviously relieved to be in the other's company. But Rachel knew that she would have to tread very carefully now. Hysterical laughter was all well and good, but it hardly made them the best of friends. She watched while Kate walked to the pram and smiled at her baby. 'Has it been hard, love?'

'Yes. Especially just lately. There's been no-one to do the shopping, so I've been sneaking about like a woman in purdah. It's . . . it's Dora and Geoff. I've been more scared of them finding me than . . . than . . . well, I suppose I wasn't really scared of you. I was just worried in case a grandson proved too much for you to keep quiet about. I mean, the number of people who know is growing by the day. There's the two Misses who have been so wonderfully good to me – amazing how much a couple of spinsters can understand about life. Then I had to tell Mel, of course. And Maureen's been in on it since I left school last July. I had to leave because I was beginning to show.'

Rachel took a few hesitant steps towards her daughter. 'Trust me?'

Kate shrugged her shoulders and put her head on one side. 'No option, eh?' She had to admit to herself a certain relief. A baby was a big thing to hide; a mother was a big thing to walk away from forever. 'Another cup, then?' While she poured, she told Rachel of her plans, about the house, about Steve and about the job. Rachel's face, which showed embarrassment when Steve's homosexuality was mentioned so openly, was creased into lines of naked hurt when she heard that a Mrs Melia would be looking after Michael. But she smiled broadly when Kate spoke the words, 'You and Arthur can come on Sundays. It's not too far, about fifty minutes through Leigh and down the East Lancs.' Then the grandmother stood and stared at the sleeping baby until, with reluctance, she agreed that it was time for the last bus.

Parcels began to arrive at nine a.m. the next day. There were flowers and greetings cards, baby clothes and toys, pots and pans labelled 'FOR YOUR NEW HOME', and some skirts and blouses for Kate. At lunchtime, Arthur turned up with a big smile and a cheque for five hundred pounds. 'Take it, lass. I've nowt to spend it on, none of

305

me own.' And his eyes were suspiciously watery as he played with Michael.

When they were alone once more, Kate picked up her son and spoke to him severely. 'Michael John,' she said with an air of resignation. 'Your ruination has just begun!'

One final hazard appeared on Kate's last Sunday. Melanie barged in to make a last attempt to dissuade her mother from the foolishness of moving to Crosby. 'I'll never be able to see you, Mum,' she wailed.

'What absolute rot. I shall learn to drive . . .'

'But I can't visit you! I can't see my own mother! If I come, then Dad will find out about Michael and that man you'll be living with. Oh, Mother! Why did you have to turn out so difficult?'

Kate sighed and patted her daughter's arm. 'We all have trouble rearing our parents, Mel. Just remember this one thing. Justice is not a right, it's a commodity that can be bought like bread and cheese. Justice can only be obtained through a very expensive lawyer – it has little to do with the rights and wrongs of a case. Your father's purchasing power currently exceeds mine by thousands. When he finds out about Michael, he will try to take him from me.'

Melanie flounced about the bare room, hands waving wildly as she spoke. 'Yet I can still come with you? Would you really take that gamble?'

'Yes. Yes, I would. My sanity is precious, child, and I am escaping to hang on to it. That's selfish. But I will not pick and choose between my children. If you decide to live with me, then we must tell Dad about Michael. But if you're staying with him and Dora, then leave me my other child.'

Melanie stayed for a long time that day. She stared at her mother for hours on end, marvelling at Kate's new prettiness and calm. The jealousy she felt towards

Michael was only natural, she told herself. And life wasn't bad in Edgeford, she was getting much of her own way. But this mother, this precious and impossible person was going out of her sphere, possibly for months and years. 'Don't forget me,' she whispered as she clung to Kate before leaving. 'I love you, Mother.'

Kate choked back a sob. 'We shall be together again, Mel. When you've finished school, go to Liverpool University. We shall find a way. There is always a way . . .'

13

For Christine Halls, it was hard to admit that life had become more interesting without Derek. Not that she could have analysed her feelings, because Christine's mind allowed her to go so far and no further. Had she known what more intelligent souls suffered, she would no doubt have been grateful for her limitations. But all Chris could feel was an occasional sense of unexpected satisfaction with her daytime life, some sadness because of Derek's departure, and a degree of concern for the poor chap next door. After all, Geoff had no wife to comfort him, no-one to look after him. Except for his mother, who was a frail soul with lots of illnesses that Chris couldn't even pronounce.

Yet, in spite of her worries about her deserted neighbours, Christine's affection for the absent Kate was not diminished in any way. Kate was one of the few people who had ever cared to confide in Chris, so this alone turned the missing friend into a heroine without stain on her good soul. But Chris was unacquainted with mixed feelings, so she usually ran away whenever Geoff or Dora started to assassinate Kate's character.

And she had plenty to run to. There were her flower-arranging classes and her baby-care lessons. Then there was choir practice, Legion of Mary, NSPCC functions and flag days, and the adult literacy scheme. Because she herself had learned to read late, she proved an ideal teacher, choosing those who asked for individual attention in preference to membership of a large class. Thus her home became a seat of learning where she took weekly charge of two separate senior citizens, helping them to enjoy for the first time ever a good old natter about their illiteracy. After chats and many cups of tea, there would follow a slow yet avid perusal of the week's *Evening News*es.

But the main reason for Christine's occasional *joie de vivre* was her child-minding. So expert did she prove, that women were putting their names on her waiting list before their pregnancies had borne fruit, because Christine would take no more than three full-timers and three after-schoolers. The happiest hours in her home were when the after-schoolers had been picked up at three-thirty and she could enjoy her large 'family' until mums or dads arrived to pick up offspring.

It was then, from about six o'clock in the evening, that Chris felt the loneliness. She would cook her solitary dinner, eat it, wash the dishes, then watch the clock until class or meeting time. When there were no meetings, she would find herself drawn towards the next house, partly because she had promised to keep an eye on Melanie, mostly because she could not face the isolation of her own living room. Standards in her house were slipping fast, though the place was always clean. But there seemed little point in poking around in corners every day when carpets had irretrievably lost that just-bought look, while chair legs and soft furnishings were chewed and child-scarred.

Kate had been gone for several months now. Poor old Dora had taken responsibility for all cleaning, cooking, washing and shopping, so Chris saw that it was plainly her own Christian duty to talk to Melanie, to make sure that the girl got some love and attention. And that was why Chris spent so much time next door.

She kept telling herself about the 'good reason' she had for visiting, yet she was filled with shame each time she went home to burn uncontrollably in her lonely bed. Geoff! He was masterful, charming, elegant, all the things her wonderful Derek had never been. He knew how to decant, how to pour, how to hold a glass. Geoff knew everything. She saw him as the father she had never had, also as the lover she might have chosen. Open choice had never been available to Christine. She had pledged herself to Derek before reaching double figures, and Chris had never been one for broken promises.

It was not unusual, therefore, for Christine to haunt the confessional box every Friday night. This was on account of her unclean thoughts. The teaching had been hammered home severely; there were sins of thought, word, deed and omission, and she was guilty of the sin she failed to recognize as desperation and loneliness. Time after time, she poured her guilt into the ear of a bored priest. 'I'm not fit to run the Children of Mary, Father. I keep thinking about him, specially in bed.' The priest usually yawned when things reached this particular stage. He knew what she meant, didn't he himself suffer from time to time? 'And if he wanted me,' Chris would wail, 'then I know I would give myself to him.'

Father Flynn would shuffle about in his uncomfortable chair. Was Christine Halls ever going to grow up? The supposed anonymity of the confessional was a farce, particularly in this case. He would have recognized that whine at a distance of forty paces. 'I can't cope with it, Father. I think I'm in love with him . . .'

'Say five Our Fathers and five Hail Marys.'

'But what about tomorrow? I'll go through it all again then.'

'Pray for strength and forgiveness.'

'Oh, is that all?'

'Five Glory Bes.'

So Christine found no help or support during her dreadful days of torment. She went on a diet. The diet consisted of lettuce, fruit and love, because her infatuation more than appeased an appetite that had, until now, been healthy and eager. Each morning, she hid behind net curtains and watched while he drove away to work, her heart almost exploding because she would be separated from him until the evening. So, while her young charges played and caused mayhem, she added to the happy mess by cooking scones, pies and cakes in readiness for her beloved's return. The scones and cakes were really for Melanie, weren't they? She asked herself this question frequently as she kneaded and mixed and rolled. It was all about looking after Melanie while Kate was away. The other problem would disappear in time. Wouldn't it?

But it didn't. As Chris began to emerge from her chrysalis of fat, Geoff started to notice his next-door neighbour. She wasn't a bad looker after all. There was a new shine to her hair, and she had started to colour in the prematurely grey bits. Gentle blue eyes looked upon him with obvious devotion, and he found himself flattered by her interest. She was only thirty-three. He preened himself. In spite of a sixteen-year age gap, she still found him attractive.

Melanie was not blind to the situation. 'Dad,' she chided one day. 'How can you allow her to make such a fool of herself? After all, you would never consider such a dumbell, would you?'

'I beg your pardon?'

'Christine, next door. She's after you now that Mum's gone.' Melanie was, as usual, blunt to the point of carelessness. 'You must put her off, tell her to stay away.'

He folded his paper. 'Why? She's good company for Mother. Mother has no-one else to talk to.'

Melanie raised her eyes to the ceiling. 'Dad! She isn't interested in Granny – or in me. It's you she comes to see. Every time she looks at you with those sad cow's eyes, I feel sick.'

'Cows have brown eyes, I think.'

'See? You've noticed the colour of her eyes. She doesn't even speak English! How can you encourage a woman who is so . . . so stupid?'

Geoff smiled knowingly. 'Brains aren't everything. Not in a woman.'

'Oh, I see. So it won't matter if I fail all my O'levels?'

'I didn't mean it that way. Chris has . . . other qualities. She can't help her lack of education, she never had your advantages.'

'Right.' Melanie's mouth was set in a thin determined line. 'I shall go and live with Mum.'

He grinned. 'If you can find her. I, of course, am forbidden to look. And she is promising to file for divorce on the grounds of irretrievable breakdown.'

Melanie sniffed loudly. 'Will she go through with it? Will you let her?'

He shrugged broad shoulders. 'Can't stop her, I'm afraid. As my solicitor put it, if one partner decides that the music has stopped, there is no way that the other dancer can continue to tango. No-one can dance alone, Melanie.'

She studied him for a moment or two. 'OK. Just don't start waltzing with Matilda next door. Otherwise, I'll be off to Crosby . . .' She stopped, aware that she had blurted out the words carelessly and stupidly. A hand strayed to her mouth. Good heavens! If she could say 'Crosby' so easily, how near was she to mentioning Michael?

'Crosby?' he snapped.

She hesitated. 'Somewhere like that. I can't remember exactly.'

His eyes narrowed. 'You know where she is, don't you? Ah yes, even a creature as flighty and thoughtless as your mother couldn't take off without leaving a contact number for her only child. You had better give it to me.'

The girl staggered back as if she had been struck. 'No!'

He waved his arms wildly in the air now. 'What if something happens? God forbid that it should, but suppose you were in an accident? How would I find Kate then? This is ridiculous, Melanie. If you know that blasted woman's whereabouts . . .'

'You'd be fined if you followed her.'

His face darkened to an unattractive shade of magenta. 'I have no intention of following anyone. But, should the need arise . . .'

'Should the need arise, Dad, then Granny Rachel will find her.'

He shook his head. 'No. Those two quarrelled, didn't they? They are not on speaking terms.'

'It's been . . . put right.' Melanie hung her head. She didn't feel ashamed of the fact that she had sheltered her mother, but there were times when it was almost impossible to bear her father's pain and petulance. 'They made it up. Just before Mum went to . . . to . . .'

'To Crosby. Ah well. If you think so little of your father and so much of your mother, then there is little more to be said.' He went off to mix his dose of cocktail while Melanie fled to the safety of her room.

Geoff nursed his martini. He did not feel particularly comfortable with himself these days. Somewhere at the back of his mind lurked a vague suspicion that he had been a less than perfect husband. Time was his problem, his enemy. There was too much of it. With Kate gone, the house seemed silent and un-lived in. The silence wove itself around him, providing a cocoon in which he was forced to sit and think about the past. Not that Kate had been noisy. But she had been . . . there. Now he thought about his adulteries, about his mother's interference, his own weakness. No! He wasn't weak! It was all her fault, she shouldn't have gone! There must be a way round this, there really must! Bugger the injunction, he would find the damned woman and drag her back here. Life was dull without her, decidedly colourless. Mother had lost her energy because she had no-one to talk to, Melanie seemed listless at times, while his bed was cold every night.

As Geoff sat and thought about bed, Chris walked in with a pot of plum jam. 'I . . . er . . . made it myself. Last year.' She stared at him with an affection she had not the wit to conceal.

He studied her. She was coming on a treat; even the malapropisms were fewer now that she'd started to look after the English of others. She might be useful. Handled correctly, this dumb devotion of hers could well be turned to his advantage. He twisted his glass. 'I've been thinking, Chris. Come here. Come and sit by me.'

Her cheeks flushed pink with girlish pleasure as she took her place beside him on the sofa. 'Yes, Geoff?' They were the eyes of a worshipping spaniel, beautiful too, softened by moss green shadow and emphasized with thick black mascara. Yes, this new Christine might prove extremely useful. 'Do you know where Kate is?' he asked without further preamble. 'Not that I have any affection for her, you understand. But I may need to contact her in a case of emergency.'

'Oh.' She folded nervous hands. 'I've no idea. Have you asked Melanie?'

'Sworn to secrecy, I'm afraid. But I do worry, Chris. What would happen if Melanie were ill? I couldn't contact her mother, could I?'

She swallowed. 'No. I suppose not.'

He took her hand, noticing how her fingers trembled in his grasp. 'Find her for me, will you? Please, love?' A renewed bout of trembling, this time right up her arm and into the shoulder that leaned against his. With a subtle change of tactic, he moved his hand to her upper arm, making sure that the backs of his fingers made contact with an ample breast. His body stirred as he felt the immediate reaction of the nipple. 'Go to Rachel on the market. See what you can find out.'

Her lips were parted in anticipation. With a slowness that was painful for both of them, he made the journey to her welcoming mouth, kissing her deeply, running his

314

tongue against mint-flavoured teeth. Now she shook like a leaf as he moved expert hands over her upper body.

When he released her, he knew she was his for the taking. Great tears hovered on the edge of blackened lashes, while a hungry mouth whispered, 'Geoff . . . oh, Geoff.'

He would have to act quickly, Mother would be back from the chiropodist at any second. 'You will find out for me?' he asked.

'What?' She was obviously in a very heightened state of sexual excitement, too keen for anything but his proximity to be noticed at present.

'Find out where Melanie's mother is.'

'Eh?' She blinked rapidly. 'Yes. Oh yes.'

He smiled reassuringly. 'Lonely?'

'Yes. Oh yes.'

Geoff checked himself for a second. What was he doing? Did he really want to get lumbered with a woman who breathed 'yes, oh yes' every hour of the day? He thought about this. Chris was ripe, big-breasted, strong in instinct. She would probably make an excellent bed-fellow, would be anxious to please and serve in all kinds of ways. Kate had pretended for long enough to be a 'yes' woman, the sort he had always wanted. Chris was the real thing! But she lived right next door, it would be silly and dangerous. Yes, and she slept next door. Alone. How easy it would be for him to slip out in the night . . . And she hadn't the brain to fight back once he tired of her. Strange, he mused briefly, how many women he had had in his time. Yet only one meant anything at all to him, and that particular one was currently unavailable. 'Do you miss . . . loving?' he whispered now. 'Do you miss being touched?'

'I miss it something awful, Geoff.'

'Shall I visit you? Later tonight?'

The confessional was a million miles away. The confessional was Fridays and this was only Wednesday.

'Yes.' With sudden boldness, she took his hand and placed it on her breast, and he marvelled at the size and weight of her warm ripeness. 'Come to me,' she mumbled, and he wondered briefly whether or not she had recently mastered the Mills and Boon school of reading. 'I shall be ready for you.' On this note of high drama, she left the room, her walk made drunken by sheer lust.

For Geoff, that night began as pure farce. At midnight, when he felt sure that the rest of the house was at peace, he pulled on his clothes over his pyjamas. Although he had seen this done in films, it was not as easy in real life as it looked on a cinema or television screen. But he didn't want to startle Chris by stripping off right down to his undies; after all, she was a reserved type for most of the time.

Then, when he finally got himself out of the house, he realized that he had forgotten his keys. This posed a difficult problem. If he were to sneak back in the morning unshaven and unkempt, two pairs of female eyebrows would no doubt be raised, so he set about breaking into his own house. The task was not an easy one. As a security-conscious chap, Geoff had made sure that his fortress was virtually impenetrable, so he found himself squeezing through the small window in his mother's bathroom. When his legs were hanging over the wash-basin, the light was snapped on and his mother's voice screamed out loud enough to wake the dead, 'Geoff! We've got the burglars!', after which announcement she set about the business of beating his posterior with the lavatory brush.

Having established the identity of her intruder, Dora wanted full details as to why and where, so Geoff made up a tale about seeing a fox on the lawn and locking himself out by accident. This led to the making and drinking of cocoa, then he was forced to listen while his mother delivered a lecture on insomnia, high blood pressure and the tendency to piles, the latter being caused, of course, by walking about in wet grass after midnight, especially in springtime. His elbow was slipping off the table, and he jerked himself awake as he remembered, with a sudden blinding clarity, that Chris had a key to his house! Of course she did! There had been no need for any of this foolishness.

The whole process was repeated at one in the morning, trousers and jacket over pyjamas, keys in a pocket, out through the front door and over to Christine's darkened house. He rang the bell. Nothing happened. Perhaps she had had second thoughts. Of course! He had a key to her house just as she had one to his! There followed several long and angry minutes while he tried, in that special darkness known only to the edge of countryside, to find on his ring the implement that would open Christine's door. Several of his own keys got stuck, and one in particular threatened to snap, so tightly did it fit.

But at last, he was in the house. He shouldn't have worried about his pyjamas, because Chris was stark naked beneath the sheets, smooth, beautiful and inviting, in spite of the fact that she had caused her mascara to run by crying herself to sleep. A small bedside lamp illuminated her luscious curves as he pulled back the covers.

The rest of the night was a blur of frantic activity. Geoff emerged early the next morning with a headache, a bad back and the sure knowledge that there had been more to Derek than met the eye. A lot more. Geoff coughed a great deal, pleaded flu, then took to his bed for the whole of the day.

Next door, Christine's batteries were fully recharged. By nine o'clock, the house sparkled and 'her' three babies were ensconced in the rear seat of the Morris Minor. She smiled benignly upon the world as she made her way towards Bolton market. Christine Halls was no longer a Catholic. No more choir practices and Legion of Mary for her. Because she had found her new husband,

and she marvelled at the fact that he wasn't even an orphan.

Rachel was selling some strange-looking ornaments that everyone seemed to be going in for these days. Hideous, they were. Each item consisted of a plastic vase-shaped base with twenty or thirty wires sticking out of the top. To these were attached little nodding balls, sometimes all silver, sometimes of one garish colour, occasionally of mixed shades. It was a confusing business. Single colours were seven and six, silver were nine bob. A mixture of colours was still seven and six, but a mixture of silver plus colour(s) was eight shillings. She was fed up with them. As soon as she got one out of its box, it mushroomed outward and bobbed about like a lot of satellites around some invisible moon. The things took up too much space, spoiled the appearance of the stall and sold like hot cakes – which was why Rachel had stocked them in the first place. One woman bought five 'to put away as presents' and Rachel shook her head as she watched this particular shopper's back disappearing in the direction of the fishmarket.

'Silly mare,' whispered Rachel to Ernie, who was bent double with the agony of trying not to laugh while she sold these ornaments that so plainly irritated her. 'Just think, Ernie, come next Christmas, there'll be five more houses with one of them things in the window. Where there used to be a nice plant or a pot dog, there'll be bouncing blinking balls. I could do with this business until it came to bouncing balls. I am going to draw the line, Ern.'

He guffawed loudly. 'You mean you ain't gonna sell no more? What will Arthur say?'

'He can say what he wants. Let him have these horrors in his shop, look at them! I can't fit any pots on me stall because of these stupid balls. Every time the wind blows, they start bobbing about like ducks on water.'

A little voice piped up, 'Can I have a shocking pink one, Mrs Bottomley?' and Rachel turned to find Kate's neighbour standing to one side of the stall. Well, Kate's ex-neighbour . . .

'Eeh love.' Rachel's tone was filled with concern. 'You don't want one of them things. They're in very bad taste.'

Christine's face fell. 'Oh, I see. Only Derek always told me what to buy, but he isn't here any more.'

'I know. And I'm sorry, lass.'

'I thought the babies might like them.' She was wearing two slings, one child fastened to her back, the younger infant plastered against her chest. A third youngster was struggling to break free of toddler reins and Rachel relieved her of this exuberant three-year-old. 'They'd pull the balls off and choke on them, Christine. That would never do, would it?'

'Oh. Well, I was going to have it high up. Still, if they're in bad taste, I won't bother.'

Rachel smiled encouragingly. 'Fair enough. Can I interest you in anything else?'

'Well . . . I just wondered . . .'

'Anything at all. As long as it's pots or ironmongery, I can get it.'

Christine took a deep breath. 'It's not exactly ironmongery at all. I want Kate's new address. See, I'd like to write to her and tell her how Melanie's getting on.'

Rachel tutted quietly. 'I'm under starter's orders, love. I've not to give our Katherine's address to nobody. What I can do, though, is contact her and tell her to get in touch with you.'

This was all getting a bit complicated for Chris. 'I need to get hold of her,' she said, a hint of desperation in her voice. After all, she would have to tell Kate about herself and Geoff, wouldn't she? 'Her and me, we were getting quite intimidated with one another.'

Rachel passed a hand across a grin as she translated Christine's meaning. 'Tell you what, then. You give me a message and I'll pass it on to Katherine on Sunday when we go and see her. Will that do?'

'It's . . . private.'

'Oh, I see. Well, what shall I do then?'

Chris hung her head in despiar. 'I'll have a thick-bottomed frying pan and tell her to phone me some time.'

'All right.'

That night, Chris snuggled up to her lover and rained apologetic kisses all over his face. 'I tried my best,' she said. 'But Rachel wouldn't tell me anything. She said she'd see Kate next Sunday and ask her to . . .'

'When? What time?'

'I don't know. She just said Sunday. Why, Geoff?'

'We can follow them!' There was triumph in his tone. 'We'll follow Rachel and Arthur to Crosby!'

'Is that . . . is that a good idea?'

'Of course it is. What a clever girl you are!' Then he set about the business of repaying her for such cleverness.

They sat for three hours outside Arthur Bottomley's shop and place of residence, Geoff cursing and shivering from lack of sleep, Chris doling out concern, sandwiches and cups of coffee from a giant Thermos. 'Don't fret, darling,' she murmured. 'We'll find your poor little Melanie's mum.'

Geoff ground his teeth noiselessly. Poor little Melanie? There'd have been no need for this charade if poor little Melanie had come up with the goods. But no. She might be living with her father, but Melanie's real loyalties plainly resided in North Liverpool.

Of course, getting away had not been easy. They were going to look for a car, that was the official version. Chris needed to change her car and Geoff was going to help her choose. Could Melanie come? The girl's face had worn a knowing look as this question dropped from her lips. No, Melanie could not come. Melanie had a riding lesson at three . . . Why were they setting out so early if they weren't going to be back by three? This astute query from Dora, who had looked decidedly suspicious. Well, there were a lot of cars advertised this week and one of them was as far away as Bispham. Dora would enjoy a trip to Bispham, Dora wanted to come, would they wait while she found her pills. No, they could not wait. Geoff had promised his mother an outing some time next week, then, after bundling his mistress into the Rover, he had set off at speed down the driveway.

He looked at his watch. Twelve o'clock. 'Are you sure she said this Sunday?'

'Yes,' replied Chris, her mouth full of sausage roll. 'Isn't it exciting?' She brushed a few crumbs from her bosom. 'It's like one of those American gangster films where everybody follows everybody else.'

Geoff thought it was more like a Keystone Kops episode, but he didn't air his view, simply because he knew his opinion would be stifled at birth by Christine's slowness of uptake. 'I'm going to need the bathroom,' he mumbled.

'Oh.' She turned her head and surveyed the surrounding area. 'You'd best go up that alley, then. There's no toilet round here.'

He juggled with his thoughts. The idea of urinating in a public passage was revolting, but so was the concept of wetting himself and the Rover's seat. Nature won in the end, and he arrived back at the car to find Chris in a state of wild excitement. 'They've gone!'

'When?'

'Just now, a minute ago. They went up this road towards the school where Kate used to teach.'

Geoff reached into the back of the car and took some items from a bag. Swiftly, he donned a scarf that came up to his chin, a trilby hat and a pair of darkish glasses. It was then that Chris made her serious mistake – she laughed. Geoff liked a joke. He was often to be found having a good old giggle at the golf club or in the local pub. Why, his sense of humour was renowned, wasn't it? But one of Geoff's major flaws was that he could not stand to be the butt. 'What's so funny?' he snapped.

'The hat! It makes you look so . . . so old!'

'Good.' There was no alteration in tone. 'I don't want to be spotted, and this is no laughing matter, Chris. There's already a chance that Rachel might recognize the car – though I haven't had it long, and she wasn't exactly a regular visitor. But we must keep cool. Sniggering like a teenager will get us nowhere.'

'Oh.' She was hurt, wounded to the quick. 'We won't get far if we sit here either, will we?'

With such simplistic logic, he could not argue. 'It's all right,' he said with a slight note of apology. 'I know where they'll be heading for and it's a fairly straight road. Now, I want you to keep your head down in case Rachel spots you. When we get a bit nearer, you can put your scarf on and hope for the best, because we might need two pairs of eyes.'

So Chris saw little of the journey up St Helens Road, through Leigh and Lowton and down towards the East Lancashire Road. It was then, as Geoff was about to turn on to this main Liverpool to Manchester trunk route, that he declared, 'Found them. Keep down, please. I'll try to make sure there are at least two cars between us and them.'

They drove through Bootle and down to the dock road, Chris raising her head occasionally to catch a glimpse of a ship as it sat waiting to load or to discharge its cargo. Then it was left for Litherland and Waterloo, up Liverpool Road and straight into the heart of Great Crosby. They passed Merchant Taylors' and, when they reached St Mary's College, Geoff saw Arthur's car making a right turn into Endbutt Lane. This area was quite densely populated, and Geoff realized that they must be right on top of Kate's house, because the avenues here were narrow. No-one would drive along these streets unless they were seeking a specific address.

He slowed as Arthur turned left off the lane, following at a snail's pace till the Austin stopped on a corner of the Northern Road. With infinite care, the Rover was parked and its occupants watched furtively while Arthur and Rachel went into the end house.

'There!' exclaimed Geoff triumphantly. 'Got her!'

Chris sniffed. 'Right. What are you going to do about it?'

'Nothing. Not just now.' Then, almost to himself, he added, 'But I'll get that lady home one of these days, just you wait and see.'

His passenger sniffed again. 'You want Kate back, then?'

'Er . . . no. Of course not. But I'd like her to see the damage she's done. Melanie hasn't been herself for a long time, and my mother has been left to run a household simply because madam decided to walk out on a sudden whim.'

She hesitated momentarily. 'It . . . it wasn't a whim, Geoff.'

'Pardon?'

'It was for her sanitary's sake. She thought she'd go mad in Edgeford. Something to do with being stifled, I think she said. You and your mother were getting on her nerves . . .' She hung her head in shame and misery.

'The word is sanity, Chris, sanity! A commodity that Kate showed a sad lack of. She had a psychiatrist for years . . .'

'I know. She didn't need . . .'

'Didn't need? Well, she is certainly unhinged now. All women are unhinged after abortion.'

'What?' Christine's jaw fell. 'You mean she . . . ? Oh no. I don't believe that, Geoff. Not about Kate. Kate's a good woman, she's my friend. No! I must go and speak to her. This is terrible, terrible . . .'

He grabbed her sleeve. 'Hang on! You can't just march in there . . .'

'I want the truth! I want to know why anyone would kill an innocent baby . . .'

Panic rose in his gorge. Chris might blow the whole thing if she walked into that house! There was the injunction for one thing, but his main worry was not a legal one – he did not wish to face the joint wrath of Kate and Rachel on this or any other day. He doubted that Kate would ever implement the injunction anyway, surely she could never be so nasty? But Rachel's temper was something he would rather avoid at all costs. 'Chris!' he barked. 'Stop this. The baby was probably not alive and it was killing Kate. It's her diabetes. Remember? I told you all about that some time ago.'

Chris nodded mutely.

'All the same, the operation will have left her weak, damaged her mind. It wasn't an ordinary abortion, you see. It was to save her life. If you go banging on the door and shouting, that will only upset her more.'

'Poor Kate.' Chris began to rock back and forth in her seat. 'My poor, poor friend. How she must have suffered. No wonder she ran away. Oh dear. Or deary me. Let's go home, Geoff. I feel quite ill.'

He drove slowly past the house, sneering as he saw how far down in the world Kate had willingly come. It wasn't a patch on Beech Gardens. For a start, it was a semi and no-one who was anyone lived in a semi. And it was at least thirty years old, with white-painted pebble-dash and splay bay windows that betrayed its geriatric status right away. 'Bloody dump,' he muttered.

'I think it's quite nice,' said Chris. 'It has . . . oh, what's the word?'

'Character,' he snapped.

'And a nice garden. I wonder if she rents it? I wonder if she lives alone?'

He turned right on to the Northern Road. 'She'll live

alone. That's what it was all about, wanting to be alone with her pathetic cartoons. Well, at least we know where Melanie's mother is.'

Chris straightened in her seat once they were out of immediate danger. 'I still need to talk to her,' she insisted stubbornly. 'She will have to be told about us.'

'Pardon?' He swerved to avoid a parked car.

'Us. She'll have to be told that we are in love.'

'What?' He slammed on the brakes and slewed to a halt outside a park gate. 'You . . . can't do that! That would ruin everything!'

'Why?'

Oh God! His mouth moved to frame the right words, but they would not come out at first. Christine's honesty and childlike trust were suddenly a burden, yet these qualities had been so attractive only days earlier. She had too strong a sense of fair play, this one.

'Geoff? What's wrong? I can't marry Kate's ex-husband without telling her, can I now? It wouldn't be right.'

'Marry?' The word was out before he could bite it back.

Her face fell. 'We will be getting married, won't we? I know it can't be in church, especially mine, but we're . . . sleeping together, Geoff. We have to get married if we sleep together.'

He cleared his throat. 'Yes. Quite. But if you tell Kate, it will . . . er . . . damage my case. I'll be the guilty party, so to speak. She left me, Chris. I didn't leave her, I was quite prepared to put up with her sudden changes in behaviour. But if she sues me for adultery, I might lose my home,' he finished, suddenly inspired.

'Why?'

'Because . . . because I'd have to pay her off. And Melanie and Mother would lose their home too. Could you do that to us?'

She thought for a long moment. 'No. I suppose not.

325

But we'll have to stop, you and I. If I can't tell her that we're sleeping together, then we'll just have to wait until we can get married.'

His lower lip protruded in an unattractive pout. 'I'll miss you,' he moaned self-pityingly.

'And I'll miss you. But I don't like telling lies, and not telling the truth is the same thing. We'll have to give one another our keys back.' She glanced at him sideways. 'You won't marry me anyway, will you?'

His cheeks were flushed. 'Well I . . . It's a bit early to tell, really.'

Chris looked down at her folded hands. 'It's just sex for you, isn't it? Derek told me about people like you. I was safe with him, and I wish he was back to bash you! No. You won't marry me.'

He coughed. 'I might.'

She pulled back her shoulders as if forcing herself to wear a mantle of pride. 'No you won't, Geoff Saunders. Because I won't marry you, see? You are not good enough for me, and you're definitely not good enough for my friend Kate.'

'Hey! No need for that, old girl.'

She turned and stared at him steadily. 'I'm not the old one, you are. You're worn out! You haven't half Derek's strength. Take me home.'

'But . . .'

'Take me home before I run back and tell Kate you're spying.'

He took her home.

Santosh Mathur was in deep mourning. His young wife Hamida had died while giving birth to a little son, and this was his first time out since the funeral. He walked like an aged man towards Rachel's stall, his hands outstretched to clasp her welcoming arms. 'Oh San,' she moaned. 'It's so good to see you. Did you want something?'

'Yes.' His usually coffee-coloured complexion was paler from lack of sleep. 'Since Mr Carter kindly took me on in his office, I have scarcely been in to do my job. I am in need of your assistance.'

'Anything, lad. Anything I can manage. See, get round the back of the counter and sit in this here chair. Ernie, take over. I'm in conference with me accountant.'

They sat among boxes and piles of pots, Santosh on a chair, Rachel perching on the edge of a stool. He sighed a deep shuddering breath before beginning, 'I have no family here. Other people in my community will help me, but I am anxious for Robert to be Roman.'

'Roman?'

He smiled sadly. 'A saying of your husband's. I gave my child an English name because he is born in your country. Also, it is a name of strength, a name I like. I wish for Robert to be fostered on weekdays. I cannot look after his needs myself. There are examinations to pass. Also, I have not much money. Do you know of a house that will take my boy?'

'Well, I can ask round, like.'

'I owe you much, Rachel. You are a good woman and your daughter is also good. On her word I was given the position of clerk with Mr Philip Carter. Your daughter got me this through my employer's wife. To pay back, I must do very well. And I cannot do well if I stay at home to look after my son.'

Rachel thought for a moment. 'That's true. But listen, lad. Wouldn't Robert be better with an Indian family? Traditions and all that?'

'Tradition I shall teach him. I want him in an English-speaking household. Many of our children do not hear English at home. For his education, I want him to speak English with perfection.'

She sighed and shook her head. 'Well, there is one woman, like. But I wouldn't say her English is perfect.

327

She's good-hearted and has no children of her own, but she does a bit of minding while mothers work.'

'Then Robert would have company!'

'Aye, but she's happen full up. I know she only takes a few at a time.'

'Ask her,' he pleaded. 'You will please ask her?'

That same evening, Chris sat in her empty house and gazed unseeing at her colour television set. Life was awful. She couldn't go next door when Geoff was about, and even when he wasn't around things were difficult, because Melanie kept passing cryptic comments about lovers' tiffs. Chris couldn't even keep her promise to Kate now, keeping an eye on Melanie was almost out of the question. And, of course, when Kate had phoned in response to Chris's message, that had been difficult too. She was suddenly ashamed, unable to tell Kate the truth about herself and Geoff, so she'd found herself wittering on about stupid things, things that didn't really matter.

She'd gone back to church, of course. Father Flynn had been very understanding about the whole matter – all she'd had to do was a novena, and she'd done many of those in her time.

The phone rang. 'Hello?' Her voice must have betrayed her misery.

'What's up, girl?'

'Oh, Mrs Bottomley.' She swallowed hard. Did Mrs Bottomley know she'd been followed? And should Chris confess her part anyway? No. That would only cause more upset, and causing upset was probably some kind of sin. 'I'm all right,' she said quietly.

'I want a favour. For a friend of mine.' And Rachel told the tragic tale of Santosh and Hamida while Chris wept anew for Derek. 'Oh, Mrs Bottomley! I know exactly how the poor man must feel.'

'Will you take the child, though? To live with you five days a week?'

Chris gasped. 'A baby? A baby living here? Ooh . . .

328

ooh . . . yes! They're gorgeous, those dark children. I've a room ready, and I've a cot and a carrycot . . .'

'Slow down, lass,' said Rachel. 'Think what you're taking on. Babies cry in the night . . .'

'So do I!' Especially since Geoff stopped coming . . .

'They're hard work, Christine. But I know you've done all them classes, so I told Mr Mathur about you.'

'Send him round to see me.'

'I'll fetch him. Me and Arthur will bring him round tomorrow night.'

Chris dried her eyes. 'And the baby? Will you bring the baby?'

'I'll mention that to Santosh, it's up to him.'

'I must clean up!' yelled Chris. 'I must find a nice frock. I want to make a good impression, don't I?'

'Not for Santosh, love. Just be yourself. There's no side to him and I know he doesn't like side.'

'Right.' Chris slammed home the receiver and dashed to get the Hoover. Whether he liked side or not, Chris was out to make that good impression.

They sat around a coffee table that held all the best china. Chris had served just a few bits and pieces with a good strong pot of Indian tea to make him feel at home. But she was distracted by the baby, so beautiful he was, in his bright shawl and blue Babygro. 'Can I hold him?'

Santosh smiled sadly. 'Yes. He is missing a mother's touch, I fear.' And this was a real mother, Santosh recognized that. It was not necessary to give birth in order to be a mother.

Chris held the tiny bundle to her chest. 'Hello, cheeky. Let's show you round the house, eh? You don't have to stay if you don't like it, but I do hope you will decide to stay. I'm lonely without my Derek. Will you keep me company? Will you?' And she left the room with the infant in her arms.

Arthur cleared his throat. This was heavy stuff for a

man who had spent many years as a lonely widower. Rachel certainly brought a lot of problems into his life. Problems, energy and fun.

'She is a good woman,' pronounced Santosh. 'Robert will do well here.'

Rachel leaned forward and patted his hand. 'There's just one problem, lad. She'll not take money. She needs Robert more than he needs her, and she's been left comfortable . . .'

'I cannot take this service for no payment.'

'You'll have to, son. She's a widow, so she feels for you.'

Santosh bowed his head. 'Then my debt will be a moral one. This I cannot consider.'

Arthur coughed again. 'Compromise,' he said wisely. 'Pay her back once you're on a proper wage. Get her to take a bit each week, threaten to take the kiddy elsewhere if she won't have a few bob off you. And if she still won't take it, then pay her in kind. Fetch her a couple of tins of ham and a chicken now and then. She might not take cash, but she'll likely accept gifts.'

Santosh grinned. 'You are a clever man, Arthur. That is a good idea.' He gazed round the room. 'This is the sort of home I wish for my son. At each weekend, he will return home into poverty . . .'

'Back to his dad, that's what's important.' Rachel's tone was firm. 'You keep in touch with him. He's an Indian boy who needs a proper Indian parent.'

'Yes, I do know that.'

Chris stood in the doorway. 'He says he likes it here,' she announced determinedly. 'I shall look after him, Mr Mathur. Though I wish I hadn't been needed. Everyone should have his own mother. I never had one . . .'

Santosh gulped back his grief, which was still raw. 'My wife would have liked you, Mrs Halls. Hamida's soul is in the boy, so he will like you too.' He rose stiffly to his feet. 'The equipment is in the car. I shall go now and carry it into your house.'

'I have everything, Mr Mathur.'

Large brown eyes stared at her sadly. 'No. You have not a photograph of his mother. She will sit by his bed so that he will know her face. Also, he has his own toys, carved in India, the things I had when I was a child.'

'Oh, yes. I'm sorry. I won't let him think I'm his mother, Mr Mathur. He'll know who his mother was, which is more than I ever did. I agree with you. This little one has to know where he really belongs. Don't worry, please. I won't take him over. But I can't help loving him. I love all babies.'

Santosh gazed at her for an uncomfortably long time. 'Yes,' he said finally. 'You are like Rachel. Your goodness is in your face.'

After everyone had left, Chris sat with the child in her arms and thanked God for sending salvation in such a warm and lovable form. And she knew she was smiling as she sat by her fire. The thing that caused her to smile was an echo in her mind. 'Your goodness is in your face.' He was a nice man. A very nice man.

14

By 1970, nothing had happened to alter Kate's marital status. She had hit a snag, a rather large one. Although Geoff had apparently made no effort to trace her, and in spite of the fact that both Melanie and Rachel had kept their promises, she was up the creek without a paddle and it was difficult to know whether to float or swim against the tide.

She could not sue for divorce: Michael John, now in the second year of his life, had been registered as Geoff's son; if she pursued the legal dissolution, then all this would come out in court, because she could not deny Michael's existence in case somebody decided to cross-refer. She had registered two children to Geoff and there was no getting away from that fact. Also, if she simply sat it out and waited for Geoff to sue – which he inevitably must in the end – then she would still have to confess that she had a son. So her basic dilemma was the fact that she fell between two stools. Should she continue to keep quiet and wait? If only she had entered Michael as 'father unknown'! No, that would have been selfish. But this was hell at times.

Apart from all that, life was great, better than it had ever been. So successful had Boothroyd become, that Kate was thinking of giving up what she called her day job at school. Three times she had travelled to London for meetings with the *Mercury*'s editor. He had introduced her to the manufacturers who would be using her drawings for greetings cards, posters and items of pottery. Boothroyd had become something of a cult figure, particularly with children, and Kate was currently negotiating a deal for T-shirts, socks and underwear. She now had her own accountant in Southport, and he was advising her to go full-time freelance because most of her teacher's salary was being wasted in tax.

But she loved her job. It was both challenging and satisfying, so she found herself juggling with time, dividing her out-of-school hours between Michael and Boothroyd. Yes, life was busy and good. Steve was fun to live with and Mrs Melia next door looked after Michael perfectly well while Kate was out at work.

It was a Sunday afternoon in October. Kate sat in the back living room working out programmes for a brain-damaged child in her class. The sun streamed through a large square bay window, and Michael played happily with wooden blocks and some kitchen spoons. Steve popped his head round the door. 'He's outside,' he said tersely.

'Who is?'

'Your husband. He sits there quite often on a Sunday, but I thought it was time I told you.'

Her face drained of colour as she pressed a hand to her stomach. This was the sort of shock she could do without, she could almost feel the sugar level reducing to nought in her bloodstream. With difficulty, she took some deep breaths. 'Good grief! How long has this been going on?'

He shrugged. 'Months. Don't go into a coma over it, for God's sake. I usually take Michael up to my room, haven't you noticed? But Michael's getting a bit big to hide now. One of these days, your old man is going to spot him playing in the side garden.'

Kate snapped her jaw shut. 'Why? Why didn't you tell me before this?'

'Because of your health. Because I knew it would put you into a flat spin. The baby was easy to hide but a two-year-old is another matter altogether. Anyway, I think you should tell Geoff. I've always thought he should know . . .'

'Are you sure it's him?'

'It's the man in that photograph you brought with you by accident. New car, same man. Didn't Mel say on her last visit that he often sneaks off at the weekends? Well, this is where he sneaks to. Where are you going?' He watched as she dragged on a coat against the October wind. 'Stay in, Kate. You'll gain nothing by tackling him.'

She pulled a wry face. 'Has he ever seen you?'

'No. I always keep the net curtain across the front window on Sundays. But it can't go on forever. Sooner or later, we are bound to slip up . . .'

She marched out of the house and across the Northern Road. He sat in a huge red Jaguar, his face almost matching the car for colour as he watched her approach. Kate hauled open the passenger door and stared down at him. 'What do you think you're doing?' she asked coldly.

He inhaled sharply. 'Oh, it's you. I'd no idea you lived round here. I was . . . just sitting. There are no parking regulations, and I've paid my road tax. Whose is the white Ford outside your house, by the way? I suppose that is your house, since you just walked out of it.'

'The car is mine.' A lie, but for a good reason.

'Passed your test, then?'

'Yes. First time.' She noticed how his teeth were gritted as he absorbed these three words. He had taken his test twice, and he could not bear to think of her beating him even at this one small thing. For a few moments she studied him, as if she were summing him up. He hadn't changed much except for a few deeper lines on his forehead. The bearing was still the same, upright to a point, shoulders slightly rounded when he felt cowed. He obviously felt cowed now. She nodded slightly. He was a man of mistakes, and she had been the biggest. He had married a young girl in order to be dominant, in order to keep the place his mother had ordained for him. But the young girl had grown into what he probably considered to be a virago.

'Working?' He tapped the steering wheel with a leather-gloved finger.

'Yes.'

'Where?'

Her lip curled into what almost became a snarl. 'I can't tell you. That was the trouble last time, wasn't it? You phoning the school in the hope that you'd wear me down or drive me insane. Or that I'd lose my job and come home defeated. But you have never defeated me, Geoff Saunders.'

'Oh dear. We are tetchy, aren't we?'

' "We" are not tetchy at all. "We" are bleeding furious. The injunction still stands. You are not to contact me and you are to stay away from my home. The limit is, I think, a mile. So bugger off.'

'Still the complete lady, I see.'

'In response to the perfect gentleman.'

He stared at the road ahead. 'Melanie needs you. She's got to that age, some big exams coming up too.'

'She seemed all right to me. I do see my daughter, Geoff. We meet on a Saturday . . .'

'And she's been here.'

'Yes.'

He decided to go for a different tack. 'Mother can't cope any more. She's seventy-five now and she has trouble with . . . well . . . with her bowels.'

Kate smiled grimly. 'So? What else is new? I got your mother's bowels served up for breakfast, lunch and supper over a period of fourteen years . . .'

'That is hardly a savoury comment to make, Kate.'

'Your mother is hardly a savoury woman. We had everything from the common cold to bloody gangrene and suppurating leg sores for every meal. But I'm not going to start about your mother; if I did, we'd be here all day and most of next week.'

'You've always hated her. Why? Why, though? A poor harmless old woman . . .'

'She's about as harmless as one of those Australian spiders that bite you in the vitals when you're on the loo. But no, I will not be drawn on that particular subject. Save to say that you could never see your mother for what she is. Until we can see our mothers clearly, we can have no separate identity. That's why you're such a blurred person.' She paused and looked at his troubled face. 'You've still no idea where you went wrong, have you? It's hopeless. You use women, Geoff . . .'

'There's no need for all this. Come back, I'll put Mother in a home.'

She shook her head. 'Putting her away will solve nothing.'

'But you just said . . .'

'Go away. You are practically on my property, and if you don't move, I shall implement the injunction immediately.'

'Kate!'

She slammed the car door and began to walk away. He wound down his window. 'Come home! There's never been . . . anyone like you. I can't . . .'

Kate stopped in the middle of the road, then sauntered back to the car. 'Don't tell me you can't live without me,' she said quietly.

'It's been a half-life. I didn't know how much I cared until you'd gone.'

'Stop it. This is hurting me. Haven't you hurt me enough?'

Tears threatened in his large brown eyes. 'I'm sorry. The other women, everything, I'm sorry. Please?'

'No. I'm happy here, happier than I've ever been.'

Sadness quickly turned to temper. 'I'll break in!' he shouted desperately.

She stepped back a pace or two. 'And I'll break your

sodding neck, after the court has dealt with you. Now, go away.'

A few middle-aged Sunday strollers pretended not to notice this exchange, but Kate was wise to the Crosby people, she knew they were taking it all in. Yet she didn't care.

'Divorce, then?' he yelled as she crossed the road.

'Yes,' she replied with volume and enthusiasm. 'This place is full of drop-outs anyway, what would one more matter?' This was said to annoy the passers-by, and Kate immediately felt ashamed of herself. Perhaps she did care after all? 'Divorce me!' she screamed. 'Get it over with! But stay away from my house!' She marched inside and slammed the door hard.

Steve was waiting with open arms, as ever. 'Come on, now, don't fret. What's the point of getting yourself into a lather about it? He's bound to find out in the end . . .'

'Yes,' she wailed. 'And what will he do then? What will he do when he finds out about the abortion I never had, and about the child I hid from him? He has parental rights and I have denied him access. Think what a good solicitor would make out of that, Steve.'

'They don't take a child from its mother. Not without a damned good reason.'

She stepped back a fraction. 'He always said I was unfit. I've had a psychiatrist. He'll tell them I've had a shrink and that I'm not fit to be a mother, won't he?'

Steve tutted, folded his arms and shook his head. 'And your headmaster will tell them – whoever "they" are – that you run a special care unit efficiently, imaginatively and effectively.'

She wiped her tears on the sleeve of her coat. 'Will I win? Will I?'

He tickled her under the chin. 'Let the war start first, Kate.' He stared at the closed door. Battle was about to commence at any time. Somewhere in his bones, Steve Collins felt that.

Kate had always thought of Crosby as a funny old place, and living here over a period of some eighteen months had scarcely altered her opinion. Although the settlement was steeped in history, having taken its name from the Norse and Scandanavian words for 'village' and 'cross', it somehow seemed, at first glance, to have little identity of its own.

Bootle, which was just down the road, was another matter altogether. Bootle had managed to become Liverpudlian, whereas Crosby housed a somewhat 'cultured' population that seemed either geriatric or itinerant. The former group had lived in the village forever, while the latter comprised those who were putting their children through the three public schools, or commuters who worked in the city.

There were, in fact, two Crosbys. There was Great Crosby where Kate lived – a vast sprawling mass of largely subsiding houses – and there was Little Crosby. To live in Little Crosby, one almost needed a letter from the Pope, for the community was solidly Roman Catholic, as was its parish church. Kate loved Little Crosby with its cluster of stone cottages, and she spent many hours reading about its history of religious purges and secret chapels.

But the more she got to know about the larger Crosby, the more fascinated she became. In Moor Lane there stood a working mill where locals bought wholemeal flour to bake their bread. Coronation Park housed an ice-age boulder, which item had been carried down by glacier from the Lake District, while the site of St Michael's Well, which stood on what used to be the village green, was marked by a suitably ancient wooden cross. There were some strange place names too. She never discovered the origin of Sniggery Wood, a place owned by the public since the jubilee of George V and Queen Mary, but she did get to the root of Endbutt Lane's beginnings;

Endbutt was a corruption of endboat, as this avenue had once held the terminus for Liverpool-bound canal boats. So while Crosby was, in its own way, an interesting place, it was a place of another people's past, and it was Bolton that Kate continued to miss.

In the here and now, Crosby village was simply a suburb of the city, a collection of shops, supermarkets and houses. It was not a market town, and Kate, coming from the largest market town in England, longed for the personality provided by a three-times weekly influx of business. The people of Crosby were kind on the whole, but they seemed aloof and terribly self-contained in comparison to the Bolton folk. As Kate's doctor told her, 'Here, you could die and no-one would notice until milk bottles stretched to the gate. In Bootle, where I used to work, sickness brought help automatically. If you want neighbours, move to Bootle.' Kate didn't feel like moving to Bootle. This was because of her long-term plan for Michael. If she could continue successful as a cartoonist, if the money carried on rolling in, then the lad could go to Merchant Taylors'. That he was going to be bright enough she did not doubt, while her faith – or lack of that commodity – in the state system of education remained unaltered.

In the evenings, after Michael had gone to bed, and after she had finished commissioned cartoon work, Kate worked on her magnum opus which, like Topsy, grew and grew. It was a reading scheme, a scheme without words. Because she understood children's love for comics, Kate was trying to invent an educational programme in strip form. Infants did not need the printed word; she was giving them the opportunity to write, with their teachers' help, their own first reading book. The cartoons were funny, simple at first, then gradually becoming more detailed in order to extend a child's spoken vocabulary. She had confidence in this system, but she needed a publisher to share her views,

339

and the time was coming when she would show what she called 'The Play Away Scheme' to some educational boffin who would, no doubt, tear the concept to pieces. But before leaving teaching, she wanted to make her mark.

On the Sunday after Geoff's 'visit', she was working on the sixth and final book in the set. Steve was in the kitchen with Michael when the knock at the front door came, and he immediately scurried through to Kate's living room with the child in his arms. 'Well?' he whispered.

Kate flung down her pencil. 'It can't be,' she said quietly. 'The injunction . . .'

'It might be. What the hell do I do?' His face was white with tension; the child's cheeks were white with flour. 'Shall I take him out? This can't go on, Kate. We can't spend the rest of our lives on the run. And what if Melanie lets it out? What if . . . ?'

'Take him out.' The doorbell rang shrilly. 'When I open the front door, you nip out of the back.'

With a huge sigh of frustration, Steve grabbed Michael's anorak from a chair and went back into the kitchen.

Kate composed herself, pushed her hair from her work-damped forehead, then walked into the hall. 'Now!' she stage-whispered. Both doors opened simultaneously, Kate gasping aloud when she found Chris standing in the porch. The back door closed softly. 'Chris! Whatever . . . ? I mean, come in . . .' She pulled Christine into the hallway so that Steve would not be seen sneaking through the side garden with the child.

As soon as she was in the house, Chris burst into tears. 'I tried to stop it, Kate. I took my key back and gave him his, but the weekends were so lonely. It was all right in the week when I had Robert and the others, but when Santosh took the baby back every Friday . . . Oh, what have I done?'

Kate studied the distressed woman. 'What on earth are you talking about, Chris? Come in, come right into the sitting room . . .' She watched through the window as Steve drove off with Michael fastened into the rear seat. They were in the front room now and Kate gestured towards the sofa, offering Chris a seat.

'You mightn't want me to stay.' There was a hysterical edge to the voice. 'Not after what I've done.'

'What have you done? I can't imagine you doing anything really bad.'

'I've come here for a start, haven't I? Maureen Carter told me I wasn't to come. Mind, she didn't know I had your address.'

Kate sat in a fireside chair, crossed her legs and waited patiently.

'He made me help to find you. Last year, it was.'

'Geoff?' Kate felt the hairs on her neck rising as her flesh crawled with this new knowledge. All along, he had been aware . . .

'I did everything he told me. Everything. I tried so hard, especially after I got Robert . . .'

'That's your little foster-boy, isn't it? Maureen told me . . .'

Christine's face lit up momentarily. 'He's beautiful. I got babysitters and went to classes for Robert. He's clever, you see. So now I've got my English and maths O'levels and I'm doing history next. I want to be good enough. Good enough for him and for Santosh. Santosh is a proper accountant again and I'm . . . I'm going to marry him. We have to get married in the registry because Santosh is not a Christian. I have no-one to confess to . . .'

'Congratulations!' Kate leapt up and shook her friend's hand. 'On both fronts. I'm glad you've taken the classes and I'm delighted about Santosh. Do you love him?'

Chris moaned and turned her head away. 'Yes. But I want you to forgive me.'

341

'What for?'

Chris spread out her hands in an imploring gesture. 'For . . . for sleeping with your husband! I had to tell you. There's no-one else to tell.'

'Oh.' Kate hurriedly squashed a bubble of laughter, arranging her features into what she hoped was a semblance of sympathy. After all, sleeping with Geoff had probably been a mortal sin in Chris's book, and should therefore be treated accordingly. But it was hard not to laugh, because she had never seen herself as a mother-confessor.

'We had this row after we found you. I knew he wanted you back, I knew he wouldn't ever marry me. All I want is to be married, Kate. Married to a man I can love. At first, when Derek died, I thought I'd never want another husband. But I do, I do! Santosh is so kind and caring, I could never tell him about me and Geoff. Geoff was awfully upset, Kate. I told him he was too old for me and he went away and . . .'

'And sulked.'

'Yes. But we still got together again.'

Kate wiped a hand across her brow. 'We all have talents. Geoff's is for sulking. Go on. Talk to me, I'm not angry.'

Chris sniffed loudly. 'Then I got Robert. It was fine at first, I didn't notice the weekends. But then I got lonely again and . . . and . . .'

'You ran next door for comfort.'

'Yes.' The woman on the sofa gulped back the choking tears. 'I need the loving, Kate. I need . . . well . . . to be touched. Geoff wasn't as caring or as gentle as Derek, but . . .'

'He was better than nothing? Look, forget him.'

Chris shivered. 'I begged him to marry me. Humiliated myself, I did. I thought if you weren't coming home, then he ought to marry me.'

Kate snorted with anger. 'He's not good enough for you, love.'

Chris's face wore a puzzled look as she mopped her cheeks with a scrap of handkerchief. 'Eh? He's a managing director!'

'He's a fool. A pompous, overbearing and spoiled little brat. Chris, he has to have his shirts folded just so, a crease in a hanky can cause world war in that house. Put one foot out of place at his works' functions and he'll have you thrown in jail. A drop of milk on a tablecloth drives him out of his mind for the day. Please, Chris, stick to Santosh. He's a good man and . . .'

'BUT I'VE BEEN SLEEPING WITH GEOFF!'

'So what? Do you want all of Crosby to know? And will you give up your chance of happiness with Santosh and Robert just because of a small adventure?' Kate rose to her feet and stamped away to the fireplace where she stood arms akimbo, staring at the wreckage before her. 'Look what he's reduced you to! When did you last have a good square meal? Have some pride, girl.'

The handkerchief was now a twisted ball in Chris's hands. 'If Santosh ever found out. What if Geoff tells him? What if . . . ?'

'Rubbish! What if the moon's green cheese? He hasn't the guts. Geoff would never admit anything that might get him into trouble. Go home and marry your Indian prince.' Kate nodded. Yes, it would probably work too. It seemed, on the face of it, a strange liaison, this joining of Catholic and Hindu. But marriage, thought Kate, came down to personalities. Santosh and Chris were both good, caring and generous people. They deserved each other. Santosh would have a loving wife and a good home for his son; Chris would be gaining a devoted and loyal husband. Differences in creed and origin were somehow made small simply because Christine herself seemed to barely question them. Ah well, it was time the poor girl had some happiness.

Chris rubbed her eyes and gazed around the room. 'Whose are those?' She pointed to a pair of man's slippers near the hearth.

Kate hesitated. 'They're Steve's,' she replied eventually.

'Oh.'

'I live with him, but we do not co-habit. Steve has . . . his own arrangements. There's no room in my life for a man.'

'I see. Don't you miss the . . . you know . . . the loving?'

'Sometimes.' Kate sniffed. 'But I don't miss Geoff, except in the way I might miss a headache after a dose of aspirin. Stay away from him, Chris. The man can be poison. He will undermine you until you forget who you are. He needs to do that in order to make himself feel good.'

Chris breathed a deep, shuddering sigh. 'I wish I was clever like you, Kate. I wish I could work people out and know why they do things. But I can't. I just felt so lonely and Geoff took that away—he made me feel wanted again.'

Kate shivered visibly. 'Chris, listen to me. He uses prostitutes, abroad, particularly when he's in Amsterdam. He once brought a souvenir back with him and we both had to be treated for crab lice.'

The small woman's face paled. 'What are they?'

'A sort of bug that gets transmitted in pubic hair. He picked up filth from a whore and passed it on to me. Oh, I forgave him. I pretended to believe that he'd slept between unclean sheets. You see, I was pregnant with Melanie at the time and still under his thumb. But I have never forgotten the crab lice. If you ever feel tempted by Geoff again, remember what he is. A dirty old man. He has been a dirty old man since he stopped being a dirty young man.'

'Oh! Oh!' Chris pressed a hand to her mouth.

'Get married. Stay away from him. Understand?'

The grey face remained still and waxen.

'I'm not telling you any of this out of malice, love. It isn't something I broadcast widely. If you were not such a good person, then I probably would have left you to get on with it. But don't ruin your chances of marriage. Derek was a kind man, one that suited you, Santosh is the same. He will be devoted and kind and he will never be unfaithful to you. If you were to marry Geoff, you would never know where he had been or whose bed he had come from. His mother made him like that, Chris. She laid herself down as a doormat and he's been walking over women ever since. A user of women is always a bad man. Please don't think of him. Please?'

Christine's head seemed to jerk as she tried to nod and shake at the same time. 'But . . . he's always so clean, so careful with his clothes and all that. You'd never think, would you?'

'He's obsessive. Many obsessives are sexually depraved.'

'I feel dirty! I want to go home and have a hot bath. I'm going . . . I'm going to be sick . . .' She ran from the room and Kate followed her, pushing her towards the bathroom. After she had emptied her stomach into the toilet, Chris sank to the floor, her legs obviously too weak to hold her. 'Oh God,' she moaned, 'what have I done?'

'You've been sick. There's no crime in that.' Kate mopped the feverish brow with a damp flannel. 'And the thing that made you sick was knowing your mistake. There's no law against making mistakes either. So you just sit there till you feel better. If you start heaving again, at least you've only to lean over the bowl.'

Chris glanced around the small pink bathroom. 'Does your lodger play with a duck in the bath? And a plastic alligator?'

Kate made no reply.

The woman on the floor raised a weak hand. 'And those pyjamas on the radiator, is he a dwarf?'

'No.'

'Oh Kate!'

'What?'

'I'm going to be sick again.'

'Then get on with it.'

She got on with it. Kate, standing by helplessly, didn't know what to say or do next. There was a child in the house; evidence of that child was in almost every room, because Michael, ever since he had learned to walk, had become something of a voyager. It was a family joke that Michael would turn out to be either a gypsy or a travelling salesman.

Chris sluiced her face at the washbasin, then groped for a towel on a nearby rail. Slowly, while patting her face dry, she turned to look at Kate. 'You never had that abortion, did you?'

'No. No, I didn't.'

'Don't you believe in it? Is that why?'

'I don't believe in it for me, but I wouldn't care to judge anyone else who took that option.'

'Oh.' Chris's round features began to clear as strength and understanding arrived simultaneously. 'You were brave, Kate. With the sugar and everything . . .'

'It didn't feel brave, it felt foolish. I might have put him through the pain of birth just for him to die. But it was OK, I had a Caesarean, so he didn't feel a thing.'

'And you?'

Kate shrugged lightly. 'He could easily have finished up motherless. They were hard days.'

'And all alone too. Why? Why didn't you tell anyone? We all thought you'd moved away to a job in Manchester . . .' She suddenly began to nod rhythmically, putting Kate in mind of a Victorian mechanical doll she'd seen years ago, smooth-faced, dark-haired and nodding. 'You did all this to keep your baby away from Geoff, didn't you?'

'Yes.'

'Why though? Is Geoff so bad?'

Kate folded her arms. 'He isn't exactly bad, but he's not strong enough to be a father. He's a weak man.'

'But . . . the baby's his too! What did you have, by the way?'

'A boy. Which is why I never went back. Though I would probably have kept my baby away no matter what its sex. Geoff and Dora have no idea with children. I didn't want Dora spoiling another child of mine. And I ran for my sanity.'

'Yes.' The dark head was bowed in deep thought now. 'I remember you telling me that. I remember you saying that if you stayed you'd likely finish up in a mental ward. But oh, Kate, what if he ever finds out?'

'About Michael?'

'What a lovely name! Yes, about Michael. You know how he always wanted a son. Does Melanie realize that she has a brother?'

'Oh yes.'

'And she's never told?'

Kate smiled broadly. 'Melanie is my daughter. Soon, he will lose her too, because Mel will not suffer fools. The trappings still attract her, of course. Horses, nice house, good clothes. But once she tries to grow up – really grow up – then Dora and Geoff will stand in her way. If I know my daughter, she'll drive through them like a bulldozer. Mel doesn't have a gentle touch, I'm afraid.'

Chris stood up and touched Kate's arm. 'He won't find out from me, you know. But he'll find out, he's bound to. Isn't he?'

The taller woman's chin jutted forward. 'Let him. Just let him try to get his hands on my son.'

Chris's grip tightened. 'He's his son too, love. You

can't get away from that – ever. I don't know much about courts and suchlike, but won't Geoff have a claim?'

'Yes.' The tone was quiet, rather too controlled. 'But to implement it, he'll have to get past me. And I intend to use every weapon, clean or dirty, to keep my boy away from his inadequate father.'

'You wouldn't . . . you wouldn't hurt Geoff? I mean . . . you know . . . go for him?'

'I might. There's no telling what a mother might do to save her child from the vultures.'

'You'll get in trouble, Kate.'

Kate looked sorrowfully at her little friend. 'I've been in trouble for years. I'm used to it.'

Maria Murphy died in the night just before the Christmas holidays. Kate, who still remembered clearly the death of Steve's sister, simply went to pieces. She found herself weeping copiously in the headmaster's office. Mr Healey blinked back his own tears before pushing a small glass under her nose. 'Take a sip of brandy,' he said gently. 'It'll do no harm if it does no good.'

'She was . . . she was fine. She locked me in the store room again last week and ran off with the key. It took Diane and Yvonne ten minutes to get the key from her . . .'

'She was a very sick little girl.'

Kate smiled in spite of everything. 'Little' was hardly the word for Maria who, at eighteen years of age, had weighed several stones over the odds. 'I thought she'd make it,' she whispered. 'She could move about, walk and so on. I never thought she'd go with pneumonia.'

'Her heart was weak, love. That's the trouble with a severe Downs, you never know the day.'

'And her parents are devastated.'

'Yes. They realized it was on the cards, always a possibility, but even so . . .'

Kate rose unsteadily to her feet. 'I don't think I can do this job, Mr Healey. I can't take the heartbreak. With the other so-called normal kids, I . . . usually . . . managed not to become attached. But Maria? Dear God, we could never find a pencil or a paintbrush! Who's going to hide my stuff now, Mr Healey?'

He shook his grey head. 'I don't know. Now, get home this minute . . .'

'But I've the physiotherapist coming! And Helen's going to be measured for her hoist! And I haven't finished my requisition forms . . .'

'Mrs Saunders!'

'Yes?'

'Don't you have the two finest nursery nurses in the world? Aren't they capable of seeing to measurements and physiotherapy?'

'Yes but . . .'

'And what am I here for? Decoration? I can take care of the unit for one day, can't I? Do I have your permission?'

'OK. You win, I'll go home.'

As she drove the short distance from Kirkby to Crosby, Kate thought intensely about Maria Murphy's family. Good and caring people, they were. Imperfect, but good. She stopped at the traffic lights on Moor Lane. Their daughter's death would cut them to the quick, however well-prepared they might have been. Maria had been special in more ways than one. So, given the brevity of some lives, given the imperfection of parents in general, who was she in particular to act like God?

And suddenly, the taking away of Michael became, in her mind, a terrible and unforgivable crime. Geoff was a weak man, just as she was a weak woman. How could she judge him unfit to rear a son? More to the point, how could she judge herself as capable?

The car behind her hooted impatiently and she crawled through a light that had probably been green for ages.

349

Like a snail, she crept round Crosby, finally parking on the front at Blundellsands, where silence reigned. This was the truly posh end of the villages, a village on its own, the sort of area where people got upset if 'Great Crosby' should be mistakenly written on envelopes addressed to them. This was Blundellsands! This was reputed to be the site where Blondell had landed with his Norsemen, and the name was probably a corruption of Blondell's Lands.

The river stretched away towards the open sea and Ireland. Below her, on the shore, a few sea-birds pecked about in dirty sand. To her left, she could glimpse a few of the dock cranes, while Wales with its pretty hills was obliterated just now by mist. On a good day, Wales was truly visible from here, as was New Brighton with its domed pavilion. But today there was just the river, grey, oil-streaked and leaden in its movements.

She folded her hands on the steering wheel, resting a throbbing head against the cushion of her arms. Maria. Michael. It might so easily have been Michael. He'd had no decent start in life; premature, a diabetic mum who had been living at the time in conditions far from perfect. And yet she had hidden herself, hidden him, taken him away from what was rightfully his. Didn't Michael have rights too? Who the hell was she to deny him a father?

Then there was Steve, that other added complication. Since Mark's disappearance, Steve had apparently remained celibate. And while poor Michael probably thought of Steve as a father, Kate . . . Oh God, no. She didn't love him! How many times a day did she tell herself just that? Her affection for Steve was invested in the fact that he posed no threat. Wasn't it? For Steve, she was just another person, a human being he valued and respected, someone he cared about. There was nothing, NOTHING! She found herself sobbing this word, wetting her hands with tears.

You will pull yourself together, Kate Saunders. Maria has died; you will show respect and go to the funeral. And you will wipe Steve Collins out of your mind this minute. He is not for you; he is not for any woman. Then, you will look at your child, really look at him. You have made your stand. Perhaps it is time for you to return, tail between legs, 'sorry, Geoff, sorry, Dora.'

She raised her head slowly and gazed across the estuary. A ship was coming in, a big and beautiful white ship from some faraway place. On the docks, they would be ready to receive her, those big burly Scouse dockers with accents as thick as treacle, hands like shovels, hearts as gentle as Larry the Lamb. But it wasn't her ship coming home. She knew that clearly enough. Perhaps hers had been lost at sea.

It was her turn this week for both car and cooking. This had seemed a sensible enough arrangement to both Kate and Steve; whoever got the car did the choosing, shopping and cooking, while the other got picked up from school, catered for; then the cateree (as Steve called the recipient of such services) took charge of washing up and child-minding. Not that this situation needed to last much longer, mused Kate as she drove through Crosby. She had enough money from Boothroyd for her own car, even for her own house. She picked him up at three-thirty, her face still red from weeping at the Blundell-sands front.

'What the hell's up with you?' he asked. 'You've not bent my car, have you?'

'Maria died.'

'Oh no!'

'And I can't cope with it. I can't cope with anything any more. I'll probably give up school and do my Boothroyding full time.' She threw a pile of papers at him. 'I've been writing that all day, can't seem to get it right.'

351

He read aloud, ' "Dear Geoff, I think you should know that you have a son and his name is Michael." ' The rest was crossed out and tear-stained. He picked up the next sheet. ' "Geoff, a child in my class died yesterday and I started thinking. Any one of us can die at any minute and it's wrong for me to keep things from you . . ." ' Steve glanced at her. 'Are you feeling all right?'

'No. My head's burning.'

He shuffled through the pages in his hand. ' "There comes a time, Geoff, for clearing the air. I ran because I thought you weren't good enough. Perhaps I am not good enough." ' The paper rustled as he screwed it into a large ball. 'You're not well.'

'No. As I said before, my head's burning.'

'If you were well, you'd have more sense than to commit all this to paper. Writing down that you're not good enough, you'll lose Michael!'

'I lost Maria!'

'And was that your fault? Was it?'

'She seemed OK. I should have noticed.'

'Her parents are doubtless saying the same thing. Stop it, Kate! You will post none of that rubbish. If you're going to tell Geoff, you will do it face to face and after Christmas.'

'Right.' She swallowed painfully.

'What is the matter with you?' He touched her forehead. 'My God, I could fry an egg on your face.'

'Then you'd better do the cooking, because I'll be sick.' She got out of the car and staggered round to the passenger seat while he slid across to drive. 'You must get the doctor too, Steve. It's nothing to do with my diabetes, this is something else altogether. Just get me home and put me to bed, will you?'

Two hours later, a concerned doctor packed away what Kate called his instruments of torture. 'Stay in bed,' he ordered. 'Tomorrow, there'll be somebody here for a blood sample.'

'What is it?' Her voice was thin and weak.

'If I knew what it was, I wouldn't be having tests done. It looks like glandular fever, but I need it confirming.'

'Oh. Do I have to go in hospital?'

'Probably not. Leave the child next door.' He turned and called, 'Mr Collins?'

Steve came in, his handsome features altered by a deep frown. 'Yes?'

'Can you get time off work?'

'I suppose so. We're allowed compassionate days for family, and Kate is as near a wife as I'll ever get. What do I do for her?'

'Fluids. And get hold of her diabetic points guide, try to balance insulin with intake. If she refuses solids altogether, she may have to go into Walton for supervision. And if she can't manage her injection, send for me.'

He left them alone together. Steve perched on the edge of her bed. 'What next, eh?'

His voice was far away, but his face remained so near that she might have reached out and touched him, so she did. 'You are so beautiful, Steve. All that lovely brown hair and those soulful blue eyes. What a waste.'

He grinned. 'Definitely delirious. You have to eat something.'

'Feed a cold, starve a fever. Get my mother.'

'You sure?'

She nodded. 'It hurts. All over my body. I am as weak as a newborn kitten. Get some sugar handy by the bed, this could be the start of a hypo. Don't tell Mel. If she rings, say I'm in bed with flu. My head is floating somewhere near the ceiling. Get Mam, Steve. For God's sake, fetch my mother.'

'I will.' He rose to leave, but she would not release his hand.

'Steve?'

'What?'

353

'Why couldn't you be normal?'

He raised his shoulders. 'What's normal?'

'You know what I mean.'

'Oh.'

She was sinking into unconsciousness, and her hold on his fingers became slacker. 'I love you,' she whispered before slipping into sleep.

Steve looked at the ceiling and blinked rapidly. 'Kate, my love, if I could have been what you call normal, then you would have been the one for me.' He stamped out of the room to phone Rachel.

Rachel took over in Rachel's famous way, deferring to nobody, showing little respect for doctors who came for samples and to check her daughter's progress. 'Glandular fever?' she snapped frequently. 'She'd never have caught it if she'd had a proper job. And if you lot were anything like proper doctors, proper doctors like what we had in my day, this poor girl would be cured by now.'

Dr Fenwick sighed and stared at the angry little woman. 'She's holding her own, Mrs Bottomley.'

'Holding her own? Holding her blinking own? It's just as well, 'cos you're doing nowt for her. And think what I'm saving the health service, eh? Unpaid nurse and skivvy, that's me . . .'

'I'll send someone in . . .'

'You'll do no such thing! She can't stand nurses, my Katherine. Nurses, teachers and social workers, she reckons they're all tarred with the same brush. And doctors and all.'

He smiled wryly. 'Then you can't have it both ways. She either stays here with you in charge, or she comes into Walton Hospital.'

'She's not going in there! I wouldn't send a dog in there.'

'They wouldn't take a dog in there, Mrs Bottomley.'

'Mother.' The voice from the pillow was tired. 'Mother, shut up. He's doing his bloody best.'

Rachel bridled. 'Aye, well. Happen his best's not good enough.' She turned to the bed and spoke gently to her daughter. 'You keep out of it, love, concentrate on getting better.' She pulled the doctor to the door. 'If owt happens to her, Doc, I'll have you separated from your stethoscope.'

'Yes. I don't doubt that you will.'

Rachel let the doctor out then returned to the sickbed. 'You've done it, haven't you?'

'What?'

'Got better. What did you think I meant? That you'd messed the bed?'

'Wouldn't be the first time. Sorry.'

'Nay, lass.' The older woman's eyes misted over. 'It's been a privilege. It's not often you get to do much for your baby once it's grown. And . . . and . . . I hope you don't mind, but in between nursing and washing, I've . . . well . . .'

'You've what?'

'. . . and seeing to Steve – hey, he's a nice lad for all he's a nancy . . .'

'Mother!'

'. . . and going next door to see if me-lad-o's all right, and shopping and cooking and counting your points . . .'

'What have you done?'

Rachel swallowed deeply. 'I've studied it. It's wonderful . . .'

'Studied what?'

'That there reading scheme.'

'Oh Mother!'

'They said . . .' Tears flowed freely now. 'Oh God. They said at school that Judith was only clever and that Katherine would leave her mark. I thought . . .' she blew her nose loudly, 'I thought you were just awkward, I thought you'd never let it out. I mean, I know you've done well with your cartoons and all that, but I was looking for the serious side. Them nuns, they said, "Katherine's vocabulary is unusual." Well, I thought you'd been swearing, didn't I? I thought you'd been listening to your dad. Then they showed me all them little books what you'd made on your own. Six years old and all spelt right 'cos I'd taught you how to use a dictionary.' The small head was suddenly held proud. 'I taught you. They never. Any start you had was from me. When your dad used to take Judith out, you and me got learning. All these years I've waited and I never knew what I was waiting for. I thought happen you'd go back and do a degree, only you don't need no degree, do you? 'Cos here you are making little books like you did at school.'

Kate sniffed. 'You shouldn't have looked at the work. It's private.'

'Private? It's brilliant! It's for general consumption, is that. And the sixth book, the one with a few words in, that's quite historical, isn't it? How did you remember all that? The gossips on the corner, him with his blessed pigeons at the end house, her that always stood at the door with a pot towel in her hand. All that detail. You noticed everything, didn't you? And the main thing you noticed was me. Oh, you've got me to a T in them drawings. No wonder you called book five "Oh Mother!" That there Nelly, she's me, isn't she?'

'Not completely.'

Rachel grinned impishly. 'Anyroad, while you've been bad, me and Steve sent it all off to some university press or other, he knows. And we had a letter back to say they're interested in what they call your pre-reading work. Then there's cheques all over the house for your pots and your tea-towels, you're a rich woman. I'm having me stall done up with all your mugs and place mats – they can buy them from the mother of KAZ! Isn't it all exciting?'

'I suppose it is.'

While Rachel raved on about fame and fortune, Kate lay flat on the bed, her mind concentrating on just one thought. She had nearly died. Again. This was becoming a habit. If and when she did eventually die, Michael would have to go through the trauma of meeting an unknown father.

It was time to get well again, time to roll the ball.

15

Dora was flicking a feather duster around Melanie's room. As usual, she had been through all the girl's private papers, clicking her tongue over scribbled homework notes, furrowing her brow while reading Kate's carefully worded letters, shaking her head at the sight of all those hidden baby photographs. These were snapshops of Melanie's friend's little brother. A handsome enough baby, though scarcely qualified to take up space in a corner of the bureau. Dora sniffed. She was a secretive child, was Melanie. Going off on Saturdays to meet her mother, walking about for the rest of the week looking like the cat who'd swallowed the cream. Which was why Dora excused herself for snooping about the room. Young girls needed checking from time to time.

The old lady sank into Melanie's basket chair, the duster drooping from her right hand. This house was too much for a woman of her age, far too much. And the female who came in twice a week was good for nothing, never touched an item above eye-level and missed a few things that should have been obvious even to one of such apparently narrowed vision.

It was all Kate's fault, all of it. If she'd stayed in her rightful place . . . Dora kicked off her shoes and leaned back in the chair. More than two years now. Geoffrey must either get her back or divorce her, he was allowing himself to become a laughing stock. The woman was making fools of everyone. Dora sniffed again. Famous now, was madam. Interviews in the papers and on the wireless – what next? Telly, that would be it.

She'd probably give a half-hour lecture entitled 'How I Abandoned My Family And Became Successful'.

The pain crept through her chest again, dull at first, then spreading its sharp needles down arms and into wrists and fingers. She popped another tablet under her tongue and waited for the spasm to pass.

It took a while. It was then, during this particular episode, that Dora really started to think. Thinking and planning somehow took the edge off things, made her concentrate on matters which, though troublesome, were slightly less frightening than her erratic heartbeat.

It was all quite simple, really. Simple and thoroughly complex. She had to get Kate back. She, Dora Saunders, would have to bend both knees as far as they would go and beg Kate to come home.

Her mouth was suddenly dry and furry. The idea of begging stuck in her parched throat, and she swallowed deliberately and loudly. But an effort must be made. She could not just wander off into death; she could not leave her poor son alone and wifeless, her granddaughter lost and motherless.

She turned her head and stared through the window. Such a mess should never have been arrived at in the first place. The ducks were quacking outside; Kate had loved the ducks, especially that white one. In her mind's eye there appeared a vivid picture of Kate, Kate running up and down the bank with a stray duckling in her hands, Kate returning triumphant after finding a duck that would accept the little bird.

The pain began to ease a little. Whose fault was the mess? Was it Kate's, Geoff's, Dora's? Oh, what did it matter now, at the eleventh hour? The past was the past and could not be mended. But the future mattered, really mattered to Dora. And a strange sensation of peace came over her as the decision finally arrived. She would contact Kate. Whatever the cost to pride and dignity, she would make the first move. For Geoffrey's sake.

Later, in the hallway, she settled herself into the telephone seat and dialled the number she had extracted from Melanie's diary. Kate had to be at home. According to recent accounts, she worked full-time from the house now.

'Hello.' The voice at the other end was so cool.

'It's Dora, your mother-in-law.'

'Oh.'

Dora coughed. 'I am phoning you because it's 1971 and I thought—'

'I do know the date, thanks.'

The older woman fought to control her erratic breathing. 'Don't come the clever one with me, Kate! It's 1971 and you have been gone for well over two years. This whole situation is beyond me. And it's certainly too much for me.'

'I'm . . . sorry.'

'You're sorry?' She must remain calm. The tablets could do so much and no more. 'Listen to me, Kate. We have not always got on, you and I, but the time for plain speaking has arrived. I have angina and an inoperable growth in my bowel. It won't be long now. Will you come home when I'm dead? Is that what you're waiting for?'

'Dora, I . . .' Kate's voice faded to nothing.

'I have to know. I am leaving my son and my grand-daughter with no-one. I have to know.'

After a short silence, Kate said, 'Don't excite yourself, Dora. Have you got medicine for your heart?'

'Yes. It's with me all the time.' She began to cry quietly. 'I know now. I know where I went wrong. You and I could have been friends, but I was . . . never mind all that. And you were wrong too.'

'Yes. Yes, I was. I'll be sorting something out soon. Please take care . . .'

But Dora wasn't going to be fobbed off so easily. 'What are you going to sort out? Will you take Melanie away from him? After all, you're a rich woman . . .'

'No. I won't be taking Melanie anywhere. But I'll be seeing Geoff soon.'

'When? When, though?'

'Soon. That's all I can tell you, Dora. Are you feeling better now?'

Dora sniffed and blew her nose. 'I've . . . missed you. I hate to say it, but I have. And Geoffrey has too. I know there have been . . . other women, Kate, but—'

'You knew?'

'I've always known. He's been spoilt. I spoiled him. He sees what he wants and goes for it.'

'Thank you.'

'What for?'

'For saying that.'

Dora wept anew. 'He loves you, Kate. Only you . . .'

'I'll see him soon. Don't worry. I have to go now. Goodbye, Dora.'

'Goodbye, Kate.'

Dora replaced the receiver, then mopped her eyes with the sodden handkerchief. Perhaps madam would deign to come home after all. Perhaps Dora would be able to die in peace?

Phil Carter scraped avidly at the last drops of his brandied chocolate mousse, not noticing that the three other occupants of the table were laughing at him.

'Why don't you lick the bowl?' asked Maureen. 'That was delicious, Chris. Absolutely perfect. Tell me, how do you two manage? For food and . . . well . . . religion and so on? Aren't there a lot of differences?'

Chris shrugged. 'I suppose there were. But we got over them, didn't we, Santosh? He bought me a cookery book and I learned to do his meals. And he's learning how to eat a bit of English food. It's give and take, all give and take.'

'And what about church?' asked Phil.

'We don't bother.' Chris's face wore an air of serenity.

'My lot doesn't want to know me, but Santosh says they'll all come round in time. I don't care whether they do or whether they don't. We've got one another and that's all that counts. Me, Santosh and our little Robert.'

Santosh Mathur smiled benignly upon his new wife. She was everything he needed. Chris had proved to be an excellent companion, a diligent student at night school, a good cook and a caring stepmother for Robert. 'I have a wonderful woman,' he declared solemnly. 'Sometimes she is too wonderful. I am afraid that I shall grow fat.'

'Give over,' chided Chris, though her face was stretched into a wide grin. 'It's not in your nature to be fat. You're like a beanpole, you are. Shall we have our coffee in the lounge?'

They repaired to the other room, where the atmosphere suddenly became serious as they drank their Kenya blend from thin Susie Cooper cups. The real business of the evening was about to commence. Santosh took charge of the meeting, while Phil, who was hearing certain facts for the first time, sat back looking amazed during much of what followed.

'It's better at Maureen and Phil's house,' began Santosh. 'This must be done with delicacy, and our house is too close to Geoff's. It cannot be done in a public place. If they were to meet in a restaurant, things could go very wrong. At least in Maureen's kitchen they will be able to shout.' He nodded. 'Yes, I fear there will be much shouting.'

Chris shook her head. 'Kate says there'll be no arguing. She's arranging something so there'll be no arguing. The first sign of a raised voice and she's off, she says.'

Phil sipped his black coffee. 'What's this all about?'

Maureen rounded on him. 'Listen, you. You'll know in a minute. And don't you say one word about this, Phil Carter. Not to Geoff, not to anyone. As Santosh says, it's a delicate business.'

They spent ten minutes or so working out dates and times. The Carter children would go to their grandmother, while the senior Carters would stay with Santosh and Chris until the all-clear telephone call.

'Will somebody put me in the picture, please?' yelled a frustrated Phil. 'Why do Geoff and Kate Saunders need my house?'

Maureen fixed him with a steely stare. 'Who mended our marriage?' she snapped.

'Kate did . . .'

'Then button your lip while Santosh tells you.'

A stunned Phil sat motionless and silent while the story unfolded itself. At the end of the discussion, the Carters walked home hand in hand. 'He'll go bloody mad,' muttered Phil more than once.

'Let him. She's doing the right thing.'

'A bit late in the day, though. And what's going to come of it? Kate can never live with Geoff . . .'

'Kate can do anything.' There was grim confidence in Maureen's tone. 'Anything she sets her mind to. Perhaps she's forgiven him after two years' breathing space. And she knows Dora's dying. She'll not leave Mel and Geoff on their own. Kate's a strong woman, she's had to be.'

'He'll go bloody mad,' repeated Phil yet again as they stepped through their own front door. 'Stark staring raving bonkers . . .'

Rachel Bottomley was as proud as punch, and it showed. Every market day, she arranged her KAZ side of the stall, announcing loudly to each potential customer that she was the mother of KAZ. (Though she didn't need to tell them, the sign above the counter declared her relationship plainly enough.) There were Boothroyd plates, mugs, infant feeding sets, place mats, tea-towels and aprons. Across the aisle, Shoe-ey Hughie sold Boothroyd slippers, while Maisie Hawthorne's stall displayed Boothroyd greetings cards, posters and wrapping paper.

Katherine was going to be a millionare at this rate! Rachel bought herself a smart black dress so that the Boothroyd apron she always wore would stand out more clearly. A jeweller friend converted two Boothroyd key-rings into ear rings, while Arthur ordered special paper bags with one of his step-daughter's cartoons printed on them. Kate was making them all rich.

But something niggled away at the back of Rachel's mind as she flashed her automatic 'customer' smile. Katherine was up to something. Ever since she'd recovered from the glandular fever, the girl had been quiet and thoughtful. When she did speak, it was often about death, her own death, and what would happen to Melanie and who would take care of Michael. It was silly, all of it. Katherine was as well as she'd ever been. With insulin and the right diet, she could survive well into old age.

Rachel paused as she handed a frying pan to Ernie. Aye, that would be it. Their Katherine was about to come clean with Geoff. She was going to tell him about the baby. Rachel retired to a stool and left Ernie to get on with it. Her emotions were mixed, churning about in her chest like the contents of an automatic washing machine. Poor old Dora was nearly out of it, Katherine had told her that. So there'd be no interfering mother-in-law up at Edgeford. But there'd be Geoff. Geoff would be furious. Geoff would hurt Katherine. And what would he do to Melanie when he found out about the child's deception? Oh God! What a mess! She decided to pack up early that day. She must get home and phone Katherine, warn her against doing anything careless.

But she was too late. By the time she reached home, Kate had already left to keep her assignation with Geoff. Steve, too, was worried about the possible outcome – the tension in his tone almost crackled across miles of telephone cable.

Rachel turned to her husband. 'Ooh, Arthur. What the devil is she getting herself into this time?'

He patted her shoulder. 'Look. You've always said she was wrong keeping Michael a secret.'

'Aye. But that was then and this is now. He's going to lose his rag, love. I mean, he's had a son for two years and never known! What will he say? What will he do?'

'You can't stop it, lass. Kate will do what she's decided, and that's that.'

Rachel half-smiled. 'She always was an awkward little bugger.'

'Rachel Bottomley! That's swearing!'

'Aye, I know. But you don't know how awkward she was . . .'

They tossed a coin. The agreement was that each could speak for up to ten minutes and that the other would not interrupt no matter how strong the temptation. Kate chose heads and won, then sat there for ages wondering where and how to begin. She gazed round Maureen's kitchen. It was posh, all newly done out in white and red, everything sparkling clean. A small cobweb hung from a light suspended low over the table, and Kate swatted this away with her handkerchief.

He coughed. She stared at him. He was clean-shaven, but the threat of dark stubble showed blue against the weak jaw-line. His eyes were still soft and brown, gentle, like Michael's. But lines had clustered around and above them, giving his forehead the appearance of a ploughed field whenever he raised his eyebrows. They were raised now. He was waiting for her to begin. She cleared her throat. It was time.

'It all goes back to my father, and I'm not going to go over all that again. I hated him, Geoff, yet I loved him desperately. He was so bad to me. No-one can ever know how bad he was. Even my mother doesn't know. She wasn't always there.

'Because of him, I married too young. And I didn't trust you, because I didn't trust any man. I loved you, well, I think I did. But there was no trust. And you treated me badly, so this allowed me to carry on disliking the men in my life.

'Strangely enough, your other women didn't bother me. Betrayal on that level meant little to me. It was the bigger things. Like the way you dominated me, the way you allowed your mother to put me down. We were married just a short time when I began to realize that your mother had an abnormal hold over you. This power of hers extended to everything she considered to be yours, and that included myself and Mel.

'There were times when I panicked beyond endurance. I felt trapped, stuck in a hole too deep to climb out of. I looked for footholds. One was my job, another was my drawing. And a third was a brief and meaningless affair with Mike Wray. Don't look at me like that. I've done nothing unusual. And whatever I did, wherever I went, I had to come home to you and Dora.

'You moved her in. By then, it didn't make any difference because she was a more or less permanent fixture anyway. I suppose I can forgive you for that. She was lonely, old and miserable. But some things are not forgivable. The psychiatrist falls into the latter category. You sent me to him because I would not dance to your tune. Geoff, I couldn't even hear your bloody tune! I didn't need him. I have never needed a shrink. Perhaps you do?

'When I got diabetes, I began to review my life. It seemed that I didn't have much apart from a couple of needles and a few bottles of insulin. Your mother had taken over my daughter. You had your women, your job and your various club activities. I was stuck in a vacuum.

'So I decided to go. Right. I'm a wealthy woman now, Geoff. I made my way in life in spite of you and away from you. That would not have been possible had I remained. At home, you are the only one allowed to shine. But I didn't go just to become wealthy and successful. I went to become myself, to find out who this woman was, this silly person who had allowed herself to be swamped by you and Dora. Leaving Mel was hard. Just as I left, we were getting close. But that child knew I had to leave. At thirteen, she could see what you and your mother were doing to me.

'Look at me, Geoff. This is so dificult. Please don't say anything, not till I've finished. If you start on me, I'll leave. I did not have an abortion. We have a son. He is two years old. I almost died having him, then I nearly keeled over a couple of months ago with glandular fever. I cannot go on hiding him. Michael has a father. You are his father, and he has a right to know you.

'Please don't hurt Mel because of this. She had to protect me; I am her mother. You, above all people, should know how a child feels about its mother. She and Michael are good friends. I don't know what we are going to do about the future, but you must see your son.

'I judged you, Geoff. I judged you as unfit to be a father. You are perhaps not a good father, but you are certainly an improvement on my own male parent. Anyway, it's simpler than that. Who am I to decide that I'm such a wonderful mother? Who am I to decree who shall and who shall not see our son?

'But I know this much. I will not have him brought up to feel superior just because he's male. I will not have him spoilt. He is a sweet and gentle-natured child, and he is thriving with me and Steve.

'OK. I must explain about Steve. We share a house, no more than that. The relationship is completely platonic, I have never been a promiscuous woman anyway.

'It is now my intention to buy a house here in Edgeford so that you will have contact with your son and I will be able to see my daughter.

'I have nothing more to say to you. Perhaps I had better make some coffee while you compose your reply.'

Kate busied herself with grinder and percolator, her hands trembling as she measured out the beans.

Geoff sat as still as a rock, fingers clasped in front of him, eyes glazed as if he were drunk. He couldn't take it in! He had a son, a real live two-year-old son! And this . . . this woman had deprived him of his rights as a father. So had Mel. The thought of Melanie plotting and scheming behind his back made his flesh crawl. How devious was womankind? Was Mother out of the same mould? Probably. Poor Mother had never seen this . . . Michael? Was that his name? Mother would be going into hospital soon, possibly for the final time.

He thought about what Kate had said, allowed the words to echo in his brain, tried to absorb the enormity of it all. His reply must be sensible and controlled. If he lost his temper, Kate would disappear forever. And he must be honest. If he tried to defend himself, she would see right through him.

He watched her. Her hair shone gold in the artificial light, and he found that he could not take his eyes off her. Long tapering fingers, a straight spine, slender legs, pride in her stance. She was his! All along, she had been his. So had Mel. So had Michael. But above all else, he wanted Kate back. And to get her back, he would have to prove himself worthwhile. After all, this was now a woman of substance, a woman with power, one who would not suffer fools for any reason. He shivered. It went against the grain but, for the first time, he would have to try to be completely honest with his wife. If he left out one fact, one detail, she would know it.

He sighed deeply as she placed the mug of coffee before him. That sigh tore at his soul. He was admitting, finally, that this person was clever, probably cleverer than he was. He would have to come clean. Completely clean . . .

'I'm hurt. It's no use pretending that I'm not. I always wanted a son, and you have taken him away from me. I can't even ask you what he looks like, because we are not allowed to converse at this point. Leave me a photograph. Of course, I'm very angry too, but there's no point in blowing a gasket, is there? What's done is done, I suppose.

'You began with your childhood; I shall begin with mine. When Father died, Mother depended totally on me. I suppose she over-depended. Life had to be perfectly regulated to keep her on an even keel. Perhaps this is why I am so fussy about everything – didn't you used to call me an old woman?

'She didn't want me to marry. But once I reached my thirties, I began to visualize myself living with her forever, getting old myself, watching her fail completely until I would be left with nothing. I chose a young wife. I wanted your youth, needed it. But I loved you, Kate. As soon as I saw your disappointed little face in that dance hall, I knew you were for me. But you became distant once we were married. In your mind, you were always somewhere else. I didn't understand you.

'Yes, Mother spoiled me. Women have a habit of spoiling me. I am used to my own way with women. I was not a faithful husband, Kate. I cannot defend my faithlessness, save to say that something was missing from my marriage. I think my idea of marriage was basically wrong. Just as you judged me, I decided that you were not a good wife. Strangely enough, I have been more faithful since you left me. There have been three women in your absence. One of them was Christine next door – I'm not particularly proud of that.

'Now for the big one. You were right about my needing a psychiatrist. I see Dr Coakley once a week. He is treating me for something called manic depression. He and I have discussed my relationship with you. He says I was too manipulative, and I am sorry for that.

'I can't say much to you, except that I still . . . care for you and that I'm disgusted by what you have done to us. Leaving Melanie was one thing; getting her

369

involved in duplicity is another matter altogether. You can put this right. Just come home. Bring the little lad and we'll pick up where we left off. But it will be better. I'll be better.

'Well, you stated the rules, missus. No conversation, no discussion, just say our pieces then leave. But to-morrow I shall be bringing my mother to Crosby. Let her see her grandson before she dies. Whatever happens from now on, Kate, is on your head. I will not sue you; I will not divorce you. I leave the matter entirely in your obviously competent hands.'

She watched him leave. They had been together for just fifteen minutes. Fifteen minutes in two and a half years! Yet in that short time, she had known him better than ever before. He was vulnerable; he no longer saw himself as perfect. 'I don't love you,' she whispered into the silent room. 'But you are likeable. For Mel, and for Michael, I have to move nearer to you . . .'

Dora had to take another of the little pills. When the pain had mercifully edged away, she looked up into the worried face of her only son. 'It's all right, Geoffrey. Just a turn. That was enough to give anybody a turn. A boy, you say? A little grandson? How could she keep him from us? Why? Are we such bad people?'

He perched on the edge of the bed and grasped his mother's hand. 'Kate must have thought we were bad, too bad for her. We didn't . . . perhaps we didn't always treat her well. I don't know what to think. And I don't know what to do. If she won't come home voluntarily, I can scarcely drag her by the hair. Nor can I sue for custody of a two-year-old. How could we look after a baby?'

Dora heaved herself up from the bed and swung her feet on to the floor. 'Well, I suppose we'd better go and see this baby before it's too late. Too late for me, at least.'

His grip on her hand tightened. 'I can't bear the

370

thought of life without you, Mother. You've always been here . . .' Yes, she'd been here too often, he knew that now. He'd always known it, yet had never admitted that fact to himself or to anyone else. And now it was too late!

Dora smiled bravely. 'It's funny. I've been ill for so long, worried sick about dying. I could have enjoyed all those years, Geoffrey. But now that it's really coming, I don't seem to mind. As long as it doesn't hurt too much. I want to go with my heart, not with the other. I don't want to die of cancer.'

He lifted her from the divan and helped her on with coat and scarf. 'Be nice to Kate when we get there,' he whispered before kissing her lightly on the forehead.

'I was always nice,' she replied smartly.

He sighed. 'Well, be extra nice, then.'

They stood in the porch for what seemed an interminable time. At last, Kate opened the inner door wide enough to let them in. Not a single word was spoken as she led them through the hallway and into the back room. Dora gazed around at the mess. The big square bay was occupied by a large desk covered in paints and paper, while the sofa and both easy chairs were covered in finished work. 'Hang on a minute,' said Kate. She cleared the room in one swift movement, gathering everything together and dumping it on to the desk where it slid about until it found its own level. 'Sit down.'

'Where is he?' asked Dora breathlessly.

'He's out. I'll bring him back shortly.'

'Out?' began Dora, but Geoff laid a restraining arm on his mother's shoulder. 'Hold your horses,' he said softly. 'This has to be done properly.'

Kate shot him a look of gratitude, then sat down in the swivel chair at her desk. 'Michael doesn't know what "Daddy" means,' she began. 'And it's time he did. He will probably start playgroup or nursery soon, and that's when he'll notice that other children have fathers. The introduction must be gradual. I don't want either of you pouncing on him and smothering him. You are just a pair of strangers . . .'

'And whose fault is that . . . ?'

'Mother!'

Kate gazed steadily at her mother-in-law. She wanted to yell, 'It's your fault, yours and your son's! I wanted someone of my own, a child who would not be reared to think of its mother as a certifiable idiot!' Instead, she spoke quietly. 'Dora, it's time to forgive and forget.'

'And what have you to forgive?' asked the old lady.

Kate paused, but did not avert her eyes. 'You led me a dog's life, both of you.'

Dora blushed, dropped her eyes, then brushed needlessly at the front of her coat. 'I expect he knows his Granny Rachel, though.'

'Yes, he does.'

'Hardly fair,' muttered Dora.

Geoff stepped into the middle of the room, as if to provide a barrier between the two sparring partners. 'Kate made the first move,' he said. 'She set up the meeting between myself and her. Whatever has happened in the past must be left aside. If you are going to carry on bickering, Mother, I shall have to put you back in the car.'

'But Geoffrey . . .'

'Enough,' he said, his voice firm. 'I came here to see my son, not to act as referee between the two of you. Now,' he looked hard at his mother, 'are you going to behave yourself? We can't have the child upset.'

Dora took a deep breath. 'I'll do my best. I've always done my best. For years I tried to . . .' She twittered on, and Geoff looked at Kate. 'Bring him,' he whispered. 'I'll keep her in order.'

His eyes were smiling, and Kate suddenly wanted to hug him for taking her side. Had he ever taken her side before?

Dora continued undeterred, 'And everything I did for Melanie while Kate went to work. No thanks. You never get any thanks . . .'

'Is she ever going to stop?' mouthed Kate.

He nodded. 'For good. Soon, she'll stop for good.'

Kate inclined her head, then left the room to fetch Michael from next door.

He ran in eagerly, pausing just inside the doorway to study the man and the woman who were new words in his vocabulary. Would they fuss him? Michael didn't like fuss. Would they give him presents? He loved presents.

Geoff turned away and swallowed a sob, his hand fumbling in a jacket pocket. 'I've got something here for a boy,' he said, his voice suspiciously thick. 'He might be called Michael. Is he called Michael, Granny Dora?'

Dora dabbed at wet cheeks. 'I think so. Oh, Geoffrey, look at his eyes!'

Kate blinked rapidly, then used her knee gently to propel her son further into the room. 'Say hello,' she said.

'Hello.'

Geoff swivelled round. 'Hello, cowboy. See in my pocket? It's a little cardboard box. I wonder what's in that little cardboard box?'

'Daddy and Granny Dora,' said Kate. 'With a present for you.'

'Present,' repeated the child, his face beaming with anticipation. 'Present for me.' He snatched the box and opened it with chubby though dextrous fingers. 'Racing car!' he screamed. 'Mummy, racing car! Red one!'

'Aw, bless him.' Dora seemed steadier now. 'And in my handbag, I've got a tractor.' She pulled this larger item from her bag. 'What colour's that, Michael?'

'Green.' He grabbed at it.

'Kiss first,' demanded Dora.

The little boy, apparently liking what he saw, climbed

on to Dora's lap. As she kissed her grandchild, the other two adults in the room stared at one another.

'God, Kate,' mumbled Geoff. 'This is too much for me. What the hell do we do?'

'Something. We'll do something.'

'Promise?'

'Yes.'

Michael jumped down from his new-found granny's lap and rushed out into the hall, from where many 'vroom-vrooms' and 'beep-beeps' were heard as he pushed car and tractor about on the parquet floor.

Dora wiped away a last stray tear. 'Well,' she said begrudgingly. 'At least I did get to see him. Thanks for that. Thanks for not taking him off to the other side of the country. I . . . I won't be here long, you know.'

'I know.' Kate's tone was subdued. 'And I'm very, very sorry.'

'Oh Kate!' cried the old woman. 'Why didn't we get on?'

Kate fell to her knees in front of Dora's chair. 'Because we're both too bossy, Granny. And Geoff was too soft to manage us. Don't cry. Please don't cry, Dora.'

'I didn't know what I was doing! He was all I had! I didn't know I was causing damage . . .'

'Forget that now.' Kate placed her arms on Dora's shoulders. There was a musty smell in the room, a smell that did not match Kate's memory of this woman. Was it the odour of imminent death? Dora's skin hung in loose yellow folds, large bags under the eyes, quivering layers where her fat chins had once been. 'Let's forgive one another, shall we? I'll be buying a house nearby, probably on the Rookery estate. Then you can see Michael as often as you like.'

'Come home.' A mustard-coloured hand gripped Kate's arm.

Geoff stepped forward. 'No, Mother. Leave it all to Kate now. I'm sure she's capable of reaching a decision on her own. Come on. We have to get home. You mustn't tire yourself.' He helped Kate to her feet. 'I love you, girl,' he whispered. 'The door's always open. Whenever you need me, I'll be there. But you don't need anyone, do you? You're probably richer than the rest of us put together.'

She looked deep into the sad brown eyes. 'There's more to life than money, Geoff. A lot more.' She smiled at her husband for what seemed like the first time ever. 'I'll be in touch.'

The accident happened on the way home from Kate's house, just as they were driving through Atherton on the main Bolton road. It was not Geoff's fault; there was nothing he might have done to prevent it. A large van travelling at speed towards them suddenly went out of control, sliding abruptly into their path. The Jaguar was crushed against a concrete lamp standard, and the impact was sufficiently vicious to kill Dora outright.

Geoff remained aware of most of what went on around him. He heard bells and sirens, caught the odd glimpse of flashing lights, knew when a needle was being inserted into his arm once the doctor found a hand space in the wreckage. He floated in and out of consciousness while the car shuddered with the vibration of cutting gear. There was little pain, but he could not turn in what was left of his seat to look at Mother.

As Geoff hung between life and death, Michael's little face kept jumping into his mind. A sweet and pretty child who liked red racing cars and green tractors and old ladies. What else did he know about his son? Nothing. Or of Kate? Just a little more than nothing. He had been wrong, so wrong to try and mould her into whatever . . . Into what? What had he wanted? Why all those other women, all those nameless and faceless creatures? Then poor Christine. Regrets, regrets . . .

They lifted him on to a stretcher, and still he felt

nothing. His mouth·opened to speak, but someone clamped an oxygen mask over his face.

When he came to again, he was in a small white room filled with people. 'Mother?' he managed.

'Sorry,' said a doctor.

'Dead?'

'I'm afraid so.'

'Just as well, just as well . . .' He drifted away again.

'Your name?' yelled a voice in his ear. 'Come on, man, save yourself! What's your name?'

'Saunders. Geoff Saunders.'

'Address?'

'Fifty Beech Gardens, Edgeford. Phone my daughter. She will be worried.'

They seemed to be studying his feet. 'There's no response,' said a nurse at the foot of the bed. 'No reflex at all.'

'I've broken my back.' Geoff's voice was small. 'Haven't I?'

'We don't know yet. It could be trauma, bad bruising . . .'

'It's broken,' he repeated sadly. 'I can feel my arms now, but not my legs. Get Kate. Tell Melanie to get Kate. I want Michael. Bring Michael. I have to apologize. To Kate. I must tell her . . . Get Kate!'

So great was his state of agitation, that the doctor, fearful that further damage might occur, decided to knock him out for the rest of the examination. All the vital signs were normal, but it did look as if the poor chap might have severed his lower spine.

Kate and Melanie came to him that night, sitting for hours by his bed until the sedative drug began to wear off. He blinked his eyes to force them to focus. 'My girls,' he smiled. 'Both my girls. At last . . .'

Melanie choked on a sob. 'Daddy!'

'It's all right, Melanie. Granny Dora can't hurt any more.' He looked at Kate. 'Where's Michael?'

'At home, love. This is not the place for him. He's a noisy little beggar at times. I'll bring him to see you when you're a bit better.'

'Will I get better? Will I?'

'They say so. I asked them.'

'My . . . my legs?'

Mel was weeping openly now. 'They don't know, Dad. They don't know . . .'

'Hush,' chided Kate gently. 'Let's look on the bright side. These things sometimes heal themselves.'

'And if they don't?' His eyes were filled with fear. 'How the hell do I earn my living?'

Tenderly, Kate stroked the hair from his damp forehead. 'Let me worry about that,' she said. 'Let someone else take charge for a change . . .'

It was a beautiful April day.

Kate drove her new car along Church Road, past the bank where Maureen had had her fracas all those years ago, past the shops and the church and the old village hall. Almost everything remained the same. In Edgeford, not much changed over the years. There was a new corrugated scout hut next to the Post Office, and Kate parked outside this building for a while. Perhaps the fights for space in the village hall were less frequent now? She needed space too, just a few last moments of aloneness during which she might think, assess, speculate about the future.

Michael was asleep on the back seat, hiccuping now and then after that bad bout of crying. He hadn't liked leaving Steve. Neither had she, because she loved him. It was a hopeless love, but that didn't make it any less strong. Steve had given so much, had taken nothing. Perhaps if their relationship had been physical, she would not have cared so much for him. The end of an era. Kate sat and studied the village stocks. The past, no matter how bad it had been, was safe because it was known. The future? What did it hold?

Michael coughed and she turned to look at her son. He had kicked up one hell of a fuss when he'd noticed his things being packed. 'Going to a nice house' and 'seeing Daddy and Melanie' meant little to him. He wanted continuity; he wanted to stay in the only home he could remember. But no-one could remain in the past. So she sat in the present, wondering, as so many have wondered, whether or no this particular present was her correct gateway to the future.

There were Boothroyd puppets in the Post Office window. In classrooms all over Britain, five-year-olds were verbalizing Kate's cartoons, taking their first steps towards reading. She had done all that. With her hands and her head, with her memories of Jemima and all the mallards, Kate had achieved a great deal.

She sighed heavily. If she hadn't left home, then Geoff would never have driven to see her on that fateful day. If she'd tried, like Maureen had tried, to be a good wife, a conventional middle-class woman, then Geoff would not be in a wheelchair now. So much to blame herself for! But if she'd stayed, there would have been no Boothroyd, no reading scheme, possibly no Kate! And Geoff might have had an accident anywhere, at any time. It was not her fault, surely? At least she had money now; at least she could replace his income.

It was going to be a long haul. She would have to learn to accept Geoff the way he was, just as he would have to accept her, warts and all. Poor little Michael was probably worst off, a new family to cope with, different surroundings, a complete change of life. It was easier for Kate; Kate had memories of this place. Michael had nothing to build on.

There was quite a crowd gathered on the open-plan lawn in front of number 50. Santosh and Chris, Phil and Maureen, Arthur and Rachel. And standing on the path was Melanie. It looked as if the girl had deliberately set herself aside so that she would be the first to welcome Mum and Michael. Her solitude touched Kate, made her feel guilty all over again. She climbed out of the car and lifted Michael on to the grass, where he made an immediate bee-line for Rachel.

Melanie opened her arms. 'Welcome home, Mum. I'm so glad . . .' The rest was muffled by tears and a tight hug. Then they all surrounded Kate with smiles, handshakes and unsteady laughter. Everyone here understood the size of the step she was taking.

Geoff trolleyed his way down the side drive, his right hand shaking on the control of his motor wheelchair. And suddenly, everyone melted away, disappeared into the house, leaving the two of them together.

She looked at him for a long time. He would never walk again. The rest of his life would be spent in bed or on a chair.

'I'm sorry it had to be this way, Kate,' he said gruffly. 'I didn't want you to have to come home. I wanted you to want to come home.'

Kate smiled. 'I'm here. That's a start, isn't it?' He needed her. For the first time in her life, she was needed by an adult. 'We'll just have to get by as best we can. Are you still in the granny flat?'

He shrugged. 'Can't get upstairs.'

'Then we'll have a lift put in, buy you a wheelchair for upstairs too.'

'Thanks.'

'What for?'

'I don't know.'

'Neither do I.'

She left him sitting there while she walked across to the brook. Jemima, or perhaps one of her daughters, was leading an armada of ducklings in a straight line through the rushes. On the opposite bank sat a perfect Boothroyd, a pure mallard with all the greens and blues that made him so wonderfully elegant and dinner party-ish.

An arm touched Kate's shoulder. 'Katherine? We've a meal on, a buffet. Are you coming in, lass?'

Kate turned and looked into the sad-happy face that belonged to Rachel Bottomley. 'I'm scared, Mam,' she whispered.

'You'll be all right.'

'Will I?'

'Aye. Come in now. That lad of yours has demolished a plate of best salmon butties already. He seems quite at home.'

'Oh, Mother!'

'What?'

Kate swivelled on her heel and looked at all of it. House, garden, husband in wheelchair, happy faces at the window. She sighed. 'I don't know what. Just, oh, Mother, that's all.'

THE END

WITH LOVE FROM MA MAGUIRE
by Ruth Hamilton

From the very first meeting of Philly Maguire and Richard Swainbank, a pattern of overpowering love, conflict, hatred, and secrecy was born. For although Philly and Richard were on opposite sides of the mill floor, the recognised – both of them – that they were equally matched in strength of character and the capacity for overwhelming sexual passion.

Thus begun the forty years of conflict between the two families – the Swainbanks, cushioned by wealth but tearing each other to pieces with the violence of their emotions – and the Maguires, proud, betrayed, and led by the vibrant and magnificent Philly.

A major saga of the Lancashire cotton mills – of the strong, violent, real people who both owned them, and worked in them – and of the dangerous things that love can do to families throughout the generations.

0 552 13616 6

A WHISPER TO THE LIVING
by Ruth Hamilton

Annie Byrne was born during one of the worst winters Lancashire ever remembered. When the doctor finally got through the nine-foot drifts of snow, mother and daughter were in a pretty bad way, but both the new-born Annie and her exhausted mother – a spinner in the cotton mill – were fighters, tough and determined not to let the world knock them down.

They needed to be tough, for when Annie's father was killed in the war, Nancy married again. And Eddie Higson – once he'd courted and won Nancy Byrne – turned into a nightmare of a man, terrorising the young girl with one secret evil after another.

She had two friends who helped her through these bad year. Martin Cullen, rough, uneducated, loyal, who knew he wasn't good enough for her, and David Pritchard, the doctor who had supported her through the worst times and who had bad problems of his own.

Together they watched her grow into a beautiful young woman, desperately fighting the legacy of her childhood.

0 552 13384 1

THE MOSES CHILD
by Audrey Reimann

Oliver Wainwright was sixteen when he first set eyes on Florence Mawdesley. He was hiding in the water of the lake on Sir Philip Oldfield's land – taking refuge after stealing a mallard duck.

She was standing at the water's edge, silk-gowned, sheltered by her parasol, the privileged, aristocratic granddaughter of Sir Philip Oldfield. Oliver thought he had never seen anyone so lovely.

That same day he ran away – left the estate and the life of servitude that had killed his father – and took the first steps towards his future – as a self-made cotton king, a mill owner, a man of property. It was in the mill that he met Rosie, dark, warm, beautiful, who began to cast her spell over him, even though she was a married woman.

But even as he rose to power – fighting Sir Philip Oldfield's vicious and vindictive revenge every inch of the way – he never forgot the vision of the beautiful girl at the water's edge.

0 552 13521 6

A SELECTED LIST OF FINE TITLES
AVAILABLE FROM CORGI BOOKS

☐	13482 X	THE SISTERS O'DONNELL	*Lyn Andrews*	£3.99
☐	13482 1	THE WHITE EMPRESS	*Lyn Andrews*	£3.99
☐	13230 6	AN EQUAL CHANCE	*Brenda Clarke*	£3.99
☐	12887 2	SHAKE DOWN THE STARS	*Frances Donnelly*	£3.99
☐	13384 1	A WHISPER TO THE LIVING	*Ruth Hamilton*	£3.50
☐	13616 6	WITH LOVE FROM MA MAGUIRE	*Ruth Hamilton*	£3.99
☐	12607 1	DOCTOR ROSE	*Elvi Rhodes*	£2.99
☐	13185 7	THE GOLDEN GIRLS	*Elvi Rhodes*	£3.99
☐	13481 3	THE HOUSE OF BONNEAU	*Elvi Rhodes*	£3.99
☐	13309 4	MADELEINE	*Elvi Rhodes*	£3.99
☐	12367 6	OPAL	*Elvi Rhodes*	£2.99
☐	12803 1	RUTH APPLEBY	*Elvi Rhodes*	£4.99
☐	13521 6	THE MOSES CHILD	*Audrey Reimann*	£3.50
☐	13413 9	THE QUIET WAR OF REBECCA SHELDON	*Kathleen Rowntree*	£3.99
☐	13557 7	BRIEF SHINING	*Kathleen Rowntree*	£3.99
☐	12375 7	A SCATTERING OF DAISIES	*Susan Sallis*	£3.99
☐	12579 2	THE DAFFODILS OF NEWENT	*Susan Sallis*	£3.99
☐	12880 5	BLUEBELL WINDOWS	*Susan Sallis*	£3.99
☐	13136 9	ROSEMARY FOR REMEMBRANCE	*Susan Sallis*	£3.99
☐	13346 9	SUMMER VISITORS	*Susan Sallis*	£3.99
☐	13545 3	BY SUN AND CANDLELIGHT	*Susan Sallis*	£3.99
☐	13299 3	DOWN LAMBETH WAY	*Mary Jane Staples*	£3.99
☐	13573 9	KING OF CAMBERWELL	*Mary Jane Staples*	£3.99
☐	13444 9	OUR EMILY	*Mary Jane Staples*	£3.99
☐	13635 2	TWO FOR THREE FARTHINGS	*Mary Jane Staples*	£3.99